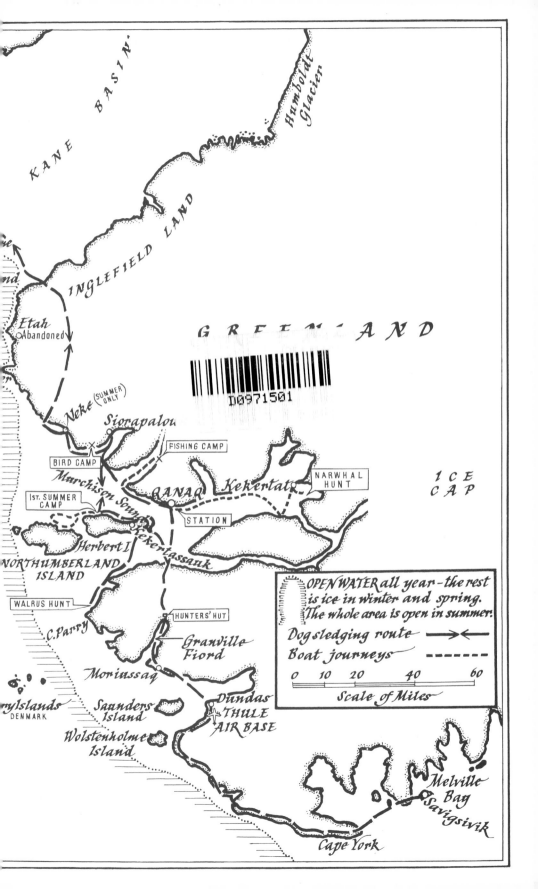

KANE BASIN

Humboldt Glacier

INGLEFIELD LAND

GREENLAND

Etah Abandoned

Neke (SUMMER ONLY)

Siorapaluk

FISHING CAMP

BIRD CAMP

Murchison Sound

NARWHAL HUNT

QANAQ   Kekertat

ICE CAP

1st. SUMMER CAMP

STATION

Kekertassauk

Herbert I.

NORTHUMBERLAND ISLAND

WALRUS HUNT

HUNTERS' HUT

C. Parry

Granville Fiord

Moriussaq

OPEN WATER all year - the rest is ice in winter and spring. The whole area is open in summer.

Dog sledging route

Boat journeys

0   10   20   40   60

Scale of Miles

rylslands DENMARK

Saunders Island

Wolstenholme Island

Dundas THULE AIR BASE

Melville Bay Savigsivik

Cape York

THE SNOW PEOPLE

1. The settlement in summer, with the hills of
Herbert Island in the background.

MARIE HERBERT

The Snow People

G. P. Putnam's Sons
New York

LIST OF ILLUSTRATIONS

1. The settlement in summer   *Frontispiece*

2. Blizzard in the village   22

3. Our hut in the village   22

4. A stranded iceberg   23

5. The children help fetch ice in winter   23

6. Avatak, with Kari   54

7. Migishoo   54

8. Maria   54

9. A picture of Avatak and his parents outside their skin tent   55

10. The children of the settlement came to play with Kari   86

11. Pouline, Inoutdliak and Martha, Maria's daughters, with Kari   86

12. The meat racks on the shore   87

13. Face to face with a team of huskies   118

14. Before the start of a winter journey, Wally checks that Kari
    is snug   118

15. A brew stop is an essential part of travelling   119

16. An overnight stop   119

17 and 18. The dogs find it heavy going over the ice ridges. The driver has to stop every few miles to untangle the leads   150

19 and 20. It can take two hunters over an hour to cut up a large walrus   151

21. The seal-hunter has to hide behind a white screen   182

22. Avatak's mother, Suakunguak, ties a newly-scraped sealskin to a frame   182

23. Dealing with a polar-bear skin   183

24. A mother stands proudly over four white whales her son has caught   183

25. The bird cliffs of Siorapalouk   214

26. One of the three old turf huts still occupied in the Thule District   215

27. Kari made friends with the old people right away   215

ACKNOWLEDGEMENTS

It is not possible to organize an expedition to the Arctic without the help of a great many people; nor at first did I think it was possible for the wife of a polar explorer, with propriety, to take up the pen and under a surname already established in the literature of the North, to write a book about my adventures among the Eskimos of the Thule District—the tribe for whom my husband has such a high regard.

So then, to those many friends who helped us along the way, and in particular to Dudley Witting, Charles and Georgina Turriff, His Excellency Ebbe Munck, Orla Sandborg and Martin Kilt, I offer my grateful thanks. And to those whose friendly persuasion and encouragement made this book possible: especially to George Greenfield who first suggested I should write it; to my dearest friends Pauline and John Alderton who have shared with me over the years so many of my anxieties and joys, and to my husband, without whom I might never have discovered that to the north of latitude seventy-five there is another world—I wish here to express my most affectionate and very special thanks.

This leaves still unmentioned the people about whom I have written; but then, this book is nothing if it does not show how much I came to love them and how deeply I respect their right to live the way they choose.

Marie Herbert

Herbert Island
Northwest Greenland
May 1973.

For
Charles and Marie McGaughey

THE SNOW PEOPLE

1

The sun caught the green copper turrets of Copenhagen as the ship eased from the quay and swung into the sea lane. The thrill of adventure and the thought of new lands swept over me. At last, after months of preparation and frustration, we were on our way. I glanced towards Wally. I could see the excitement in his eyes.

For me it was more than excitement. Two years before, Wally had returned from an expedition which had taken him on foot across the Arctic Ocean from Barrow in Alaska, via the North Pole, to Spitzbergen. For the last two years he had been shackled by office life, burdened by debts and harassed by deadlines. Now at last he was on the move again. He seemed to have been re-born.

Thule was our destination. The very name was exciting: it conjured up pictures of a strange and beautiful land inhabited by unknown creatures. Ultima Thule was the name given by the Greeks to the farthest region of the world as they knew it—the last outpost between civilization and obscurity. 'Beyond it were haunted seas, darkness and nameless terrors that would strike fear into the bravest hearts.'* The earliest explorer Pytheas, born around 350 B.C. in the Greek colony of Massalia (now called Marseilles), discovered a land to the north of Britain which he called Thule, where there was no night in summer and 'where neither earth, water, nor air exist separately, but a sort of concretion of all these.' He describes meeting with 'sluggish and congealed sea which could neither be travelled over nor sailed through.' These are the conditions which polar explorers often described and this was what lay in store for our little ship as it turned its head into the North Sea.

* From *Polar Deserts* by Wally Herbert, published by Collins International Library Series.

The Ultima Thule we were heading for was in Northwest Greenland. There, at Smith Sound, 800 miles within the Arctic Circle, lived an isolated people—the Polar Eskimos. These were the last descendants of a tribe of Eskimos that had migrated from Canada over a thousand years ago. Apart from a few Eskimos on the East Coast, these were the only true Eskimos remaining in Greenland. This small and scattered group of people are the last of a race who still call themselves the Inuit—the 'real people'. They live by hunting and, like all predators, are resigned to a pattern of alternating feast and famine. They live from day to day, and when they die, they die a thousand deaths : for, according to their belief, each time a Polar Eskimo dies his soul seeks out a newborn child and takes possession of its body.

These were the people we had chosen to live with for a year. For Kari, our little girl of ten months, and for me it would be a tremendous new experience. For Wally it would be the fulfilment of a dream. He had a deep respect for these people. He had lived with them through the long polar night, and travelled with them in the spring. He had driven their dogs from Northwest Greenland fifteen hundred miles across some of the roughest country in the Arctic, retracing the outward route of Dr Frederick Cook, who claimed to have reached the North Pole in 1908. And he had driven their dogs nearly four thousand miles across the top of the world from Alaska, via the North Pole, to Spitzbergen. Now he felt it was his duty to return and help the Polar Eskimos in the only way he was able—by filming, recording and writing about them, and by making, with their help, a record of the closing scenes of a dying culture.

We had with us a friend of Wally's, Tom Sharp, who was a sound recordist. He was able to stay six weeks to help us set up home in the Eskimo village and we hoped he would be able to film for us our arrival on Herbert Island.

The trip across the North Atlantic was less dramatic than I had expected. I had pictured tempestuous seas that would keep me strapped to my bunk, but most days I stayed on my feet. Wally and Tom took turns looking after Kari so that I could have a few days' relaxation after the hectic weeks of preparation.

'Make the most of this trip,' everyone told me. 'It will be a long time before you can enjoy the luxuries of civilized living.'

Kari was very spoilt by all the crew. At mealtimes she sat on the Captain's lap and ate daintily from his plate. She was both adored and adoring. But as Kari gurgled and cooed at her admirers I wondered what sort of life I was taking her into. The ship, with its running hot and cold water, its electricity, its heating at the turn of a switch, suddenly seemed comforting. We enjoyed the occasional evenings chatting with the crew over drinks. Living with a people who didn't speak our language, would we miss this type of companionship? Neither of us spoke Greenlandic—might we not get very lonely? What would we do in an emergency to explain our needs? The closer we approached Greenland the more the problems occupied my mind. We were to be living ninety miles north of the US Strategic Airbase of Thule. We would be isolated from the Greenlanders of the West Coast by treacherous sea ice, and from the Canadian Eskimos by the 'north water' of Baffin Bay. To the east was a desert of ice, and north of the few settlements in the Thule district there was nothing but wasteland.

'How do you think you'll stand the isolation and the cold?' they asked me.

'I don't know,' I replied truthfully.

On our tenth day at sea we expected to sight land. There was a message from the Captain after breakfast to say that we were approaching some large icebergs. I felt very excited. There is something magical about those floating crystal jewels. I rushed on deck with Kari, swaddled in sheepskin, in my arms. Ahead of us two giant bergs, aquamarine streaked with deep turquoise, rose majestically, like two pillars at the entrance of some fabulous kingdom. Emerald-green waves splashed against their bases, sending up showers of tiny sparkling gems. Irregular in shape, the bergs towered high above us. A curving spine surrounded gaping mouths which seemed to call us to them. There was something sinister about their beauty. As we glided tremulously between them, I held my breath, expecting any moment that they would draw together and crush our tiny ship.

'You know it can be very dangerous, sailing near these bergs,' the First Officer commented. I nodded without speaking, afraid to waken the spirit that might conjure the bergs into life.

Once past the bergs I felt our adventure had really begun. There was no going back now. We had entered the gates of the North. It was a calm day. For a while nothing disturbed the glassy surface of the sea, which reflected the deep blue of the sky. During the morning we sighted distant mountains, partly covered by mist, and as we sailed up the West Coast of Greenland more and more bergs appeared to delight the eye. The colours turned throughout the day from palest grey to brilliant white. Deep fissures of peacock blue contrasted with the green-black sea. The sun picked out random bergs which sparkled like many-faceted jewels. Great monuments towered like Sphinxes over clusters of conical 'tents', while across a limitless sea a giant's sculpture lay strewn in shattered heaps. Overhead the gulls wheeled and dived. Small white-bellied black birds bobbed on the water and disappeared. I suddenly felt overawed at the prospect of my year in Thule.

Two days later, on the 28th of August, we crossed the Arctic Circle. There were no great celebrations, but I felt pleased and I wished Kari could appreciate what was happening. Every day seemed to be getting colder. There was great excitement when we passed a school of whales. We circled round them and admired their grace. This was whale country. In the seventeenth and eighteenth centuries these waters had been busy with whalers, mainly from Holland and England. So great had been their toll that the large Greenland whale became almost extinct. But the whalers had not confined their activities to the sea: their friendliness towards the locals resulted in a new mixed race of Greenlanders—the ancestors of the West Greenlanders of today.

As we went north we came closer to land. The weather was crisp and sunny. We passed copper cliffs veined with black and coloured with large patches of white—the bird cliffs, stained by hundreds of years of bird droppings. Through the binoculars we could see clouds of birds in endless motion against the dark backdrop. Patches of green here and there were the only signs of vegetation against the stark rocks.

Further up the coast several long, smooth-backed mounds rose from the water. All of similar height and length, they looked like giant sea creatures that had slunk into the shadows to sleep. Not far from them groups of bergs glittered in the sunshine. Inland, clouds guillotined the tops of the mountains and left them collars of new snow.

We continued past coves and inlets. On the horizon I saw my first mirage—islands and ice cliffs hung suspended in air, between tall obelisks.

One evening we were delighted to see a little red fishing boat, from the nearby town of Upernavik. After days of travelling, without a sign of human life, such a homely sight was welcome. We were not scheduled to stop at Upernavik, but the Captain decided to give us a close look at our first settlement. As if anticipating our visit, the little boat turned course and blazed a trail for us into its home town. There seemed no sign of life. The hospital, a large red, timbered building, dominated the settlement. Scattered around on different levels about sixty little boxes clung to the stony ground. They had been painted red, blue, ochre, or green and had different coloured roofs. They perched haphazardly on the hill which was one of thousands along the coast. The temperature was above freezing but we shivered in the cold wind.

It seemed such a desolate little place—miles from anywhere. 'A town of drunks,' said the Captain. 'They are so lazy here—just sit in the street and drink beer. Half the town is always in the hospital, and the other half takes them water and removes the refuse.'

'What a life!' I thought, wondering whether or not to believe him. I hoped it wasn't like that at Thule. 'They aren't hunters here,' the Captain continued. 'They live on subsidies from the Danish Government. They have nothing to spend their money on but drink.'

Very few of the settlements in Greenland could support hunters. Only further north and on the Northeast Coast of Greenland did hunting communities still survive. The decline of the seal and the increasing warmth of the climate over the last fifty years had caused the towns down the West Coast of Greenland to turn from seal to cod as a source of livelihood. As we left Upernavik, I hoped I would find the atmosphere of Herbert Island more attractive.

After supper, Tom called me out to look at the receding land. The coast now looked like a scalloped frieze, changing from blue to palest grey. The tiny bergs were like clusters of pink shells around the brilliant orange jewel of the setting sun. At intervals sparkling ice pillars flashed its reflection. The Arctic was magnificent, and I went to bed entranced by its beauty.

There were two more days to go before we expected to reach Qanaq, the administrative capital of Thule. Eighteen miles across the Sound from Qanaq lay Herbert Island. Wally and Tom were itching to get ashore and get down to work. The journey had been dull for them. And the fumes from the central heating had given everyone a headache. They had decided that I should stay in Qanaq or on board ship while they had a look at Kekertassuaq—the village on Herbert Island. As the end of the journey approached I began to feel uncertain. The ship had become a cocoon. I felt protected by it. I knew once I left it I would have to brave a new way of life. I didn't know if I was ready for it.

As we passed Cape York someone pointed out the plain, tall obelisk of Peary's monument. Beyond it, the Crimson Cliffs supported meandering ice roads. We were near enough to see the jagged walls of the glaciers which had 'calved' from time to time, sending huge icebergs growling out into the sea. The sea was covered in brash—broken pieces and pans of ice, in all shapes and textures. Some had broken off bergs, and their undersides now showed where the current had worn them smooth. Some of the pieces were beautiful shades of blue. Others had large patches of rubble imbedded in them.

We were expected to reach Qanaq in the early hours of the morning. In the evening we had a little party. I dressed in my prettiest clothes. I would be roughing it soon and I wanted to make the most of my last night on board. I stood on the bridge for a while before going to bed. I felt excited but a little in awe of this great country that I had been watching unfold. Wally said he would call me when we passed Herbert Island. I tucked Kari under the blankets and wondered what adventures I was letting her in for.

I dozed fitfully. About 1.30 a.m. I felt a tug at my sleeve and a dark figure leaned over the bunk. 'We're just passing Herbert Island,' whispered Wally. 'It's worth a look.' I shot out of bed, my heart pounding. We were in sight of our destination. I scrambled into my clothes and went quickly up on deck. Peering out of my parka, I saw mountains capped with snow, and glaciers spreading like ravenous tongues around them. 'Is that Herbert Island?' I asked, half asleep. 'No, I'll show you in a second—you had better tie your shoelaces first.' Wally guided me round towards the bridge.

'Darling, there's your island,' he said.

A razorback ridge of featureless rock stretched on either side. No light shone on it or was reflected back. The bleak monotony of it was broken only by the scars and scratches of the cutting winds which had swept it clean. There seemed no space for man or beast on this barren rock: and this was where I had brought my baby to live for a year. My vision blurred. I thought I would choke. I could say nothing.

Sensing my distress Wally said lamely, 'It looks better in daylight.'

I nodded and hid my face in my parka.

2

The ship was bound for Qanaq. There it would unload a large supply of food and non-perishable goods before returning to Copenhagen. The unloading would take a day or two, and the Captain suggested we stay on board until our heavy equipment was ashore. We had a lot of cabin baggage—expensive filming equipment as well as our personal luggage, and several cases of canned baby food to last us till all our supplies were delivered to Herbert Island.

I stood on deck as the ship glided very slowly across Murchison Sound towards Qanaq. Several large icebergs loomed ahead. Through a beautiful natural archway in one I caught sight of the tiny houses nestling in the hillside. All around were fiords, mountains, and glaciers. I wondered how anyone could have the courage to live in so barren and hostile a country. As I gazed over the side of the ship a seal popped up its head, looked round, and disappeared. It did this several times. It looked so friendly I couldn't help grinning at it, half expecting it to grin back. But it finally vanished and left me alone with my thoughts. It was below freezing, but I did not feel the cold. I felt sleepy, yet I wanted to stay up till the ship dropped anchor.

We were very close to Qanaq. It was 2.30 a.m. and still twilight. The sun had sunk below the horizon for the first time two weeks earlier. Wally could not hide the thrill he felt to be arriving. As we passed a line of glaciers, which had gouged precipitous paths out of the mountains, Wally pointed and explained that along one of them was the route we would take when we visited the Airbase in winter. I felt weak in the pit of my stomach. 'Route?' I thought to myself, 'what route—it looks a hell of a ride.' What conceit had suggested that I could fit into this harsh environment? Polar books were full of the stories of courageous and hardy men who had lost their lives in these icy wastes. I had the baby, how could I cope? With a great rattle we dropped anchor.

I snatched a few hours' sleep before breakfast. Tom breezed in with a cheery good morning.

'Well, what do you think of your island then?' he asked, rubbing his hands together.

'Hmm, black and bleak!' I said soberly.

'Black!' he exclaimed. 'It's not black, it's a beautiful shade of pink— you should have seen it when I got up this morning. The sun was shining on it. It looked lovely.'

I looked searchingly at him to see if he was teasing. I could never tell with Tom. His eyes had a perpetual laugh in them and his beard disguised the expression of his mouth.

'I bet he's having a good chuckle to himself,' I thought.

Wally and Tom had decided to go ashore to find someone to take them to the island later in the day, so that they could see what needed to be done to the hut to make it habitable. Then we could buy the necessary wood and paint in the store before we went across with our baggage. I decided to stay on board to finish packing. I would have plenty of time in the next year to visit Qanaq. Besides, we had been warned that between 1 and 5 p.m. low tide would uncover a reef skirting just off the beach and no boats could get to or from the shore. Five hours was a long time to carry a baby around in the cold.

I sat on deck and scanned the settlement through binoculars. The village was so small I could follow the movements of the whole community. There were about sixty houses in all, divided in two sections. To the left, separated from the smarter houses by a road leading up the hill, was a collection of tiny, drab shanties—about thirty of them, united under a cloud of dust and smoke. Over the years the reds, blues and greens of the woodwork had bleached and blistered and peeled, leaving scrofulous patches. The roofs were patched, and stained with rust from the dripping chimney pipes, while smudged sheets of plastic flapped in the breeze over cracked and missing panes. Layers of rubble, which had rolled down from the khaki-coloured hills behind, lay in a patchwork of crazy-paving, cemented together by piles of blubber and dog excrement. Bow-legged crones, clad in a mixture of native and western dress, waddled between the houses, accompanied by rosy-cheeked children, while broad-shouldered hunters in polar-bear pants and blood-greased anoraks hoisted the carcasses of fresh meat on to the racks above the heads of the howling huskies. Beneath the wooden scaffolds, black and sticky from blood and oil, pools of shiny grease covered the discarded yellowing blubber. Here and there an occasional dead dog or pup lay beneath the heavy odours and flying dust.

In contrast to the hovels along the beach were neat rows of well-kept houses perched on tiers sloping gently up to the snowless hills that fronted the dome-shaped icecap. Workmen had restored ageing roofs and worn paintwork. Hothouse plants flourished in the centrally heated rooms behind spotless windows framed in pretty curtains. Wooden arteries protected the electric cables and waterpipes that pumped life to the heart of Qanaq. Here the Danish Administrators and workers and the more prosperous Greenlanders lived in apparent harmony in the shadow of the school, the hospital, and the church.

Below the level of the tenements the beach bustled with the movement of men, machinery, and dogs. Heavy vehicles roared into the water to retrieve stranded cargo. As they hauled their loads away from the grasping tide, the onlookers peered enquiringly, and the dogs sniffed suspiciously.

There was no jetty. Instead of the fleet of barges or floating pontoon I had expected I saw nothing more sophisticated than a shallow metal raft on to which the cargo was dumped. This was then pulled by a small fishing boat towards the shore. Then, just before the boat threatened to beach itself, it turned abruptly and left the floating platform to travel up the beach. All that prevented the precious cargo from slipping into the sea was the rim, one foot high, around its three sides. It was left to God to protect the other side. The occasional box toppled off, and had to be retrieved by boat hooks before the water had time to penetrate too deeply. I watched with some alarm as a few boxes eluded the hook and floated short of the shore. I hoped our valuable equipment would stand the short transfer from ship to shore without a similar immersion. When the speed of the 'barge' was not sufficient to carry it up on to the beach a heavy tractor ploughed into the waves to give it the necessary shove from behind.

Summer is not the best time to visit an Arctic settlement. Refuse which has lain throughout the winter hidden under a blanket of snow is suddenly uncovered. Old clothes, tins, broken bottles, sunbleached bones, and other litter strew the ground. Even the dogs looked dirty, their pelts covered with coal dust.

I turned from the village to look at the sea. The snow-capped mountains ringing the horizon caught the sun, its colours turning through the shades of grey and blue to a delicate pink. Birds circled and dived around the bergs. The ice sparkled like a cluster of opals—greeny-blue during the day but afire with the brilliance of a burning sun at night.

Wally and Tom returned to say they had been offered a lift to Herbert Island in the boat of Orla Sandborg, the Danish Administrator. I had not yet met him, but I knew he had been one of Wally's greatest supporters during his trip in Thule training for the trans-Arctic journey He invited us all to stay at his house for a few days before going over to the island, but Wally had thought it best to get me there as soon as possible—in case the comforts of living in Qanaq made me change my mind about the whole affair.

I can still remember the future picture I had of myself on Christmas Eve 1969—the day I married a 'polar explorer': a devoted wife vicariously following her husband's hazardous journeys through his despatches, which would arrive smudged and battered, having travelled perhaps for thousands of miles in a sledge bag before they could be posted at some remote settlement in the frozen North!

I knew already that Wally had set his heart on returning to Greenland to the Polar Eskimos he had wintered with in 1966 at the settlement of Qanaq. From there he had made a dog-sledge journey of fifteen hundred miles, across some of the roughest country in the Arctic, to Resolute Bay, in the Canadian North West Territories. In those nine months the expedition had tested, under harrowing conditions, the equipment and techniques that were to be used in the more lengthy and difficult trans-Arctic journey.

The British Trans-Arctic Expedition set out on February 21st 1968 from Point Barrow, Alaska, to make the first surface crossing of the Arctic Ocean, via the North Pole, to Spitzbergen. Before we were married I followed with fascination their despatches in the press—the account of a journey by dog sledge of three thousand eight hundred miles over shifting, fracturing ice. It took sixteen months, which was the longest sustained sledge journey in the history of polar exploration.

As a friend, then, I had been concerned, but now as a wife I was to become a participant, totally involved. I accepted as a matter of course the possibility of separation while Wally made more exploratory journeys in some inhospitable part of the world. My surprise was all the greater when, in the euphoria of wedlock, Wally suggested I should go with him on his next assault on the unknown. I accepted with alacrity—reckoning that there would be time enough later to repent.

In the next year Wally's plans to return to Greenland crystallized. And without my realizing it, he gradually built up in my mind a colourful mosaic, until all that was needed to make the Arctic come alive was the lament of sledge dogs and the laughter of Eskimo children. With infectious enthusiasm he talked of 'a pocket of good hunting territory' about ninety miles north of the US Strategic Airbase at Thule, in Northwest Greenland. 'To their east,' he said, 'is a desert of ice : to the north not a living soul of their own race.'

Immediately I wanted to meet this small scattered group of people called Polar Eskimos. These were men, Wally told me, whose ways were those of the animal. In spite of their skills and ingenuity, their intelligence and their powers of reason, they were predators, resigned during their hunting journeys to the alternating pattern of feast and famine.

With a newly arrived baby daughter to look after, I was thrown into the whirlwind of activities that make up the organization of an expedition. Any glamour I might have imagined was soon lost in the triangle of typewriter, telephone, and baby. The task was formidable, and at times I was disheartened. But I learnt that with Wally you don't give up. The scales seemed heavily weighed against our meeting the shipping deadline. Yet, when the day came we were on board the ship that took us from Copenhagen to our destination in Greenland.

We were very lucky to have been able to hire a hut from the community for a year. It was the same as those the Eskimos lived in, and was usually used by visitors from other settlements. We had brought with us a Parcol Housing Unit. It was like a large semi-cylindrical padded tent, and was made specifically for the Arctic. Wally's party had used it with great success during their winter drift on the Arctic Ocean. We would have preferred living in the Parcol, because it was so much warmer and better ventilated than the hut we were offered, but we thought it might be more tactful to live in the local house. At least it was in the centre of the village. Wally could set up the Parcol away from the village and use it as a workroom and store. It was to become a marvellous retreat for Wally when our tiny house was crammed with children—a daily occurrence during the winter !

It was some time after supper when Wally and Tom arrived back at the ship, ravenous and cold. They had been kept waiting for their Eskimo guide for a couple of hours after the agreed departure time. (We were to learn that time means nothing to the Eskimos. They go when the spirit moves them.) I had spent hours gazing at the sombre island. Except for early morning and late evening, when the sun bathed it in a deep pink, it seemed perpetually in shadow. I tried to pierce the distance to see where the settlement could be, but nothing relieved the monotony of the long ridge except a few folds that slanted down to the sea. I wondered what sort of a life would I lead there.

I had managed to keep some food and some hot coffee aside for Wally and Tom. They sat down like two conspirators enjoying a secret. I was bursting for news, but tried hard not to show too much curiosity. They were equally anxious to tell their story but we all avoided the subject—till I could stand the strain no longer. At last I gave in.

'Well,' I said at last, 'what's it like?'

They shot a glance at each other and smirked.

'It has atmosphere,' said Wally.

'Which means very primitive,' laughed Tom.

'Place is covered with muck,' continued Wally.

They looked hard at me to see my reaction. I kept an inscrutable silence.

'We have found a marvellous place to put the Parcol—away from the village on a plot gazing out to sea, surrounded on three sides by water —it is really fabulous,' enthused Wally, his eyes shining.

As Tom left the room, Wally whispered, 'You are going to love it. There are lots of kids running around, and when we have cleaned up the hut it will be really cosy.'

That night Wally spoke to the Captain about getting our equipment to Herbert Island. All the gear from the ship's hold was to be transferred to the coaster which was leaving in a day or two for the three other settlements in the district. We were rather concerned about our personal baggage and filming equipment as transporting it would mean a couple of trips from Qanaq by small boat. We had to get a lot of wood for shelves, glass for the windows, paint buckets, and other hardware, besides some food to last us the few days till our provisions arrived from the other ship.

'If you talk to the pilot, we might be able to drop you off at Herbert Island on our way out tomorrow,' the Captain offered.

'That would be great,' responded Wally, and he hurried off to look for him. Later, he returned beaming to say it was all fixed—the ship would drop us off. It was a great relief.

The next morning we got up early and hitched a ride on the barge between bales of caribou skins, which the Eskimos use for making clothing, and for sleeping on during their journeys. Wally had Kari in a papoose carrier on his back. A week or two before leaving England I had twisted my back and it was still rather painful. We knew that Eskimo men never carried their children this way, but Wally decided that a serious back injury would be worse than any loss of face.

On shore, as soon as we passed the huge warehouse we were greeted with squeals of delight and mirth. Old crones came over to coo at Kari, their faces screwed up like crumpled parchment, and their almond eyes hid in the folds of their high cheeks. They looked from Wally to me with some amusement and commented in unintelligible guttural sounds. As they noticed Kari's shoeless feet their faces dropped and they muttered anxiously. They were all wearing kamiks—sealskin boots lined with a sock of dogskin. I had put several pairs of thick socks on Kari and felt sure she would be warm enough for the short trip, though I intended getting some local footwear made as soon as possible. I studied the clothes of the old folk. Unlike the youngsters who favoured western dress, they stuck to the traditional costume. The men wore polar-bear breeches and a light-coloured cloth anorak. A few of the elderly women wore kamiks that reached the top of the thigh. With these they wore a short floral anorak with a cummerbund of a different pattern. Others wore bright jerseys instead of the anoraks, or combined dresses with short kamiks.

Lots of children and young girls stood about. Their beautiful, dark slanting eyes shone from smiling light brown faces, glossy with health. They gathered round Kari, and she gurgled pleasurably at the attention. I seemed to read their thoughts: 'How strange of these white people to let the man carry the baby on his back.' They giggled and pointed at Wally—but he strode through them unabashed.

Wally wanted to show Orla his new family, so we went to his office first. He was hard at work so we did not stay long, but we were very pleased when he offered to lend us a folding table and a couple of chairs to take to Herbert Island with us. Within half an hour we were laden with goods which were too much for us to carry and we had to get help from the other passengers and crew.

We rushed through our shopping. The store had a surprising variety of luxuries—it catered for the Danes in Qanaq as well as for the Eskimos. Most of the things available were of good quality, but I had no time to examine them too closely. We had to make sure we got down to the beach in time for the last launch.

Lunch was a celebratory affair. The Captain had asked the chef to make a special curry for me, as he knew I liked it. Wally had bought some wine. The conversation was lighthearted and amusing. We felt like castaways about to be stranded on a desert island for a year—but a desert island without sunny beaches or palm trees. Many jokes were made about our probable appearance in a year's time.

'Mr Herbert—do you think the natives are friendly on this island?' asked the Captain flippantly. 'Should I send some men with rifles to form a bridgehead while you land?'

We all laughed, recalling stories of cannibals lurking amongst the lush vegetation of tiny tropical islands.

'Well,' someone said, 'at least there are no trees here for them to hide behind.'

After lunch the men loaded all our gear into one of the lifeboats. Tom was to go ashore first with most of the gear, and we would make the second trip with just a few odds and ends. Wally had been thinking hard about the feasibility of filming our arrival on the island, and had decided to abandon the idea. Firstly, it would be very complicated to arrange, and secondly, but more important, we felt it would be rather boorish to turn a battery of cameras on an unsuspecting people. We felt it would be wiser to let the locals get used to us before we tried invading their privacy with the ruthless candour of the camera.

Practically everyone on board had turned out to see us off. We turned from Qanaq towards the long vertical ridge of rock. It looked beige in the rather flat light. Wally pointed out a dip in the spine, where a fold swept down to a wide apron of land and where the village lay. We skirted the chain of bergs at the head of the Sound and soon after 5 p.m. reached a spot opposite the village. The anchor dropped and the lifeboat was lowered into the water.

Accompanying Tom in the boat were the Captain, the First Officer, and the Chief Engineer. A group of figures appeared on the raised rocks near a tiny cove. Behind them a cluster of small huts clung to patches of flat ground between the tiers of uneven rocks that sloped gradually to the hills behind. At the rear of the houses, fifteen in all, a red building stood out from the rest. It was larger than the others, and marked with a small white cross. To the left of it the Danish flag fluttered on a flagstaff that rose out of a mound of rocks. There seemed to be lots of dogs around. There was something about the place that I liked. Wally pointed out the small red hut in the centre and said that was ours. A score of binoculars fixed it in their sights. A few people sneaked glances in my direction.

The boat pulled away from the ship with great aplomb. The Captain, a very handsome man, looked very dashing in his smart uniform. We all hung over the sides and followed the boat's progress towards the shore. About fifty yards off the tiny craft gave a belch of smoke and came to a spluttering stop. The pause that followed seemed infinite, though it could not have been more than a few minutes. Everyone tried to keep a straight face.

'I bet the Captain is furious,' someone said.

'Especially as he's got his cap on.'

'Oh, those ruddy engines are always stopping.'

We were cut short by a new burst of life from the boat. It quickly off-loaded Tom with our gear, and returned to the ship.

We shook hands with the Captain, and thanked him for the trouble he had taken on our behalf.

'We'll come and collect you next year,' he offered. I wondered what stories we would have to tell him.

After a long journey I usually find leaving a ship rather sad, but this time I felt more excitement than nostalgia. We had taken an irrevocable step. We had disembarked on to a tiny, barren island, only eight hundred and sixty miles from the North Pole. We had cast away the trappings of civilized life and chosen to live 'primitive' among a strange people we could not talk to.

I gazed, fascinated, at the natives of this desert island. A huddle of children stared wide-eyed at the approaching boat. Their elders hardly spoke, except for an occasional comment, till we had almost reached them and they caught sight of Kari. Then a chorus of exclamations and friendly laughs filled the air. As I looked for a footing on the slimy green rocks, a young woman stepped down to steady me. I handed Kari to her, and several pairs of hands reached down to take her to safer ground. Within a few minutes our eager helpers had carried everything up to the drier rocks.

For a couple of minutes we all stood grinning at each other, rather em-barrassed. A little circle had gathered round the woman holding Kari, who gurgled appreciatively.

The First Officer and Chief Engineer shook hands with us and wished us luck. As gracefully as two courtiers they backed up to the boat, started the engine and pulled away, still smiling at us. As one of them waved, the other raised his hat and bowed graciously. It would have been most moving and impressive had they not been heading straight for one of the boats anchored in the cove. A gasp of alarm rose simultaneously from us all, and we stood rigid waiting for what seemed an unavoidable crunch. Our friendly officers, sensing some disaster, looked round and jerked the boat away from its collision course in the nick of time. We all waved and burst out laughing. The ice was broken. I felt at home. I knew I would be happy here.

3

Our gear lay around us like the washed up litter from a wreck. We grabbed a few things and followed the young woman who had helped me from the boat.

Our hut rose like a red growth out of a heap of rubble. Trash was strewn all around. A couple of decayed walrus heads stuck to the roof and a greasy dogskin lay pinioned to an outhouse. The stones around were yellow and oily, cemented together by layers of blubber. Dogs sprawled about amongst a pile of bones.

A minute porch led into a kitchen where there was a coal stove, an old grimy storage unit, and some hooks on the walls. There were two dirty shelves on which an assortment of odds and ends were scattered. Opposite the front door a second door led into a larger living room, in which there was a wooden platform, which served as a bed or a seat, a chest of drawers painted pink, and a rickety table made out of packing cases and painted a dark brown. The walls of this room were dark blue with muddy patches showing through. All the woodwork was pink, and the paint had blistered and peeled. The windows, though double glazed, let in the sounds of the Arctic through the broken and cracked panes. There was a slight chill in the place which could not disguise the heavy odour of seal and walrus. The wood floor was stained with blood and blubber. It would need a lot of work to make it cosy!

We introduced ourselves to our new friend. Her name was Savfak. She invited us to her house for a cup of tea. I was delighted with the idea, and took a bottle of milk up with me for Kari. Wally and Tom decided to bring our gear up to the hut first and said they would join us later. I followed the tiny round figure up the hill to a house next to the church. Like most of the other houses—ours was one of the exceptions—it was raised a few feet above the ground. Unlike ours, the first room was bigger than the bedroom. In one corner was the stove, and there was a wooden bench around two of the walls. In the middle of the room was a table laid with cups and saucers.

There were cheap religious prints on the walls. A basin of dark meat lay near the stove on the floor. A rather battered radio stood on the table —my hostess pointed to it and said something. I could only smile and shrug my shoulders. From where I sat I could see out of the window over the rest of the village. Everyone was helping the men carry the luggage up to the hut. A few minutes later the ship blew three blasts on the siren. The sound was beautiful and resonant and I suddenly felt a little nostalgic as I watched it turn again towards the way we had come. I ran to the door with Kari, and waved. I hoped the same ship would return for us next year.

Soon Wally and Tom arrived, followed by Savfak's husband, Rasmusee (the Eskimos had a habit of adding 'ee' to names ending in 's' or 'f'), and their teenage daughter. Our host was wearing polar-bear pants, held up by braces attached to a broad sealskin waistband. The hair on the seat turned outwards in all directions like a posy of ducks' tails.

Rasmusee looked unwell, his face was drawn and he gasped and spluttered for breath. The remains of a tubercular cough rumbled through his respiratory system, and he grew blue in the face. We all held our breath, as if willing him to breathe again. The room filled with the sound of throats clearing. I was relieved later to discover that TB had been practically eradicated in Greenland, and a strict watch was kept on those who had had it. But that afternoon I just wanted to get out of the house as quickly as possible. Kari's antics had our host gasping for air; at times I thought he would collapse.

We were delighted when we got back to the hut to find the fire roaring away, a bucket of coal beside it and another filled with ice on top. The floor had been swept and a lamp lit. No sooner were we in the door than several visitors arrived and settled themselves on boxes in the kitchen. They were all very jovial and chatted to us in a mixture of guttural and nasal sounds, strung together in apparently endless sequence. Our expressions of blank incomprehension had them rolling on their seats with laughter. Eventually they tried the one or two words of English they had learnt from the occasional visitor. Their total vocabulary consisted of counting to ten and three expressions, which sounded like 'Wuteez-yornem', 'Howar-yu' and 'Iddunno-me'. They told us their names—which sounded to us like a rumble in their throats. Our inadequate attempts to repeat them had them all giggling helplessly. 'It seems very easy to please them,' Wally laughed, caught up in the infectious merriment.

We made coffee and served it in cardboard mugs given us by the Chief Steward. The door burst open and a gang of inquisitive children poured into the room. The house was crowded. I did not particularly welcome the intrusion of a horde of gaping youngsters. I made up my mind I would teach them to knock before they came into the house.

But my first problem was very basic : I whispered to Wally, 'Where is the loo?'

'There isn't one,' he grunted.

'Well, where do I go?' I asked anxiously.

'The whole of the Arctic is yours,' Wally said generously. 'Just find yourself a spot with a beautiful view, and squat.'

This is very easy to find on Herbert Island, but privacy was a different matter. Every time I stepped outside the door a flock of children rushed up to grab a hand; vying with them was a pack of dogs, who found the seal trimmings on my coat too good to ignore. At last, desperate, I rushed inside again and picked up some gear, including the baby's potty, which I shoved up my parka.

I pretended to be storing things in a little shed behind the hut. I had to bend double to get in. It had a raised floor and a false ceiling and I crammed myself in and closed the door, plunged in complete darkness. With great difficulty I held the door ajar with one hand to let in some light—at the same time letting in the noses of a couple of huskies, which had been attracted by the unusual activity. Knowing how hungry they can get and that they eat absolutely anything, I sat petrified a couple of inches from the sniffing snouts. In an attempt to scare them off I hissed loudly. But this only succeeded in attracting more of them. They began to paw at the door.

Dropping one's pants when wearing ski-pants, long-johns, and a thick parka is a bit awkward even without the added difficulty of bending double and holding the door an inch ajar, but I managed it. I dug in vain in my pockets for a bit of loo paper. I could hardly believe my luck when I spied a roll of paper in the corner. I noticed in the chink of light from the door that it was as thick as wrapping paper. 'Good lord, they must be tough up here,' I thought, remembering the soft, double-layered tissue rolls I was used to. Anyway, I was not going to worry about little luxuries like that. My relief was somewhat short-lived when I discovered that the paper was gummed on one side. I found out later that it was used for sealing cracks in the walls.

When I eventually opened the door of the shed, I found a group of curious dogs and children waiting for me. I stepped out, as nonchalantly as the occasion would allow, and walked away, carrying the potty at arm's length above the heads of the crowd, to find a place to empty it. However, the sight of the yellow vessel was too much for the nearest husky. He let out a howl of delight. Immobilized by the sound for one moment, the stray dogs of the village looked for its origin, and then with a mighty roar all sprang in my direction, pounding over the rocks in their mad rush towards the outstretched yellow potty. Paralysed with fright, I took one look at the beasts tearing towards me and hurled it into the air. Turning tail, I did not stop running till I had reached the hut and sat in breathless sanctuary behind the closed door.

After our guests had gone we did the minimum of unpacking and clearing up before having a meal and crawling tired and contented into our sleeping bags. I lay for a while listening to the sound of the dogs howling outside. It was eerie but I liked it. My hip bones ached against the hard bed and the room felt stale and airless. It was quite dark, as it was the end of summer. I wondered what the villagers were really like. Would Kari and I be safe when Wally went away? A million thoughts crowded through my head till I at last fell asleep.

The next morning the fire was out. When we did get it going and started to cook, the heat made me feel ill. It seemed to draw the smell of seal from the woodwork and the air was heavy and stifling. We would have to ventilate it better, even if it meant making another 'nose', as the Eskimos called the small breathing hole.

I had to go for a walk. It was a gorgeous, crisp, sunny day. We wandered through the village after breakfast, picking our way through the scores of dogs. Most of them were tethered outside the houses of their owners, but quite a few ran loose. Some were only puppies, but they looked quite big. They seemed very friendly and waddled along, waggling from side to side, taking friendly bites at our fists and tripping us up as they darted between our legs. They kept getting in the way and made deep growling noises as they nibbled at us. 'They are not really growling,' explained Wally. 'They are talking—just shove them out of the way if they bother you.' He demonstrated with an inelegant shove up the backside of one. 'Trouble is, they like that,' he laughed, as the dog returned for more.

Not all the huskies were as friendly as the few woolly ones that accompanied us. Some of them looked very powerful and fierce, and I remembered the advice I had had from someone who knew Greenland—never to leave Kari unprotected. Every year there are cases of children badly mauled by dogs and occasionally these injuries are fatal. I kept a clear distance from the teams. As we passed one house I noticed a puppy waddling away from its mother towards some bigger dogs. These were just ready to set upon it when the bitch dived after it to rescue it. She gathered it up in her mouth and dropped it further away, giving it a sharp nudge with her snout.

Our first necessity was water. If there were no meltstreams we would have to look for ice on the beach. Wally and I decided to explore the hills for streams. We took a bucket with us, and we had not gone twenty yards when an old man appeared and called out to us, gesticulating towards the shore. We waved and thanked him and continued on our way, unable to tell him that we wanted a walk first. But the old man obviously thought we had misunderstood and he stood frantically yelling and gesticulating till we had to go and investigate. He walked down with us and pointed to two large pieces of ice on an upturned boat. Wally showed me how to break it up with a pointed knife, using sharp stabbing movements.

There was very little ice washed up against the shore in that first week. If the locals did not leave some for us on the boat, Wally or Tom had to walk a long way to find a stranded berg. My back was giving me trouble, and Wally suggested I should leave the heavy jobs to the men. But, although collecting ice was heavy, it was considered women's work and I often went down with my bucket to collect a load.

At first I had great difficulty handling the ice knife. I knew that ice had a grain in it, and that I should strike along the grain, but I just had not got the knack. A beautiful lump of clear ice would be reduced to a shattered heap of splinters in no time. I felt guilty wasting so much ice, and would try to scoop up a few clean handfuls, where it had fallen in the slime. The characteristic of freshwater ice is that it shatters easily, with beautiful tinkling sounds, unlike sea ice, which is cloudy and difficult to break.

We spent the first two weeks cleaning up the hut and burning mounds of rubbish. We cleared the old walrus heads off the roof and the bones and litter from outside. We scraped the blood off the floor and woodwork, and washed everything. The smell of seal and walrus we imprisoned under two coats of paint. Tom made shelves and a complete L-shaped working area in the kitchen.

We laid lino on the kitchen floor, and in the other room we fitted a thick red carpet of nylon pile backed with foam, to insulate it against the damp. Kari was at an age when she would be spending a lot of time on the floor and we thought this a necessity. We were very glad in the winter that we had the carpet, as the hut was very cold, especially at floor level.

Our efforts were watched with great interest by the locals. They came in and sat and drank coffee at any time during the day. I had a kettle on the boil the whole time, and it was no wonder that we had to make several trips to get ice.

Someone arrived at most meals and we had always to be prepared to feed several guests. Conversation was limited. We felt the silences very keenly, but our visitors did not seem to feel any embarrassment. We longed for the arrival of the coaster with our books and equipment, so that we would have some pictures to show them. We racked our brains to be entertaining. If Wally had not been able to draw so well, I doubt if we would have made ourselves understood at all.

Greenland is a 'province' of Denmark, but few of the Thule Eskimos spoke anything but their own tongue. Most textbooks for Greenlandic were in Danish, and to speed up the process of learning I had brought a Linguaphone course in Danish so that I could translate the texts. But once I had learnt a few basic phrases in Eskimo, I built up my own vocabulary and concentrated on one language only.

The Eskimo language is unique. A series of ideas can be explained in one word, simply by adding affixes to a stem, which sometimes has a meaning on its own but often has not. There is no limit to the number of possible affixes—but even an Eskimo would get confused if a word is too long. We found that when the Eskimos spoke to us they used very short words which were easy for us to understand. That explained why we could not understand them when they spoke amongst themselves. An example of a simple Eskimo word-sentence is: 'Kekertassuakakakakaok' —which means, 'The large island has many hills.'

From the two windows in the hut we could either gaze inland towards the village and the hills behind, or out to sea, across the Sound that divided the island from the mainland. Gigantic bergs drifted past, growling as they scraped against the rocks and roaring like distant thunder when they capsized. On the far mainland huge glaciers gouged a path through the sheer rock that formed a ring around the mighty icecap. Colours changed constantly. Turquoise bergs floated in a green-blue sea, against a backdrop of sun-fired mountains; the black rocks of the island seemed stark against the lace snow cover of the hills behind. The Arctic was decidedly magnificent!

2. In winter the island was often whipped by blizzards, which drove the people indoors and the dogs into tight balls of fur. Only the hungry bitch with young would prowl for food.

3. Our hut was in the centre of the village, very like the others, but a bit smaller. The store hut in the foreground was a good place to keep furs out of the heat of the kitchen.

4. We often passed stranded icebergs when travelling over the ice. Huge blocks break off from time to time, and some of this ice—up to 2,000 years old and quite unpolluted—is now being shipped to the U.S. for use in drinks. provides delicious drinking water.

5. The children often helped me fetch ice in winter. Sometimes Kari would come, well wrapped in furs, for a ride on the little sledg

4

The arrival of the coaster was a great event. It brought the community their supplies of fuel and coal for the winter and it brought us the food, clothes, and heavy equipment that had to last us for a year. At the first sight of it the children ran around yelling, 'Umiarssuak'—'The big ship, the big ship'. The houses poured forth scrambling toddlers and adults. Some of the old folk ambled down to the cove with pipe in mouth.

The Eskimos were paid for the hours they spent carrying the coal sacks and fuel drums up to the village, and they worked very hard. When all that was done, they trouped down with Wally and Tom to help them with their gear. Wally had chosen a beautiful position for the prefabricated hut which we had brought, about three hundred yards from the village, near a tiny cove. Men, women, and children struggled over the slippery rocks with our stores. It took ages, but no one complained. Many of the boxes had come apart during the voyage and one of the boats was littered with cans of food, but everyone scrambled genially in the bottom of the boat to pick them up.

Our first meals were strange combinations of food. We just picked up what came to hand. The meat racks in the village were bare and it was a week or two before the hunters brought in any seal. We had decided to bring our food with us so we should not be a burden on the community. When possible we would eat the local food but we would often have been very hungry had we not brought our own.

The men's first task was to erect the prefabricated hut. They set to with great energy, while the locals marvelled at the ingenuity of the design and the speed with which it took shape. It took a few hours to put it up and install the fire and unpack the bed. The latter was a very clever piece of furniture, made up of twin beds, one of which folded up and nestled beneath the other when not in use. It was very practical for our cramped quarters.

The new hut was to be Wally's retreat when he wanted to work, but as it was so bright and airy we decided to sleep in it till the house in the village was ready. There was a marvellous atmosphere to the place and magnificent views all around. From our beds we could see the haloes of fire and burning furnaces of sunset. From the other window in the morning we could see the delicate hues of sunrise.

The ground around was stony, but uncluttered with the trash of the village, and the smell of the sea wafted through the ventilators, instead of the thick smells of dog and seal that blanketed the settlement. The water slapped against the rocks, and sent clouds of glittering spume into the air. A few Arctic terns, beautiful streamlined grey birds with white breasts, hovered balletically before swooping in a graceful arc to snatch some morsel from the sea. The place was magical.

That night in the new hut I felt the pulse of the Arctic for the first time. Soft flakes of snow drifted down and settled for a while on the sloping roof before slipping with a whishing rush down the slithery fabric. In the distance a dog howled—a wild sad lament: the sound swelled as other dogs added voice to it, sending ripples of pleasurable fear down the spine. Two hundred heads lifted to the moon, and the cry grew louder and more plaintive, rising again with even greater intensity. The howl ebbed and flowed. I snuggled deeper into my sleeping bag. Wally was asleep and Kari seemed oblivious to everything. Suddenly the sound ceased. Only the wind could be heard, gently flapping the fabric of the hut. I filled my lungs with the sparkling air and dropped off to sleep.

The night promised the bliss of an untroubled sleep, but I was to have a rude awakening. With very little warning Kari became very disturbed and hysterical. Between fits of screaming and wild thrashing she was very sick. Wally had to go down to the beach to get some water to mop up, and then had to make a second journey to cool the water I had brought in a flask. Kari seemed in agony and I was frantically worried.

Our medical kit was still packed and there was no way of getting medical help quickly.

Other than finding someone to take us across by boat (which could take a couple of hours) the earliest I could reach a doctor was by radio to Qanaq at 10 a.m. How would I explain the problem to the locals? What a god-forsaken country I had brought Kari to. I remembered the advice of a doctor friend, who warned me of the danger of dehydration when a baby loses water through sickness or diarrhoea. Here was Kari with both, and there was no water to give her. At last Wally returned. He did not seem at all agitated. I sat with Kari for most of the night, spooning water down her throat. I was determined she would not die of dehydration.

As the hours passed, the wind picked up. The hut, whose gentle rustling had seemed so soothing earlier, became animated with dreadful spasms. The frame quivered and groaned as it wrestled with the wind. Wally had warned me that the wind sounded worse in the hut than it really was, but I could not get out of my mind the story I had heard of a family that had moved a few years ago from Herbert Island to Qanaq, because their wooden house had turned turtle during a storm. The whole family had been in bed when it happened. They had had to feel their way around in the dark for clothes as the wind whipped them through the broken windows. It was completely dark outside and they were almost choked by the heavy blizzard which filled the air with thick flakes of snow. Clinging to each other they had crawled helplessly about in the dark for hours before they found one of the other houses, where they took refuge. I thanked God when day dawned. Kari slept and the wind stopped.

We got in touch with the doctor by radio that morning and explained the symptoms. He suggested a bland diet of oats and water for a few days, and some sort of brown powder which I could get from Savfak, who acted as nurse and kept the medicine chest in her house. Within a week Kari was back to normal with a new tooth to show for her pains.

Greenland is an explorer's paradise, and it was not long before we took to the hills. We left Kari with Tom, and Wally and I climbed a couple of very rocky tiers that led up to the foot of the hills themselves. Every few yards I stopped to pick up a stone which caught my eye—there were so many pretty pebbles—pink and green and smoky white. 'The trouble with taking you for a walk,' complained Wally, 'is that you keep stopping to collect stones. It takes twice as long as it should, and I have to carry several pounds extra weight.' I thrust a few more stones into his pockets.

We passed a shallow crater which looked as if it would be a meltpool in summer. A carpet of moss, with tiny rusty leaves between the clumps, stretched across it. Further on, close to the sea, on a grassy shelf we made an exciting find—the site of an old village, camouflaged by the grassy hillside. Several large cairns, made of circles of flat stones piled on top of each other, indicated where meat was stored in winter, out of reach of dogs and other animals. Between the large stones smaller ones had been inserted, together with various bones, to make the rocky mound impregnable. The top rocks were greasy from the blubber of the cached animals. These cairns, we learnt later, were still used by the villagers to store their meat.

The ground was strewn with huge bones, which looked as if they came from whale or walrus. Tufts of thick coarse grass sprang up everywhere. The Eskimos used it in their kamiks as insulation, and in the old days it was used as padding for the sleeping platforms. We could also see it sticking out of the sides of the old houses, where it was used with the moss to hold the stones together. The bases of these houses were circular. When built they were made completely of slabs of stone, moss and grass cemented together to form a house similar in shape to the snow house which we call 'igloo': actually 'igdlo' is the Eskimo name for any sort of house, and the snow house is called 'igdluigak'. These were entered by a long low tunnel, sunk beneath the level of the house so that cold air from outside would be trapped. A visitor would take off his heavy fur parka, brush the snow from it and leave it in the passageway before stepping up into the room.

Near the bed platform was usually a smaller platform on which stood the oil lamp, made of soapstone and shaped like a half-moon with a small rim to catch the oil from the chopped seal or whale blubber which was burnt in it. Dried moss was used as a wick. Above the lamp was suspended the cooking pot, usually made out of soapstone, and the drying frame on which skins were stretched and clothes hung to dry. A certain amount of light came through the window of stretched seal intestine sewn together. It was impossible to see out of this except through a tiny hole. Another large hole was made for ventilation, and this could be plugged with grass if it became too draughty.

It was very warm in the winter houses, and people sat with as few clothes on as possible. The men wore only their polar-bear pants, and the women only their short fox pants. The children ran around naked. The houses everywhere looked out over the sea and the same sites were used by generations of travellers. When the spring came the people moved out of the houses into tents. Today the Eskimos do the same thing.

It was marvellous to see these old houses and to realize how simply people can live. The Eskimos had very few possessions—their knives, cooking pots, hunting tools and skins were all they carried. This way there was very little to take on a sledge, and moving home was an easy matter. To this day, the Eskimos live as simply. These houses had been lived in as late as 1958.

We got back to the hut just as a little red boat arrived. Tom was trying hard to amuse Kari who was struggling under the arm of an elderly woman who deftly changed her nappy. The door flew open and half a dozen children burst into the kitchen. They stood in silence for a minute or two while their bright eyes flashed a penetrating look around the hut. Noticing Kari in the other room they gradually approached the door. Then, gaining confidence they sneaked inside. In seconds they had Kari surrounded, cramming her with biscuits and jostling for a chance to pick her up.

She seemed terrified by the sudden intrusion, the noisy chatter and the grasping hands. Her cries showed her alarm, and I had to rescue her frequently from a tiny youngster who clasped her precariously around the waist and swung her round upside down, her head an inch from the floor. Her admirers meant her no harm, but their enthusiasm was overpowering and I wondered how long it would take before she learnt to cope with it. It is not surprising that the first English phrases the children learnt were 'what's the matter' and 'be careful!' They were so used to hearing them that as soon as Kari squawked they would ask her 'wotz-a-matta?' while someone else would shout 'bee-car-fool!'

For some reason Kari's name confused them, and to begin with they all called her 'Cow-ree'. Each time it was mispronounced I would tell them, 'It is not "Cow-ree". It is "Kari".' I was so used to correcting them that the first day they all called her Kari I found myself calling her 'Cow-ree'.

The children were the loveliest urchins I had seen—down at heel and bursting out of their clothes at the elbows and knees, the seams of their pants always split. Any zips that worked at all were always at halfmast. They gazed inscrutably from eyes as dark as ripe berries and kept all their smiles for Kari, whom they watched with devotion. Her hair fascinated them and they could not resist fingering her curls, so different from their own straight black hair. Like most children brought up away from the refinements of civilized life, they had no embarrassment at performing natural functions. They farted loudly in our presence, picked their noses, snorted constantly and wiped their sniffles on their sleeves. They ran outside for a pee, creating the most hazardous approach to the hut, when the yellow snow turned to ice. Together with the dogs, who insisted on leaving their card on the doorstep, the children were responsible for most of my falls near the hut in the dark months.

It took a while to get to know everyone on the island. Some were away visiting other settlements, and among those that remained it was difficult to distinguish residents from visitors. Our introduction was sometimes less formal than we expected : one young Eskimo serenaded us through the window, with a bottle in his hand, before tottering in and putting a heavy arm around the neck of Wally and Tom. Turning to each with a vacant look in his eyes he said politely, 'Thang yow very much,' and then shook hands. He clicked his heels, pulled himself up and saluted Wally, exclaiming loudly, 'Yu eengleesh—me Eskimo. Eskimo no good,' at which he burst into laughter. Then he shook hands solemnly with us again, and thanked us warmly.

He turned to go but caught sight of Kari and stopped. I was a bit alarmed in case he hurt her. I had heard stories of the dreadful drunken fights that take place amongst the Eskimos, and our visitor looked quite wild-eyed and savage. The Eskimos love children, and their violence is never directed deliberately towards them, but when a man is drunk he often does not realize what he is doing. I watched him like a cat watches a mouse, ready to snatch up Kari at a moment's notice. She was in her cot and seemed a bit puzzled at the antics of our visitor but otherwise undisturbed.

The door opened slowly and a head poked round. An old man with jet-black hair cut in a bowl shape peered in. I smiled in welcome and slightly hesitatingly he shuffled in, followed by a refined-looking but scruffy woman whose age was difficult to tell. She could have been in her late fifties. She seemed ill at ease and kept glancing towards the young man who was crooning uncertainly to Kari.

She pointed to him and said he was her 'piccaninny'. Where she got the expression I cannot think, unless it was from a film she had seen at Qanaq sometime. I nodded in response wondering what her 'piccaninny' was going to do to my 'piccaninny'.

The old man sat down on one of the boxes, beer-bottle in hand, and turned a radiant smile on the four of us. The man had a certain quality about him which was warm and instantly likeable. He was very gentle and with great charm offered me a sip of his beer. I was so captivated by his personality that I was very tempted to accept and wondered if it was rude of me to refuse. He sat relaxed and lit his pipe. His son became more vocal while his mother stood restlessly, watching him rather sadly. From time to time he would stand up and shout 'Eskimo no good' which upset the old woman. She turned towards me distressed commenting 'whisky no good'. I felt sorry to see her so unhappy and agreed with her confiding 'Eskimo good—whisky no good'. She nodded with relief and took the cigarette Wally offered her. To our surprise, the three of them left soon after with many goodbyes and expressions of thanks. It was not the only sign of drunkenness we were to see that day.

We had just sat down to a meal. I was facing the window that looked towards the village, and Wally and Tom sat on either side. Suddenly a tremendous commotion broke out. Outside one of the other houses I noticed a lot of activity as kids darted around a young drunken man and a woman who appeared to be his wife. They struggled violently with each other. She tried to run away, and he fought to restrain her. He shouted abuse at her, and she spat back at him. Her long hair fell in disorder around her face and shoulders. The two of them swayed and stumbled drunkenly. With a heavy crash they fell to the ground, locked in a hostile embrace.

Several people joined the group, while the children huddled together at a short distance, frightened but curious. The young couple staggered to their feet. It was early evening and rather cold but the woman wore only a thin sweater and trousers. She resisted all efforts to drag her back into the house and flayed wildly at her man. He cuffed her viciously across the face, and tugged her by the hair. A thin trickle of blood oozed down her face and on to her jersey.

One of the newcomers put a restraining hand on the man and tried to reason with him. He spoke then to the woman, who screamed wildly at him and beat him with her fists. An older woman pushed the girl towards the house. She whipped round and slapped her. She stood shivering, her hands in her pockets, swaying slightly. Her husband looked towards her. He seemed torn between compassion and outrage—one moment slipping off his sweater to cover her and the next threatening her with the handle of a harpoon, as she slung the sweater back at him.

Suddenly, as if seeing her chance to escape, she darted away from the group, past our house, towards the sea, stumbling and sprawling over the jagged rocks. The rest stood embarrassed for a minute, looking towards our hut and muttering amongst themselves, but on impulse they too began to run. By this time the victim of the chase had reached the rocks which lay uncovered by the tide. She turned towards her pursuers and screamed at them. They stopped in their tracks uncertain what to do. Her man continued to close the distance between them, lurching unsteadily from side to side. There was a shout from everyone as she disappeared over the rocks. They all tore towards the sea, shouting and gesticulating frantically. Minutes later they dragged up a stumbling, wet creature who looked half dead from fatigue and cold. She was ushered quickly and without ceremony to her house.

Wally and Tom refused to look, out of principle, but I am afraid curiosity got the better of me and I sat fixed to my seat. I was evidently not the only voyeuse. A minute later an old crone crept in. We pulled our chairs aside to let her sit down and gave her a cup of tea and a cigarette. She picked a chair opposite the window and watched out of slanting eyes for any further developments. We made no comment when she gestured towards the other house with a simpering smile.

She had not long to wait before the participants in the drama appeared once again on the scene. The young woman was dressed as though ready for a journey, a small suitcase in her hand. From the composure with which the group made their way towards the boats it looked as if an amicable settlement had been reached. Their silence disguised their feelings, but these became all too apparent when the moment to depart arrived. As if with second thoughts, the young woman snatched up the youngest of the children. She was very quick and her movement took the others by surprise. But before she could reach the boat, an agonized scream rent the air as though the father had been seized with a sudden pain.

He sprang forward and intercepted his wife, hitting her brutally in the face as he wrested the child from her. The poor woman staggered from the violence of the blow. She bowed her head as if her spirit were broken and clambered silently into the boat, which was ready to leave. A young couple in the boat made as if to help her, but she brushed past them and sat down. The drama was over and the boat pulled away. The scattered group broke up and the hunter walked unsteadily towards his hut, carrying his child. The door closed behind them. Our visitor clucked disapprovingly and sneaked a glance in our direction. We sat in silence.

In the next two weeks Wally was busy sorting out the stores, unpacking them and storing them in the hut. We had to get this done before the heavy snows set in. On a couple of occasions it did snow and once it rained in the middle of the night. We made a mad dash to cover everything.

The daily chores took so much time. Every morning ice had to be collected and melted. Coal had to be brought in and the fire cleaned and built. Fuel for the lamps and stove had to be bought. This took ages. We had to go to the little store and wait our turn in the queue. The store is the social centre of the village. Here gossip is exchanged and items of importance discussed : and it is here that the hunter exchanges his skins and tusks for money. It is an important place, and little wonder there seems no necessity to hurry. There is all the time in the world to mull over the merchandise, though the items rarely change and the choice is hardly apparent.

In one corner a large oil stove takes the chill out of the large, rather bare room. The shelves were always sparsely covered—with assorted nails, files, spare parts for lamps, rubber boots, bales of sombre material and a collection of other necessities. Fuel has to have a chit written and when everyone else is finished the buyer accompanies the storekeeper to the fuel drums. There then ensues a lengthy hunt for the barrel tap and the barrel wrench, without which the fuel cannot be tapped. Once the ground is covered with snow it becomes almost impossible to find either of these implements, although the whole village uses them regularly. If it ever occurred to anyone that they should be kept in a special place, no one does anything about it. So every day they are lost, and every day hours spent looking for them.

To speed up the process of getting fuel we decided to buy ten forty-five gallon drums, which we kept apart from the rest. Unfortunately, we lacked the necessary tools to draw from them and we still had to join the daily hunt. Wally would come back exasperated after wasting a couple of hours ferreting under the snow before he could tap any fuel. It was difficult to explain to a community who don't live by the clock just how important time is to us. The Eskimo lives an irregular life. His movements vary from day to day and from season to season. He is not obliged by diurnal darkness to keep an eight-hour day like most other people in the world. Dictated to only by the weather, which affects the movements of his prey, the Eskimo is a creature of impulse.

The children rushed around 'helping' till they were rewarded with a bar of chocolate each and sent away. One day, however, we had opened several large cases of Heinz baby food and a huge crate of Heinz Ready Made Meals. The packets were colourful, and the children let out squeals of delight when they saw them. We had been working hard and decided to have a bit of a rest before cooking the evening meal. I was most concerned about all the stuff that was still outside and asked Wally whether it should not all be locked away in case any was stolen.

'Oh, the Eskimos would never steal anything—they have far too much pride,' he said emphatically. 'Put it right out of your mind.' I felt rather guilty at having been so nasty, and marvelled at the integrity of the people we were living with.

I stretched out for a few minutes while Wally stood at the window smoking his pipe. An exclamation from him made me start up, and he declared incredulously, 'the kids are pinching the stuff.' I scrambled to the window to have a look. There they were completely oblivious to the fact that they could be observed, sneaking between the boxes and stuffing handfuls of various foods under their jerseys and down their pants. As I darted outside to catch them in the act they scurried away towards the village while cans of baby food spilled with a clatter at their feet before rolling noisily down the rocks. I called after them with all the authority I could muster. They stopped in their tracks and turned round with blank faces. They walked slowly towards my beckoning finger and stood inno- cently till I pointed to the peculiar lumps jutting awkwardly from their clothes. With a slight blush from some of them they dropped their loot, producing it from the most uncomfortable hiding places. I glared in silence at them hoping to strike terror into their hearts, but the only re- sponse was an infectious giggle from a three-year-old. 'You are very, very naughty,' I said sternly. 'Never come here again,' I said trying to mime the message to my uncomprehending audience. There was a moment's silence while I could not think of anything else to say, but I frowned as if it were intentional and I was letting the words sink in. My audience tried to keep a straight face and with a peremptory goodbye I dismissed them. They scampered away clucking to each other till they reached a safe distance when the main culprits—twins—yelled something unintel- ligible and stuck out their tongues. It seemed my 'angels' had a touch of the demon in them.

5

The crisp morning air was fresher than a cold shower, and easier on the senses. In the little cove near the hut the fishing boats leant askew on the rust-coloured seaweed uncovered by the ebbing tide. Turquoise lumps of berg lay stranded on the pink rocks at the water's edge, and the stones showed dark out of the snow. Our footsteps crunched through the sparkling crystals and left deep imprints. We breathed deeply.

Our feet were cold by the time we reached the hut. I decided to get measured as soon as possible for kamiks and for the fur clothes that we would need during the winter. We had beautiful suede coats which had been specially designed for us in England, but with the varying seasons in the Arctic we would need several different types of outer clothing. For winter it was best to have the fur outside so that the snow would slip off.

That morning I was in the kitchen when I heard a noise on the porch. A hand was fumbling and rattling the door knob, but without effect. I hurried to open it. A face the texture of dried fried fruit appeared. Kind brown eyes looked in, then disappeared into tight folds as Migishoo smiled. Granny Migishoo, one of our regular visitors, shuffled in, holding a frightened little boy by the hand. He looked round and cuddly in his polar-bear pants. He pressed against the door, unwilling to get too close to the strangers who spoke with gruff voices. His grandmother squatted on the low bench in the kitchen and chuckled. Wisps of hair fell away from the strange little bun at the nape of her neck. The old woman bent towards the child. I could only make out the word 'Kasdlunas', as she pointed a thin finger at Wally and Tom. The sight of two hairy men peering round the door was too much for the child. He screamed and stamped his feet, tugging at the worn skirt of the old woman.

The woman chuckled and muttered to herself. She turned to me and said, 'Ivdlit Kasdluna, uvanga Inuk.' 'You Kasdlunas, me Inuk.' The Eskimos described everyone other than themselves as Kasdlunas. They called themselves the Inuit—which simply means, 'the people'. For centuries, since they never saw anyone else, they believed they were the only human beings in the world. The word 'Eskimo' is a French corruption of a Cree Indian word which means 'eaters of raw meat'.

Kari had been asleep when the old woman and the child arrived, but she woke at the noise and looked in amazement at the tiny newcomer. The child seemed so distraught with fright that the old woman felt obliged to take him out. She cackled as she turned to go and indicated the beach, holding up eight fingers. In response to our puzzled enquiries she beckoned, as if letting us in on a secret. Tom and I followed her; Wally stayed with Kari.

A small group gathered round a young hunter and his wife as they flensed eight newly caught seals. The coats of the dead animals shone sleek and silvery. Their large doleful eyes looked reproachfully from their pretty faces. The hunter laid each one on its back and with a quick movement cut a straight line down its middle, as if unzipping a tight-fitting wet-suit. His wife used a woman's short curved knife, called an 'ulu'. Together they deftly cut the skin away from the thick layer of pinkish white blubber beneath. The skin was then dropped into the shallow water so the blood could soak off. As each creature was skinned it was hauled aside.

There was something repulsive, almost obscene, about the naked carcasses. The eyes, robbed of their protective mantle, protruded hideously. The black flippers, which were all that remained of the outer skin, looked like ridiculous boots which someone with a morbid sense of humour had put upon unsuspecting corpses—a joke in bad taste.

It was a cold job. The woman stopped occasionally to nurse her blood-stained hands. Children darted about, shouting happily, as the few adults stood and watched. A score or more dogs hung around waiting for scraps. A few brazen ones sneaked in amongst the crowd towards the carcasses, but a hail of stones and shouted curses sent them squealing away.

When the last seal had been skinned, the men in the crowd helped the hunter hoist the smaller ones on to the meat rack. The larger seals were cut into three pieces. The meat was black and very bloody. 'Ugghh!' exclaimed Tom, as the livid guts spewed out. 'I think I can live without that.' It did look most unappetizing, and I wondered how anyone could eat it raw. It would not take us long to change our attitude.

The hunter looked towards us, 'Do you want some?' We shook our heads, embarrassed that he might have thought we were waiting to be asked. An Eskimo will always offer onlookers a share, if he knows they have none of their own. In the old days the hunters shared the catch with the community. Now, however, Eskimos usually have to pay for the meat they get from a hunter—a practice some of them consider very strange.

As the last of the meat was slung on to the platform, the dogs made a dive for the pool of blood that lay between the rocks. They lapped it up greedily and turned with livid noses to look for more. We returned to the hut for something less gory.

The hut was crammed with children. It soon became a habit for them to come every day, livening the place with their gay chatter. Kari soon grew to expect them, and she squealed with delight at their arrival. They strove very hard to make amends for their earlier bad behaviour and returned all the food that was still missing. Some of the packets were nibbled at, but even an Eskimo child finds dehydrated curry difficult to take. As a peace-offering each child had brought a lump of ice. Some of these were very big, and their bare hands were curled up into their sleeves as they handed the dripping objects to me. In the face of such a gesture I could not bar the door.

I decided they should learn another lesson, and I beckoned them to follow me outside. They looked anxiously up at me. I closed the door behind me and told them all to watch. I then knocked on it and pretended to listen. I told them to practise, while I went inside and called 'Come in'. Of course, this was completely new to them, so they went on knocking while I grew hoarse yelling 'Come in'. In the end, however, I managed to explain the meaning of the words and we practised some more. On the whole they remembered this lesson, though occasionally they would knock and appear before I had time to answer.

Kari very soon learnt to take their rough handling, and after a few months I was more concerned for the safety of her playmates than I was for her. Unlike most Eskimo children of her age, she was very chatty and she soon learnt how to command. I often wondered how I managed to cram so many people into a room 14' × 11'. Needless to say, I was always stepping over several bodies stretched on the ground.

Unlike children in other countries, the Eskimos played no games of war. They played with imaginary rifles and harpoons, but these were never directed against people but against the formidable beasts that haunted the vast wastes of their land. Wrestling on the floor, they mimicked the fierce dogfights outside their homes.

One day Tom brought back a large egg that he had found lying amongst the stones during his evening walk in the hills. The children were very excited, and he gave it to one of the little girls. She dashed away, and reappeared a few minutes later stirring some sugar into it. She ate it raw— and to the envy of all her mates.

Occasionally some of the children would join us at our evening meal. Their diet normally consisted of meat, without any accompaniment, and it was a change for them to eat our food. They would wait for us to start before handling the knife and fork, somewhat uncertainly. They were used to holding a lump of meat in their hands and slicing bits off with a knife. They were always very dignified in these situations, watching the procedure with large black eyes.

The children noticed my passion for collecting stones. Within a few days I was swamped with a load of rubble, gathered in handfuls. At last I had to tell them to stop bringing them. I suggested they take them to their parents instead. They led me to understand that their mothers would not appreciate them the way I would.

By the end of September the weather was beginning to get much colder. Tom had left for England. He had been a marvellous help to us and we would have liked him to stay longer, but he had commitments back home. Savfak brought Kari's kamiks on the same day I got mine. The stitching was minute. The outer kamik was of creamy sealskin from which the hair had been scraped. It had been allowed to dry in the frost, out of the sun, till it became quite white. (The sun would have turned it yellow.) The inner sock was made of dogskin, from a young pup (probably one that could be spared from a large litter). Savfak had also made a beautiful outfit for Kari from the skin of a newly born seal. It was beautiful, silver grey, with a blue-black streak down the back. The trousers came down to her ankles, though sometimes the children had them just to the tops of their kamiks. The jacket was trimmed with blue fox. Kari looked really lovely in this new outfit.

Now that it was getting colder it was not so pleasant fetching ice. The driving snow, like hard pellets, stung my eyes and burnt my cheeks. I wondered how much colder it would get in winter, and how I would be able to stand it. The wind whipped into the skin and left it red and raw.

It was only after Wally had got us squared away for the winter that he had any time to think about filming. The enormity of the problem he had undertaken suddenly dawned on us. He had come to Greenland, happy with the thought that this expedition would put him back in the field and at the same time give him scope to use his artistic and creative talents. Neither of us had taken into account the technical problems when one person becomes producer, director, script-writer, camera-man, sound recordist, technician—all rolled into one. This apart from being husband, father, general helper, and protector!

The idea had originally been that I would help Wally when possible, if I could find someone to look after Kari. Failing that, Wally would get one of the locals to help him hump the gear around. In practice this did not work out. Invariably when Wally wanted to film it was inconvenient for anyone to babysit. And we found that the hunters of Herbert Island were very proud, and could not be employed as casual labour. So Wally was stuck with the job himself.

Soon after we arrived on the island we realized that three crates of equipment were missing. In them was Wally's large radio set which he hoped to use to call me when he went travelling. Also among the missing items were the B.S.A. tapes he needed if he were to film with synchro-nized sound. Wally had brought a beautiful precision-made Eclair camera, but it had to be protected against damage with an enormous metal case and when all his equipment was put together it became a for-midable weight to carry. Besides this he carried two battery belts, each weighing fifteen pounds, a tape recorder, which weighed fifty pounds, besides tripod leads, and mikes. Added to this, in winter there were lights and their batteries, bringing the total to about 230 pounds. When film-ing something like the spring walrus hunts, all this had to be carted for several hours across the ice, without the help of a dog team because dogs would have disturbed the walrus. The problems were enormous—quite apart from the possibility of the cold making the batteries lose their charge and the film snap inside the camera.

It was a long time before Wally's kamiks arrived, and he complained that his feet were being 'pushed out of his gumboots by the snow'. It was so much warmer in kamiks. Savfak showed me how to stuff them out with grass between the two layers. It is easier to walk on snow or ice with the flat sole, provided one shuffles, but they have no grip on a slope. Most kamiks are close-fitting round the top, as well as having a fringe of polar bear which stops the snow from getting inside. On long journeys, and especially in a storm, the men usually tie a cord around the top so that the snow cannot seep down. We used sheepskin for the inner socks on many of our kamiks, as this was very warm and did not smell. One of the worst smells in the hut was that of worn kamiks, especially if the inner socks were made of dogskin.

Every night the kamiks had to be separated from their liners and hung up to dry. If they had got very wet they had to be turned inside out. They must not get too dry or they would be impossible to wear without a lot of softening. This was one of the first things the women always did when they came to inspect our kamiks. They would pull them apart and spend ages softening them on a long stick with a broad blunt steel end. The soles were stretched and pulled over this till I thought they would tear, but they were very strong. In the old days, before they had steel, the Eskimos used to soften their skins by chewing them. By the time the women were old their teeth were completely worn down. Even today when a woman is sewing new skins she will often chew them first to soften them, and the men will sometimes chew polar-bear skin before it is worked on by their wives.

I often wondered how the women had any time to do anything after they had seen to the kamiks of the whole family. The sight of the scrofulous-looking kamiks was not something that would have encouraged me to chew them, especially as I knew where they had been. The most difficult part of putting the two boots together was to arrange the stuffing evenly between the two. Our kamiks never looked like those of the Eskimos. Ours were always lopsided, with the enormous sole inching up over the instep while the toes and heels curled up like protuberant lips. We looked positively deformed when they were on.

As the days became colder, the nights became darker and the sun sank lower in the sky. On 23rd September we had twelve hours' darkness and twelve hours' light. From now on the days would get shorter and shorter until the sun would finally disappear. Yet every day the colours of the scenery were entrancing. Even on the coldest days, when sky and earth merged in shades of grey, there would be a burst in the cloud, and the sun would sprinkle the bergs with a delicate lemon light. On these days the growling sea wrestled with the huge chunks of ice and dashed them against the rocks, milling them into a grating flotsam. I had never before felt so much alive, nor so much at peace.

But my moments of euphoria were sometimes shattered unexpectedly. One morning we were in the hut when suddenly a maniac cry rent the air, followed by squeals of terror and pain. We rushed out of the house. Beneath the meat racks dogs were fighting, a cauldron of flying fur. Women screamed at youngsters and snatched up toddlers. A hunter struck at the writhing mass with a harpoon. Again and again the weapon landed with a dull thud against bony heads. The snarls of the attacking dogs sunk to a low rumble as the agitation ceased. The dogs parted. But the victim did not stir. A trickle of blood dripped from its broken neck.

This type of incident was to become painfully familiar to us. From other settlements we heard tales of children badly mauled and needing surgical treatment; and over the radio one day we heard of a child attacked by a runaway team, who had died from his wounds. No wonder children were taught to protect themselves with whips and stones at an early age. The Eskimo rules his team by fear. It is the only way to teach them obedience. And it is the only way to protect his family from the bloodthirsty pack which can put to flight even the fearsome polar bear.

The husky is not always a vicious animal. On the contrary, it can be a very playful and affectionate pet. But like the wolf, it is unpredictable. The pups are as endearing as any small animals, but once the dog joins a team it becomes a savage creature, contending for position in the pecking order. When trained properly it is a marvellous worker and can pull an amazing weight for its size, providing one of the most exhilarating forms of transport. A good team is a hunter's proudest possession.

We acquired our own team one afternoon with very little warning. That morning we received a message that Orla Sandborg wanted to speak to Wally over the radio. He had to place fourteen dogs that belonged to a woman whose husband had just been drowned. Did we want them? Orla wanted the answer as soon as possible. The widow could not provide for them and he had promised to find a buyer. It was a unique opportunity to get a team, but it was two months sooner than we had planned to buy one. It would entail a lot more work for Wally, and more expense. However, it would save him the problem of training a team from scratch. He decided to take them.

That afternoon we were just about to go for a walk when I caught sight of a small fishing boat arriving, crammed with dogs. 'They must be ours,' I said to Wally, with some surprise. He went down to the beach to have a look. He had hardly got there when a flash of fur shot over the side of the boat. Seconds later several dogs bounded over the ground in the direction of the village, while their less fortunate mates floundered around in the icy water trying to get a footing on the slippery rocks. They shook the water from their coats, then galloped after the others through the village, leaving a trail of havoc behind them as they plunged through the teams of resident dogs. From every direction frenzied howls greeted the intruders.

An Eskimo limped ashore from the boat and awkwardly approached Wally. Standing crookedly, he made a gesture of handing over the dogs, saying emphatically, 'Fourteen'. We thanked him with some embarrassment and turned to follow the new arrivals. Most of the men were away but the women and children joined in the chase which led us backwards and forwards through the village, for well over an hour. The job was made more difficult by the fact that only two of the beasts had harnesses. The others had only a frayed bit of rope attached insecurely to them.

I had joined in eagerly, without actually considering what I was going to do with a dog once I had caught it. The reality of finding myself anchored to a bristling brute proved so alarming that I dropped the ragged rope and ran as fast as I could away from the dogs I had been pursuing for over an hour. But the children kept appearing with protesting dogs, which they insisted I take in tow. The bigger ones I let slip through my fingers, but I held on to a couple of cringing creatures whom I discovered did not belong to us in any case.

Eventually we had thirteen tethered to the rocks outside the hut. We had no idea if they were all ours or if we had inadvertently tied up a loose dog from someone else's team. We spent a few anxious days waiting for some reaction from the returning hunters, but fortunately we had made no mistakes. The fourteenth dog eventually turned up, but he fitted in so badly into the team that we were glad when one of our neighbours eventually relieved us of responsibility for him.

The locals all visited us soon after to cast an appraising eye on our team. They all stated the obvious—that we needed harnesses and leads for them. They offered suggestions about grouping them. Wally had his own ideas, but he often took their advice, so as not to seem churlish. We found very often that the locals would see us start a job and would come along and take over. It was meant out of kindness, of course, and we realized this, but at times we found it rather bothering to be treated like children. It was more of an aggravation for Wally when he was travelling with the Eskimos than it was for me at home.

Dogs need constant looking after, and can eat a family out of house and home. If they are not fighting and half killing each other, they are getting their traces into such a tangle that they nearly choke themselves to death. Hours are spent making harnesses and leads which can be bitten through within half an hour, after which the dogs launch themselves on the village. It is no fun to be constantly renewing and repairing these items. If a dog does this too often he has to have his teeth knocked out. This is a painful and noisy business and not a task the hunter enjoys. But on frequent occasions we heard the squeals of pain during these operations.

Our dogs seemed a bit thin and they fell upon the pemmican Wally gave them as if they had not eaten for weeks. Often in summer the dogs do go hungry. The Eskimo resents having to feed animals that are not earning their keep. On occasions dogs will be left for ten days or more without food if the hunter is rather lazy or if he is 'unlucky'. We would have to find some way of getting fresh meat for them. We were not allowed to hunt ourselves since the Danish Government only gives permits to the Eskimos. We had brought a fair amount of pemmican, but Wally wanted to save this for his journey in the winter.

Our first task was to make a set of leads and harnesses for each dog. Wally showed me how to splice the ends of the rope and how to lay out the harnesses, and the two of us set to to make them. We were interrupted several times by villagers. They picked up the harnesses and measured them. Everyone came to the conclusion that they were not quite right, but maybe they would do. They pointed out that such and such should be as long as an arm, another should be the width of two fingers, another three fingers, and the last the width of a fist. They seemed to make no allowance for the fact that some dogs were bigger than others (or even that some arms were longer than others). They laughed when they saw me sewing the harnesses. I was doing a man's job. But Migishoo said it was a good thing to see Kasdlunas doing things for themselves instead of asking the Eskimos to do it for them.

The division of labour was fairly strictly followed by the Eskimos. The man hunted, and provided the meat and skins. The woman scraped and washed and stretched the skins; she made the clothes and cooked the meals, she tidied the house and fetched water, and she carried the baby, on her back, in an Amaut. The men looked after the dogs, but it was the job of either to untangle the traces whenever the team was at home. The woman controlled the dogs with the whip while the man hitched them to the sledge, and it was her job either to walk ahead of him swishing the whip in front of the dogs to find a route over the tide crack, or to guide the sledge from behind to enable the man to jump on at a moment's notice when the dogs took off.

They must have thought us quaint, as we always shared the burden of work, although Wally always insisted on doing heavy work alone. We never insisted that a particular job was the responsibility of the other person alone. We did what we felt we had to do ourselves and if there was time we helped the one who had not finished. It worked out marvellously, though Wally always did more than his share. I talked to some of the women about our 'partnership', and some felt that they would like a similar arrangement with their menfolk. But others laughed at such an idea : it was such a Kasdluna's way of looking at things.

We found looking after the dogs a very time-consuming business. Cutting meat for them in the cold stung our hands till they were red and raw. Every dog had to be seen to get his fair share. Usually the bullies in the team pounced on the weaker ones and paralysed them with fright while they gobbled their portion. The dogs are merciless in their fights and invariably the weaker animal is set upon by the whole team—the cowardly ones giving the prostrate beast a furtive bite under cover of the larger assailants. Unfortunately the strongest workers were not always the best fighters, and sometimes a good worker would be ruined by its team mates.

6

Towards the end of September it became very murky inside the hut by about 10 p.m. Wally showed me how to light the pressure lamps. Lighting them was difficult and this was the job I detested most while living in the wilds. If you don't take great care they burst into flame, sending up great sheets of fire. It is as alarming as it is dangerous, and I was always afraid something would catch fire. The ceilings were so low and there was never enough water to put out a blaze. In such a tiny hut, made completely of timber, a fire would have been a very serious thing. I could never hide my failures : the clouds of acrid smoke, in the wake of a dozen coughing and spluttering children, would tell the village 'kutdlek ajorpok'—'the lamp was no good.'

Another hazard to my well-being and to Wally's peace of mind was 'can tops'. I have never had so many cut fingers as I had during those first few weeks on Herbert Island, when we lived almost exclusively out of tins. I got to the stage when I would try and hide my hands from Wally. Each new plaster brought a pained expression to his face, and sometimes he would say, 'You'll have to go home—you will never survive more than a couple of months at this rate.' Each time I would promise to be more careful, and remind him of the number of times every day he bumped his head on the door frame.

One evening though I thought my time had come to be deported. I was in the kitchen at about 8 p.m. cooking a meal, having spent most of the day melting down water so that I could wash my hair. I had two full buckets of water near the stove. They gave me a good feeling every time I saw them. I had never felt so rich in my life as when I looked at all that water I had so painstakingly melted down. Wally had just come in after a hard day's work outside and was exhausted and cold from long exposure to the wind.

I could just about make out what I was doing in the kitchen by the light from the other room. It was stifling in the kitchen from the heat of the stove, and I could not bear a lamp contributing to the heat.

I had cooked a curry, which smelt delicious, and I was just putting some chocolate sauce that I had made for afters at the back of the stove to keep warm when I felt the 'redhot' stove pipe against my arm. My howl of pain set off a chain of events, all with suitable sound-effects. I whipped back the chocolate sauce, which banged against the curry pot, which fell into the water bucket, with such a clatter that I stepped back into the slops bucket, which turned its bilge all over the floor.

It is too horrible to go into the details of the hideous sight of the kitchen when an ashen-faced Wally brought in the bright light. Enough to say that he generously helped me with the Herculean task of clearing up and, tired as he was, went to fetch fresh ice to make up for the two bucket loads that were lost. Towards midnight we sat down to our meal. We ate for a few moments in silence before Wally pointed to the enormous plaster on my arms. 'What did you do this time?'

'Burnt myself,' I said rather meekly.

He shook his head. 'Oh well, everyone is entitled to a few mistakes,' he said understandingly.

'Trouble is,' I muttered rather sheepishly, 'I seem to have used up my share, and we have only been here a month!'

As the evenings began to get darker I began to feel a sense of isolation in our tiny hut. I spent my days typing out the Eskimo language-book Orla had lent me, trying to translate the Danish into English. The job was long and laborious and I could not be sure that the translation was correct. There was an added problem: in Thule they spoke a dialect for which I had no vocabulary.

Migishoo was one of our most regular visitors, and I was glad of the old woman's company. She made a great effort to talk to us and was the first to notice if there was anything we needed. She would bring fresh grass for our kamiks, and was always clucking to herself about the fire and the lamps. One day she brought a pair of kamiks for Kari. She waited till all the children had left before she brought them out from under her anorak. They were badly made and grubby, although they were new. Obviously the person who had made them did not take much pride in her work. They were far too big for Kari, but I felt I ought to buy them because she had been so thoughtful. However, deciding a price for anything is always very difficult with the Eskimos. The first answer you will get when you ask is 'Naluvara'—'I don't know.' We spent ages trying to sort out a fair price. Migishoo's face had become rather anxious during the discussion, but she burst into a broad grin as soon as she saw the money, and she thanked me profusely for it. We bought lots of things from Migishoo during our stay on Herbert Island. She had a nose for our needs and would be shoving a fox tail or a new pair of gloves into our hands before we realized we actually needed them. There was always the same anxiety as we ferreted out the price she had in mind, and always the radiant smile once we had agreed on it.

Migishoo was a great old woman, the mother of five grown-up children, two of whom lived in the village. Her husband, a dour old man, who rarely smiled, was unable to hunt because he had bad hands. She therefore had to depend on her sons for meat, if she did not get any herself. Without a dog team, there was not much a woman in her position could do except shoot birds in summer, or catch seals in a net laid under the ice in winter. So she was grateful to earn a bit of cash from us or from odd work, like stacking the coal. For several days she and a couple of other old women could be seen humping the heavy sacks on to a small sledge which they hauled up to the centre of the village.

The first social call I paid was on the old woman. I was fascinated to see how she lived, because from the outside her house was the most interesting in the village. On three sides the wooden hut had been protected by a wall of stones and turf, on which lay a few old walrus heads and scattered bones. I took a presentation box of cigarettes as a present. All the Eskimos smoke profusely.

I hallooed from outside to give her warning that it was me. A friendly call answered as the old woman opened the door. Her little grandson peered sheepishly round, then scampered inside with a flash of bare bottom. The kitchen was tiny, even smaller than ours, and the remains of a meal were on a little table. She pointed proudly to a fox she had trapped. The wet skin had been turned inside out and stretched on a frame above my head. The thin legs stuck out at strange angles. On a wall were the wings of a gull, fanned out and sewn together.

She beckoned me into the other room which was about four times the size of the kitchen. There were a couple of sleeping platforms strewn with an assortment of grubby bedclothes. The floor was cluttered with scraps of skin (as I discovered later, she hoarded them like gold). There were some dusty plastic flowers on the table, and a plastic mobile caught in my hair. Migishoo gathered things up and shoved them under the bed. Her eyes lit up when I handed her the cigarettes and she hurried to get some cups for 'Tsee'. I was surprised how bare the room was, and how ordinary compared to the Eskimos' huts. There were several large religious pictures on the wall, and a huge poster of a pin-up in flimsy sugary-pink baby doll pyjamas.

Migishoo fumbled amongst a collection of things on the bench to find her glasses—an old-fashioned pair with small round lenses and black frames. Then she showed me an American magazine, dated 1925, dog-eared and torn, and without a cover, that had published an article about the Smith Sound Eskimos. There was a picture of her, taken when she was about twelve. She laughed loudly as she pointed to it. The tea was cold, and she apologized for not having any milk or sugar. From time to time she would pick up the magazine and open it at her photo and roar with laughter. She scrummaged through drawers full of rags and old clothes to find a few wrinkled and faded photographs. She pointed out various people whom I assumed were her family. When there were no more photos to show I thought maybe I ought to go. As I left she pointed to an old hand-machine and said she would sew some curtains I had started making by hand. 'Oh, no, don't worry,' I told her—thinking I would do a better job myself. But she called half an hour later to collect them.

Towards the beginning of October, when the snow covered everything, the air had a strange luminescent quality. At times the hills flattened into two-dimension, like an immense mural, but suddenly the evening sun would pour yellow vapour out of the clouds, as if from some distant furnace glowing behind the hills. Ribbons of burning light would spread across the grey sky and fire the tops of the bergs. Patches of thin ice floated in a wide band out on the Sound against a back drop of glaciers, which flowed like molten gold.

The children enjoyed every season. I often went for walks with them into the hills. They would skate on the thin ice of the shallow lakes or would run ahead and wave to me to come and see a mound of rocks which they said was a grave. One day they pointed to a little patch outside the church which had a white cross on it and a wreath of plastic flowers. They chattered excitedly, and pointed, but I could not understand what they were saying. At last they performed a grim pantomime of someone shooting herself through the mouth. They lolled about grotesquely with open mouths and hanging tongues and collapsed indecently on the snow. A young woman had committed suicide on the island the year before we had arrived, leaving a husband and three children.

The children loved to imagine on these walks that just round the next boulder there might be a polar bear. Many times they cried, 'Nanok!' These days it would be unusual to see a bear near a settlement, but once in a while their spoor was found on the ice on the far side of the Sound, and three years before a cub had been washed ashore near the village. Ten years ago bears were plentiful. Now the hunters had to travel north to Smith Sound or south to Savigsavik. Despite the reassurances from everybody not to be afraid they told stories of tracks being seen on the island, and I never felt completely comfortable going for a walk on my own in the dark.

On my trips through the village I would stop and chat with the locals. Some houses were more accessible than others. One of the biggest obstacles was the pile of refuse that towered outside most of them. Everything was thrown on to this pile, from slops to old tins, bottles, boxes, and old clothes These awful dumps spread like a huge cancer over the rocky ground. We threw only the slops outside: everything else I collected in a bin and dumped down one of the huge cracks in the rocks near the shore, away from the huts. Whenever anything was thrown out, a score of dogs would tear across to examine it. They seemed ready to eat anything except hardware. Surprisingly, though, there was a lot of blubber lying around which they ignored.

Once we got our own dogs I felt that the time had come to get rid of the hangers-on that did not belong to us, and with a noisy attack on them I made the symbolic act of chipping away all the yellow snow and ice which plastered the surround to the porch. I had no doubt that one of our own dogs would perform the same ritual pee up against the door, as the other dogs had done, and I felt if any dog was going to do it, it might as well be one of our own.

One day Wally asked me to go and untangle the dogs' traces. It would save him a lot of time if I could do this, and I might as well start now, he said, because if he were ever away without the dogs I would then have to do it on my own. It was very cold and rather windy, so I put on a heavy parka and thick woollen gloves. As I approached the team all thirteen got up and growled a soft resonant welcome deep in their throats. But a few could not resist taking a nip at a neighbour who might have got too close, and the victims howled as if they were being tortured to death. My steps faltered and I stopped on the edge of the lunging group. My peculiar attitude excited them and they began jumping up in the air to get at me

—whether in love or hate I could not tell. I could not be sure that they recognized me as the wife of the provider. And I was not too keen to find out. I glanced back to the hut, to see Wally watching out of the window and I pulled a face as he smiled encouragement.

This was the first time I had actually seen our specimens, and I did not particularly relish the sight. There was one huge black dog, one-eyed —as were two others—and almost twice the size of the rest, who was obviously the lead dog. Contending for leadership was a thick-set white dog with one ear so deeply cut it looked as though it would fall off if he shook his head. All the rest were either scarred or moulting. I had never owned so many ugly beasts.

We still had not got a whip, and so I had nothing to control the howling pack. A pair of snapping jaws caught on the edge of my coat and I yelled in terror. As I jumped back there was a cackle behind me : the ubiquitous Migishoo with a thin whip in her hand. She flicked it over the heads of the dogs and they cowered as it cracked. 'This is how you do it,' she said, cracking it again over their heads as they slunk to the ground. 'Don't say "shoo" to them,' she told me. 'Say "Hhhaaarrraaaooouuu".' The sound rumbled in her throat and I thought, 'If I heard that in the dark, it would scare the life out of me.' Together we tackled the job of untangling the traces, and Migishoo checked the dogs at the first sign of insubordinance. I had to take my gloves off to manipulate the rope. It was bitterly cold and the job complicated. The rope was covered with blubber and frozen dog excrement; my nails broke and my fingers ached.

At times it was difficult to get meat for the dogs and we had to feed them on pemmican, but usually there was a variety of meat for them— seal, walrus, or whale meat. Our first seal was given to us by Avatak, the young Eskimo who had 'serenaded' us that first evening we arrived on Herbert Island. He generously insisted on Wally having the largest of the seals he had brought in that day. Together they hauled it on a sledge towards the dogs, who grew frantic with excitement. When they cut the seal open they discovered a tiny foetus, perfectly shaped. Avatak brought it over for me to look at. I was upset—and even more when he laughed and threw it to one of the dogs. A large foetus, almost ready to be born, has beautiful white, downy fur. It always seemed such a shame, such a waste of life, but the Eskimos did not think of it in this way. Besides, there was no way of telling that the animal one hunted was pregnant.

Sometimes when we were short of meat, we arranged to buy some through the storeman. Wally would have to go down to the cove to get the seal weighed. But the weights, like the barrel tap, were nowhere to be found. Buyer, seller, and storekeeper would then get shovels and dig in the snow until they unearthed them. There was a set price for a kilo of seal meat and the sum was always worked out on the snow. The transaction could take up to a couple of hours while they looked for weights and then each of them did the sum.

On one occasion the problem was to multiply .90 kroner by 30. Wally stuck a harpoon between the 9 and the 0, to indicate the decimal point, and multiplied by three. The Eskimos said this could not possibly be right. They mutliplied by five, then by two—where they went after that Wally was not sure, but it was a long time before their answer tallied with his. And in the meantime both the Eskimos had reached different figures and had to start all over again. Wally would come back exasperated from these transactions. 'We can't go on like this,' he complained. 'What with getting fuel and buying dog meat there is no time left in the day to do anything else.'

We partly solved our problem by buying a thousand pounds of shark meat from the Greenland Trading Company. But the dogs did not like this too much. It was smelly and very oily, and the Eskimos said that the dogs would get intoxicated and very sick if fed too much on it. Orla said that it was only fresh shark meat that did this and that the stuff he sold us was several months old. But certainly there was a marked difference in the dogs' reaction to seal meat.

The seal is a marvellous animal because the whole of it can be used. From the skin the Eskimos make kamiks, or clothes for children, or the Amaut—the garment which women wear when they carry the child on their backs. Sealskin bags are used for storing birds in summer: and when inflated a sealskin bag makes a very good bladder to attach to a harpoon. In the old days, before the Eskimos used stone or steel cooking pots, they would sometimes hang up a sealskin with hot stones and water to cook the meat. Seal blubber was used as an alluminant, and the meat is food for man or dogs.

As the locals got to know us better they would occasionally bring in the huge liver, which they regard as a delicacy, especially when eaten fresh and raw. I found it to be the tastiest liver I had eaten. The meat is very good, and gives a very thick gravy because it contains so much blood. It has rather a pungent odour, however, and I always preferred to eat seal meat in the open.

We discovered that Avatak was the father of seven of the children who used to visit daily. They were very endearing and I grew more fond of them than of any other children in the village. I think I learnt most of my Eskimo from them, and before long we communicated quite satisfactorily. They all called me Maria, with the result that Kari eventually called me Maria also. They very soon began mimicking both the way we spoke Eskimo and the way we spoke to each other in English. Whenever Wally entered the house he would be greeted with a chorus of 'Halloo darleeng'.

They were fascinated by kissing. Eskimos do not kiss their children; they demonstrate their affection in a charming way of nuzzling the child in the neck or just under the nose, and giving the barest suggestion of a sniff. As Kari became more responsive, her kisses were in great demand and I once found a couple of three-year-olds practising 'how the Kasdlunas did it'. They clasped each other in a passionate embrace, kissed each other firmly on the mouth, and dissolved into a fit of giggles.

In the evenings the hunters came in with their catch, their boats covered with gore. An occasional damaged kayak showed where a walrus had attacked the frail craft and the hunter had perhaps barely escaped with his life. The walrus is one of the most dangerous animals in the Arctic, very aggressive and strong. A large bull can weigh as much as two and a half tons. The only creature not frightened by them is the killer whale: even polar bears steer clear of them in the water, though on land the walrus is slow and cumbersome and easier prey.

Walrus meat is very tasty, but it has to be cooked for a long time to get rid of possible parasites. It is good food for dogs because it is not too easy to digest, and so stays in the stomach a long while and the dogs do not get so hungry. Although the Eskimos know that it is dangerous to eat undercooked walrus flesh, if they are very hungry they cannot resist it. Before the newly killed animal has a chance to freeze they cut off meat and eat it—and invariably suffer the consequences.

One evening I made a great pile of pancakes and sent them over to Avatak's house in a large saucepan, to which I had added a delicious orange sauce. It was this gesture I am sure which prompted Maria, Avatak's wife, to visit. She had not been on the island when we arrived and, although I had noticed her several times in the village, I had not spoken to her. Wally thought her rather sullen, as she always avoided our gaze and seemed wrapped up in herself. I think it was just that she was rather shy. She visited unexpectedly one evening while I was cooking. I felt ill at ease and made a great effort to make her relax. She did not smile much, and it almost seemed as if it had been a great effort for her to visit. I took down one book after another to entertain her—showing her books on string craft, macramé, and needlework, but she barely flipped through them. It was only when I brought out my book on the Eskimo language that she took any interest. I discovered later that she hated sewing, because she had so many clothes and kamiks to make for her large family.

I was glad when Wally arrived from the Parcol hut, where he had been working, and a little later Avatak and little Eto arrived. I cooked a meal for them, and as the evening wore on our guests came out of their shells. Maria offered to teach me the Thule equivalent for many of the Southern Greenlandic words in the book I was using. We had been talking and drawing for six hours when they left at 1.30 a.m. The effort of wearing a perpetual smile had left us with aching cheeks, but the foundations were laid that night for a very close relationship between the two families.

Maria was not a Thule Eskimo. She was from Upernavik. Unlike most of the other Eskimos, she was fair-skinned. By strange coincidence she was the same age as me, and Wally was the same age as Avatak. She had married at the age of eighteen. I found she was as eager to communicate to me as I was to her, and was very interested in reading and learning. She went to great lengths to help me understand.

The more I knew Maria the more I liked her—a brittle shell covered a soft core, and her sarcastic tongue disguised a deep compassion.

Wally used to go to the Parcol hut every morning after breakfast. The children would arrive after an hour's school in the morning, and stayed for most of the day. But I insisted they left at meal times. I could not afford to feed twelve other mouths on our rations and I did not enjoy looking into twelve pairs of eyes following every mouthful.

'I suppose we are just as bad when we want to film the locals,' I said .to Wally once. The same thought had been going through his mind. He nodded disconsolately. He did not enjoy prying into other people's lives. He suddenly felt he had no right to be there.

'They are not interested in the record of their dying culture,' he said. 'They just think I'm a damn nuisance.'

We talked round and round the subject. It was true that the villagers were indifferent to the work we had planned to do here. We had hoped to win their confidence before turning a battery of cameras on them. We did not want to manœuvre them as if they were animals in a toy zoo, but we did want a true and artistic account of the last of the Polar Eskimos.

Wally had hoped that the Eskimos would be sympathetic because many of them knew him and because he had proved himself capable of tackling their environment, with their dogs and by their methods, but without their help. He felt this would be a bond with them, and was bitterly disappointed and hurt when he found this was not the case. What we did not realize then but which we discovered later was that the Eskimos did admire and respect him for the man he was, but they could not identify with him as film-maker.

Wally made some enquiries about accompanying the hunters on some of their boat trips. He was willing to pay for the inconvenience as long as he could film. There were many young hunters on Herbert Island and they had the reputation of being some of the finest in the district, but nobody offered to take him with them. Wally was irritated and despondent. There were no boats that he could hire for himself. We found out later that the hunters were afraid Wally would get in their way; but they were more than willing to take him with them if it was for the pleasure of joining in the hunt.

Eventually the storekeeper offered to take Wally out on a walrus hunt. But Wally had to hang about for days while they waited for good weather. On two occasions they started and turned back (though other hunters went on) because the man was afraid there was too much wind. Eventually they did go off and were away overnight. They caught a glimpse of a walrus a couple of hundred yards away. The Eskimos could not understand this was not worth filming and with great impatience shouted at him 'Kasdluna'—'FILM!' The rudeness startled Wally and he made a pretence of filming, but he realized that he must have appeared very slow and incompetent. Unfortunately he did not know enough of the language to be able to explain.

The fact that he was called 'Kasdluna' and not Wally as he had been addressed all morning showed just how impatient the Eskimo was. When they stopped for a brew Wally discovered he had left his mug behind. With great reluctance one old man produced a spare—but not without expressing his thoughts on those people who did not carry their own. Wally offered the Eskimos a couple of large bars of chocolate each, but they did not bother to share their hardtack biscuits with him, or even to ask if he wanted water.

We could not understand this lack of manners. For years writers have been singing the praises of Eskimo courtesy. They could not have changed overnight. It was some time before we realized that it was a custom that young people never drank from the same cup as old men. There were many similar taboos—usually for health reasons.

Wally remembered the incident, but the others obviously forgot: as soon as they caught a couple of seals their good humour returned and they offered Wally a trip on another day. When word got around that he was not such a difficult passenger he was offered a few other trips. But these were primarily to hunt, and filming gear was considered an unnecessary encumbrance. In the end, Wally got some excellent film, but the effort was always physically and emotionally draining.

We always locked our door when we went to bed, though the Eskimos never lock theirs. One morning at about six o'clock we were woken by a tremendous hammering and tugging at the outside door. Wally went to investigate. One of Migishoo's sons, Kaudlutok, thought Wally might like to go seal hunting with him. He was leaving in ten minutes. This was a typical Eskimo invitation—always about ten minutes to get dressed, grab a bite of something to eat, and collect one's gear.

It was a cold dull day, and they had to make their way over the frozen waves in the cove to get to the boat. I did not envy Wally his trip. They got back around seven o'clock that evening. I stood at the door while Wally came in and noticed Avatak cutting up a seal for his dogs, while Maria controlled them with a whip. The dogs clamoured, but they were held back with angry words and with the stinging lash. Avatak drew out the guts, squeezed the blood out of them between his fingers and handed them, in coils like a length of rope, to his wife. The children loved to eat them boiled.

As the end of the boating season approached the loose dogs were rounded up and added to the various teams. They were fed more regularly in preparation for the strenuous journeys they would make on the sea ice. A new season was soon to begin.

7

The young pups darted in and out of the small bergs which had stuck fast on the underwater ledge, held together by thin sheets of pancake ice which had sneaked between them in the calm night. The cove was beginning to freeze in. The rocks down to the water formed a marble staircase of ice, on which a red carpet of blood had frozen. Where the carpet ended 'the little hunter', as we called Kaudlutok, leant over the side of his boat chipping away the frozen gore. He had let the seal heads drip over the side of the boat so that the blood would not stain their pelts.

The candles of light on the horizon had only another week to burn before the sun disappeared completely from the Arctic for four months. Soon the fishing boats would make their last journey of the year. The men would gather on the boats and rock them from side to side to break through the thickening skin of ice. As a symbol of the season to come, the hunters would muster the dogs to haul the heavy boats ashore. Kaudlutok had a small boat—a hunter's boat that could stay on the water a little longer.

But after that the race began, the race to be the first hunter to run a team of dogs. There was no open challenge, just the instinct of competition. The hunters worked all hours. The dogs which had been running wild all summer were caught and tethered outside the huts. Strong fingers spliced ropes and fashioned harnesses. New whips were made and tapered to a fine point, and the unkempt sledges were repaired and the runners filed smooth. The work was long and laborious and much of it was done in the open. While the men made their repairs, the woman stitched fur clothes. The hunter needs at least three pairs of kamiks. Unlike the summer kamiks, which are smooth and furless, most winter kamiks retain the fur. They can be made from a variety of pelts—polar bear is magnificent and tugto (caribou skin) can be very attractive, but kamiks are also

6. Avatak, with Kari.

7. Migishoo.

8. Maria.

9. Eskimo houses are very bare, with only a few pictures or ornaments they buy in the store or have been given. Photos have pride of place, and this one was very special—a picture of Avatak and his parents outside their skin tent. It was given them by the doctor who took it, and was a source of endless interest. Avatak insisted that Wally should have it because he was his good friend. To fill the space Wally drew a picture of Avatak's five daughters.

made from the common Ringed Seal and the Harp Seal, while the thick soles come from the tougher Bearded Seal.

For sledging the man always wear polar-bear pants which reach from below the knee to just above the hips. They all have a wide cummerbund of sealskin attached. The parkas that the men and women wear these days are made of tugto and they reach to the top of the thigh where they hang in a fringe, either of the same material, or of polar bear. The hood is framed with foxskin. These are very serviceable and warm, but they can be very stiff if the skin has not been properly prepared. Very often in the old days the Eskimos wore parkas of blue foxskin. These look beautiful and very warm, but they are very fragile, and useless if they get wet (as in a thick snowstorm). When wet, they hang quite limp, snow gets knotted in the fur, which then freezes. Once frozen they are so brittle that the slightest pull would tear them.

Although the women often wear polar-bear pants when travelling, their usual costume is a parka, short fox pants of blue and white fox, and long kamiks which reach the top of the thigh and which are trimmed with a long fringe of polar bear. These kamiks are usually lined with tugto and are very warm on the legs, but the feet often get very cold. The Eskimo women have very dainty hands and feet, and they like to have their long kamiks close-fitting to show off their small feet. This means that sometimes there is little room for padding. To compensate for this, on a very long journey in winter, the women will often add to them a pair of tugto overshoes. This makes a tremendous difference, although on a large person they look rather clumsy. Long kamiks are not as flexible as polar-bear pants and they restrict movement, so women will sometimes wear polar-bear pants in preference on a very long journey.

Winter brings with it a new sound to the village. At the start of the 'day' the cries of men, children, and dogs ring through the village announcing the frustrations and excitement of the new sledging. Bellowed curses accompany a kick in the ribs as the brawling dogs grapple with each other, twisting their traces into tangles. The sharp crack of the whip threatens the struggling mass of fur as the dogs fight for precedence. Eventually the dogs are separated and the team finally settles into shape. The king dog takes the lead and the others follow, spread out like a fan.

Unlike most of their cousins in Canada and Alaska, who use motor toboggans to hunt and make the rounds of their traplines, the Greenland Eskimos still use dogs to haul their sledges. It is a far more romantic way of travelling, but it takes longer to look after dogs than to maintain a

snowmobile. We had brought with us two 'Skidoos', which Wally had used
to ferry some of his heaviest gear during his journeys. They were a beautiful chrome yellow, and the Eskimos exclaimed in delight when they saw
them. 'Not as dependable as dogs,' they commented, as their fingers
strayed over all the buttons.

The great advantage of the Skidoo is that it can pull very heavy loads
and still go three or four times the speed of dogs. There is no great sweat
looking for pickets on arrival anywhere, and of course none of the chore
of buying meat and cutting it up. The Eskimos would admit these were
advantages but they always maintained that on a long journey they would
prefer dogs.

'Why?' we asked, surprised at how concerned they seemed about it.

'Well, for one thing dogs don't break down,' they commented. 'And
secondly, when you run short of food, you can't eat a Skidoo.'

We had decided to use both forms of transport. Wally thought I ought
to try and overcome my fear of the dogs by handling them more often. He
suggested that I should feed them while he was in Qanaq for a couple of
days. I felt quite responsible as I went out, knife in hand, to cut the meat
up. We had most of it on a meat rack, but Wally had brought some
down and put it in a hut outside so that I could get at it. The 'meat' was
very cold and hard, and so oily that I had to take my gloves off. While I
was working at it Maria came over to help. My hands were swollen and
aching with the cold. The wind snatched and picked at my face and I felt
quite sick with the chill. I really wondered how I could face the winter
and the outside jobs, in temperatures of the ⁻30s° Centigrade. Maria
smiled sympathetically when she saw me struggling with the meat. She
got an axe and hacked at it.

When I had enough I put it in a box and carried it round to the dogs.
They were frenzied with excitement. I threw them the meat, but a few of
the large dogs pounced on the smaller ones and took their share. The king
dog was worst. He seemed to be everywhere. I was very annoyed, but
helpless. Fights broke out all around me. One poor one-eyed dog could
not even see the pieces I threw him when they were right under his nose.
I really felt sorry for him as the big black dog plunged over, snarled viciously, and snatched the meat. As if in answer to prayer, Migishoo
appeared, whip in hand. She seemed to have a sixth sense for knowing
I was in trouble, and she set to to quell the unruly team. With her help
we saw that each dog was fed.

I was glad when Wally returned and I could hand the chore back to him. Looking after dogs was really a full-time occupation. Although my father was a vet, I had no aspirations to follow in his footsteps. On the contrary, I was terrified of most animals and especially of huskies. However, I realized eventually that they could be quite friendly despite their fierce looks.

Wally tried to explain to Avatak and Maria that my father was an 'animal doctor', but as neither of us knew the word for animal I suggested he use the word seal instead. Maria roared with laughter at the thought of anyone wanting to cure a sick seal. So Wally drew a picture of my father at work, explaining that my family had lived in Ceylon for many years, and that the animals he had had to treat were very different from those found in the Arctic. The sketch of a tiny figure injecting a huge elephant had the two visitors rolling with laughter.

I felt a need for some sort of communal game to entertain the locals. Wally hated games because he thought them such a waste of time. But even when we knew a fair amount of the language we found conversation difficult. I always found it easier to talk to the women when their husbands were not around, but in company, after we had discussed the weather and the hunting there was nothing left to say, unless we drew from our own experiences. They rarely asked questions, and if we were not talking about things that we hoped would interest them, we were constantly asking for information of one kind or another.

I think it was easier to talk to the women alone because they often liked to talk about personal things, and sometimes about their husbands. I think if I had to live in the Arctic for several years I would find the lack of intellectual stimulus one of the most difficult things to overcome. The boredom that settled on the village when there was no work to be done was distressing to see. It seemed such a waste of life.

One person whom I felt craved some sort of intellectual outlet was Maria, although I do not think she was consciously aware of this. She visited me almost every day, even if it was for only a few minutes. Sometimes she would pore over our books. There were a few books in the schoolhouse which the locals could borrow, but she had read all these and they had not been renewed for a couple of years.

Maria told me how she loved reading. She would read aloud to the family when new books arrived, until the early hours of the morning. Everyone would fall asleep, but she could not put the book down. When there were no books she got very bored. There was no dance hall or cinema on Herbert Island, as there was in Qanaq.

As if to compensate for the lack of entertainment, Maria took it upon herself to help me learn Eskimo. She was a marvellous teacher and very patient. My grammar was bad and she could not explain how to put it right, but I built up a wide vocabulary with her help, and with a bit of mime I found we could talk about anything under the sun. A strong bond soon grew up between us.

There was a little newspaper produced in Qanaq which provided local news and a larger paper was sent up from Godhab for those who wanted to be better informed. Otherwise the Eskimos listened for international news to the small transistors that every household possessed. The joy of the little transistors was that one could hear all the telegrams being passed to the various settlements from Qanaq, together with news of those who were travelling and the conditions of the ice in various places. It was of great value in the lives of the Eskimos.

The meat racks had been empty when we arrived. Now they gradually began to fill, as hunters brought in seal and walrus. On the way to the cove one evening I passed a dog hanged from one of the beams of a rack. I had seen it running around that morning, and I had noticed its beautiful coat. I was obviously not the only one, because here it was hanging by the neck—its beautiful fur standing out and its eyes glazed and staring. The skin was needed for lining boots, or for breeches for children, in place of polar-bear pants. Dogskin is very warm and is much less stiff than polar bear. The Eskimos will never shoot a dog if they want to use its fur for clothing, as they say it spoils the pelt. Often I would be amazed at those dogs I would find strung up, but the villagers explained that they were not good workers and therefore they were more of a liability, so they might as well make use of the fur.

As I arrived at the group of figures silhouetted by a couple of paraffin lamps down by the shore one of the older village boys noticed me and yelled, 'Kasdlunagguak, Kasdlunagguak!'—'The white woman is coming.' There was something impertinent in his manner which I disliked. I was tired of being called a Kasdluna. They all knew my name—why did they not use it?

Rasmus had caught a Bearded Seal and a walrus. The Bearded Seal is very big and has a very tough hide. Its skin is too tough for clothing but it makes good soles for kamiks. Cut in a spiral, and stretched, it makes excellent ropes, which can be used as traces for dogs, bindings for sledges and lashes for whips. In the old days when the Eskimos lived in stone or turf houses, the window-panes were usually made of the intestine of the

Bearded Seal in preference to the common Ringed Seal. They were split and dried and sewn together, then framed with sealskin.

The next morning when a couple of the children addressed me as 'Kasdluna', I told them that they were to call me 'Marie'. I tried to explain that they would not like it if I called them by another name than the one they had been given. The children spread the word around and when Migishoo visited she said 'Ivdlit Inuk, Ivdlit Kasdluna nagga.' 'You are an Inuk—you are not a stranger.' I explained that my name was Marie and liked to be called that just as she liked to be called Migishoo. She asked what my husband's name was. When I told her, she mouthed it very carefully and went out of the house still memorizing 'Ooallee, Ooallee'.

One evening I went with Savfak to one of the houses in the village to get a sealskin for my long kamiks and to buy white and blue fox for my fox pants. It was very dark, and she clung to me to guide me. Even with a torch it was difficult to make out the dips and mounds in the snow, and we kept lurching into hidden hollows. To avoid making a wide detour we had to cross the thin ice of the tiny cove, and I slithered dangerously at first, until I realized that I should shuffle.

The house we entered was spotlessly clean. Three men sat on a bench and a young, sullen-looking woman sat beside the sink cleaning her nails. Savfak sat on a stool and I stood awkwardly, wondering how long it would be before I was invited to sit down. Eventually one of the men indicated that I should sit on a chair near the table. This was the first house I had been in where no attempt was made to welcome me, and I felt disinclined to stay long. Savfak chatted for a while, but soon came to the point of our visit.

We picked out the skins we needed. They were frozen and inside-out, so we could not really examine the pelt. A few days later, when they were ready for sewing, Savfak told me that they were very inferior. Without my realizing it, however, I had been charged twenty kroner above the price for prime skins. I felt disgusted with this dishonesty, and resolved to be more careful in future. Throughout the whole of our stay on Herbert Island this particular family remained aloof, except on the rare occasions when they visited to ask us to sell something they wanted.

Compared with most of the other huts in the village our hut was very cosy. It must have seemed so cluttered to everyone, since theirs looked so bleak to us. Our books and tape recorders and camera equipment lined one wall. Against another was the bed. I had made a big bolster of sheepskin from skins we had been given. I was going to drape the whole bed with these, but Wally said it looked too like a boudoir. We put up a few of Wally's drawings of Eskimos, and these were admired by all our visitors. The carpet made a tremendous difference, both in looks and in comfort, and I think without it the cold would have been unbearable for Kari, who spent most of her time on the floor.

We had not brought many ornaments with us and I was glad one evening when Aima visited and brought with her a tupilak figure which she had made from the lower jaw of a walrus. The beginnings of this form of art began nearly two hundred years ago in Angmagssalik, a town on the East Coast of Greenland. Originally, the Eskimos believed that tupilaks were a kind of troll animal. Originally they were made from the bones of children or certain animals in order to get rid of an enemy. They were made in great secrecy and the bones had to be put together by the thumb and little finger alone, or else they would not function. Earth or seaweed was used to fill out the shape: then the body was wrapped in a piece of skin and a magic song was sung over it, to give it life.

The tupilak was supposed to attack in the shape of the animal represented. In some cases it was thought to steal a person's soul. Then the body became very sick, and it would need an Angakok or witch doctor to get the soul back.

The creature I got from Aima had no such evil intention. It stood on our shelves for a long time with no harm to anyone. I was not sure if it was a gift or not. I did not want the locals to think that I would buy anything they brought, so I said nothing about the price. I did notice my visitor's knees showing out of her threadbare stockings and I thought if anyone needed spare cash it would probably be her. However, I gave her some cigarettes and decided to pay her a visit the next day to work out a price.

I entered a room as large as our living room. The green paint, blackened by layers of coal dust, was curling away from the walls. Sheets of Christmas wrapping paper were plastered over various parts of the room, together with a huge blonde pin-up in tight jeans, her full breasts pale against a tanned body. A picture of Christ gazed vacantly from the opposite wall, and there were the usual dog-eared family photographs.

The black stove was covered with pots containing water of different shades of grey, and alongside it on the floor was a large metal container catching the drips from a carcass of dark meat suspended from the ceiling. It had thick coarse 'skin' of a deeper hue where it had been exposed to the air for a long time. Cluttering the shelves alongside one wall and also on the floor lay a selection of used pots, mugs, plates, and cups, smeared with the remnants of long-forgotten meals.

Seated at the table, in a space she had made for herself amongst the clutter, was Aima's teenage daughter. She twiddled her pencil over some homework, while her mother bent over a small basin on the floor washing some worn clothing. The only ornaments in the room apart from the wall decorations were a couple of brightly coloured pieces of beadwork slung carelessly around the neck of an empty bottle. A brimming pee pot stood in the centre of the bedroom.

I was greeted loudly, with great friendliness, by Piautok. He hummed to himself and ran through his meagre vocabulary of English words a couple of times. I liked the old man. Aima was a bit put out to be caught doing her chores, so I did not stay long. It was difficult to make myself understood, and it was some time before they realized that I wanted to pay for the tupilak. At last Piautok suggested that ten kroner would be all right because it was partly a gift and because I had given them some cigarettes. I was ready to leave when they asked if I would like some tea. I refused as graciously as I could as I did not want to deplete their stocks —as I passed the cups caked with layers of several days' usage I was not sorry.

8

The boats were up. There was now no way out of Herbert Island until the ice formed. Until the dog teams could take to the ice we were cut off from the rest of the world. The only way out, in an emergency, would be by helicopter from Thule Airbase. The air rescue service was part of the agreement made when the Airbase came into being in 1952. The helicopters are alerted from Qanaq, but the only way to contact Qanaq is by radio. But the radio on Herbert Island was now out of order —so we were really cut off.

The dying sun, as if to compensate for its disappearance, put on a kaleidoscopic display of colour. I would wake in the morning to see a pale moon and an orange sun together in the blue sky. The dogs lay in pools of pink between the black rocks. Against the horizon dark and light bergs alternated : those nearest blushed delicately in the sun. As the day wore on, icebergs like green fortresses sailed into view, outlined in petrol blue and covered with snow. At night their colour deepened into mauve.

When the ice was four inches thick it was safe enough to walk on, though not thick enough to take a dog team. My first venture on to the new ice was a thrilling experience. I went with Taitsianguaraitsiak and Suakuanguak to lay a net under the ice. Each carried a harpoon and the old man had an old tattered canvas bag slung over his shoulders. His wife carried the frail rifle which always seemed to point in my direction, whichever way I moved. It was a cold day and we walked for over half an hour along the coast while the old folk looked with practised eyes for the slight bulge in the ice which suggested the breathing hole of the seal. It was 23rd October—the next day would be the last day of sunlight. Already there was a wide band of ice around the island.

We kept close to the shore line, up and down the rocks and around the tiny inlets, while the squat old man peered out of his good eye towards the blue-grey band of ice. (His other eye had been badly injured several years before when the tip of his whip caught it.) They explained that in places the wind had blown away some of the ice, and that was no good for netting. Eventually, however, we climbed down the steep bank on to a drifting floe near the shore. Stopping first to make sure I was safe, the two of them then skipped across several more floes and waited while I followed gingerly. It is a really strange sensation to walk on sea ice for the first time. An old Alaskan Eskimo Wally had filmed said, 'Sea ice flexible like plastic, fresh ice break like glass.' I was ready to test his theory, and I felt all the thrill and excitement of the beginner explorer. From time to time the old man struck the ice with his harpoon. He sucked contentedly at his little pipe and his wife and I waited respectfully for him to lead the way.

As we left the safety of dry land I thought of the icy water just a few inches beneath me—water that could paralyse the body in a few minutes. Before long we reached a hummock in the ice like a huge boil frozen as it was about to burst. Taitsianguaraitsiak picked a spot about four yards from the mound and began to chip a hole in the ice with the pointed end of his harpoon. He made a hole about a foot in diameter. Then Suakuanguak scooped the mush out with an old frying pan. I could not help noticing how straight their backs were whenever they bent over. They seemed to bend from the hips—'chevron-shaped', as Wally called it.

The old man explained that the seals would come up for air into the little hummock: then, on their way back, they might get caught in his net. 'Imaka. Imaka nagga.' 'Maybe. Maybe not,' he laughed as he said it. His wife chuckled too. The Eskimos always used the word 'Imaka', 'Maybe', when they talked about anything.

It was lovely to see how well these two old folk worked together. They seemed so dependent on each other, so much in tune. I liked their ready smile and the concern they showed that I should be safe and not too cold. It was easy to see in them the spirit that had made their ancestors survive in this inhospitable environment, without the assistance of white men and without the accoutrements of civilized living. These old folk had been brought up the tough way, before the village of Kekertassuak had sprung up. These were the last of the pioneers, the true Inuit.

When the old couple had made three holes, five or six feet apart, they began to put the net together. They stretched it across the ice to unravel any tangles, and tied small stones to one side to weight it down in the water.

The skill came in getting the net into position beneath the ice. The old man tied a length of gut to one of the top corners of the net, and the other end of his harpoon. He then threw the harpoon like a spear through one of the holes in the direction of the next. Suakuanguak or I had to catch it as it glided past. I did manage to catch it after a few attempts.

When the gut line was running from each corner of the net down through the centre hole, and out to the holes at either side, all that remained was to lower the net carefully through the centre hole, tighten the lines, and anchor them so that the net hung taut in position beneath the ice. A quick look into the middle hole and the old man was satisfied that the net was hanging right. We kicked the snow back into the holes to cut out the daylight, and the job was done.

We rubbed our hands together to restore the circulation and looked round for a place to walk ashore. 'When do you think a seal might get caught in the net?' I asked, in Eskimo. 'Akago, imaka.' 'Tomorrow, maybe,' replied Suakuanguak with a mischievous look on her face. 'Kisiane imaka nagga.' 'But maybe not.' We all laughed. These two people were so used to hunting and the joys and disappointments that went with it. If there was a seal they were glad, but if there was not they accepted it calmly.

The ice soon grows. It was only a matter of days before the hoarse cries of men and dogs rang through the village to announce the start of the sledging. At the start of a journey the difficulty is to get the team on to the ice. The ground is strewn with rocks which snag the traces and dogs are often pinioned to the ground and run over. If the load is light they escape with slight injury, but occasionally a dog is killed. The owner of the team, or his wife, walks ahead of the dogs cracking the whip from side to side to slow down the excited team.

Then, apart from the rocks, there is the tide crack to get over. This rises or falls over a range of twelve feet. It is a jumbled mass of small bergs with a sharp, serrated edge. At high tide a broad band of water separates it from firm ground and it is impassable. At all times it is hazardous, being both steep and slippery.

Normally the sledge slithers to a halt on the crest of the 'wave', then topples over at tremendous speed. Dogs slither frantically down the slope to escape the sharp runners hard on their tails. Sometimes the hunter will ride the sledge over the crack, but often he too struggles for a foothold with his dogs. The sledge hits the surface, squealing and lurching.

Quivering momentarily from the shock, it leaps into life after the heaving huskies, and the hunter jumps aboard. The whole thing happens so quickly, there is no time to think : you have to act on impulse. But what a marvellous sight it is to see a team of huskies breaking out on to the frozen sea!

My own first ride by dog sledge was like a romantic and exciting dream. As on most mornings, the whole village was alive with the bustle of sledging; screams, yells, and howls intermingled in the frosty air. Wally struggled across with his camera equipment to where Taitsianguaraitsiak was hitching up his dogs. We had arranged to accompany the old couple on a trip to film the net laying.

The sun had set on the Arctic a few days before. Now there were only a few hours of twilight each day. As the old man gathered his dogs in groups of three and brought them to the sledge, furious fights broke out. Suakuanguak lashed at them with the whip. The gentle old man roared at them with a fury I would not have thought him capable of, and beat them with the butt of a harpoon till they fell apart. Finally, all were hitched to the sledge, with bright blue traces.

Except for Wally's camera gear the sledge was lightly loaded. A couple of tugto skins were spread along it for us to sit on. A brew box, a tent, and a rifle were the only other items. Suakuanguak looked gorgeous in a beautiful fawn tugto parka, trimmed round the hood with blue fox. She had on a pair of polar-bear pants, but still managed to look the essence of femininity. She glanced at my ski-pants and asked if they would be warm enough, but I assured her I had plenty on underneath. She was not convinced, however, and fetched a warm blanket for me.

'Jump on.' The words were so unexpected I had hardly registered them before the sledge began to move away. I hurled myself after it and grabbed hold of the ropes to lever myself on. Wally leapt aboard and Suakuanguak glided on to it beside me as it whipped past her. I sat with my legs in front of me to avoid the rocks and ice knobbles. Suakuanguak sat side-saddle with her feet over the side so that she could jump off at a moment's notice. We had a run of about two hundred yards down to the sea ice. The men jumped off from time to time to guide the sledge from some obstacle. I held on tight as we straddled the gaping tide crack and tipped precariously to one side. Once over, the dogs broke into a gallop on the flat ice.

The only sound was the panting of dogs and the rasp of runners on occasional rough patches. One by one the dogs hobbled along for a stretch like deformed creatures as they emptied their bowels. They always did this when they started a journey, and the first five minutes of every sledge ride are characterized by the heavy odours of the excited dogs. In time it ceases to be offensive—though I heard a story of one 'explorer' who was so disturbed by the smell that he had a screen erected between himself and the dogs.

Taitsianguaraitsiak slumped on the sledge like a rag doll and turned to us with a broad grin. He lit his pipe and chatted to us about the team as it galloped at a steady pace, parallel to the coast. As we approached an obstacle he muttered a simple command, 'Hako, hako', 'Left', or, 'Achook', 'Right'. The dogs obeyed almost immediately. He hardly ever had to use the whip. His team was one of the best in the village. He had trained them all since they were pups and his face lit with pride as he demonstrated how easily he could manœuvre them.

We drove for a few minutes, then stopped at the site of the first seal hole. 'Imaka puisse perengilak.' 'Maybe there's no seal,' they both said. They scooped out the ice from the centre hole and the old man peered down. 'Ajor—puisse perengilak.' They both burst out laughing, as if the very idea of there being one was very funny. We drove on, and the performance was repeated at a second hole a couple of miles away.

At the third stop we were supposed to film, but it looked as if there was a net already laid there.

'Whose is that?' asked Wally, surprised.

'Ours,' they said, as if it were obvious.

'But I thought you only had three nets.'

'Yes, we have,' they agreed.

We stood and looked at them for a moment, hardly daring to ask, 'Well, what about the net you are going to lay today?'

'Oh, we have not any more—we laid it yesterday,' they said, pointing to the hole.

Wally's face sank. 'What an utter waste of time,' he breathed aside.

The old folk sensed there was something wrong. They both glanced anxiously at us, their happy faces screwed into a worried frown. I was sorry to see them upset, and equally sorry that Wally's time had been wasted. 'Well, since there are no seal, let's us go and look at the old stone houses,' I suggested. I knew they had lived in them at one time.

A look of relief crossed their faces as they agreed with enthusiasm. The old man laughed as he got back on the sledge. 'It was a really good house when we lived in it,' he said.

As we neared the houses the old man pointed out a hole in the cliffs which he said had once belonged to him. 'It was where we stretched our skins,' explained his wife. We turned towards it and stopped the sledge underneath the black cliffs. Thick, jumbled ice led up to them, and there was a white band, three feet deep covering the base, where the tide had risen and fallen several times and drops of water had frozen on the cliff face, gradually getting thicker.

We walked to the cluster of stone houses and they pointed out with great pride the house they had lived in before they had moved to the village in 1958.

'It was very cosy in here,' said Suakuanguak nostalgically, 'and we could see lots of seal and walrus from the window.'

'There are not so many nowadays,' her husband commented. 'The motor boats have frightened them away.'

Suakuanguak pointed out the space where the window used to be, explaining that it was made of seal gut. She hummed to herself as she began pulling up clumps of the coarse grass that grew around the house. 'Very good for kamiks,' she murmured.

We made our way back down to the sea ice. 'I will get some more netting and make a new net tonight,' Suakuanguak said, 'and you can come with us tomorrow and film.' She looked anxiously at me to see if it would be all right.

The trip the following day was more productive. The old couple found two seals in one net. It was a cold clear day with a bitter wind and the horizon was dotted with tiny black figures staking their claim to likely spots for seals. The spot the old man chose was near an iceberg. While he chipped away at the ice holes, Suakuanguak lit the primus and got a brew going underneath the frail tent that they had stretched across the sledge, leaning on a couple of harpoons. It was very cosy inside and we were glad to get in out of the cold and warm our hands and feet.

Savfak had worked hard to make my fox pants and long kamiks. The pants were very warm, but I felt a bit ungainly in the kamiks. They were so stiff it was like wearing plaster casts on both legs. I had to be helped into them, and could not bend my knees when I sat down. 'They will supple up in time,' Savfak had promised me. I was much warmer than I had been a few days before, however—it was obviously sensible to dress like the Eskimos.

It was marvellous to stand for a few moments and gaze at this vast amphitheatre. The ice creaked and groaned around us like a door swinging on rusty hinges. The dogs sprawled on the ice licking their paws and scratching in the fresh snow to slake their thirst.

I walked between the two bergs near us. They stood thirty feet high. I had never been so close. I could actually climb on them. As I stood on one, I noticed that it was moving faintly up and down, in unison with a strange grating sound. I scampered off quickly to the safety of the tent.

The ride back was very bumpy. We caught against ice knobbles frequently and the dogs yelped as they were pinioned to the ice. On a couple of occasions the sledge just missed running over one of them. It squealed and lunged away from the runner, and it was a wonder it was not strangled in its terror. We missed it by a hair's breadth.

'What would happen if we hit one?' I asked Wally.

'It might be badly hurt, or even killed. In which case they would put it on the sledge and use its skin.'

We bumped and lurched over ramps and slammed down the drops, rattling every bone in our bodies.

That evening our two travelling companions came for a supper of seal liver. Suakuanguak was to make polar-bear pants for Wally and took out a bit of string to measure him. At each measurement she would make a knot in the string. Eventually there were so many knots that I wondered how on earth she would remember what they all meant. As if reading my thoughts she suddenly burst out laughing and said, 'Oh, I will have to do it again. I have forgotten which is which.' When she left she still looked puzzled.

It was becoming more and more difficult to get ice. The rocks down to the sea ice were very steep and slippery. The cracks in the ice went down several feet, sometimes a couple of feet wide. It is very frightening for a newcomer to the environment. It was so wet at times, and I fell so often. At first I did not know which was good ice and which was salty. There is a great difference in the texture. Ice from the bergs (which is freshwater ice, and which can be as much as 2,000 years old) is a lovely crystal colour. It is very clear and breaks off with sharp tinkling sounds. Part of this ice would be salty, where the underside had been thrown up, but this was very cloudy and difficult to break. Often, however, the water would cover all the good ice, and so two or three inches had to be chipped off all round the berg to get at the good ice.

As the twilight grew shorter each day I wondered how I was going to manage to get the ice in the dark of winter, with only a torch or a petrol lamp to light this huge black void. As the winter closed in, the environ-ment became more and more frightening.

One evening I sat in the hut gazing at the thin film of ice that covered the windows. It had formed into beautiful fern shapes and it sparkled like some exotic bead-work. Kari had had a bad cold and I had kept her indoors for a few days. I felt quite housebound and depressed not to be able to enjoy the few hours of twilight. How would I feel in winter after even the twilight had gone? I did not like going out in the dark by my-self, but I would have to fetch coal and ice and run the gauntlet of the dogs when I went visiting.

Some of the dogs looked really menacing. How much worse it would be in winter, when I might flounder into them unexpectedly. It was so easy to lose the sense of direction when there were no lights to follow. How would anyone know where to look for me if I did get hurt or lost? I had enough problems looking after Kari, keeping her healthy and amused.

'What's up?' broke in Wally unexpectedly.

'Oh, nothing,' I said.

'Come on, tell me what's the matter.' I really wanted to unburden my-self, so I poured out my worries—not the least being the fear that I might be caught by a polar bear while we went sledging in the night and Wally might not even know because he would be sitting at the front of the sledge and would not hear me if the wind was blowing in my direction . . .

Wally listened patiently and talked over all the problems, trying to reassure me. That night I found a little note slipped into my sleeping bag :

'For Marie from your loving husband—regarding the coming of winter's darkness.

> 'Ghaist nor bogle shalt thou fear;
> Thou'st to Love and Heaven sae dear,
> Nocht of ill may come thee near,
> My bonnie dearie.'

(Robert Burns)

As Kari grew more used to the villagers she became more responsive, and soon they began to recognize Eskimo words in what appeared to us childish mumblings. Their delight at this was quite charming and I realized just how much they appreciated our efforts to learn their language. I was thankful that she had been so healthy since we had arrived, although of course, she had the occasional coughs and sniffles that the other children got. Kari was quick to learn from them and it was not long before she, like her playmates, was wiping her nose on her sleeve.

One night I left Kari with Wally and decided to go for a walk. The first full moon of winter bathed everything in a brilliant silver light. The whole world, as it seemed from our island, was veiled in snow. No sound or breeze disturbed the serenity.

I skirted the houses, so as not to walk into anyone's dog team, and made my way towards the far cove, in the direction of the old huts. The water had filled in a wide scoop which led into the cove and this had frozen over. In the silvery light the new ice looked waxy, and it bent under my foot. I liked this walk because it was in sight of the lights from the village and I drew some comfort from them. I did not want to go up into the hills because they were too eerie in this light, and I would have died of fright if I saw man or beast.

I was about halfway across the ice when it began to dip quite noticeably under my feet. My courage began to drain away. To go on was impossible, and to return was almost as bad, but at least I had got that far, so I should be able to retrace my route. I shuffled back, slithering like a cork on slippery patches and breaking the thin skin in other places.

I would gladly have gone straight home when I reached firm ground, but I could not bear to seem such a coward, so I followed the edge of the ice round the cove and up the bank to the stone huts. I saw the deep footprints where Wally had walked a few days before when he was filming. They were comforting, but the place was very spooky and the dark rocks looked awesome. Strange figures peopled the shadows and I actually thought I saw a person sitting near one of the meat cairns. As I moved the figures seemed to move too and I kept stopping quickly in my tracks to see if I could catch them out.

I told myself that it was a waste of beautiful scenery and that I should stop frightening myself and look at it. So I stood on the high ridge overlooking the pagan camp site, where the bones of the dead shone in the moonlight. All around the land was white, merging into a flat shimmering plain which stretched far to the horizon in one direction, and guarded by mountains on every other front. A sphinx-like berg dominated the vast desert of ice, broken up by occasional oases of light radiating from ice castles. Myriads of sparkling gems littered the ground and crunched beneath my feet. I felt like an explorer gazing on a new planet, unearthly and beautiful.

One day, a noise from the coast line attracted us all, and we went to investigate. Two teams of dogs had arrived from Qanaq. The tide crack was a formidable wall, and there was a gap of a few feet between it and the shore. As dogs slithered and fell the drivers shuffled to the front to inspect the ice. Their lanterns swayed above the silhouettes and I saw that one of them was the storekeeper. The sledges were piled high with packages. I hoped there was mail. There was much heaving and pushing while the drivers urged the dogs forward with the words, 'Huk, huk, huk'. I left them to it and speeded home to put on the kettle. If there was mail we would have visitors.

Minutes later the door opened and the storekeeper's gawky teenage daughter shuffled in with a blue cloth bag. There definitely was mail. She dropped on to a chair in silence and sat like a fallen sponge while I made some tea. I sat trying to make conversation with my limited vocabulary, with no response from my visitor, till my patience gave out—throwing etiquette to the winds I picked up the bag and sorted through the letters.

We sat reading the post till the early hours of the morning. We read and reread letters from home to make sure there was nothing we had missed. We fell with hungry eyes upon the magazines. Often we had wished for a few minutes' relaxation with a magazine, as a change from the literary desert we found ourselves in. But we had forgotten how hedonistic was the society we had left, and the articles and pictures shocked us into an awareness of its depravity. These—a cross-section of magazines you could read in the dentist's waiting-room—seemed obsessed with pornography, abortion, homosexuality, violence, and drugs. Sensational erotica glared out of the glossy pages. The contrast with the simple society we were living in was infinite. I felt ashamed of them and hid them so that the Eskimos would not see them. I did not want to expose them to the worst aspects of our culture. If this was what they were supposed to aspire to, it was a sad reflection on our civilization. We went to bed with troubled minds and thought of our Eskimo friends—how blissful was their innocence.

The best feature of winter is the companionship that people begin to draw from each other. We soon had visitors every night. One evening, Kaudlutok visited, bringing six bottles of beer. The gesture was most unexpected and extremely generous, as liquor is rationed in Thule. We felt embarrassed to take his share. However he insisted, and we each took a bottle, persuading him to join us as well. He had already been drinking and was very friendly and loquacious. I liked Kaudlutok, a slim strong man with a handsome face. A slight moustache enhanced his strong features and his hair, when he was not wearing a woollen cap low on his forehead, curled up in a great sweep away from his face. He told us that many people would be drinking tonight because they had collected their ration. He predicted that there would be fights. He laughed and added that Wally and I would probably be at loggerheads later.

As he was chatting, the door opened and Migishoo rolled in on rubber legs. She stood unsteadily for a minute at the door to the living room, her eyes large and vacant. In her fingers a cigarette hung on its last shreds. She found a seat near her son and snuggled into it like a bug creeping into a hole in the wall. From time to time she caught my eye and drew circles in the air behind Kaudlutok's back, jabbing in the air towards him to indicate that he was drunk. Kaudlutok was explaining the rationing system to Wally.

Migishoo staggered over to me. I had still half of my first bottle in my hand. 'Drink up,' she said, 'and have another.'

I told her that I had already had enough. Why didn't she have a bottle? No. It was for us; she would not take any. However, the strain of waiting for me to finish seemed too much, and she struggled to open a new bottle.

'You and me will go seal hunting tomorrow,' she whispered. 'I caught two seals in one net today and there may be more tomorrow. Leave the baby with him.' She pointed to Wally. Her nose wrinkled and her eyes disappeared completely into the folds of her skin. Pointing to Kaudlutok she described another circle in the air, and shuffled out unsteadily, slamming the door behind her.

Not long after, Inaluk, Kaudlutok's wife, arrived. 'Ah, she has come to fight me,' joked Kaudlutok. They stayed till 1.30 a.m. Then they offered to get more beer, but Wally thought we had had enough. Before finally going to bed Kaudlutok returned with an old rope dog collar, fastened with ivory, which he insisted Wally take. We had complained that evening that one of our dogs kept biting through his harness, and talked about putting him on a dog collar and chain. This sort of gesture is typical of the generosity of the Eskimos.

If ever I was firm with Kari the Eskimos were shocked. To them a child could do no wrong. What did it matter if they were indulged—they were only children? My efforts to explain were always cut short by a look from Maria which seemed to say, 'You Kasdlunas are all the same. You have no heart, and no love for your children.'

At last the day came when Wally was ready to take his dogs on to the ice for a trial run. He had been trying for so long to get a sledge, and had eventually bought a very long one, made of oak. It was very heavy, unlike the usual lightweight Eskimo sledges, but it had travelled many miles and seemed in good condition. The handlebars needed repairing, and Kaud-lutok insisted on patching them up for Wally, although he would have preferred to make a new pair himself. At times the Eskimos were too thoughtful. They took the responsibility out of one's hands, and it always seemed churlish to refuse their kindness. Yet we would often have been better off doing things our way, which we knew best, rather than adopting Eskimo methods.

It was a very cold day, with a strong wind that ruffled the fur of the dogs. Before he left the house Wally started to make a loaf of bread.

'This is going to be a beautiful loaf,' he said, 'I will enjoy some of that after my ride.'

I had learnt how to make bread but Wally occasionally made some to give me a break. I stoked up the fire, and made a mental note to slip the bread in the oven just before I went down to the tide crack to help Wally with the sledge.

The dogs were frenzied with excitement, jumping about as if possessed. The big black dog threw his weight into every skirmish, sometimes adding to the noise, sometimes quelling it. It took Wally's whip, as he collected the dogs in threes and attached them to the sledge. He took the weakest first and then the stronger ones. I had to stand at the head of the team and swing the whip over their heads to keep them from running off. The whip was difficult to manage. The lash was thirty feet long. There is an art in handling it which only the Eskimos seem to have mastered. In my inexpert hands it became an instrument of self-torture. As each new group of dogs reached the sledge, they fell upon each other like wild animals. I lashed at them with fright—and screamed with pain as the whip stung me in the face. The fighting animals lurched towards me, snapping and snarling, and the sledge began to move after them. I was afraid it would run me down. I slashed in the air to beat them off as I stumbled back.

The whip is like panic itself: it flies around aimlessly, slapping one on the back of the thighs, snagging on the rocks, catching on the guy ropes of the huts. All bedlam was let loose when the last of the dogs were added to the sledge. Tying the leads to the centre trace Wally suddenly found himself in a mass of writhing, snapping fur. Thirteen fighting dogs engulfed him, and he was almost pulled to the ground. He kicked out, as the traces tightened round him, and snatched for the whip which I flung to him. With a bellow from the depths of his lungs, he avoided the threatening muzzles and smashed the handle of the whip into the middle of the many-headed fiend. Eventually it fell quivering apart. The whip cracked again and again over the heads of the now cowering beasts as Wally restored order amongst them. He picked out a few of the more vicious dogs and let the sharp point of the whip sear into their flesh, until they howled with pain. In a few minutes they were silent. They were ready to go.

As the sledge moved off Migishoo rushed up with a tugto skin she had been softening for us, and threw it over the sledge. In our excitement we had not remembered to put down any padding for Wally. She brought a small whip with her and told me to call, 'Arechit!' to the dogs while I wielded the whip. That was the way the Eskimos quietened their dogs.

We jostled our way over the uneven ground towards the tide crack. Wally strode in front with the whip and I trotted behind pushing the sledge away from the many obstacles. At the tide crack he kept ahead of the dogs and I slid down the steep walls of ice on my seat. 'Unhook those traces, they are caught on that knobble,' directed Wally. I slithered awkwardly as my feet went in opposite directions down the angular ice and eventually crawled over to the knobble. As I pulled at the taut rope which anchored the sledge, Wally got ready to dive on. The straining dogs shot across the floes as the rope was released and with a wild whoop, Wally hurled himself after them. He landed on his back on the sledge and waved to me as the team whipped out over the ice.

I laughed to see him go. He loved sledging and was as proud of his team as any Eskimo. He was so generous when it came to sharing experiences, and was so patient with my mistakes. His confidence in me gave me courage when I was afraid. I watched as he disappeared out of sight.

When I got back to the hut it was stifling. The door of the stove was still open : it was red hot. I rushed to the oven to look at the bread. It had risen to magnificent proportions—but the crust was black. I wrapped cloths around my hands and levered it out. But the tin was so hot it burnt through and I dropped it. A clatter from the water bucket made me freeze. Surely this time Wally would not forgive me—there was a limit even to his patience. All I could do was to scoop the soggy loaf out of the bucket. As it fell apart I could tell the texture was perfect, a beautiful specimen. I had to do something to try and save it, so I cut off the crust and put it back in the oven to dry out.

Maria came in just as I was putting in the second part. She looked at it askance. 'Well, I suppose Wally is in Canada by now,' she laughed. She had obviously seen the team take off.

'Yes, he said he might be back without the dogs,' I commented. Although it was a common enough experience amongst the Eskimos none of them liked to admit it and Maria obviously enjoyed the thought.

We need not have worried, however, because a couple of hours later Wally returned with team intact. He had had a marvellous ride, though the dogs had not responded to any commands. His eyes fell on the bread. 'How strange it is,' he said, cutting a slice. 'Yes it is rather,' I admitted, without explaining why.

A lot of care has to be given to the men's clothing when they return from a sledging journey. The kamiks have to be separated from the inners, dried and then softened before they are worn again. The polar-bear pants have to be turned inside-out, and when they are dry they have to be kneaded with a blunt ulu to keep them supple. A woman will spend ages rubbing the skin between her fists to keep it from becoming stiff. The snow must be brushed from the tugto parka before it is brought inside or the moisture will freeze, making it most uncomfortable to put on. Wally's parka always looked and behaved like a suit of armour, and at the start of a journey he could barely move his arms. After several hours' exertion when he began to sweat, the parka would lose its stiffness, but then overnight the same thing happened again. It took a while before I learnt how to cope with the skins.

Often these days the men would fetch the meat from the caches they had made in summer. There was great excitement when they brought back 'kiviak'. This dish is a delicacy no Eskimo would refuse. It is made by fermenting little auks in a specially prepared sealskin bag which has still a thick layer of blubber on it. We would see next year the men at summer camp hauling out the carcass of a seal through the mouth of the 'bag' so that there would be fewer holes to sew up. The stuffed skins are placed in a shady place between layers of stones so that the sun cannot get through to the skin to make the contents rancid. The fat seeps into the birds which in time ferment. The birds are not plucked or gutted but put in the bag intact.

On one of my visits to some old folk on Herbert Island I interrupted a feast of these. In their hands each held a small bird, denuded of feathers, except for its downy head, which lolled from side to side as they sucked the raw flesh from its tiny frame. Their mouths and hands were livid and the juice trickled down their chins on to their anoraks. They were a little embarrassed to be caught in such a state. The kiviak has a foul smell, which lingers on the fingers even when they have been washed. If this did not put one off, the sight of the bedraggled blood-stained feathers certainly would. When the last bits of flesh had been picked off the carcass and the head crunched between their teeth to get at the brains, the carcass was thrown away, another bird would be peeled of its skin in one quick gesture and the feast continued.

I slipped on to the little stool that had been shoved towards me, but felt that my presence was out of place. I explained I was only visiting for a few minutes with Kari. As I left I was invited to take some birds with me. 'Maybe just one,' I suggested. They all laughed and made a gesture as if to hold their noses. I took home my delicacy with some curiosity. I had heard so much of this strange 'dish'. I stripped it outside the house and just took the limp carcass inside to cut a tiny portion off it. It was stronger than the strongest cheese I had ever tasted. No—it was definitely not for me. I wrapped it up well and took it furtively to where we dumped the rubbish.

9

Talk of Christmas began when families started to visit from afar, taking advantage of the good ice to travel with their dog teams. Some had been held up a few weeks when the ice fractured and split around their villages. But sooner or later the ice had to harden and no time was lost before the teams set out.

'There's a dog team,' the children would scream and rush to the scene.

Dogs and people mingled in noisy confusion. The arrivals had no time to catch their breath. Although I didn't know half the people that arrived, except that they were brothers, sisters, cousins, aunts of the people who lived here, I was always informed of their arrival as if I was expected to drop everything and join the throng of onlookers.

Another reminder that Christmas was on the way was the sound of the children practising carols. These days most Greenlanders are Lutherans or Christians of some kind or another, and they celebrate Christmas like all Christians, with services in the church and a general celebration in their homes.

For centuries the Eskimos believed only in the supernatural powers of the Angakok or Shaman. God had no place in their belief, and they worshipped no divinity. The Danish colonists brought their faith with them. In 1721 Hans Egede, 'the father of all missionaries' in Greenland, settled to christianize the Greenlanders.

A favourite game of the children was 'priest and laymen'. The 'parishioners' would line up to receive a blessing from the 'priest', who devoutly intoned a passage from a book. At first Kari was hauled up with the multitude to receive 'Communion', but then they decided it would be better if the roles were reversed. They propped her up on her two pins, feet apart and bottom out, and came and knelt before her, first giving a short bob in genuflection. She sensed the solemnity of the occasion and treated them to a stream of garbled sounds which they listened to with great devotion.

The dark never kept the children from playing outside but when we went to get ice they insisted we went in threes. The tupilaks, they explained, hid under the ice, and could appear at any moment and carry one away. My own fears of the dark were merely practical. The cracks in the ice were frightening. Still, the little kerosene lamps provided some light and I had a horde of followers on most occasions to help me pull the sledge. So I hid my fears.

Kari loved it when we bundled her into a pile of furs and took her for a ride on the sledge. The light from the pressure lamp bobbed from side to side and when it went out, as it frequently did, we would stand for a minute till our eyes got used to the dark and would walk home with only the lights of the stars for company.

One night an injured dog broke loose. Eventually we noticed him skulking round the village. He was very attractive—white with deep black rings around his eyes—but he was very nervous and inclined to snap, and we were afraid he might attack one of the children. At last we discovered he had joined Avatak's team, and seemed to get on well with them. Avatak suggested he look after the dog for a while. He pointed out that he was a strong animal with good muscles. We were grateful as we did not want to shoot him. At Christmas Wally gave Avatak the dog to keep.

The hut was getting colder, with temperatures below freezing in the living room. The Eskimo women complained that ours was the coldest hut in the village, and we decided we would have to get some sort of oil heater to back up the stove in the kitchen. Kari, of course, was always at floor level during the day, when she was playing, and that was the coldest part of the hut, but there seemed no way of raising her.

One morning as I bent to retrieve something from under her bed I noticed thick clumps of ice stuck to the wall. Some of her toys which had lain there for a few days were covered with a thin film of it. Even our clothes began to freeze to the wall overnight and the sleeping bags would be stuck to the wall in the morning when we woke up. Yet we all remained very healthy during the winter, except for the colds, which everyone else seemed to suffer at some time or another.

One day as I was changing Kari's nappy I asked Maria how the Eskimo woman had coped without nappies in the old days. She explained that they sometimes used a bit of sealskin, or any soft skin that came to hand, but when the children were carried in the Amaut (the sealskin jacket with a pouch at the back) they were usually naked. The mother would occasionally put in some absorbent moss which could be changed regularly, but sometimes they did not bother.

Towards the beginning of December, the children became very excited, because 'Nihima', their name for Father Christmas, was to visit all the settlements with presents for the children. We asked the children how he would arrive and they replied, 'By helicopter of course.' We told them that in our country Father Christmas came by sledge, which was drawn by tugto (reindeer). The children laughed at this and said they didn't believe it, because everyone knew that he arrived by helicopter. Every year the Americans visit the settlements with presents for every child. It is a joint Danish-American gesture of goodwill, and the weeks of excitement beforehand are evidence enough that it is a very worthwhile mission.

We had been expecting Nihima for a couple of days, but the weather had been too bad for flying. When he did arrive our family was quite unprepared. Wally had come back from a hunting trip in the early hours of the morning, after battling through dreadful weather conditions. He had travelled for twelve hours in complete blackness. He could only tell he was approaching a berg when the stars were suddenly blocked out of view. We had just finished breakfast when children darted in breathlessly to tell us that Nihima had arrived, and we were to hurry and bring Kari up to Savfak's house, where there was to be a party.

Eventually I sallied out in the dark with Kari wearing white dogskin pants and a very pretty foxskin parka. Without realizing it I wandered into the neighbour's dog team. A deep-throated growl from one and a couple of swift forms leaping up in the light from the window made me jump back in terror. The ground billowed in great waves of drifts and I was having difficulty finding my way up the hill. A torch suddenly appeared out of the dark as if by its own volition and bobbed towards me : Maria whisked Kari out of my arms and ran up the hill with her. When I reached the door to Savfak's house I could hear the sounds of high spirits bursting the small room.

All the children were dressed in their festive clothes. The little girls wore pretty dresses, or long kamiks and foxskin pants, with bright anoraks. The boys all wore white anoraks over dark trousers or polar-bear pants. The lights from the candles shone in their laughing eyes. They were very happy. There were many parents in the room and several huge Americans, together with the Danish Liaison Officer from the Base who was responsible for keeping goodwill between the Danes, the Greenlanders, and the Americans—sometimes a difficult task.

Each child was given a red stocking full of toys and sweets, and a large present. The Eskimos insisted on pushing Kari forward to get a present, although Wally and I felt that it really was not her privilege. But the locals did not bother about questions like that—she was a child and that was all that mattered.

The few weeks before Christmas are busy ones for the Eskimo women. Traditionally, at this time everyone gets a new anorak and a new pair of kamiks. In a family with many children this means a great deal of work for the mother. Skins have to be scraped, stretched and dried. There is a lot of sewing to be done. The women leave their long kamiks out in the frost to bleach them. Because I am taller than Eskimo women, mine were made out of Harp Seal, but they were as white as the Ringed Seal kamiks worn by the Eskimo women.

I had a lot of presents for the villagers, but still needed to buy a few more things, so we decided to make a quick trip to Qanaq. We could not decide whether to go by dog sledge or by Skidoo. The advantage with the Skidoo was that it was quicker and more direct and we could get to Qanaq and back the same day. We could also park it where we liked in Qanaq. The main disadvantage was that it would be colder, as there was greater wind chill.

Wind chill is one of the most important factors to consider when dressing for a journey in the cold. The faster the speed and the stronger the wind the greater chill the body has to contend with. Thus, if there was no wind and the temperature was $-5°F.$, and we travelled at a speed of 25 miles per hour, the equivalent chill would be $-51°F$. If, however, there was also a wind blowing the chill factor would increase. Weighed against this was the length of time it would take to get to Qanaq by dogs—possibly three hours as against the Skidoo's 30–40 minutes—and the chore of looking for somewhere to picket the dogs at the other end. This was sometimes difficult if there were other teams visiting. The dogs have to be near snow, as they get very thirsty during and after a journey, and there is no water available in winter.

We decided to take a chance and go by Skidoo. But I set to to make a thick sheepskin bag with a hood on it, inside which I put Kari's sleeping bag. The whole lot we put inside a wooden box which we anchored to the sledge. That would save me the trouble of holding on to her all the time.

As we were leaving, Migishoo came down to see us off. She brought a cotton tablecloth which she said I should put over the box. She showed me how I should feel inside from time to time to make sure Kari's face wasn't too cold. Good Lord, she will smother, I thought to myself as I saw the cloth put over the face of the sleeping child. I didn't realize there is enough air trapped for a baby inside the folds of the cloth and that this protects their delicate faces from the cutting wind.

We had no goggles, as these steam up in the cold. But we needed some protection for our faces and I made sheepskin masks, with holes for the eyes, to cover our noses and cheeks. We didn't dare put them on till we got out of the village, for fear of scaring anyone who caught sight of us. Even the adults were obsessed with imaginary spirits, which they said flew underneath the ice and which could appear at any moment and 'get us'. These things were said half in jest, but there was more than a touch of superstition in the ideas.

For some reason I had decided at the last minute to take Kari's little sledge on the larger one, which would be pulled by Skidoo. I thought it might be useful.

There was enough moonlight for us to be able to see clearly. Setting out was a glorious feeling. The sledge swung like a pendulum from side to side, down the rafted ice in the cove, till its nose pulled round towards the open pack. The Skidoo roared into the silent night and we raced after it. Raised prints of paw marks shone like strange ⅃. wers on the frozen sea. It was exhilarating to swish over the moonlit ice in whatever direction we pleased without battling with the wills of thirteen dogs, who always wanted to go the wrong way.

I had just begun to relax—when the wooden shaft which joined the sledge to the Skidoo snapped. Wally managed to fix it. But when it came to starting the Skidoo again it just would not work. Nothing could make it go. It would start, and then peter out in a few seconds. Wally did everything in the book, including changing the spark plugs, but it was no good. It was as dead as a doused fire.

We were about five miles from Herbert Island and still thirteen miles from Qanaq. We couldn't tell what was the matter, but repairs would have entailed putting up a tent and getting a primus going. It was too long for Kari to be outdoors in such an uncomfortable situation. Wally tried the Skidoo again.

'Oh, hell, who'd ever bring a wife and baby to the Arctic!' he blurted out. 'If you were a man I could have left you here and gone back to get the dogs. But I can't leave you alone with Kari—anything might happen. You wouldn't know what to do if a polar bear appeared. Besides it is too cold!'

I nodded glumly. Poor Wally. He had so many things go wrong with this expedition already, without the responsibility of Kari and me.

'Let's push Kari back on her sledge,' I suggested, thanking God I had brought it. Wally agreed there was no alternative. By this time Kari was crying hysterically. I felt inside but she seemed quite warm, just frightened. We pacified her and started the walk back. It was sweaty work in all our polar clothes. Wally trudged ahead, pulling, and I pushed from behind—a silent trio. Wally carried the gun and I had the ice axe. I couldn't help looking round every few minutes to make sure that the forms I saw silhouetted against the light sky were not animal.

The return journey seemed endless and by the time we got back we were exhausted. The runners on the small sledge were rough from the scratches of the rocks at the island. Our clothes were soaked in sweat when we returned and we had to strip them off as soon as we got inside the house. Of course the fire had gone out, and it was cold and dark, but we soon had the place cheered up. We discovered later that the trouble with the Skidoo was water in the fuel. Wally had taken tremendous care when he had mixed the petrol and oil but we learnt that some of the fuel drums already had water in them. At Orla's suggestion we added spirit to the mixture and had no further trouble. When Maria heard about our adventure she told me several stories of adventures she herself had had. She spoke of one occasion when she had been underneath an overhanging cliff, and there was a sudden avalanche : it just missed her and the children, but formed a huge wall of snow between them and her husband. Thinking they could not possibly have survived, he was overcome with grief, and sat on his sledge and wept. By great good luck, they managed to worm their way round behind the wall of snow and came out several yards ahead of the unhappy man. He was in some doubt that it was really them. But her teasing assured him that 'no angel would speak that way.' He still gets embarrassed if the incident is mentioned.

Maria explained that there were two reasons why women carried their baby in the Amaut when they went sledging. Firstly, it was warmer and the child could be twisted round to the mother's breast without taking off any clothes. But, as important was the fact that sledges sometimes went through the ice, and if a mother was trying to save herself from going under, she often had not time to save the baby as well, and there had been many cases in their history of children being lost when the ice gave way. My heart froze as she told me this: and I made sure when we made Kari's travelling cot that she was easy to get at in case I had to snatch her up suddenly. But the thought of travelling with her seemed less agreeable, and I decided that as soon as I could find someone who would look after her, while we went away on short journeys, the better.

We decided to use the dogs for our second attempt to get to Qanaq. It was very dark the day we left. We had made spare harnesses and leads, and Wally had spent eight hours filing the scratched runners of the sledge. When he eventually came to collect Kari and me from the hut he reported that six dogs had broken loose and at the moment were on their way towards Canada! I fumed. I didn't realize that sometimes even the Eskimos lose their dogs this way.

We decided to carry on without the six that had run off. They were bound to return—if they didn't get their traces caught on an ice knobble. In any case, I was not prepared to wait till they were found. We had a head torch with us, but its beam gradually faded and the batteries I had brought to replace them were so cold it would not function till Wally warmed them against his skin. The beam was still not very strong, however, and we only knew we had reached an iceberg when the dogs suddenly veered off course, and we would rub shoulders with a huge dark spectre. But after a while I found my eyes got used to the dark.

Every couple of miles the sledge had to be stopped so that we could untangle the leads. The dogs' eyes lit up in the beam of the torch. Part of the journey was very rough. I clung on to the ropes as Wally called out from in front, 'Don't let the sledge catch on a hummock.' As he said it we slammed into a mound of ice. I was supposed to jump off the sledge whenever it looked as if we might hit anything and steer it away by the handlebars, or by running up to the runners and giving them a sharp pull or push. As Wally had the torch I couldn't see a thing, and to make matters worse I kept tripping over the jagged lumps that stuck up everywhere. I did not like being at the back of the sledge with so much space behind and no one to keep me company. So instead of running along behind I would climb on it from time to time and let it look after itself.

I felt very warm although with the wind the temperature (or chill factor) was equivalent to $-60°C$. My eyes were the only part of me that felt the cold air. From time to time I put my hand inside Kari's cot to see if she was still breathing. There wasn't a murmur from her, but she was very snug with a pocket of warm air round her nose, fast asleep. My hands froze every time I took my mitts off and I stopped feeling her after a while as I thought the shock of feeling a cold hand against one's cheek must be most unpleasant.

It was difficult to keep to the trail, and we found ourselves going off course at quite a tangent as we looked for a route through the rough ice. Weaving in and around the bergs in the dark, it was easy to lose one's sense of direction. Suddenly the whole sky seemed alight with a mysterious brightness. It was an aurora, Wally told me—the Northern Lights. I had heard so much about these, and now I was to see them for myself.

A panorama of colour swept across the sky—their tiny fingers of light burst into flickering beams of greeny brightness, waxing and waning in a variety of shapes. For over an hour we watched the spectacle while hills and bergs flashed into view against a backdrop of brilliant and unusual colours. We watched in silence while the dogs followed the trail of sledge tracks suddenly visible. Wally looked like an embalmed figure as he sat in front, his parka haloed by the distant lights.

As we neared Qanaq the lights from the lamps shone like jewels at the foot of the hills. I had no more fear of polar bears. We were in sight of habitation. I thought I heard the crack of a whip in the still air—and got a shock to see a dog appear suddenly at my elbow. Before I could turn, a team appeared within a foot of me and almost ran into our own dogs. As I watched them being swallowed up in the dark, I thought, how absurd, being run down by another team in all this space.

We were ages looking for a picket. There were several dog teams taking up the spots that Wally usually used. There was little snow elsewhere and we grew weary searching. While we were looking, an Eskimo woman came down and invited us to her house—we thanked her but said we had somewhere to go for the night. It was midnight. With all our detours and stops it had taken us five hours to do a journey Wally could do on his own in two. The climb up to Orla's house was agony carrying Kari and our gear. We were embarrassed to be arriving at such an hour, but a most gracious Orla greeted us and we felt at home immediately.

Qanaq was festive! Decorated trees shone in the windows of some of the homes, and a large one with electric lights stood outside the church. The store was crammed with bright things. Happy faces milled around the counters buying candles, decorations and a hundred and one other things.

We had a little party at Orla's as we would not be in Qanaq at Christmas. We picked up a pile of mail that had collected for us and left Qanaq in good spirits. The ice had opened up in places and two dogs fell in a lead. They thrashed around till Wally hauled them out whimpering. We crossed other frozen leads where jagged six-inch ruffs of ice stood up, razor sharp. The dogs' paws get very sore if fresh sea ice gets between the claws, because the salt irritates the skin.

It was cold and Wally trotted beside the sledge for a while to get his feet warm. Mine felt cold too so I jumped off to join him. The sound of our footsteps galvanized the dogs into sudden action. They began to gallop. At that moment Wally slipped and landed headlong on the ice. I was left behind, mincing along in my stiff kamiks, while Wally scrambled to his feet and tore like the very devil after the runaway team, yelling 'Ai, ai, ai', as the Eskimos do to stop the dogs. The faster he ran the faster the dogs went. At last the two traces collided round the opposite sides of an ice boulder. Wally reached them before they had time to recover, and I caught up a couple of minutes later. Wally's words don't bear repeating, but mine were more thankful. I imagined the commotion if a sledge rolled into the village with only a baby on it. That would be something we would never live down.

From the noisy welcome we got as we reached the island we realized that the lost six dogs had returned. The tide crack was impassable by sledge, and almost as bad on foot. We could not get a footing and kept slithering on our faces, until we eventually rolled over the rim of the ice wall, and slithered the last few feet on our sides.

In the dim light Wally's hut looked like a morgue. Carcasses of seal dripped into the tub beside the fire. I couldn't bear the thought of thawing meat in our tiny kitchen. There was the danger that Kari would fall into the gory tub, and the smell would have impregnated all the books. Yet it was not the most inspiring sight for Wally either, when trying to work out his film scripts. In the end Avatak offered to thaw the meat for us in his house.

Just before Christmas there was the last-minute rush to sell foxskins in the store, so that the villagers could make a quick trip to Qanaq to buy presents and decorations. Feelings ran high these days, when a hard-won pelt which the owner considered first class was given a lower grade by the storeman. Maria burst out at the storekeeper, 'You are not an Eskimo, you are a Kasdlunas!' She felt this the supreme insult for being cheated.

The 24th arrived at last. This is the day the Eskimos celebrate Christmas, starting in the evening. We got up early to get our chores done before anyone called. It wasn't long before a stream of children poured into the hut dressed in their new clothes and beaming above their sparkling kamiks. They shook hands a score of times and wished us 'Jutdle Pidluarit'. The festivities began, as with most festivals, in the church, and I thought I ought to grace the scene to be sociable.

Dressed in my long kamiks, foxskin pants, and new turquoise anorak, I clawed my way up the bank to the church. The catechist was already reading the service when I arrived, and rows of devout heads bowed in attention. The men sat on one side and the women on the other. Shocks of black hair contrasted with the white anoraks which fitted snugly with the tops of the polar bear pants. It was impossible to tell from behind who were the old men and who the young, except by the cut of the hair. The old men favoured a round bowl cut, but the young men had more modern styles. One seldom sees a grey-haired Eskimo (unless he has some foreign blood in him), and bald heads are equally rare.

The women mostly had long hair, caught in the nape of the neck in a bun and divided horizontally by a ribbon. The new bright-coloured anoraks were a good contrast to the stark figures across the aisle. The white kamiks of the young women, trimmed at the top with a long fringe of polar-bear skin, which hung in bouncing fronds of spun silver, supported curvaceous buttocks clad in foxskin. The children shuffled and fidgeted in the pews, their polar-bear skin pants worn to a smooth black patch on the knee and rump.

Outside, the service over, a little crowd gathered. The cold air checked the dribble from the children's noses and tickled the throat with a moment's coughing. As I slipped down the slopes to the hut voices called out, 'Don't forget the children's party.' The darkness was broken by the flicker of waving torches—whose sudden disappearance meant another tumble down the slippery banks. There was much laughter and toing and froing. I felt very contented.

At the hut there was just time to see Wally and Kari into their coats before the three of us faced the hill, yet again. The teacher's house was right next to the church and the pink glow of the many candles through the window waxed and waned as figures passed the frosted panes. The sounds of singing announced the party in full swing. The open door framed a beautifully decorated miniature Christmas tree around which two circles of children danced in opposite directions. Parents hugged the wall and I pressed myself into a corner with Kari. When the dancing and singing stopped, everyone was given a packet of sweets and biscuits. Then they all disappeared to their own homes.

10. The children of the settlement were constant visitors. Even the little boys played with Kari (these are wearing the traditional polar-bear pants).

11. Pouline, Inoutdliak and Martha, Maria's daughters, were daily visitors, and they spent hours amusing Kari. Here Kari is dressed in a Canadian *amaut*, which one of the women lent her to carry her Teddy bear in. Eskimo women carry their babies on their backs until they are over a year old. This photograph was taken in summer: the rocky ground is littered with empty cans.

12. The meat racks are stocked with walrus, and the snow on the shore is stained with blood. The *kayaks* are upturned—waiting for summer and the icefree sea.

The essential part of Christmas is visiting and being visited. We didn't know who should take the initiative. What happened when people met halfway—did they pass each other and pretend they were going to another house or did they turn round and come back home? There must be some sort of procedure. We decided to wait and see if anything happened.

We had hardly been back five minutes when Avatak, Maria and the seven children exploded into the kitchen. They were laden with huge, brightly wrapped parcels which they showered upon us. It was so sudden and so unexpected I felt quite overcome, and had to busy myself bringing out homemade Christmas cake and chocolate biscuits and sweets, nuts, dates and bottles of juice. Everyone devoured the sweetmeats as if they were starved—including a plate of mince pies which would have passed for rock cakes.

I couldn't wait to give our presents to them and to see their reactions as they opened them. And then of course we unwrapped ours. The first delight was a beautifully made sledge from Avatak for Kari. It was a replica of the kind the hunters used and had been bound and varnished with great care and artistry. Wally had a magnificent pair of walrus tusks which Avatak had polished beautifully: Maria had made him some sealskin mitts. Lots of tiny presents were thrust into his and Kari's hands from the children.

The first present I opened for myself was a large sealskin which Inoutdliak had begged her mother to give me, because I hadn't had new kamiks for Christmas. Then I opened an attractive wall tile, with a picture of a kayak skimming over the water. What I had kept to the last, and what really intrigued me, was a large parcel I had shoved behind me on the bed.

'I worked all night on that,' said Maria as I picked it up. I noticed one corner was soggy and it seemed very heavy. I couldn't think what it could be. Bit by bit I began to uncover a gorgeous white fox fur. 'Oh, Maria!' I exclaimed, 'How clever of you. How did you manage to stuff it?' I had unwrapped the whole parcel. 'It looks so real.' Everyone was convulsed with laughter, rolling around in their seats and looking at me. I suddenly realized to my horror that the fox I was holding was frozen stiff, straight out of the trap. I let out a shriek and dropped it, more in fun than in earnest, and they howled with delight.

When I did pick it up, I saw how its last agonies had frozen on its face —the skin had flattened where it had fallen over and pushed one eye together, as if it was winking. One leg was bent and its tongue between its teeth was beginning to thaw, though the eyes were still glazed with frost. Its belly too began to thaw and drip. The fur however was exquisite.

In the midst of the revelry, Migishoo arrived with her grandson. She presented Wally with some white sealskin for mitts. She had already made a pair for Kari. To me she gave her ulu. It was a marvellous gift. Her precious possession which had been worn smooth by constant handling. I was very touched. This was a sample of the generosity which the whole village showed us. We were quite overcome by the unexpected kindness of them all.

As Avatak's family turned to go the children cried, 'Tomorrow's Christmas as well.' They darted off to join the other children in their tour of the village. Each hut was visited in turn, and the occupants treated to several choruses from one of their songs. The singing over, a sea of upturned faces paused hopefully for some small token of our appreciation. Presents were fondled, scrutinized and exhibited, before joining the other gifts secreted about their person. Bubbling over with excitement and curiosity, they flitted off to the next fireside, disappearing into the darkness like fireflies. Dancing lanterns weaved intangible patterns throughout the night, linking the huts together. There was very little sleep.

The 25th December—our Christmas Day—was fresh and crisp with no wind. The temperature was ⁻25°C. A half-moon—deep blood-orange—hugged the slopes of the hills near Qanaq. The children were early visitors. Again they shook hands with us and rushed outside to sing songs at the window.

We started our own little tour of the village, taking our presents with us. As it happened, in the first house we went to, the man of the house was asleep. A very bleary-eyed Kaudlutok got out of bed. It was 1 p.m. but he looked as if he needed several more hours' sleep. It was a great strain to be sociable with a yawning host, and we delivered our gifts and departed smartly. 'We are celebrating this evening,' said Inaluk. 'Please come back.'

We wondered if we would get the same reception in the other houses. We decided to try Migishoo. She was delighted to see us and sat us down to coffee and so many cakes I thought my sides would burst. I wondered how many more cakes I would be offered that day, and how I could possibly get through them.

It is customary on occasions like Christmas to send a messenger to fetch the family you would like to entertain. Avatak's eldest boy came to fetch us. We had some more presents that we had saved for our visit to them, and we burst in on a very gay scene. A tiny Christmas tree was covered with lighted candles and bright baubles. Of course the trees had to be imported.

A table laden with sweet things was in the centre of the room. 'Marie, would you like to try some mattak,' asked my hostess, indicating a large portion of newly thawed whaleskin. The thick grey skin had a thin coating of blubber on the inside. 'Yes, I'll try a little,' I agreed, not too sure whether I could eat it or not. Maria cut a couple of strips for both of us and for everyone else.

The whole family tucked into the raw whaleskin. The first few mouthfuls went down beautifully and I was surprised to find it tasted like fresh coconut. But the more I had, the more difficult it became to swallow. Beneath the thick grey flesh there is a layer of the toughest skin I have ever come across. Only the sharpest knife could pierce it, and it is impossible to bite through. The secret lies in cutting minute squares, which pop down the throat with hardly any chewing, once the fleshy part has been eaten off. In an effort to finish quickly I had cut rather large portions which even an Eskimo might have found would stick in his gullet. I chewed and chewed, assuming that sometime the skin would get softer, but it just rolled around, a great lump in my mouth. I couldn't swallow, in case I choked. But I couldn't sit chewing all evening. I tried to join the laughter of the cheerful crowd by smiling with the 'bulge' in the centre of my mouth. To have continued chewing after that would seem ridiculous. I sat for a few minutes in silence (which was unusual for me) and tried to think of a solution to my problem without admitting what had happened. At last I succeeded with great dexterity in removing the lump from my mouth and I shoved it down the only space possible—the tops of my kamiks.

We had hardly got home when Inaluk, Kaudlutok's wife, came to invite us to her house for coffee. There were several more invitations after this and by 11.30 we had had enough. Then the flash of a lamp at the window and the sound of beautiful singing held us captive. It was enchanting. The singers had gone from house to house and they burst in on a wave of cold air to greet us. We gave everyone a glass of wine and some cake and the group chatted for about half an hour. Several of the visitors were newcomers to the village, but the atmosphere was very relaxed and friendly.

I was very tired when our visitors left and anxious to get out of my fur pants and long kamiks, which were very hot. As Wally helped me pull off the tight-fitting leggings a grey lump fell out on to the floor.

'What on earth's that horrible-looking object?'

'Oh, it's the mattak,' I remembered suddenly.

'What a revolting thing to carry round in your kamiks.'

The next evening the whole village was invited to Savfak's house for a party. It was meant for adults but of course children crept in throughout the evening, and were allowed to stay a couple of hours. A long table had been put the full length of the room. Each woman drew a name from a box to see who should be her partner at the table. Ribald jokes greeted each announcement and the partners claimed each other with titillating joviality. By sheer coincidence I picked Rasmus, and Savfak picked Wally. Near us was Maria and her partner, a very fat fellow called Massana. There was much laughter and noise and I guessed there would be no inhibitions that night.

Everyone brought a gift, and they were all put in a large basket. A few days before, each person in the village had drawn a name from a box in the store to see whom they should give a present to. It was a good way of seeing that everyone got something.

On this one night in the year the men looked after the women. They served them, even putting sugar in their coffee and stirring it for them. Of course the women loved this, and ordered the fellows to do all sorts of favours for them. The 'meal' started with ice cream, which the Americans had brought in a large can. The portions were enormous, and I wondered how anyone had the stomach for so much, but it all disappeared and was followed quickly by cakes and coffee.

After this the present-giving ceremony began. Everyone had to unwrap his gift and hold it up for inspection. Loud applause was given for really original gifts. Sometimes the gift would be made up of several small items and a message would be read out to go with them. Part of a gift could be a length of rope, 'for a hunter whose dog is always biting through his traces'. Another 'some ivalo (sinew) for someone who's always bursting out of her clothes', or 'a mirror for someone who always has a smear of soot on her face'. The comments were greeted with hoots of laughter, and no one took offence.

A very noisy game was played after the things had been cleared off the table. An object was passed from hand to hand beneath the cloth, and each person had to try and guess what it was. No one was allowed to look at it except Savfak, who retrieved it if it fell to the floor. This was the rowdiest and most enjoyable game of the evening and everyone entered into the spirit of it without embarrassment.

'The thing' was supposed to feel repellent and it certainly did. It was roundish in shape, clammy and rough in texture. It is not surprising in a community of hunters and their wives, that the suggestions as to its origin were pretty basic. I must admit that my own thoughts were fairly crude. As it landed in the lap of each woman she shrieked with horror and disgust. The men added to the fun by imitating the shrieks of the women. Everyone was in stitches of laughter. It was amusing to see people who were quite used to the blood and guts of countless animals pretending to be revolted, but by the end of the game everyone was worked up into a real frenzy of anticipation. When the game was finished and no one had guessed correctly, Savfak held up a frozen egg which had been wrapped round with strips of wet fox fur. She was roundly applauded for her success in fooling everyone.

After the children were put to bed the adults returned for more games. One popular one was to tie a present to a long string suspended from the roof. Each person was blindfolded and turned round several times and then launched in the direction of the object to cut the cord. Whoever did so got the prize. A jubilant Migishoo carried it away. Several other rowdy games kept us amused for a couple of hours. Then everyone began to dance. The tape recorder was very old and the tunes like Scottish dancing. Everyone joined in the fun.

By 2 a.m. all the men—except of course Rasmus—had disappeared. He looked very tired as he sat and watched the dancing, and I was sure he wanted to go to bed. But Savfak said I was not to worry about him—he would survive! The women still wanted to dance and were not put out by the fact that there were no men left. They partnered each other. I had several dances with old crones who steered me round the room as they would a sledge through a field of rocks, with sudden jolts and stops and sharp turns.

It was at Christmas that I got to know Nauja for the first time. She had spent little time on the island since I had first seen her, but Inugssuak, her husband, decided to use the village as a base till the summer. Nauja was full of fun at the party and I immediately warmed to her. 'You're very clever to have learnt some Eskimo,' she told me. 'I know a few words of English,' she offered—and rattled off a stream of words, which included 'matches, cigarettes, knife', the phrases, ' 'ow are you' and 'thank you very much'. She laughed as she looked at me and asked cheekily, 'Aren't I clever too?' I agreed she was very clever.

By three o'clock I felt so sorry for Rasmus that I felt I had to leave. The others decided they would leave with me and six of us trouped out together. We parted in the middle of the village as if walking the imaginary spokes of a wheel. I sighed with contentment as I closed the door of the hut behind me. This had been one of the best Christmases I had ever had and I would never forget it.

10

The old year sounded a noisy retreat. To hasten its departure and welcome the new year the hunters discharged their rifles over the head of the
fleeing spectre. Balls of purple fire exploded into fountains of stars which
drizzled down on to the upturned faces. People ran from group to group
outside the huts shaking hands and wishing everyone a happy new year.

Throughout the day children kept thumping against the walls of the
house. When I had rushed out, exasperated, they told me, 'No one knocks
on the door today.' 'But you must thump the side of the house to get rid
of the Tupilaks that are hiding inside.' That evening I visited Maria and
Avatak. Maria told me she had woken up a few nights before, having
dreamed we were leaving. I told them some famous stories of dreams I
had heard, and went on to tell them some ghost stories I had read. Avatak
told me that he had seen a couple of angels once near Thule Airbase, and
pointed to one of the little tin cherubs, with puffed cheeks, wafting in the
breeze beneath the doorway. I burst out laughing, but Avatak and Maria
were quite serious, and they didn't think it amusing when I suggested
he might have had too much to drink.

Aima visited me in the early hours of the morning. We hadn't gone
to bed : we found that we were keeping the most extraordinary hours.
As it was dark all the time, except when it was moonlight, we fell into the
same habits as the Eskimos—going to bed when we were tired and eating
when we were hungry. Aima had had rather a lot to drink. She told me
how happy she had been with the necklace I had given her for Christmas,
and how she kept thinking of the day when the big ship would arrive to
take us away. 'Aaiiee!' How she would cry! She kept burying her face in
her hands, and wept a little. I made her a cup of coffee. Before she left
she hugged me several times. Wally was completely unmoved by the scene
—he never had any sympathy with drunks.

The bluish light cast by the winter moon lit up everything as brilliantly as on a summer's day. Maria and I loved going for walks in the moonlight. She asked me if it was true that in England the summer days were dark during the night. 'What a shame,' she said. 'How do you stand it to have the sun for such a short while?' I explained that we had the sun with us throughout the year, and that it balanced out. 'I like it much better our way,' she told me.

She turned towards the moon and asked me about the Americans who had visited there. Had I heard about it? I told her I had watched their arrival on the television. This fascinated her. Was it hot or cold, she wondered? I told her what I had remembered from the news, and tried to imitate the nebulous walk of the astronauts. She wondered if there was a flag there and asked me if I knew that really the moon belonged to the Eskimos. 'How do you account for that?' I asked. 'Well, because the angakoks went there long before the Americans.' I wondered how many of the Eskimos really believed this.

In the old days, it was the task of the angakoks, or witch doctors, to invoke spirits to help cure sickness, or lack of game. Sickness was considered to be an affliction of the body as a result of the soul being stolen. Sometimes the soul would be robbed by the 'man in the moon', and the angakoks had to go on long and perilous journeys to retrieve it.

Maria was always very respectful of the old customs of her people, although she had been taught differently by the missionaries. I showed her a couple of pictures which Migishoo's husband had given me at Christmas. They obviously depicted an Eskimo story of some kind. Maria said they must be of Kagssassuk—an orphan boy who was turned out of every house in the village because he was so filthy. He was stunted and weak, and young and old alike tortured him. At last he was adopted by a poor old woman and she was very kind to him. In those days everyone ate communally. Kagssassuk was too small to climb up the step into the houses and had to wait till someone lifted him in. This everybody did by putting two fingers in his nostrils and hauling him up. Naturally he became rather hideous as only his nostrils grew. He was given only the merest scraps of meat to eat and whenever a new tooth appeared it was immediately pulled out by the men so that he would not be able to chew.

One old man took pity on him and advised him to go to a mountain and call on the spirit of strength to make him strong. When he did, a very strange animal appeared, with a human face, the body of a fox and a huge bushy tail. The beast told Kagssassuk to hold on to the tail, and with it he hurled the boy through the air. Toys fell out of the boy's pockets as he did so—but after several tumbles he suddenly found himself possessed with tremendous strength.

On returning to the village the boy performed amazing feats. He lifted a huge trunk of driftwood which would have taken all the men in the village the whole day to move. He killed three polar bears by picking them up, and dashing them on an iceberg. He was fêted and flattered but he got his revenge by crushing everyone to death except the stepmother and the old couple who had befriended him.

I could never tell what was the point of many of the stories I was told. Many of them seemed to peter off without even a moral. Some would take hours to tell. It was only later that I learnt that it was considered a good story teller, in the old days, who could send his listeners to sleep.

Maria came to show me how to skin the fox she had given me for Christmas. She thawed it out completely and with a sharp knife cut the skin away from round the mouth, exposing the teeth. Gradually she cut away from round the eyes and, when the whole head was uncovered, she dispensed with the knife and pushed her hand down between the skin and the flesh, working the skin away from the body with strong fingers. It was difficult around the legs and tail, but eventually when it was all loosened she wrapped a cloth around the head of the creature and pulled. With a loud slurp the beast parted company from its skin. I gave an involuntary gasp and looked away, expecting blood to pour over the floor. Maria laughed and said, 'Well, you wanted to see how it was done!' Not a drop of blood was spilt. The pointed tail hung crudely from the naked flesh. And there on the floor, ready for scraping, was the thick white fur.

Nauja became a regular visitor like Maria. It was good to have another woman for company. And Maria had suffered the criticism of people in the village for being so friendly with a Kasdlunas. It had hurt Maria and we had decided that maybe we ought to visit other people in the village more often. Unlike Maria, Nauja loved sewing, and she was fascinated by any magazines on knitting or crochet. I taught her how to crochet and in return she showed me how to work with beads.

She told me that her husband would be going north in the spring to hunt polar bear. She hated it when he was away. After Christmas most of the hunters thought about their spring journeys. Most of them liked to go bear hunting to Savigsavik in the south, or up north towards Smith Sound. For those who went north there was always the attraction of a visit to Canada.

Wally decided to do both. He would have a practice run to Savig-savik to break in the dogs before making a journey in the spring to Grise Fiord—an Eskimo settlement on the southern coast of Ellesmere Island in Canada. Wally hoped to have a friend of his, Geoff Renner, to accompany him. Geoff was a geophysicist and had been on the short list of candidates for the Trans-Arctic Expedition, but had had some unfinished scientific work from which he could not be released. Wally needed someone to give him the assistance I could not provide and we waited anxiously to hear if Geoff could accept the offer to come up for three or four months.

Wally's choice of Eskimo companions was Peter Peary, with whom he had travelled when he was last up in Qanaq, and Avatak, who was also to accompany him in the practice run to Savigsavik. As Wally was not so fluent that he could converse freely with the Eskimos, he decided he ought to give Avatak the choice of taking a friend with him on the trip to Savigsavik, as company in the evenings when they sat in the tent. The journey was six hundred route miles—a long while, Wally thought, to freeze a smile on his face. When we suggested this to Avatak he laughed. 'I haven't any friends,' he said.

January is cold, but there is surprisingly little snowfall in areas as far north as Thule. In fact the further north, the less snowfall there is. The hunters go out even in the darkest days of winter and it is usually possible to see the faint outlines of the mountains and the shadows of the obstacles on the ice.

There were a lot of things to be done before Wally went off. All his filming equipment had to be tested, the battery recharged, the sledging gear attended to, and food and clothing to be got together. I had to do a tour of different houses to see that kamiks, mitts, and other articles of clothing were ready in time. In Suakuanguak's house her husband was sitting nursing a sore throat with a white fox tail round his neck.

By about mid-January the temperature was ⁻26°C. At mid-day there were two hours of twilight—enough to see the hills right across the bay. I could even see the distant horizon. It was cheering to know that the sun was slowly inching its way back to the North. Before it reached us, however, we should have to go through the coldest time of the year— February and early March.

I gradually began to notice how grimy the hut was beginning to look, with patches of brown on the walls and ceiling where the lights had been too hot, and a thick grey film of greasy soot on the walls. The paint had peeled off the wall in the kitchen near the stove in huge curved fronds like a large chrysanthemum.

All Kari's bottles of orange juice burst in the cold. I was really upset about this. Unlike the Eskimos who got their vitamin C from the mattak and from various parts of the animals they ate, Kari had to rely on artificial means of getting hers. I was sure that when Kari was ready for it she would eat local food. By the time she left Greenland she would tackle anything, with a preference for seal or bird flesh.

I lost count of the number of times I was asked before leaving England, 'Aren't you worried?' or, 'Isn't it a little irresponsible to take a small baby to the Arctic?' Of course I *was* worried. But I had weighed up the risks and had decided that they were not insurmountable. If it was as dangerous as most people imagined there would be no Eskimos left today. There are certainly less diseases in the polar regions than in any other part of the world and those that are found here were mostly brought by visitors. Apart from teething troubles and the occasional cold, she was bouncing with health throughout our time in Greenland.

As Kari learnt to talk she seemed to pick out the Eskimo words and discard the English ones. Her intonation was definitely Greenlandic. The Eskimos were delighted that a child so obviously European in looks should yet speak like one of their own. The locals would spend ages talking to her and watching her. Her curly hair was fondled and admired and I even saw a little packet of cellophane hanging on Maria's wall with several very familiar curls showing through. We had wondered why Kari's hair took so long to grow!

As the twilight increased I took Kari out for longer walks. The children helped me push the sledge till we came to a large patch of inland ice. Then they would rush to skate across it on their knees or bellies. They rolled across, flapping their arms like seals. This was how their fathers used to stalk these creatures. The hunter would imitate the movements of the seal till he got near enough to kill it. Now if they stalk them across the ice, they hide behind a protective screen of white material pushed along on miniature skis with a hole through it for the rifle. As I watched the children I realized why they always had so many holes in their clothes. Kari would watch till she fell asleep and would only wake when we took her inside.

On one of our walks the children took me to one of the old stone houses which they said had a skull in it. Beside the large ring of stones that made up the house proper was a little cave of rocks, similar to the shelters they made for pups. Several of the stones had been knocked off or had rolled away and there in a dim far corner was the back of a human skull.

There were a couple of other bones around which looked like leg bones, and there was a lower jaw bone from which several teeth were missing. Those that remained were worn down, tiny and flat. I assumed from this that it must be a woman as the women used to chew the skins to make them supple, and wore their teeth down to a row of flattened stumps.

I was fascinated by the find and had a morbid curiosity to have a look at the front of the skull. I picked up an old whale bone lying nearby and tried to prod the skull out of the frozen turf.

'Don't!' screamed the kids.

'Why not?' I asked.

'Because!' they shouted.

'Because what?' I insisted.

'Because the tupilaks will get you in your bed tonight.'

I dropped the whale bone and hurried away. I didn't believe in tupilaks, but I did believe in angry Eskimos. Suppose I had broken some old taboo? I surreptitiously dropped the tooth I had kept to show Wally, and said a silent prayer that nothing would happen to me.

Of course the children told their mother, and that evening I guiltily admitted what I had done. She laughed and said the children had complained that I was beating the head of a corpse.

'Why?' she asked incredulously.

They didn't know.

'Well, if Marie dies here, I'll beat her head with a bone too,' she said to pacify them. She laughed as she told me. I managed a weak smile.

Wally and Avatak left for Savigsavik on the 26th January. A grey pall hung over the sea ice and through it the moon shone like gossamer. Wally's sledge shrank till it vanished from sight with a final flash from his torch. Maria accompanied Avatak out on to the sea ice, dressed in her finest clothes. The husband goes off leaving his wife looking her most beautiful: he would always think of her as he saw her last. I had been up most of the night with Wally doing last-minute things and I went straight back to bed after they had gone.

Maria put on a show of bravado in front of any of the other women, and said it was a good thing our husbands had gone away as there would be hunters visiting from the other settlements on their way north and she would enjoy the change of company for a while. The others laughed and pretended to be shocked. But Maria's cheer would sometimes drop for a while as we chatted intimately together.

She was glad the winter was almost over. It had been unbearable to be cooped up for so long in the house. Didn't we feel the same boredom? Both she and Avatak felt restless during the long dark night. But at least the men knew that in the spring they would go on their long journeys—the women had nothing to look forward to. It was worse for those with a lot of children, like herself, because they rarely got a chance to travel, except in the summer to a camp. That was why she loved summer so much. Sometimes the women got so bored that they fought bitterly with their men.

She glanced at the books on the shelves and pointed to one that she would like to look at. She never remained miserable for long—it was if she thought it a sign of weakness to feel unhappy just because her man had gone, and Maria hated to admit weakness. She pored over the pictures in the book. I watched her, fascinated. Her features were not remarkable, except for her sloping forehead and fair complexion. Like all Eskimos she had almond eyes and high cheek bones. Her thin mouth set itself in a smirk whenever she was with other people as if she found them a constant source of amusement, and she could never resist a laugh at their expense. But at moments I thought her beautiful.

The women in the village were so different in their attitudes to me. There were those like Maria, Nauja and Savfak, who seemed genuinely to treat me as a friend. There were a couple who ignored me, as if I never existed. Others kept our relationship strictly an acquaintanceship, except at those times when beer loosed their tongues.

I used to love to hear these women come alive, when they forgot their shyness. They would go over the old stories of who had fought with whom in the village. There were often quarrels when two hunters set out after one animal. This had happened a few years ago when a bear had appeared on the scene. There were only two old men around and they had both harnessed their dogs simultaneously and dashed out after it. The old custom of dividing the fur into two was forgotten. They had skinned the animal between them and began a furious tug of war. The stronger of the two rushed off with the skin to his own home. His wife proudly scraped it and as usual hung it on the drying frame in the open air. The loser, however, sneaked down and slashed the skin in several places so that it could not be sold or used to make breeches. The battle continued over several months, till they drowned their anger in an orgy of drink.

Nauja loved to tell stories of calamities that had befallen people on their travels. The worst victims were always the Kasdlunas, though she admitted occasionally to some losses on the Inuit side. She was delighted to be able to tell me a couple of tales of cannibalism, which she assured me had happened a long time ago. She remembered a story of an expedition when both Eskimos and white men ran out of food. They could not hunt because they were in poor gaming territory. Eventually the Eskimos had eaten the dogs and survived till they could find a walrus. But all the white men except one had been too squeamish to eat dog meat and had perished.

There were times these days when all the men in the village were away. The women spent their time visiting from house to house. If there were no skins to prepare or no kamiks to make there was very little else to do. Women without children could not bear to be in the dreary houses by themselves and they spent the whole day visiting their neighbours. There was no recreation they could turn to other than sewing. The few books in the 'library' had not been renewed for a couple of years. They had read them all and didn't see the point in reading them over again. They suffered all the depressions and ills of boredom.

It was when their menfolk were away that I got to know the other women in the village better. They enjoyed the brightness of our home and the many books. I made a great effort to entertain them although I much preferred to listen to their stories. One night Nauja and I had spent the whole evening together chatting about our relationship with our husbands. She admitted that she had been *given* in marriage to her husband.

'My mother was rather frightening when she got angry—she always told me not to sleep with a man before I got married. The priests said it was a very bad thing. But one night she found me sleeping with Inugssuak after a dance. She was very angry and told him he would have to marry me.'

'But surely you like him?' I asked.

'Oh, I liked him, but there was another man I liked better.' She described how she wept behind the smile she forced at the wedding. The first two years were stormy, while they lived in his parents' house, with four of his sisters. It was a happy day for her when they got their own home.

I handed her a cigarette, which she smoked vigorously. At last she looked up. 'Was it true that white men never beat their wives?'

I told her that on the whole they didn't. They might have bitter arguments, but some married people managed to discuss their difficulties without being nasty to each other and this was the way Wally and I preferred.

'That could never happen amongst the Eskimos. The men think the women are inferior and should be kept down. They have no understanding of women. They are vicious when they are angry, especially when they are drunk.' She went on rapidly as if a torrent of feeling had been unleashed. 'I try not to fight back when he hits me and I just say yes to everything he demands, but sometimes I get fighting mad too. I often want to run away—far away, and take my two girls with me. I get so bored cooped up inside while he goes away. "Go outside," he says, "if you don't like the house." As if it is as easy as all that!' She stubbed out her cigarette as if it required all her strength.

I hesitated before I asked, 'Do you love Inugssuak?'

She thought for a moment, frowning. 'I don't know—I don't know what I feel for him. He is sometimes so difficult—I don't understand him!'

I felt sorry for her. From all appearances Inugssuak seemed a fine figure of a man—a good hunter and a loving father. But I heard from other people that when he was drunk he was like a man with a devil in him. His liquor ration had recently been stopped after a very violent argument he had had in another settlement. 'He is difficult,' Nauja repeated reflectively '—but sometimes maybe I love him. I don't know.'

There is always at least one occasion in the winter when ice has to be collected in a blizzard. If I used up my stocks of ice and delayed fetching more, bad weather could blow up and I would have no alternative but to go out in it. One such occasion happened while Wally was away. I had not in fact finished all the ice : I had left some just outside the door to save going round to the back of the hut. Unfortunately the dogs had made it unusable. It reminded me of the time in the winter when I had asked Wally to bring in a lump of ice from outside.

'It's no good, the dogs have peed on it,' he said.

'Oh, never mind. It's only for washing my hair.'

'My, you have changed since you came to the Arctic !' he exclaimed. 'You would never have dreamt of saying such a thing when we first arrived !'

Stepping out into a blizzard is like walking into a wall in the dark, but colder and more uncomfortable. Often the ground surface has been polished by the wind, and the effect is something like walking in the opposite direction to a moving pathway which has been covered in grease. To make it worse, millions of large hard pellets swirl into the face blocking the passages of the nose and stinging the eyes. As one opens one's mouth to breathe, the throat constricts, as a whirl of snow, like a ball of cotton wool, threatens to lodge in it. Bare hands are whipped by myriads of tiny lashes which cause them to throb as they swell and redden.

The ice on the windows was very thick now and Maria joked that soon I wouldn't have to go out to collect my ice. It was depressing not to be able to see out. Savfak's windows for some reason were never frosted up, and when she was alone she often dimmed the lights so that she could watch all the happenings outside. Her house was on a higher level, and she looked out over the whole village. One evening as I stood at her window, I noticed two dog teams arriving from the direction of Qanaq. One of them came into the village and was picketed like the spokes of a wheel outside one of the houses. The other was anchored to the ice. To do this, the hunter made a narrow tunnel in the ice through which he threaded the rope and tied it in a loop. These ice bridges can take a tremendous weight if nothing sharp is attached to them, but somehow that night the dogs pulled free and took off towards the north.

During the next few days it seemed as if a fever had broken out amongst the dogs. One old hunter walked into the settlement half an hour after his runaway team. A visitor slipped the traces of his dogs as he was about to tie them up and lost them completely. The first runaway team was eventually found hooked around an ice knobble, but the dogs from the visitor's team were never found! He had to hitch a ride back to Qanaq. Migishoo had been left in charge of Kaudlutok's team while he went off with another hunter! She was seen shuffling out in pursuit of a riderless sledge.

All the women could drive dogs, but some were much better than others. One Sunday Savfak asked me if I would like to go out for a sledge ride. I was delighted. It was a beautiful, crisp day with a few hours of twilight showing the trails across the ice. It was lovely to get close to the bergs again. I had seen them last in the beam of a torch on my winter journeys to Qanaq.

Savfak's dogs were smaller than average and they trotted daintily out of the village, responding faithfully to her soft commands. We sat like two ladies taking the air in a fashionable park, and stepped aside graciously to let the big dogs of the hunters pass by in a whirl of vapour from their hot breaths. We stopped near a small berg and chipped a lump off for tea. In no time the little primus was spluttering gallantly under the melted snow which had stuck to the bottom of the pan. It was marvellous to be out in the fresh air, and we waved as Migishoo came into sight with one of her sons and passed us. But our complacency was shattered— and our tea upturned—when our dogs suddenly decided to follow the other team. They lunged after them, throwing us on our backs with our feet off the ground, and yanking the harpoon that held their traces out of the ice hole. Savfak handled the whip with authority. Even so, it was some time before we had regained our composure. Our tea was lost, but we did not worry. It had been a good ride and we were ready to go home.

We rode back gently till we got to the little cove where most of the dog teams came in. The smell of the village excited the dogs and they flew over the tide crack as if jet propelled. I held on tight while we rose in the air and landed with a smack on the other side. Before I could catch my breath they galloped up the hill straight for another team. I rolled off in a heap before the inevitable fracas. A very stern Savfak went up the slope behind them. With a few deft cracks of the whip she separated the two teams, before they had a chance to get too embroiled.

One of the big tasks I had to face while Wally was away was to make a tent to use on journeys, as ours had been lost 'in transit'. Maria showed me an Eskimo tent, and we cut the new one out together. She helped with most of the stitching, and in two or three days we had an enormous red tent which opened down the front with an adhesive fastening. While we were sewing it the children were all in the hut and there were several visitors besides. The noise was deafening. I wanted to rush outside into the open, away from the close atmosphere. How could people live without privacy? Surely they needed a few moments to themselves? I think at times the women did get tired with the strain of children running in and out all the time, but they thought it was infinitely preferable to being lonely.

There was a different atmosphere in the village when the men were away. It was quieter, since the only dogs left were a few bitches with pups. There seemed to be less light. The women confined themselves to one room and did not bother to put a light in the other. I found myself doing the same. I never bothered much about meals. On a couple of occasions I invited the women in for a meal. I made a great effort to cook something tasty, and fished out the cases to look for something nice to wear. I felt marvellous after I had dressed up and put on my makeup and done my hair nicely. I opened a bottle of wine left over from Christmas. We had a very merry evening indeed.

I was amazed to find that hardly any of the Eskimos had a friend— as *I* think of a friend. Nauja said she had had one but when she died she decided not to have any more as there was no one suitable. I got the same answer from Savfak and Maria. They had both had a friend but in one case she had committed suicide and in the other she had died in some tragedy. They lived very much their own lives. They helped each other in things that affected the common good, like hauling up the boats, carrying in the stores, stacking up the coal, but on a more personal level each family looked after its own and left others to sort out their own problems.

I asked various women why they did not take it in turns to look after each other's children, so that they could have a chance to go to Qanaq. They shook their heads. 'It does not happen that way here—people are not really friendly.' Maybe they saw so much of each other that they felt the others knew too much about them already.

'Everyone is such a gossip,' explained Nauja.

During our conversations I learnt that most women had had at least one miscarriage and some more. One woman, who was still young, had had seven miscarriages and was still childless. 'It is because we get so tired and we have to work so hard,' they said.

'But couldn't you ask someone to help you scrape your skins and fetch ice?' I asked.

They shook their heads as if I wouldn't understand.

It was obvious from the women's conversation that most of them craved the intimacy and affection of friendship. And I think it was why both Nauja and Maria were so honest with me. I told them about a friend of mine, whom I had known for many years: for me she possessed all the virtues a friend should, and none of the vices. I brought out a clipping my parents had sent which showed a photo of Pauline Collins dressed in Edwardian costume from a TV series, and her husband, John Alderton, who was also in the series.

'She is an actreece,' I said, hoping that they would understand if I pronounced it in a foreign way. They shook their heads. I was sure there was a word the Eskimos would understand because there were regular films in Qanaq.

'Feelme-star!' I tried again.

They nodded their heads admiringly and examined the photo more closely.

I told them that Pauline and I had been to drama school together and had shared a flat for three years. We had never quarrelled, but of course at times one did something to upset the other, and we had an agreement to 'talk about anything bad'. I told them that we would occasionally spend an evening going through each other's faults while the other listened politely and maybe explained the reason for a certain apparent thoughtlessness. When all the faults were done with, we then went on to the good points, and ended up the evening thinking we were both marvellous.

My two listeners thought this hilarious but also a very good idea.

'Are all your friends like that?' they asked with great curiosity.

'Oh no,' I replied. 'Imaka ilane ikingut sordlo Pouline—ilane kisiane.'
'Maybe occasionally you will have a friend like that.'

11

The first of February brought a stream of visitors to Herbert Island from the surrounding settlements. Ours was the only village with any meat. The Eskimos resented paying for meat, but the old days of barter had passed. And even in the old days, a community would help its own members and let neighbouring communities starve.

The present Thule Eskimos are the descendants of Eskimos who depended for their existence on sea mammals, with occasional birds or fish. Because many of these sea mammals, such as whales, were very big it was necessary for several people to cooperate in small communities to hunt them. When a community grew too large, it split up so that the resources of one area would not be exhausted.

The community could not tolerate burdens. Therefore it was a matter of course that disabled children were exposed to the harsh weather to die. When they felt they were becoming a nuisance old people committed suicide by giving themselves up to the sea on a lonely beach. And often orphans were left without assistance to starve to death.

These days Greenland is an integral part of Denmark and the Greenlanders enjoy the same social privileges as the Danes, although the methods of administering these must necessarily be different. The poor and sick are cared for and the homeless housed. Aged folk need not be a burden on the family as the 'community' provides for them. In Thule many of the old folk had adopted a child to keep them company in their old age.

One of the most enjoyable pastimes for many was the daily radio broadcast which transmitted local news and telegrams. By carefully fiddling with the knobs, some people were quick enough to hear the messages passed to and from Qanaq and the various other settlements. The telegrams always sounded the same. People had arrived safely and were well, the weather was either good or bad. Whatever the message it was exciting to hear your name over the radio and Maria and I listened every day for news of Wally's and Avatak's arrival at Savigsavik. These messages were not just a courtesy measure, but were essential in an environment where the journeys were sometimes perilous. If travellers took an abnormally long time to arrive at their destination, people would have to go looking for them.

On the 2nd of February we were glued to the set. The radio operator had said there was to be a message for both of us.

'Marie, soon I will bring back the sun,' was the cheering message from Wally. Just that morning I had looked out of the door to see a huge ball of fire refracted above the horizon. It was like a tight knot of glowing embers which gradually disintegrated and sank again.

That evening several of the women came to the hut. I examined the kamiks some of them had made for Wally's trip to Canada. At a sound at the door I went to investigate but found nothing.

'It means Wally is thinking of you,' said Maria—adding, 'as he lies in the arms of another woman.'

We all laughed but Migishoo said, 'You tell her that Avatak is probably enjoying another woman—come on, tell her.'

I did so to please her and she burst into a roar of gleeful laughter. We laughed as well, and Maria said, with mock conceit, 'Oh, no, not Avatak —never.'

It was true what Wally had said. He was expected back in Qanaq on 17th February, and that was the day the sun would appear in our part of the world. It would still take three weeks before it would be seen above the hills by us at Herbert Island, but its nearness could be felt in many ways.

I had read that you would know the sun was definitely on the way back when you first noticed the colour of your dogs. Indeed, it is most startling when you suddenly notice colour for the first time, after the long period of monotony. Migishoo's dogs had been wandering around outside the hut for days, but one morning I realized what marvellous blue-black pelts two of them had, which contrasted vividly with the bright yellow tinge of part of their fur. I mentioned this to Maria and she said that because there was so much snow around it made everything else look off-white. Even polar bears, she explained, could be spotted easily at this time of the year because they looked so yellow against the brilliance of the ice around. She explained that polar bears were very intelligent animals, because they knew that their fur was yellow and their nose black—so when they stalked seals, they often carried lumps of ice to act as a screen.

We heard by radio that a sudden change of plan made Wally decide to go walrus hunting. Now they would be coming back on the night of the 9th February. That morning Maria and I were discussing the reason for the change of plan. We decided that it would be very late at night before the men arrived. She told me that before Avatak had left he had been very despondent one night. 'Ajor!' he had said to her, 'if Wally dies on the trip everyone will think I have murdered him. If I die everyone will think he has murdered me. Ajor!'

A noise outside made one of the boys peer through a chink in the ice-covered windows.

'There's a dog team outside,' he said.

'Who is it? Who is it?' yelled Maria.

There was a mad scramble to the door.

'Atata! Atata!'

'Avatak's here,' shouted Maria.

'Impossible!' I answered, knowing only too well how they loved to joke. 'Go and look for yourself.'

I ran to the door and there sure enough was Avatak in his thick tugto parka and polar-bear pants, unhitching the dogs. I scoured the horizon for Wally.

'He's probably dead,' said little Eto, encouragingly. 'A polar bear's probably eaten him.'

Suddenly he appeared from behind a berg. His dogs were tearing along in their excitement to get at the other teams. From all around there were the sounds of dogs welcoming the new arrivals.

I rushed back into the house to fetch Kari. Everyone was running in circles, not knowing what to do first. 'Tea,' yelled Maria to one of the kids. That was all there was except for a half carcass of walrus hanging from a hook in the corner. We collided in different directions, laughing at how unprepared we were. I had no makeup on. I hadn't even lit the lights in the hut. I tore across to put on the kettle and light the lamps.

Ten minutes later Wally came through the door. Ice covered the hairs of his moustache and ringed his mouth. His clothes dripped melting snow as he stood by the fire, like a giant in his furs. Kari looked coyly at him as he stooped to give her an icy embrace.

We talked late into the night, grinning till our cheeks ached at the delight of being together again. The men had travelled hard—twelve to thirteen hours a day, of which only about two or three hours were in twilight, and the rest either dark or moonlit. They had been battered by blizzards along the coast and had travelled through them over ice worn away beneath by the currents, until in places it was only a few inches thick.

Wally's dogs had been very difficult to handle. They were very lazy and he had had trouble the whole way, until Avatak had suggested changing teams for a while. 'It was like changing from an old family saloon to a de-luxe sports car,' said Wally. He tore off and didn't see Avatak for another three hours. The ride was not without mishap, however. As usual he stopped several times to untangle the traces, but once, before he could tie all the dogs back on the rope, they took off. The rope was fortunately threaded through the loop of the main trace, which was attached to the sledge. As the team galloped away Wally held on. He would not let go, though he was dragged on his stomach for over a mile, with the sledge almost on top of him. When the dogs did eventually stop, he found he had dropped Avatak's one and only whip. It was a supreme effort to drive the dogs back along the route without a whip until he had found the one he dropped, but he managed it and sat waiting for his companion to catch up. An exasperated Avatak arrived a couple of hours later cursing Wally's dogs as the worst team he had ever driven. He never offered to lend his own team again.

Wally was glad the Eskimo had had a chance to test the dogs for himself. The locals get a great delight in boasting that nobody can drive a dog team like the Inuit.

'Who has the best dog team in the district?' asked Wally, as Avatak proudly took back his own team.

'I have,' he answered without hesitation.

'Well, who has the second best team?' asked Wally.

'My father,' he replied.

As a travelling companion Wally had found Avatak difficult. He either forgot or did not bother to flash his torch back at Wally during a long stretch of coast which was unknown to Wally. It was blizzarding quite hard, and the sledge tracks were obliterated in no time: it was also dark. For some reason Wally's tent had been put on Avatak's sledge, so he could not stop and camp. He was always greeted by a cheerful smile and great friendliness when he caught up, but even Eskimos would have found this sort of travel very difficult.

As if Wally's problems with his team were not bad enough, he discovered that the two bitches in the team were on heat. This caused the most dreadful disturbance, as the dogs fought constantly. Every few hundred yards the team would come to a complete standstill while the jealous dogs attacked each other viciously. The usual procedure if there are two teams is for one team to tie the bitch at the back of the sledge so that the dogs following are excited into keeping pace. On only one occasion had Avatak done this, and he had to hang around for hours till Wally caught up. However, at one of the villages Wally exchanged the bitches for a dog and at Savigsavik he bought two others.

There were no polar bear around, so they had decided to go to the walrus grounds. The next day they set off. Maria came to see me after they had left, quietly instead of in her usual bouncing, busy way. She asked if Wally had enjoyed the trip. I wondered what Avatak had asked her to find out. At last she mentioned two incidents. I had already heard of the two occasions, when Avatak had yelled in fury for Wally to stop where there was a new lead in the ice, and another spot where there was thin ice. Wally had been annoyed at the time, but had not argued. I pointed out to Maria that Wally had spent sixteen months on drifting ice and that in that time he had learnt a thing or two. She nodded appreciatively.

It was while we were chatting that Maria commented on a remark I made recently when I tried to explain why Wally wanted to make a film. 'Many people think you all live in snow houses,' I had explained to her.

'How sad it is that they don't know more about us,' she said.

I pointed out that if the Inuit didn't like people filming and writing about them, it made it very difficult to show people how they lived. We talked about the differences in the way two cultures thought and that sometimes misunderstandings could arise because people looked at things from different points of view.

Was it true that I had told the children recently I was not a Kasdluna? she asked.

'Yes, that's true,' I replied.

She laughed sarcastically and said, 'Well, do you think you are Inuit?'

I explained that I thought it very impolite to call someone 'Kasdlunas' to her face if you knew her name. In my opinion it was unfriendly to remind people constantly that they were foreigners—people were people whatever their nationality.

My talk with Maria convinced us that we obviously misunderstood each other at times and gave cause for annoyance unwittingly. She swallowed the pill I had given her without anger, but returned one which hurt me deeply.

She began by telling me that she was not 'angry' but she was most surprised by something I had said one day after Christmas, which had seemed very rude; but she had told Avatak later that maybe it was just a misunderstanding because we spoke a different language. She hesitated as if she would change her mind but I urged her on.

'Marie, I would rather speak about things than bear a grudge, and I think you would too, isn't that right?'

'Of course,' I agreed, wondering what on earth I could have done.

'Do you remember the night you came and told us that Avatak's mother had come to ask you for ivalo?' she asked.

I did remember. Avatak's mother was making a caribou parka for me, and had asked for some sinew to sew it with. She knew I had some, because she had given me a bundle as a Christmas present. I had thought it so charming and ironic that she should have to ask me when it was usually the other way around—I was always asking the locals to provide some essential local produce. And she was having to ask me because she had been so generous at Christmas to give me all hers. I had told the two of them this, assuming they would see the humour of the situation.

'Well, we were astonished when we heard you say that she had asked for some back. You should know that it is the custom to provide the sinew if anyone is sewing anything for you.'

I had not known this, but still did not see what Maria was getting at.

'Well, what did you think when I said that, Maria?'

'Well, we thought it very rude of you. Suakuanguak didn't ask because she wanted any for herself. She has plenty.' She seemed glad to have established that fact, although she spoke harshly and abruptly. 'We were all concerned at Christmas because you were far from home, and we thought you might be lonely. We decided to try and make you feel at home and everyone decided to make you a little present.' She trailed off.

I still did not understand what I had said that should make her feel so upset. I hadn't yet grasped what was their interpretation of my statement.

'Did you think me very bad, Maria?' I asked.

'Of course!'

'But why?' I was almost afraid to ask.

Her face looked hard when she was serious. 'Because we had made so much effort for you and we had tried so hard to be friendly.'

'But I know that, Maria,' I said, distressed at the distance that seemed to be creeping between us.

'Then why were you so ungrateful?' she accused.

I couldn't speak. The accusation was so unexpected and so painful. I had to try and put into a foreign language all that milled around in my mind. I grasped feebly for words to explain that it was a mistake—that I had been misunderstood—that far from being ungrateful we had been overwhelmingly touched by their generosity. I wanted to say I was sorry but didn't know how the hell to say it. All I could say was, 'Ajor, Maria, imaka uvanga ajorpok, kisiane imaka ivdlit passiva nagga.' 'Maybe I am bad, but maybe you don't understand.' I tried to explain that far from expecting their wonderful presents we had been so overcome with their kindness. I could only blurt, 'I cried in my heart at your goodness.' By now the enormity of my offence seemed so unbearable I couldn't control the stream of tears that poured down my face. I lit a cigarette and handed her one. She knew I never smoked but I had to do something to regain my composure. I could only repeat that 'I was a bad woman'—it wasn't at all what I meant to say, but there was nothing else which would have illustrated my remorse.

My reaction completely disarmed Maria, who in turn became very miserable. 'Oh, I feel bad because I have upset you. It is I who am a bad woman.'

We smoked for a while in silence.

'Ajor, I thought it must have been a misunderstanding,' she said, concerned, at last. 'Let us forget it altogether!' She stole across the room, put her arm round my shoulders and pressed her cheek against mine. Her hand gripped my arm gently, then she slipped out of the room and closed the door silently behind her.

12

The end of February and the beginning of March is the coldest time of the year in the Arctic. Winds whip across the white desert, scarring the land. Blizzards blind the hunter and keep his family indoors. But there is one thing that lifts the depression and soothes fraught nerves—the sun. Each day it climbs a little higher, till it inches its way above the horizon. Not everyone at the same latitude sees it on the same day, but even if the hills obscure its view its presence is obvious by the band of pale pink across the pale sky and the frieze of lights on the hills around. Kekertassuak is always the last settlement to see the sun. It would take about three weeks from the time the inhabitants in Qanaq saw the sun on 17th February before it scaled the heights of the hills behind our village.

Wally's trip to the walrus hunting grounds had been cold and arduous. He and Avatak had sledged for six hours and then walked for a further five. For those five hours Wally had dragged a heavy sledge, loaded with camera, tape recorder, lights, battery belts, and batteries, together with spare leads and tripods. He was exhausted by the time they stopped. He had got some film but not enough and he would have to go again another time.

He was cheered on his return to get a telegram from Geoff to say that he could come, but only on the 7th March. That was the date that Peter Peary had originally suggested they should all leave for Canada, but of course the departure would have to be delayed a while.

I had decided I would sledge with Wally to Dundas, the village just outside the Airbase, to meet Geoff. The distance was about ninety miles, part of which was over a glacier. It would be too risky to take Kari just for a joy ride, but Maria had offered to look after her for the five days that we expected to be away.

The couple of weeks before Geoff's arrival were spent preparing for the long trip to Canada. I made a new set of harnesses, a couple of sleeping-bag covers, and a white tent to go inside the red one that Maria had helped me with. It all took a long time. Wally had a hundred and one jobs to do. By cutting two feet off the back of the sledge he had lightened it quite a bit, but it was still a considerable weight compared with the other Eskimo sledges.

I had to get a tugto parka and three pairs of kamiks made for Geoff. I also had to see that Wally's parka was in good condition after the last trip, and that he too had enough pairs of kamiks for the trip to Canada. It is much colder in Canada than in Greenland. The sealskin mitts which the men wore over woollen ones wore out very quickly while sledging and they had to have several pairs. I hoped Geoff would fit into my polar-bear pants, which were a bit large for me. It would be difficult and expensive to get another pair.

Nearly every day Maria used to take Kari over to her house for several hours. It was a great relief for me to have some time to myself. It meant I could do my chores without hauling Kari along beside me. Her hands were always straying into Wally's equipment and books. There was so much in our hut which was either too hazardous or too valuable for her to fiddle with.

In contrast, the freedom of Maria's house was bliss. Kari could roam through the two rooms at will. Her every wish was indulged. There was no danger of her upsetting the paraffin heaters as they were well out of reach. The ceiling in Maria's house was much higher than ours and lamps could be hung from it. There was rarely much on the stove except the usual pot of boiled meat. There were no jagged tins of stores to hurt her, and the large basin of seal meat would have provided a soft but malodorous cushion if she fell in. She would sit on Avatak's knee, twiddling the knobs of the radio as if she owned the place.

To our great surprise the last week in February was unusually warm. The days were very clear, with flecks of pink floss in the blue sky. A dart of orange light heralded an advancing sun, expected at Herbert Island on 7th March. I could hardly believe this was February—the coldest time of the year!

If the weather held, it looked as if we would have a good trip over the glacier to Dundas. We had decided to go to Qanaq first to tell Peter that the Canada trip should be postponed till at least the 10th March—so that Geoff would have a day to prepare himself for the journey. One of the

Eskimo hunters with a good team and with no load had done the ninety miles from Qanaq to Dundas in fifteen travelling hours, but we expected to take two days. The glacier itself is about 18 miles long, including a stretch of frozen river-bed that we would have to follow down to the sea ice. It rises to a height of 2,500 feet. It is not considered dangerous, except in bad weather, when it can be treacherous, but of course it should not be traversed by anyone who does not know the route.

On the southern side it is badly crevassed in places, but the Eskimos know where to avoid these. Wally had been over the glacier before with Avatak and felt no need to have a guide a second time. Normally two sledges travel together over the glacier, especially if the party comprises people other than Eskimos. In our case we felt confident enough to go on our own.

When we mentioned that we were leaving in a few days for Dundas, the villagers shook their heads anxiously at the thought of us going alone. I reminded them that Wally had had several years' sledging experience but they felt that a Kasdlunas could not know their land the way they knew it and that no Kasdlunas was really safe on his own. We did not argue.

Friday the 3rd March was a fine, mild day. Maria brought in a pair of tugto overshoes to put over my long kamiks as extra protection. They were very warm and less slippery than the smooth sole of the kamik. She also brought a plate of walrus heart for us to try. It was steaming hot and the juice trickled down into my upturned sleeve. It was very tasty. 'Eat some of the fat with it, it's delicious with the meat,' she urged. I have never been fond of fat but I tried it and found that it went excellently with the meat. 'You must chew it at least thirty times or you will get indigestion,' said Maria.

While Maria gathered some of Kari's things together, Avatak came in and whisked Kari outside. She sensed something unusual in all the activity and began to fret, but he quickly distracted her. I hated to leave her but I knew it was the best.

We had taken the barest essentials with us to compensate for the heavy sledge. It still seemed a lot by Eskimo standards. For one thing we always carried food for ourselves and pemmican for the dogs. Unlike the Eskimos we hadn't family scattered in the various settlements that we could rely on for hospitality. We had six days' food for ourselves and three days' for Geoff. We anticipated at the most using four day's food for ourselves and two for Geoff. There was a possibility that at Moriussaq, a village along the route, we would be entertained by the family Wally had stayed with on his travels with Avatak. At Dundas we were to be the guests of the Danish Administrator, Jens Zinglersen.

Apart from food, we had a change of clothes for Dundas and a complete set of polar clothing for Geoff—kamiks, polar-bear pants, two sets of underwear, two jerseys, woollen and sealskin mitts, light and heavy socks, foxtails to tie round the top of his calves to keep out the draught between his kamiks and breeches, and an enormous tugto parka. The bundle was very bulky. 'Thank goodness Geoff will have this lot on him on the way back,' said Wally as he heaved it on to the sledge. We had a sleeping bag each, two tugto skins, one thin foam mattress, a couple of inflatable rubber mattresses, a brew box with billies, a rifle, and an assortment of camera and film equipment. An inner and outer tent completed the load.

Although it was a mild day the sun was hidden through a curtain of haze. Our first stop, after we had picketed the dogs, was at Peter's house. There was something immediately engaging about him. A shock of black hair crowned a well chiselled, olive skin face. But it was his smile that was so disarming.

Flashing a perfect set of teeth, it lit up his whole face. Although his manner was relaxed, I sensed a burning energy beneath the surface. He had a reputation for knowing exactly what he wanted and was never irresolute. How could so small a frame contain so much spirit? I wished he could have been taller, as I watched him cross the room—and what a pity he was bowlegged!

Peter agreed to the new arrangement. 'I'll be at Herbert Island on 10th March at nine o'clock.' We looked surprised. It was unusual for an Eskimo to be so precise about time.

We were persuaded to spend the night in Qanaq instead of camping at the foot of the glacier as we had intended, but next morning we were up and away by 8.30. Across the bay we could see the mountains intersected by several glaciers. Ours was the lowest and the least steep. Several miles to my right I could see the dark side of Herbert Island, lit now by the sun. It still looked pretty bleak. More mountains and fiords came into view as we got into Inglefield Bay.

The dogs were going well except for a strong bias to the left. We had put the bitch in the lead, as an incentive. She was more nuisance than help, however, and flirted outrageously, skipping between the traces of the other dogs. As she ran from one to the other, nuzzling up to them, she wove a complicated pattern in the leads. And as each dog jostled with his neighbour to get more room they snarled even more. They hopped over and under the traces like circus dogs till they were hopelessly entwined. As dogs were ousted they nipped the offending neighbour, sending him careering out of the way, knocking the whole team sideways. Soon the whole team was running in and out, snarling and snapping, till the knot in the leads got so high up the rope that they had hardly room to move at all.

This is a situation every sledge driver tries to avoid. In this case the bitch was the root of the problem. She was just out of reach of the whip, at the head of the team, and there was no way of correcting her but to take her aside and punish her. This Wally did, while the others strained to get at her and join in the punishment. A few smacks of the whip at close quarters brought her soberly to her senses, and we had no more trouble from her. Wally growled the order to move off and the dogs surged into life.

When we were about five miles from the glacier Wally pointed out a wall of rock at the foot of it.

'That's a terminal moraine,' he explained.

'What's that?' I asked.

'It's eroded rock and debris carried down by the glacier and deposited at the foot. As the ice receded it left a ridge of rocks and stones. It is quite high—about thirty feet. We have to skirt it to get to the foot of the glacier.'

'It doesn't look that high from here,' I said. 'Couldn't we cross it?'

'Oh, heck, no. There's no snow on it and it would play hell with the runners. No, it is completely impassable.'

I looked up at the glacier. It seemed to be very steep, greeny blue with flecks of white, with black blotches here and there.

'It looks very steep,' I said, quite awestruck.

'It always looks steeper from this distance. We can either go up the centre route or up the right-hand side if there was enough snow. There doesn't seem all that much though,' said Wally casually.

I gazed at the ice fall in front of us. 'Ah, I can see a trail on the left,' I said with some relief.

'How can you?' asked Wally, puzzled.

'There is a long line of dog droppings.'

'Dog droppings! From here? That is an enormous lateral moraine. Not even an elephant could do them that size. Those are huge rocks—just wait till you get up to them. Dog droppings!' He chuckled to himself.

'They look awfully small,' I persisted.

'Well, they are about three miles away.'

Soon after, we skirted the enormous wall of angular rubble into a wide bowl at the base of the great tongue of ice. On either side the mountains rose sheer. From where we were the glacier looked as if a huge slice had been cut out of it. The centre ridge sloped dangerously steep to a high drop. Great marble-like boulders fell away from it in jumbled confusion.

'Good Lord, suppose the sledge slips sideways on the ice down that?' I exclaimed anxiously. 'The drop is about forty feet.'

'Don't worry, it won't,' said Wally reassuringly.

While I walked off to get some ice from the chunks lying around the base of the glacier Wally picketed the dogs.

'I'll have a look up the right-hand route to see how much snow there is,' said Wally.

As I got the brew box out and made the tea I got a feeling of complete isolation from everything else in the world except the team of dogs, stretched out nearby. Wally was lost to view, and it was at least ten minutes before a distant halloo reached me. It was some time before I could make him out against the rocks. In his polar clothing he was completely camouflaged. I called to him that tea was ready and held up a cup for him to see. His words were lost on the breeze and only a distorted echo reached me.

When Wally returned and we had had our tea we walked round to the lip of the glacier. The route he had just explored was impassable. From where we stood great waves of blue ice flowed down, in horizontal and vertical stripes. Tiny ripples scored the face all over with tiny snow-filled crescents.

'Yes, this is definitely the better way up,' said Wally. 'You go ahead of the dogs, picking up the trail, and I'll keep them going from behind.'

'How will I know where the trail is?' I asked, rather alarmed at the prospect of leading the team into some unfathomable predicament.

'Oh, just follow the pee marks,' said Wally casually. 'Don't worry about crevasses, there aren't any on this part of the glacier.'

I looked for the familiar yellow marks and sure enough they seemed pretty obvious. I stepped over a thick coil of scorched rope.

'Whew! Look what the friction's done to that!' exclaimed Wally.

'What friction?' I asked, puzzled.

'Well, that's a rope brake. The sledge must have been coming down at such a lick, it burnt right through the rope!'

13. It can be a startling experience, walking through the village in winter, to find oneself face to face with a team of huskies. Their eyes glitter evilly in the light of the torch. Wally's king dog was a great one-eyed bully. The dogs have to be tethered near fresh snow, as they have no other way of getting moisture in winter.

14. Before the start of a winter journey, Wally checks that Kari is snug—well wrapped in fox furs, inside two sleeping bags, protected in turn by a wooden box strapped to the sledge. The rifle is essential equipment, in case of wandering polar bears. Wally is dressed in polar-bear pants and a wolfskin *parka*. I have on a fur *parka*, of musquash, beaver and wolfskin, worn above the long *kamiks* which are the traditional dress of the Thule Eskimos.

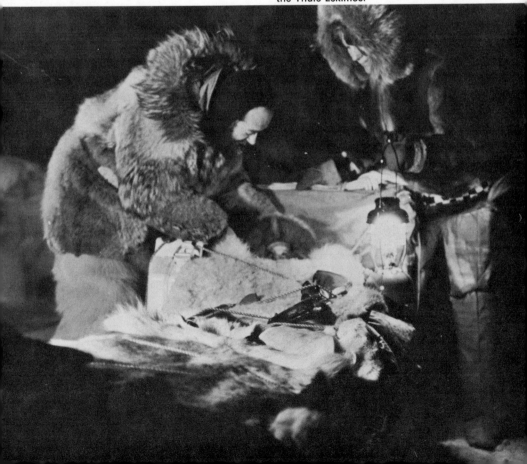

15. A brew stop is an essential part of travelling. It gives the dogs a chance to rest and eat some snow—they get very thirsty when they are working.

16. Even in the winter darkness the Eskimos travel with only a torch to guide them. They put up the tent over the sledge so that it acts as a sleeping platform, and the tent is heated by the primuses on which they brew tea. The dogs are anchored to an ice hummock nearby.

My muscles stiffened as I gazed in horror at the gigantic ice-ramp before us.

A few spots of blood stained the snow.

'You had better take your parka off,' suggested Wally. 'You will get pretty sweaty.' I took it off and threw it on to the sledge. It was most unpleasant when the sweat began to freeze so it was better not to get too hot in the first place. I called the dogs to me and started walking ahead. The first hundred yards were not too steep. The surface was very smooth, with enough snow patches for the dogs to get a grip. In a few seconds I was having to run to keep ahead of the panting animals tearing up the slope behind me. I jumped over the occasional crack, leapt up a 'wave' and down the other side, pursued relentlessly by the hot breath of the huskies.

My fear of the glacier itself was replaced by the more tangible fear of being swallowed up by our own dogs. I leapt wildly from one side to the other as I tore ahead in a desperate attempt to put some distance between me and them.

'Whew!' I gasped from a safe elevation, 'I'm exhausted. I can't keep that pace up.'

Wally laughed as he drew level. 'They were pretty close, I must admit. But that was very good going. It gets a bit steeper here so you won't have to worry about the dogs overtaking you.'

I looked up the slope. 'You know it doesn't look so high after all,' I said.

'Oh, yes it is. That's only the first tier you are looking at. There are four tiers in all, and they get progressively steeper. I think we may even have to put the dogs on an extended trace for a while.' As Wally sorted out a length of rope to make the trace, I sat on the sledge to catch my breath.

'I think you should keep closer to the dogs now—they won't overtake you but it will just excite them enough to make them pull,' explained Wally.

We set off again. As he had predicted the dogs didn't overtake me. In fact they had a tough job moving the load at all. With half the team a few yards ahead of the others it meant that at least a few dogs were on snow all the time, thus helping the rest to keep a footing. In an hour and a half we were up the first ridge. We were pretty pleased. The load was a heavy one—at least the sledge was very heavy. From then on for a while I could ride on the sledge while Wally picked out the route. From time to time he too rode.

'I always feel rotten making the dogs pull me uphill,' said Wally, 'but the Eskimos think you are crazy if you don't. They say you should make the dogs work.'

We plodded on, occasionally jumping off the sledge to whip the dogs into some concerted action to get them up a particularly difficult slope. While Wally spurred them on with the whip I added my small efforts from behind the sledge, or shoved a bit of rope behind the runners to stop the load slipping back. Every inch became a milestone till we could budge no further.

We had crossed over to the snow cover at the right-hand side of the glacier. As I looked over my shoulder a thrill of horror ran down my spine. It looked so steep I could not imagine how we would come down it without hurtling completely out of control. It was difficult enough stopping the blunt end of the runners from slipping backwards. How on earth would we stop the sledge when it was turned the other way, with the runners curving up?

'It will be no problem,' said Wally. 'We will be using the rope brakes most of the way down.'

I glanced at the rather narrow ropes slung neatly over the back handlebars. 'Are they really good?'

'They are pretty good. But we will use the chain on the ice.'

A few minutes later an exasperated bellow from Wally startled the dogs as they strained against a steep slope. They just could not exert enough effort to move the load any further. The ground was very slippery and it was difficult to keep a footing. The sledge kept slipping back and we had to work hard to keep it from sliding all the way down, taking the sprawling dogs with it. We thought of relaying, but that was always the last resort as it entailed making two trips instead of one. In any case the sledge was the heaviest part of the equipment.

We had to move off the path we were on as it led into a cul de sac. 'Huk, huk, huk!' Wally roared at the dogs, and hauled on the rope. The muscles in their necks and shoulders strained, but their feet kept slipping beneath them.

'If you can just lead them up over that brow, we will have a brew at the top,' encouraged Wally.

I stepped gingerly from behind the sledge, which was just holding. My feet however slid from under me and I fell face down in the snow. My long kamiks splayed out at an awkward angle. I got up with difficulty. I dug the ice axe into the packed snow to support me, but my feet just slithered from side to side. The dogs got up, slithering and slipping. Only a thin rope brake held the sledge from sliding all the way down again.

'The dogs can't keep a footing. And neither can I, for that matter,' I complained.

'O.K. Come back and sit on the sledge for a while,' he said, long-suffering. He took the ice axe from me and scratched several broad clefts in the snow.

'Now try it,' he suggested.

Bit by bit the heaving dogs inched the sledge up. When we got on to the glacier again they collapsed in contented heaps. While Wally lit the primus I walked off the trail to chip some ice from the great tongue of it beneath us, for tea. It was marvellous to cup the warm mug in my hands and gaze out over the vast panorama that lay to the north. Mountains ringed a frozen sea with the tip of the icecap showing above. The world seemed to drop away beneath us. As I looked, Wally pointed out the route we would have to take when we returned. It looked frighteningly steep from where I was sitting. I remembered the burnt-out rope brake I had seen at the bottom of the glacier.

'Just hang on to the sledge bag while I turn the sledge on its side. I'll use that bit of tea that is left to coat the runners.' Wally dipped a piece of fur in the pot and ran it quickly along the whole length of the steel runner. He repeated the process several times till a coating of ice, one-tenth of an inch thick, ran the full length of it. 'That should make the going a bit easier from here.'

Towards the last part of the climb we noticed the mist gathering behind us, rising like a cushion of hot air. We had started the ascent at 3 p.m. It was now 6.30 and we were several hundred yards from the top. I rode on the sledge and Wally either walked ahead or joined me for the occasional breather. The snow was soft and deep in parts, and the dogs' paws left heavy prints. I noticed a thin trail of blood, probably from a cut paw, running alongside the sledge. I couldn't tell whether it was from one of our dogs or from a previous team.

The blue was gradually disappearing from the sky. As the wind increased we were suddenly engulfed in mist. We could only see a few yards. It was like pushing our way through a thick layer of cotton wool.

We had hoped to make it to Moriussaq that night, but it looked as if we would be delayed for quite a while. The route down the other side was a more gradual slope and longer. It would be possible to feel our way down, but I didn't like the idea of that at all. I preferred to see what the hazards were.

We crept forward in silence. In no time we had lost all sense of direction. It is difficult, without any perspective, to check the vagaries of the dogs and we had the feeling we were beginning to circle. Somewhere en route the compass had dropped out of the sledge load so we had only our own judgement to go by. At last Wally decided to call a halt, in case the weather turned too rough. It would be better to camp now.

I received his suggestion with relief. While he prodded the snow for a camp site, I started to unpack the sledge. There were several thin cracks running near us, but he soon found a suitable place for the tent. The wind was picking up. It was still impossible to see more than a few yards. I held on to one tent pole while Wally put the other in place. The tent flapped agitatedly in our grasp. There was enough snow to hold the tent pegs, which meant we would not have to make ice holes. We put the tent over the sledge so that we had a platform running the full length of the tent.

It was not long before we had a meal of meat bar mixed with onion flakes, soup powder and butter. This made a rich goo which was tasty but impossible to finish. It was comforting to snuggle down into the sleeping bag and listen to the wind moaning outside. The tent flapped wildly and I wondered if we would blow away from our moorings and slither down the slope. It was a strange, exciting feeling camping at the top of a glacier. All the strange stories of adventure flitted through my mind.

'Pity you can't come on more journeys,' mused Wally, as we sipped a warm cup of tea.

'What would I do with Kari?' I wondered.

'Hmmm, bit awkward taking a baby on a journey, unless you carry it in an Amaut like the Eskimos. Imagine putting up a tent every time you wanted to change its nappy or feed it.'

We chatted on for a while before turning off the primus stove. I could feel the chill as soon as its hissing stopped. I had never felt so small as I lay on the sledge, thinking of the vast space around us. 'You need more adventure,' murmured Wally, as the night closed around us.

I prayed for none that night, and sank into sleep.

13

The next morning we awoke to a beautiful day. By about 9.30 we were ready with the sledge loaded and the team harnessed. The dogs seemed rested, and excited at the prospect of moving on. They stretched and wriggled round each other, nuzzling up to their mates with a full-throated rumble. An occasional snarl singled out the victim of the king dog. A mean, pugnacious, one-eyed colossus, by far the strongest in the team, he strutted from dog to dog bullying and provoking them to fight. Most lay on their backs, fawning, their tails sweeping the snow in an attempt to placate him.

As we crested the glacier a tremendous radiance lit the scene. The dogs, bathed in a pink glow of sunlight, crunched underfoot a carpet of shimmering snow crystals which reflected a million sunbeams. The land seemed ablaze with colour. A sparkling roadway sloped away from us. In the distance a large ice lake had formed at the head of a fiord, ringed by mountains divided by mighty glaciers.

The dogs bounded along at an easy pace. Their tails bounced and bobbed like the plumes of an exotic hat. It was a long slow drop of several miles. The sledge gathered speed, and it looked as if it would run into the dogs, floundering up to their shoulders in a sudden patch of deep snow. Wally threw a rope brake over a runner and brought the sledge to a halt beside them. A blow from one of the runners could be fatal, and sometimes the driver cannot avoid his team in time.

As we sped over the ice the slope became steeper. The sledge began to bounce and buck like a vicious animal. It reared over humps and slammed into hollows. My body ached from the jolts and blows. I clutched the ropes as it slithered from side to side, then lurched violently over a rise and plunged down the decline. I gasped as it slammed to a halt a hair's breadth from the cliff face. Then I was knocked back as it lurched into life along the base of the cliff.

Wally stopped the dogs at a gap in the moraine. He walked ahead up the jumble of rocks to look for a route. There was hardly any snow. It was a wall of torn and jagged rock.

'Christ, this will play hell with the runners,' Wally complained. He pointed out the route I was to walk so that as the dogs followed me the sledge would slip sideways along a narrow path. I walked along a diagonal line up the slope, calling to the dogs while Wally urged them on from behind. As we reached the top together they bounded across the flat stretch. I flicked the whip from side to side in front of them and by good luck rather than by good management I managed to stop them before they fell headlong over the other side.

The drop was very steep but covered in snow. It led into the river-bed and continued at a less dangerous slope for about five miles. It was impossible to ride down the bank on the sledge, but sometimes the Eskimos might ski down such a slope on their feet, holding on to the handlebars. This slowed down the sledge and meant that the driver could twist it in the right direction when it reached the bottom. As Wally got the dogs moving, I held on to the handlebars to steer it away from any large boulders, as the dogs went over the top. The dogs burst forward. I was pulled over the uneven ground. The dogs disappeared, but the sledge continued towards a huge boulder. I swung it violently round. It pointed straight at Wally. 'Look out,' I yelled. He jumped back, stumbling over the rough ground. The sledge whipped past him and leapt into the air. I watched in horror as it shook convulsively and hurtled down on the tail of the staggering animals. They had gone down at such speed that they had tumbled in a heap at the bottom of the dip. The sight of the leaping sledge about to descend on them galvanized them into action, and they tore hell for leather up the slope opposite. They were halted with a jolt half-way up the steep bank as the sledge bit into the deep snow. We slithered down to join them.

We sat and relaxed for a few minutes. Wally pointed out the route we would take through the fiord across the frozen lake. It was a fascinating and exhilarating ride down—on one side moraine and on the other mountain. We passed huge rocks sticking out like great thumbs from the palette-shaped wind scoops surrounding them. In places the highway between these obstacles was just wide enough for the sledge. Wally had to jump off to push the sledge away from the yawning hollows. I was amazed at the speed with which we wove our way through the obstacle course. I couldn't afford to daydream. I had to follow the route and anticipate which way I should lean, so as not to slide off the sledge as it tipped precipitously to one side. Eventually the gorge opened out into a wide delta, then it joined the flat sea ice.

'Right, let's stop here for a brew!' suggested Wally.

I went to cut snow while he untangled the dogs. I looked round at the glaciers that fed into the lake before us. In some places they were heavily crevassed. Lines of deep turquoise scarred the pale blue, indicating a fault or crack in the surface. Rising behind the glaciers the white tip of the icecap contrasted with the black and reddish tinge of the rocks flanking the fiord. Wally pointed out a little hut on the far shore. It was used frequently by travellers. He thought I ought to have a look at it while he filed the runners.

It was midday. As we left the delta, I noticed a thick coil of rope, obviously ditched by some sledge driver. At the end of a journey the Eskimos always throw away their rope brakes. We stopped the sledge and I ran over to pick it up. It was in perfect condition and much thicker than any of ours. I was very pleased with my find.

It took me about twenty minutes to reach the hut. It was of wood, built on skis, about 12′ × 8′, like a caravan. The floor-level was about two feet from the ground. It was littered with half-eaten meals and campers' trash. Hunters do not bother to clear up their mess, though they might clear away the trash that someone else has left before they start to eat. A ventilation hole in the roof let in the snow, which had melted into a pool on the floor. A broad wooden platform stretched the full width of the hut. It could sleep three people, and more in an emergency. It was badly warped and slanted towards the ground at the far corner. I was glad we were not staying there. A tent was more comfortable.

I went over to Wally, who was still busy on the runners, and offered to help.

'Why not untangle the dogs?' he suggested.

As we started out into the fiord I looked back at the glacier. It stretched through a dip in the icecap, a long green arm with thick black veins, like the gnarled extremity of some gigantic creature. It was a welcome change to be travelling on the flat. The surface was very good. The clean runners made a tremendous difference to the ride and the dogs seemed to enjoy their freedom. I leant right back against the handlebars and took in the shapes and colours of the land around me. This was obviously a wind funnel. The rocks on either side were patterned where the wind had etched its way through the soft rock and left only hard ridges.

I remembered that some of the oldest known rock in the world was recently found in Greenland—by a friend of Wally, Vic McGregor. I wondered what scientists think about when they look at rocks? Did they people them with gods, as I did? I could see why the so-called primitive tribes invest their land with spirits. Otherwise, what a waste—with all this beautiful country—mountains and glaciers and fiords, and no spirits to go with them. Everyone knew there were fairies in the glens in Ireland. Surely there were giants in the mountains of Greenland. Of course the Eskimos originally believed in the existence of strange creatures that inhabited the interior of their land. They were not gods to be worshipped, but they were spirits to be respected.

As we neared the Cape at the head of the fiord I was sure I could smell the sea. Ahead of us was the huge pack ice of Baffin Bay. Wally was by now quite tired. With their bias to the left the dogs had prevented him relaxing over the long trek down the fiord. His voice was hoarse from repeating 'Achook! Achook!', and his wrist was tired from the constant use of the whip. As we turned the Cape in the direction of Moriussaq the strange flat-topped Dundas Mountain appeared in the distance.

'It will only take an hour or so to get to Moriussaq,' said Wally. 'We might go on to Dundas tonight. It is about another four hours' travelling. We will see how we feel after we get to Moriussaq.'

The words were just out of his mouth when a gust of wind hit us full in the face, whipping up the loose snow and stinging our eyes. We were not sure where the village was, as Wally had last been there in the dark. He had exchanged three dogs when he was there and, as visibility got poorer, we decided to let the dogs find their way back to the village.

It was about six in the evening. We were both beginning to feel very cold and hungry. 'Oh, I'd love a plate of seal meat,' confessed Wally. The mention of it set my mouth watering and seemed to make the cavity in my stomach even larger. We wondered if anyone would offer us meat. Visitors were usually given a meal, but the Eskimos often thought it a waste to offer a Kasdluna meat, as many of them did not like local food.

After about an hour in the driving snow, the dogs suddenly turned to the left and led us over a heap of pressure. It was very difficult to see anything, but we could just make out dark outlines, which we presumed to be huts. We could not understand why there were no lights. We reached dry land before we realized that it was not the village, and that the dark objects were rocks. We retraced our route with Wally leading the dogs back over the pressure. As the sledge slid quickly down a steep ramp, I called to Wally to look out. He turned just as the sledge swung suddenly to the side, throwing me headlong on to the pressure. 'Aiee, Aiee!' called Wally to the dogs, grabbing the handlebars of the sledge. The dogs stopped and I hauled myself up. I was glad I was so well padded.

A few minutes later we rounded a wall of rocks and were cheered to see lights of the village. It was almost dark and there was not a soul about. We found a hole already made in the pressure ice beneath the village and picketed the dogs as quickly as possible. A few children crept out of the dusk and watched silently. They were followed soon after by a woman who stood shivering in a light anorak. She invited us in. We thanked her for her invitation but explained that we were looking for Kaviarssuak's house. The children pointed it out to us. We bent forward to shield our faces from the wind. Empty meat racks stood between quaint little shacks of varying shapes and sizes. We came to a halt in front of a hut sunk low into the ground, surrounded by a high drift. As we approached, the door opened and out of the tiny opening a huge figure of a woman appeared.

She stood amazed at the sudden apparition. 'My goodness, there's people!' she exclaimed, taken aback at the sight of two cocooned and icy strangers. Still surprised she stood, torch in hand, gazing at our dishevelled appearance. She rubbed her eyes with the back of her fist as if she half expected the two of us to disappear. When she saw that we were still there and that the light was not playing tricks with her, she found her voice. 'Go in, go in,' she urged in some embarrassment.

We stepped down three steps cut from the hard-packed drift. A tiny door made us bend double before entering a low-ceilinged storeroom. We passed through another low door into a large partitioned room. It was our turn to feel embarrassed at the state of our clothes, which were beginning to drip on to the clean dry floor.

Opposite me as I entered sat an old grey-haired man, with a most striking and pleasant countenance. Very gentle and dignified, he got up in some surprise to greet us, while his wife told him how she had found us outside the door.

We introduced ourselves and explained that we had been sent by Orla Sandborg, who also sent his best greetings. The couple smiled acknowledgement and recognition. We stood rather awkwardly for a minute until they entreated us to take off our damp clothes. Our arrival was so unexpected they still had not quite recovered from the surprise. We put our parkas and my overshoes in the hall and sat down on the simple sofa. The room was warm and cosy. The usual oil stove was in the corner opposite the bed with its brightly covered blanket and neatly rolled-up duvet in a spotless white cover.

I stole a glance at my hostess and caught her eye. We both smiled. She was amply endowed by nature with a figure of great roundness. She looked more Polynesian than Eskimo. Her husband was fair-skinned, with almost European features.

They asked about our journey and where we were going, and seemed dubious at the thought of us continuing to Dundas that night. 'It is very windy out there now. You had better stay till morning. You can have that bed in there if you like.' They pointed to a bed just visible behind the partition. 'My son normally sleeps there,' explained the old man, 'but he is away at the moment with his wife.' They laughed as they told us how a very fat couple had been sleeping on it once and during the night they heard a big thud as one of them fell out. We joined in the laughter. Our hostess's smile filled her face and her body heaved and gasped with amusement. We were all feeling more relaxed now, and the old man turned to Wally. 'Aren't your feet cold in those wet kamiks?' he asked.

'Oh, they are not too bad,' answered Wally.

'Take them off,' urged Bibiane. As Wally handed them to her, the old man muttered something and went out of the room. He returned with a beautiful pair of white kamiks which he told Wally to try on.

'What a marvellous fit,' exclaimed Wally. 'These are the best-fitting kamiks I have ever worn.' The old couple beamed with pleasure. 'They are beautifully made,' continued Wally. It was true. They were the first pair of kamiks ever to fit him. All his own were too big, and the Eskimos never seemed to be able to make a well-fitting pair for a foreigner.

'You must be hungry. Would you like to eat?' the old man asked. We accepted with alacrity. Bibiane went to the stove. My glance strayed to the room about us.

The walls were lined with photos and religious pictures. A bunch of plastic flowers stuck rigidly out of a cheap vase. Over the old man's chair a most impressive document caught the eye. It was from the Royal Greenland Trade Company and spoke of journeys of exploration and hardship which the old man had undertaken in his youth. He had been a companion of Rasmussee over many thousands of miles and had the reputation of being a great storyteller. We were dying to draw him out but felt this was not the moment to probe into the past too deeply.

'It is only walrus, we have no seal meat,' the old man said apologetically as bowls of thick walrus stew were placed before us. We tried to find a suitable reply. The smell of rich gravy filled the air. Both Wally and I swallowed in anticipation. The gravy was a dark brown colour and filled out with rice. It looked appetizing and nourishing.

'You will need knives,' the old man explained.

'I have one,' said Wally. 'You can share it, Marie.' Bibiane searched in the chest of drawers and found one for me. We all ate in silence, except for our occasional comments on the delicious meal. As if reading our thoughts, a pot of steaming tea was put before us, with fresh, homemade bread. 'Delicious, delicious,' murmured Wally.

It was a feast. We sat back warmed and renewed, and thanked our hosts. The conversation was freer after we had eaten. We explained that we were living on Herbert Island, and they told us that they had spent a few years at Kekertassuak. It was only then I remembered that we were living in the house that used to belong to them before they had sold it to the community.

Before turning in, around 11.30, Wally went out to collect the sleeping bags. The old man insisted on accompanying him in case he needed help. I sat and chatted with my hostess. The men came back and we excused ourselves and retired to our side of the room. The murmur of conversation from the opposite corner was punctuated by the sound of peeing into a pot. It reminded us that we ought to go outside before turning in for the night, and we waited for a suitable moment to creep out. A huge basin of walrus meat stretched below part of the carcass hung from a nail near the door. Beside this was a small hand basin with taps, but no running water. We clambered thankfully into bed.

The next morning we were woken by a fit of violent coughing from the other room. Warm water was placed in the basin for us and a towel provided. I washed, savouring the feel of the warm water. As I crossed the room to sit down I caught sight of myself in the mirror. A more unkempt looking figure was hard to imagine. My hair was lank and knotted. I felt in my pockets for a comb. I could not find one and tried to drag my fingers through the matted strands. Bibiane gave me her own comb.

Our tousled host turned on the radio for the weather forecast, while his wife poured tea and cut bread. We were just about to get up when a pot of fresh coffee was placed on the table. The Eskimos alternate between tea and coffee without comment, using the same cup for both. I must say I enjoyed it that morning.

The ride to Dundas was good. There was just a slight fog, which blanketed the Dundas Mountain from time to time, but a trail of trash, blown from the Airbase, littered the rout. Within four hours we were at the foot of the flat-topped mountain. The sprawling buildings of the Airbase came into view, and soon we were running parallel to the road to Dundas—a distance of only a couple of miles.

Cars sped to and fro along the stretch of road lined with marker flags. A large sign warned drivers to watch out for dog teams: I was amazed to find we had right of way! We crossed the road at right angles and hitched the dogs on to the sea ice. A couple of Eskimos came down to watch and help if need be. One of them, I learnt later, was Kaviarssuak's son. The Danish Administrator drew up in his car nearby.

'Welcome,' he smiled, holding out a hand. 'Good to see you.'

We hopped into the warm vehicle and sped the last hundred yards to his home.

14

It looked a beautiful day when we set out from Dundas on the return trip to Herbert Island. For Geoff it must have been exciting. He was used to polar travelling in Antarctica, where the dogs were hitched to the sledge in a long double line and passengers rarely rode. We were employing the fan trace method and had every intention of letting the dogs carry us most of the way home, if not all. I had my doubts about several parts of the glacier, but on the flat the dogs soon went well.

I had enjoyed my two days in Thule. It had been amusing meeting new people and dining in style at the Officers' Club, but I looked forward very much to getting home to Kari. The cabaret in the Club had hurled us back into the world we had forgotten. A pretty, bosomy youngster was introduced to us at the bar.

'It is an honour to meet you, sir,' she said to Wally. Some moments later she stepped into the centre of the tiny stage.

A harsh record blurted over the microphone. She looked out over her audience who stared back at her tight-fitting 'hot pants' and low-cut blouse. 'I would like to dedicate this dance to Wally Herbert,' she announced in a soft American accent. The boards hummed beneath her as she moved abruptly to the discordant sounds. All grace was centred round her hands which wove simple but delicate patterns in the air. I looked at Wally. He seemed completely mesmerized. 'I have never had a dance dedicated to me before,' he confessed. 'What am I supposed to do?'

'Enjoy it, it may never happen again,' I teased. 'I should thank her for the honour.'

'That was great, thanks very much,' he said warmly to her when she rejoined us.

'It was a pleasure.'

The naïvety of our young entertainer was charming, if not a little sad. 'I am disillusioned with men since coming to Thule,' she confided, looking up at me with beautiful blue eyes. 'They think all girls are stupid. I think when I get back to the States I will join Women's Lib or something, just to prove I've got brains.'

The ride to Moriussaq was fast and uneventful. The extra load did not seem to slow the dogs much. We had stopped by the weather office the day before to read the forecast. 'There is a big wind approaching,' we were warned. 'But we cannot say how fast yet.' We thought we ought to get away early to avoid it. Wally cast a penetrating glance behind us. There seemed no sign of bad weather as we turned our backs on the Airbase.

It was about noon when the sledge slid to a halt below the village. Swarms of children scampered over to inspect us. Each child carried a whip or a clumsy imitation of one, boys and girls repeating the same movement over and over again—perfecting a simple technique which would one day make them master sledge drivers. I flinched as a leather serpent recoiled from my feet. I darted an angry look in the direction of the young showman. He split the air with a couple of final salvos. I secretly envied him his skill.

A good-humoured clamour followed us through the village. For some reason the 'frill' on Geoff's caribou parka was an irresistible attraction to the children and it was tugged in all directions. Geoff's ready smile encouraged the teasing, and it was a surprise he had any hairs left on the hem at all. Kaviarssuak greeted us at the door with great friendliness and dignity. At the sight of him the children stopped their torment and stood back respectfully. Our parkas were taken from us to be hung up and we were beckoned into the house where a beaming Bibiane welcomed us.

The delicious smell of boiled seal wafted from the stove. Once again we were invited to join the family meal. Kaviarssuak's son and daughter-in-law were there with their little boy. The young man chatted about his day's hunting. He had caught three seals, and they were all very proud of him. It was a good feeling to have meat in the house. I had brought some presents for Bibiane which she took with delighted surprise.

We told them that bad weather was expected, so we hoped to get to the hunter's hut at the foot of the glacier before it broke. It would be a sturdier shelter in a storm than a tent. If the weather allowed we could cross the glacier the next day and possibly even carry on to Herbert Island.

It was about 3.30 when we got up to go. Our hosts wished us a safe journey, adding with a mischievous smile that if the weather turned bad we would probably be back. The children followed us out on to the ice, clambering aboard whenever they got the chance. Wally looked round. 'No wonder the dogs are making heavy weather of it,' he said. The children grinned back at him, and tumbled off in a heap on the ice. We waved at them till they were lost to sight.

Once they were gone I felt we were away in real earnest. The sky to the south was overcast and seemed to get darker every minute. In no time it had spread gloom over the whole area. After about an hour we began to round the first Cape that led to the fiord. The distance from here to the hunter's hut was about eighteen miles. Wally was worn out trying to keep the dogs on a straight course. The bitch was in the lead and kept veering to the left. By now the clouds were thick and grey. As we rounded the Cape, the winds howled down the rock face and cut across the dogs' snouts. They pulled up suddenly, and huddled together to escape its blast. Then, within seconds, we were whipped by a sudden gust from behind which enveloped us in thick swirling snow.

The sledge surged forward under the weight of the wind. The dogs' fur sprang upright like a collar around their quivering rumps. Geoff's parka was plastered with snow and I felt my clothes flattened as a cold chill gripped me. The gap between my kamiks and nanoks was soon filled with a layer of snow. I scooped out as much as I could, but with each handful I retrieved, more crept in. I remembered I had been warned that fox fur was useless when wet, and wondered how soon it would be before it hung limp around me. It would be impossible to travel if our clothes got too wet. I remembered reading once: 'The first cardinal rule of survival in the cold is to keep dry, as water conducts heat away from the body about twenty times as fast as dry still air.'

Wally called a halt. 'I will have to untangle these traces before the weather gets worse. The dogs are tying themselves in knots trying to get some shelter from each other. It looks as if a hell of a wind is blowing up. It could take at least four hours to get to the hut, if visibility does not deteriorate so much that we stray off course! We have to avoid the far side of the fiord as the ice is always very thin there.' He struggled with the tangled traces while the dogs whined at the discomfort. 'I am inclined to think it would be better to return to Moriussaq where we can at least dry out. It will be agony facing into the wind, but at least it will be over that much quicker. What do you think?'

Geoff and I both agreed that to return was the lesser of two evils.

As we turned Wally called to me to look away from the wind. I felt I ought to share the ordeal and tried to face the way we were going, but in a minute or two I found it was too much for me. Thick granules of hard sharp snow cut into my skin and scourged my eyes. I had to look away.

I turned towards Geoff who was at the back of the sledge guiding it away from obstacles, and helping to keep it on the right course. His face was red and raw. Snow plastered his eyelashes and eyebrows. He leant towards me, 'I wish I had had that pee back there,' he said, grinning.

'Me too,' I answered. We had wanted to wait till we were out of sight of the village. It was more difficult for me than for him. I had either to remove my long kamiks and stand on the ice in my stockinged feet, or contort myself into a most difficult and ungainly pose. Either way I preferred a bit of privacy.

Wally walked ahead of the dogs. By now visibility was only a few yards and the dogs were bewildered and uneasy. We kept to the tide crack to avoid losing our way. The air grew thicker and visibility diminished even further. We could not see the icebergs till we were upon them, and the sledge teetered precariously over the hummocks in its path. Broken up by the wind-battered bergs, the ice formed wide cracks revealing deep trenches. We had been travelling for over an hour and there was still no sign of the village. We realized it must be fairly near, but to reach it from this angle we had to circumnavigate a wall of pressure. At this particular point there was so much pressure that we could easily follow the wrong ridge and pass the village, or lose ourselves in the bay. By now the dogs were hopelessly tangled and seemed just as blinded as ourselves. They were puzzled and alarmed and herded together for comfort, hugging the centre of the pack, ousting one another from this place until the leads were plaited into a thick coil.

The chill down my back intensified. My clothes were clogged with snow. With each breath I felt my lungs choked. All sound was muffled. We slid through a nebulous world like phantom figures driving a white hearse. All colour was lost behind a thick veil. The dogs all looked the same, transformed by the snow.

Before long we called a halt. Wally came back to the sledge. 'I cannot see a thing. Even the dogs can't see where they are going. I think we have no alternative but to pitch a tent while there is still a bit of light, and sit it out.'

It seemed the only thing to do. Once we had made the decision we lost no time in setting up camp. The dogs had to be untangled and anchored to an ice hole. The tent had to be erected so that it would offer the least resistance to the wind. We turned the sledge on its side to act as a wind-break. While Wally saw to the dogs, Geoff and I unloaded the sledge. All the gear was placed leeward of the sledge with me on top of it to stop it blowing away. Geoff went off to help Wally.

I was frightened and lonely. It was a horrible sensation—slow burial. A thick blanket of snow clung to the fur of my parka, and filled the gap between my kamiks and thighs. I was very cold and wet. The mask of snow covering the muffler around my mouth and chin had turned to ice, and was creeping up to join the icy visor hanging from my hood and fringe. The gap around my nostrils narrowed. I tried to shout, but could not. My mouth was gagged and the sound died in my throat. A trickle of tepid water ran down my forehead, divided and slunk down the sides of my face and nose into the collar of my jersey. My lashes were heavy with snow and clung to each other when I blinked. The effort to open them was too much, so they froze together. My hands were immobile, without sensation, frozen around the objects they clutched. I had to escape.

Writhing and twisting from the waist, I snapped the hard mantle around me. I jerked my head in several directions, cracking the brittle mask which almost smothered me. The bags I gripped had been anchored by a mound of drift, and that left me free to move one hand. I raised my frozen mitt to my face and clumsily fumbled to free a passage around my eyes and nose. I pulled the cover from off my mouth and called to Wally. 'Wally, Wally!' I yelled.

'He is seeing to the dogs. Are you all right, Marie?' came the reassuring voice of Geoff from somewhere in the darkness.

'Yes, I am O.K. I just wanted to make sure you were still there.'

'Oh, well, don't worry, we will have this tent up in no time and you will be able to get in away from the wind.'

While Wally untangled the knot of snarled traces and dug ice holes to anchor the dogs, Geoff was putting up the tent. It flapped convulsively and the ropes were torn through his hands. Poor Geoff—what a welcome to the Arctic!

I sat and wriggled on the wet tugto skins, unable to understand why I should feel so cold. I was wearing foxskin pants which were normally very warm. I had a collection of items attached to me to prevent them being blown away in the blizzard. Nothing in our gear was superfluous, so I had to be very careful not to let go of anything. Sleeping bags, airmattresses, tugto skins, kerosene and the primus stove came under my protection, together with rucksacks of spare clothes and a foam mattress which formed a thin padding between us and the sledge load.

'I think you should crawl into the tent, and we will erect it over you,' suggested Geoff.

The thought of exchanging one shroud for another was none too attractive, but the choice was either that or face the elements while the men pitched camp.

I was bundled with all my baggage first under the outer red tent and then the inner white one. It was even darker than outside, and the heavy material slumped damply all over me. It was difficult to breathe, and I lashed out wildly with my arms to hold the dreadful pall away from my face and head. A harpoon stuck into the ice halfway down the sledge and acted as a tent pole. Normally we used two, one at either end of the tent, but the wind was so strong we wanted to have as little sail area as possible, so instead of anchoring the other end of the tent at parallel height, we dropped it to the ground and anchored it to an ice hole. Viewed sideways the tent looked like a right-angled triangle, and we could sit with our backs against the sledge wall.

'Wally, what is happening?' I called.

'We are just tightening the guy ropes. Be with you very soon. We'll have a primus going and a brew.'

'What is wrong with the inner tent?' I insisted. 'I feel as if I am suffocating.'

'Hang on. I'll come in and have a look.'

After a rustling and heaving, a panting Wally spoke from a couple of feet away.

'Good Lord, I cannot see a thing,' he exclaimed. 'Wait till I get my lighter.' After a couple of seconds a flame illuminated the other side of the white wall. 'Where are you?' he asked, puzzled.

'Here,' I answered, hauling up the inner tent. A cloth cave opened up to me with Wally in the centre holding up his lighter.

'You must have crawled through two thicknesses of lining,' he laughed. 'Poor old thing, that must have been very unpleasant.'

It was lovely to see Wally and feel his companionship after the long wait. 'I will just go and help Geoff put snow on the valance and we will be in in a minute.' He ferreted under the folds of the tent and eventually found the opening. He looked so uncomfortable inching over the ground on his belly beneath the tunnel of tenting. It was not easy to crawl through four feet of heavy material in polar clothing.

'Marie, can I hand you in a few more bits?' called Geoff. The brew box, ration box, and several other items that were in the sledge bag poked through the flap. I laid the wet tugtos on the floor with the foam matresses over them. I opened the brew box. Wally crept in after Geoff. I felt inside the tops of my kamiks and pulled out handfuls of snow. Near the knee there were small lumps of ice. The lower edge of my fur pants was braided with bits of ice that I had to melt in my fingers, before they could be pulled off. As the ice began to melt, some of the water saturated my long underpants and trickled down inside. It was most uncomfortable. 'I will have to take these clothes off,' I said.

'Well when you have, crawl inside your sleeping bag,' suggested Wally. 'You will soon be warm with the primus going.'

I struggled to get out of the fur clothes, which clung to me like a second skin. As I held them up to see what damage had been done to the frail skins showers of snow fell out. The fox pants were sopping wet and torn; together with my parka, they looked like the pelts of diseased, emaciated animals. I dropped them in a heap in the corner. They could not possibly dry by morning.

Lying in my sleeping bag in damp underclothes I surveyed my two travelling companions. Geoff half sat, half lay, on the other side of the tent with his back to the sledge. He was pulling the pieces of ice off his balaclava. His mitts curled up in derision where they lay on the floor. Huddled over the primus, Wally painstakingly melted the thick mask of ice that covered his face. He had never been so iced up before : another fifteen minutes outside and the mask would have smothered him. It took him over an hour to clear it.

I pulled at my fringe and broke the band of ice which held it. As I turned my head the rods of ice jingled against each other. Slowly they thawed in my fingers and slipped off the strands of hair, leaving it wet and clammy. I took off my woollen helmet, but had to put it on again as it was too cold to be without a head covering. It would have to dry on me. In silence we nursed our worn bodies.

It was not long before we had a steaming mug of tea. Cupping it in both hands, its warmth seemed to shoot through the body setting the limbs tingling. It seemed that Wally's efforts to light the lamp would never succeed. It was iced up, and just would not light. The wind set up an imbalance of air within the tent, which instantly blew out a match or lighter. It was frustrating and annoying. We had almost given up when it miraculously caught light. The wind battered without relief. Where the tent touched us it hammered unmercifully. We all leant forward to avoid the pounding over our heads and tried to get some rest.

The night dragged on. From time to time we snatched a half-hour's sleep, but the cold gnawed at us and our muscles ached. The tent was too small to allow anyone to stretch out fully. Two of us could rest, while the other curled round our feet and boosted the primus when it petered out. The men gallantly took it upon themselves to alternate on primus duty. At intervals throughout the night the walls bulged outwards as the cumbersome figures changed places. Every hour a new head leant against my bent legs.

The tent stood up very well to the battering. At times it seemed as if it had reached its limit and that more pressure would rend it in two. But it held its ground. The men had left nothing to chance, and instead of using ice pitons to anchor it, had made ice holes for each guy rope. The sledge had been anchored also on three sides to ice holes and acted as a strong barrier against the force of the blizzard.

Morning never seemed so welcome. With it came a great calm. Heaving his way through the folds of material which were plastered down by the drift, Geoff broke through the wall of snow to greet the day.

'It is not brilliant but you can just make out the sun through the clouds.'

His words were almost lost in the roar of the primus. Puffs of steam billowed into Wally's face as he poured the tea leaves into the bubbling pot. A huge lump of butter oozed over the thin skin covering the hot porridge.

'Ready for breakfast?' called Wally, as he scooped spoonfuls of tugto hairs out of the cups. 'I tried drying your fox pants over the primus, but I am afraid they are still as wet as ever,' sighed Wally. 'But here are your gloves. They are nearly dry.'

'Where were they?' I asked, amazed how warm they felt.

'I wore them last night to dry them off,' he said casually.

I watched as he worked his way into his own frozen mitts.

We decided to return to Moriussaq to dry out my clothes. I had on an old pair of ski trousers, with my long kamiks over them. I was glad we had brought a couple of old wolfskin parkas with us. They had travelled right across the North Pole with Wally but were still warm, except for a few worn patches here and there. My fox parka was frozen into a grotesque shapeless mass. It was impossible to wear—the slightest tug would tear the delicate skin.

While the men did the outside jobs I tidied up inside the tent. The temperature dropped quickly once I turned the primus off. I hurriedly rolled up the sleeping bags and brushed the snow off the rest of the gear. Snow had crept in everywhere and most things had a thick patchwork of ice or snow on them.

It was a relief to get outside and stretch my legs. The dogs too emerged from their white cocoons and shook themselves free of snow. They walked slowly as if on stilts while the blood began to flow in their cramped limbs. With another shake and a stretch they came to life. Their limp tails sprang up and fanned the air.

While Wally dug up the ropes from the snowed-in ice holes, Geoff and I pulled down the tent. It was heavy and unwieldy. As we rolled it up we brushed as much snow away from it as we could—it still had patches of ice clinging to it. We loaded the sledge haphazardly. It would have to be rearranged before a long journey. The sledge bag was stuffed with snow and all our cameras and other gear buried in it. The priority was to get to Moriussaq as quickly as possible so that we could dry out our clothes and get to the little hut later that day.

As we expected we were only about three hundred yards from the village. We left the sledge as it was, and took only our wet clothing up with us to the little house—which was becoming very familiar to us. Rather sheepishly, we stood before our host for the third time. 'Hello again,' we said, clutching our wretched clothing. His eyes reflected a secret amusement, but he did not laugh. He helped us take off our parkas.

Once again Bibiane welcomed us with open arms. She insisted we came into the warmth before shedding any more clothing. We hesitated, looking at the clean floor, but she insisted. The sight of me in long kamiks without the fur pants brought roars of laughter. By now the house was full. Bibiane's son and his family filled one corner, while we spread ourselves around another. As each wet article was shed, a cry of approval hastened its progress to the rack above the fire. When we had exhausted all available space, both above us and around the walls, the remainder of our gear was spread among the neighbouring houses.

The smiling face of Bibiane turned to us through clouds of steam from the stove. She lifted a rounded arm and wiped away the sweat from her forehead. The odour of damp clothes mingled with the smell of boiled walrus. The old man handed Wally his kamiks, delighted to lend them for a second time. He brought a new pair of polar-bear pants for Geoff to put on while his dried. Then he sank into his chair. His thin hands strayed across the worn patches of the pair he was wearing. 'What does an old man want with new polar-bear pants?' he said, half to himself. 'I am finished hunting!' I caught a look of nostalgia as he gave Geoff a friendly glance.

The two women busied themselves around the stove.

'You must be hungry,' said our host.

'A little,' I admitted. An enormous rumble from my stomach made me wide-eyed with embarrassment. All pretended not to notice.

Bibiane told us that many people had returned to the village from the storm. They had been very worried about us and had stayed up till three o'clock expecting us back. When we did not turn up, they had not been able to sleep. The ferocity of the wind had surprised them, even though they were used to violent storms. We learnt later from Thule that the wind they had recorded at one of their satellite stations around the Base was the second highest recorded on the face of the earth—gusting to 207 m.p.h. (the highest was at Mount Washington, USA—225 m.p.h.).

We were anxious to get moving as soon as possible in case the weather turned rough again. But my clothes would take almost a full day to dry out. Bibiane arranged for me to borrow a pair of fox pants, which I could return to a relative of hers in Qanaq. As we were about to leave she fished under the bed for an old case and took out an enormous navy skirt. 'Put that over your nanok if the weather gets bad. It will protect your pants and stop the snow from going down your kamiks.'

After sending a telegram to Maria to let her know we were leaving we set off once again. The old couple came down to see us off. 'Inudluaritse', 'Goodbye', they called as we moved off. As we passed the line of empty meat racks a dog sat on its haunches and lifted its head towards the sky. A howl of anguish followed us. I noticed one of our team become very agitated, straining at the lead to get at the howling dog. I recognized it as one Wally had exchanged the first time he visited the village—it was our old one-eyed bitch.

The trip to the hut seemed endless. The wind cut into us, and it was impossible to keep warm. Geoff and Wally had to run alongside the sledge to try and keep their circulation going. They wrapped me in a sleeping bag and they tied it with a thin rope, so that I would not have to hold on all the time. My back ached, and even to look into the wind was paralysing.

The light was just fading when we eventually stumbled round the last cape. The hut was dreary, especially as we discovered we had left the light behind at Moriussaq, but it was a safer retreat than the tent. We had a quick meal and stretched out on the warped platform. It was cold, but we soon fell into an exhausted sleep.

The next morning was beautiful, and we decided to do some filming. The cameras had been specially winterized, but they were frozen. I carried one inside my parka, with a couple of rolls of cine film down my kamiks to prevent the film snapping from the cold. The men were too busy manœuvring the sledge up the narrow gorge to be able to carry extra weight.

'Try and avoid the rocks,' Wally called. 'Every scratch on the runners means an extra quarter of an hour's work later.'

It took us three and a half hours to get to the moraine which separated us from the glacier. Three times we tried the steep rise over the moraine and each time the team got stuck halfway. The ground was so slippery that Wally had to cut steps for the dogs and myself. I was sent ahead to lead them over the top of the moraine, while he uttered such a wild whoop that they were galvanized into action. I, in turn, was so startled by the avalanche of dogs that in my haste to get out of the way I missed my footing and slithered sideways all the way down the slope again. But Wally got the team up the slope and stopped them before they broke loose over the flat stretch at the top.

We looked down the other side of the moraine and Wally pointed out the route he was going to take. Geoff was hidden behind a boulder halfway down, to film what we had not been able to do ourselves on our trip over. I was to follow Wally and see that the sledge did not slam into any big rocks. I preferred this to walking ahead of the team. 'Put a rope brake over the runner when it reaches here,' said Wally, pointing to a stone just over the brow of the hill. I felt a sinking feeling in the pit of my stomach. I had the dreadful vision of missing the runner and the sledge slamming into the boulder and smashing up. I was poised like an acrobat, but I was hindered by the clownish clothes. Wally called and the dogs strained. The sledge would not move. I had the rope in both hands like a lasso.

'Give the runners a shove!' called Wally.

'Oh, Lord,' I thought, 'I will never get ready in time to put the brake on.' I pushed and tugged at the runners to break the friction. The sledge inched forward. 'Huk, huk, huk!' came Wally's command. The dogs jostled and pulled, packed tightly in a bunch.

In the mêlée dogs started snapping and snarling. I handled the runners and added my war cry to the effort. With a quick jolt the sledge leapt into life. Hurling the rope towards the runner I watched it balance precariously on the upturned limb before it slid over it to the ground, biting in just before the momentum could snatch the sledge up into the air. I grabbed the handlebars as it passed. I was pulled stumbling over the rocks. I had the choice of holding on and helping to guide the sledge through the rocks or letting go and leaving it to its fate. I held on and jumped on to the sloping ends of the runners before the bottom of the slope. We careered over a few feet of flat ground and then charged up the sloping wall of the glacier to stop in a wide shallow bowl.

We stopped for a brew, and there suddenly appeared from behind and from down the glacier, six more sledges. Everybody had the same idea as ourselves and stopped for a brew, but after offering the first comers a drink we packed up and moved off. It was 4 p.m. We were anxious to cross the glacier before dark. It should have been possible, as there was just enough light to see still at 9 p.m.

We had not gone far before we met five other sledges. A great caravan of dog teams appeared suddenly out of the mist. We were warned by one of the Eskimos that there was a lot of wind up ahead, and that we would be better off to put up a tent soon. He suggested a little well-protected hollow to our right.

We were soon caught up in the blizzard, but the men got the tent up in no time. We placed the sledge crossways along one end of the tent. While the men put snow on the valance and battened everything down, I cooked a meal. We had to have it finished before dark, as we still had no light.

After supper we got into our sleeping bags while the wind howled around us, flapping the sides of the tent. My feet and head were wet and cold, shrouded in loose tent. We had purposely pitched it low. I was on the sledge. I could not bear the feeling of damp material around me, and I kept sitting up to get air. When Geoff turned the primus off a blanket of darkness engulfed us. There was not even a faint glimmer of light to be seen. There was no form or substance to anything. It was a most strange experience and a wave of claustrophobia swept over me. 'Wally,' I whispered, 'I am frightened.' His hand, meant to reassure, crept over the side of the sledge to find mine. The very fumbling unnerved me. I had never felt so helpless. The wind buffeted at the tent. It pounded against my head and shoulders and hammered against my feet. I was keyed up to all the dreadful sounds of the storm but I could not see a thing. Without a light, what could one do in an emergency, miles away from anywhere, halfway up a glacier in the dark? I felt very agitated. It was cold and uncomfortable. I could not sleep.

The hours dragged by. I dozed off in spasms, to be woken by the flapping of the wet tent around my face. I looked at my watch—the only glimmer of light was from its luminous dial. That, at least, was a comfort. At last the light began to appear through the flap of the tent. Geoff woke early and lit the primus. Its faint warmth was welcome.

Wally had a walk after breakfast up on to the glacier to see how the weather was. 'You can never judge from the tent,' he explained. I waited impatiently for him to return.

'We may have to rest up for a day till it clears.'

I could hardly believe we would have to spend a full day and another night here.

'There's hardly any visibility,' he explained. 'It would be crazy to break camp only to find we would have to pitch it again on the glacier because of bad weather. There could be a lot more wind later. At least we are a bit more protected here. We will have to stay here today and hope for an early rise tomorrow.'

'Oh how boring,' I burst out. I could not bear the thought of another cold, clammy night, cramped in the tent.

'What on earth do we do all day?' I complained. The prospect was appalling.

'We stay in our sleeping bags to keep warm. But don't worry about it. Just try and relax. It's a pain in the arse to hear someone complain about it all the time.'

'Well, that makes me feel marvellous!' I retorted. 'It's really nice to know I'm a pain in the arse.'

'I didn't say you *are* one. But you'll become one if you continue.'

I fumed. I had not moaned at all up to now, but I felt bothered and miserable. I was beginning to worry about Kari. I knew she would be perfectly safe but I missed her. Besides, the storm was pretty ferocious and I did not know how long it would last. We would have to watch we did not run out of kerosene.

There seemed no sign of the storm abating. I resolved to pull myself together. But I had five minutes' self-indulgence, glowering at Wally to show I was none too happy at his choice of words. I wrote in my diary. 'How do you spell arse?' I said breezily.

He laughed. 'Oh, Lord, I have really done it now, Geoff,' he said. 'She's never going to forget that—the trouble is you have to watch what you say to Marie or she'll end up quoting you!'

There seemed no sign of the storm abating. The monotony of our situation was relieved by the occasional cups of tea or soup. We chatted and told stories. The walls of the tent were getting a thick coating of rime. To keep it from sagging too much I had propped it up with my long kamiks. They looked grotesque. It was very cold. Geoff offered to change places with me so that I could sit up a bit. Everyone had cold feet and at least one cold shoulder where the tent had flapped around it.

I wondered how long such a storm could last and what happened when people ran out of food and fuel. We had enough fuel for another day and a half, but we would have to move before then. 'What happens if people run out of food?' I asked Wally.

'Well, if it gets desperate they eat the dogs,' he said.

I would have to be very hungry before I would do that. I thought of Maria's stories about people being lost in the Arctic without food and how only the ones who ate the dogs had survived.

'Lie-ups are all part of sledging,' commented Wally, breaking my train of thought. 'The best thing to do is to read a good book and you will find you will not bother about travelling—in fact you will want to lie-up till you have finished the book,' Wally said convincingly.

We had not brought any reading matter with us. I thought of how long we had been away. It was putting unnecessary responsibility on our friends who were looking after Kari. They might begin to worry about us. The worst of the journey was still to come. Descending the steep side of the glacier was a challenge at the best of times. We had no way of knowing how the ice conditions had changed.

That evening we turned off the primus early to save fuel and snuggled under the covers while it was still light. It was much less frightening to watch the light fade naturally than to have everything blotted out at the twist of a knob. There was a draught from somewhere and fine grains of snow had sifted in and covered everything that lay against the wall of the tent. My fox parka was covered with ice. Our gloves and mitts hung from a line above our heads. They smacked one rudely on the face if one sat up. Soon the light vanished. Another long night began. I was warmer than I had been on the sledge, although it was still damp. I could hear Geoff rubbing his feet together in the sleeping bag. Wally seemed undisturbed—or else he did not mention it.

As the wind howled and battered around us, several huge gusts made me exclaim with fright. I could almost feel the sensation of being sucked out of the tent. I kept an uncomfortable vigil till the first rays of light cheered the scene at about 6 a.m. I hurriedly lit the primus and made some tea and porridge.

'Lovely,' said Wally as he put down his bowl. 'Now I will just have five minutes' siesta.'

'Siesta !' I almost shrieked.

'Yes, I always like five minutes after breakfast. It stops you getting indigestion.'

I cleared up, trying not to look impatient. I was desperately hoping there would be nothing to stop us getting away today.

'Have a look outside,' suggested Wally.

A wall of drift obscured my view but I tunnelled a hole through it and gazed up. 'I can see the hills,' I shouted excitedly. There was a bit of mist on the col and it was still blowing, but I was sure it was good enough to travel.

An unhurried Wally had a look. 'Yes, we will get going as soon as we can. We should make it to the col in a couple of hours and get down the other side in another two.'

We set about breaking camp. By 9 a.m. we were away. 'If we are lucky we could get to Herbert Island today,' I heard Wally say. I was excited and very happy.

We had been travelling an hour when the mist rolled down. The higher we climbed the stronger the wind. For a while we followed sledge tracks, but soon we were on our own. Either the tracks had been covered, or we were off the route. We had to keep on a central line, up over the col and then pick a good route down the side of the glacier on the left.

We could see nothing to indicate where we were. We had to be careful. The col joined a ridge which ran at right angles to several precipitous glaciers—parallel with ours, but far too hazardous to descend.

Wally was walking ahead of the dogs, trying to find a route, or even a familiar landmark. 'I think we had better follow our sledge tracks back,' he said. 'The trouble is in this light all these mountains look the same.'

The wind cut past us, driving fine white snow over the tracks we had just made. 'Geoff, you've got a white spot on your cheek,' Wally warned, as we turned into the wind. The tell-tale signs of frostbite began to appear in small patches on the men's faces. Geoff rubbed his face to get the circulation going again. I sat huddled into the second wolfskin, facing away from the wind. I had put on Bibiane's voluminous skirt over my warm pants. It was a ridiculous outfit.

After a few minutes Wally came across an old deep sledge track. 'It is pointing the way we have come, so I think we were all right. I am pretty sure that is the hill we have to keep to our left.'

'The wind is still in the same direction,' said Geoff.

Once again we turned about, following the sledge tracks until they petered out.

'Put a rope brake on, Geoff. We might meet a sudden drop, and we had better be prepared.' Once again Wally led. Geoff walked behind. I held the wolfskin around me and peered after Wally as he trod his way carefully in front of the dogs. We were beginning a slight descent and he swished the whip from side to side to keep the dogs from overtaking him. A sudden shout from him made me sit up. Wally's feet seemed to sink under him. His head just missed the sledge runner as it shot after him.

The ground fell away beneath us. Dogs and sledge hurtled down the spine of the glacier. Scrambling to his feet Wally hurled himself on the nearest runner clawing the ground with his feet to break the momentum, and risking breaking his back if he let go. 'Another rope! Quick!' he shouted. I tried to turn towards Geoff but had to hold on for dear life to avoid being thrown off. Geoff, too, by this time was glued to the handle-bars, trying to drag his feet, or dig them into the smooth surface.

The dogs slid and fell, unable to get a footing, and every second the sledge got nearer to mowing them down. There was little I could do except cling on to the sledge. I stuck a foot over the side to try and break the speed, but felt my limb nearly torn from me. Eventually the men swerved the sledge sideways into a hollow. We were all badly shaken, but unhurt.

'Christ! Do you think we are on the right glacier?' blurted Wally. 'It is far steeper than I remember.'

'My God, I hope it *is* the right one,' I replied. I glanced at Geoff. He said nothing, but looked around for signs of other tracks.

'There are some tracks here,' he pointed to our left.

'Yes, I can see the trail of blood marks we followed up,' said Wally, relieved.

I tied the second wolfskin to the sledge. It looked as if I would need both hands free.

'I will have to walk ahead to look for a route and you can follow with the dogs. You had better put that other rope brake on for the next bit just in case.'

Wally moved off. Walking was very difficult. Unrelenting blizzards had polished the surface of the glacier till the snow cover was as slippery as the blue ice. Unable to keep his footing, Wally was hurled to the ground and blown across the surface like a rag doll. Halted at last in a dip, he got to his knees—only to be knocked sideways by another gust, and dragged helplessly out of sight. Eventually coming upon him in the mist we had to watch him fall a thousand times as he navigated a route for the dogs.

We had to get off the central tongue of the glacier into the gully at the side. Once again Wally set out to look for the easiest route down. The further he went the worse it seemed to get. He carried the ice axe now instead of the whip : with the rope brakes on there was little danger the dogs would overtake him, and the ice axe would make him that much more stable. Again and again he rose like a punch-drunk boxer, only to be knocked to the ground again. He clawed at the snow with the axe, but it hardly penetrated the packed surface.

Eventually Wally signalled to us that he had found a route. We had both rope brakes on. The sledge would not budge. I could not walk, as I had lost one tugto slipper—whipped away by the wind. I could not keep my footing in the slippery kamik. I had to stay on the sledge and let Geoff do all the donkey work.

'I'll take one brake off and get started and I'll slip it on immediately we get going,' said Geoff. It was still difficult to start. Geoff lunged at the dogs, pulling the runners back and forth. The dogs took off, but Geoff landed heavily on the ice, the runner just grazing his woollen helmet. I glanced anxiously back. He seemed all right. Meanwhile the sledge was going too fast : it could tip over the edge. I inched towards the runners and took the rope; I leaned forward with a foot on each runner and threw it. It missed the runner. Grabbing it again I took more care. This was my last chance. The rope slipped over the runner and bit into the snow a few feet from the drop. I thank God we had found that second rope brake on the way to Dundas, or our story might have been told by someone else.

A sprawling Wally hurled curses at the circling dogs. He was sore from his falls, and furious that he could not stay on his feet.

'You can keep kamiks in weather like this,' he fumed. 'They're bloody useless.'

'How about tying rope around them? That might help. You too, Geoff.'

They fished in the sledge bag for some thin rope and wound it round their kamiks. It seemed slightly better. 'This seems the easiest route, but it's steep,' commented Wally. 'I think the sledge might hold better if you both sit on it. We'll put another little rope on to be certain.'

I sprawled across the sledge, holding on to both handlebars. Geoff held on to the ropes that anchored the load. There was a drop of about thirty feet to a snowy path that ran up against a scree-covered mountain. Wally slid down and called the dogs to him. The sledge burst into life. 'Hold tight, Marie,' he called. I gripped harder. The sledge quickened pace. There was a sudden lurch and it began to swing sideways, tearing askew down the slope. The slope was too steep, and I waited with horror for it to pitch. If we got off, we would fall in its path : we had to hold on.

I catapulted headlong from the overturned sledge. Rolling over, I scrambled out of its path as it passed me—in pursuit of Geoff. He too dodged it by rolling out of its way. It stopped on its side a few feet from us. We got up shakily.

'You O.K. ?' asked Wally, walking towards me, his face drawn and pale.

'Hmm,' I murmured, somewhat winded.

'How about you, Geoff ?'

'Oh, fine, fine,' he said, with conviction.

We looked at the sledge. The load was bulging peculiarly. The handlebars were smashed and had to be cut free. We had to relash the load so that it would not slip off the back. We would have to use the rope brakes more often, as we would not be able to manoeuvre a sledge without handlebars. 'It is not so bad from here,' said Wally reassuringly. I nodded glumly. I wanted to slide down on my seat. I had had enough of the sledge.

'I think you'll find it easier to ride—there is no way of keeping a footing or even of stopping yourself once you start to slip.'

I sat on the sledge once again, wishing I could wrap myself up. It was very cold and in places my parka had worn thin. We all had a thick mask of ice on our faces. Wally and Geoff rubbed the white patches that had appeared on their cheeks. My fringe had slipped out of the hood and was beginning to join the lower part of my mask. Geoff and Wally felt more stable with the ropes on their kamiks, but I still could not stand without holding on to the sledge. The sole of my white kamiks was made from the same shiny skin as the rest.

We took a rope brake off to get started. Wally walked about thirty yards and stopped. This way he could keep some control over the dogs.

It was like riding down a steep road with a high camber. Every few yards we swerved into the hillside, banging against boulders and bridging enormous, gaping wind scoops. From time to time Geoff jumped off to deflect the sledge. A couple of times we could not stop the sledge soon enough, even with all the brakes on, and it tipped obliquely into a wind scoop. I had learnt by now to sit on the edge of the sledge and jump off at the first sign of danger. The men had to wait for me as I inched my way after them. Occasionally they had to come back to give me a hand.

Fog makes distances seem deceptive. Even the angle of a slope seems distorted : at times mistakenly easy, at others hopelessly difficult.

A couple of hours of agonized travel brought us in sight of the base of the glacier. We had the choice of continuing on the same route in the hope that there was a good snow cover on the cluster of 'slag' heaps at the bottom, or of going down the centre of the glacier. The danger of the latter was that we had only one chain to act as a brake. With no handlebars to hold on to it seemed too much of a risk. We decided to stick to the route we were on.

The wind had never ceased. Our bodies were tired and aching from the constant battering. Wally's lower lip had been forced down by the weight of the mask of ice, uncovering his lower teeth. Geoff looked red and raw. I wondered what I looked like myself. From where we were we could see out over the bay to the hills of Herbert Island bathed in sunlight. We had about five hundred yards of difficult terrain to cross before we were on flat ground. We did the first two hundred yards in short bursts with the two ropes on. I had completely lost faith in the safety of the sledge, and insisted on sliding down. Once in motion it was like being caught on a big dipper that had been greased by mistake.

About fifty yards from the start of the rocky slopes Wally tethered the dogs. It was so steep and slippery here that he and Geoff thought it would be easier to manhandle the sledge. Without handlebars to manœuvre with they were afraid the sledge would overrun the dogs.

Wally cut steps in the ice towards a wind scoop which had formed around a boulder. 'You sit here while we have a look at the route. We will come back for you as soon as possible.' Wally put down a sleeping bag for me to sit on. It was twenty minutes before they reappeared. My only company was the dogs. My thoughts were of Kari.

When the men returned I noticed Wally wince as he helped me out of the scoop. He had dislocated his shoulder when the sledge overran him. His wrist was sprained from the last journey, he had frostbite, and now a dislocated shoulder. The two men saw to the dogs while I made my way down the steps they had cut, keeping to the rocks where possible. Soon we were at the string of rocky mounds.

The men had decided to unpack the tent and brew box so that I could get into the warmth and make a cup of tea while they brought the rest of the gear over, with the help of the dogs. Everywhere there were scars in the rocks where the heavy sledges had bitten into them in their painful passage. I wondered how Wally and Geoff could induce the dogs to pull the heavy sledge over such terrain. What state would the runners be in after such punishment? How many hours' work would it be filing them down before they could be used on the sea ice?

I clambered up the last rise and looked at the bowl of sea ice thirty yards below me. What a marvellous sight. It was a tremendous relief to be at the end of that dreadful journey. I inched my way down. At times my feet sank through the snow that surrounded the rocks. No wonder people sprained wrists and ankles on these long journeys. Practically every foot of the way was hazardous one way or another.

At last I set foot on the sea ice. It was firm and flat. I shuffled over it to a spot where I thought we could pitch the tent. I collected some ice from the foot of the glacier while the men put up the tent. I felt almost lighthearted as I lit the primus and arranged the sleeping bags and tugto skins on the ground. I imagined it would take the men a good hour to get the sledge down, and I passed the time in preparing a meal.

Three hours later I heard the dogs panting as they came up to the tent. The stew had been off and on the primus stove a hundred times. The men were exhausted, cold and hungry. They had put the dogs on an extended trace to help them to pull the load but it was tortuously slow. They painstakingly removed the ice from their faces so that they could eat and drink. It was almost dark and we were too tired to travel any more that night. We did not know what the sea ice was like after the storm, or what the ice conditions were round the island. It made good sense to camp for the night.

We were too tired to care about the wind that night. The tent was well held down. Our bags were icy and cold. 'I wonder how Kari is,' I thought aloud.

'Fine, I should think,' grunted Wally.

The next morning was beautiful. Not a breath of wind stirred the land. Crystals of blue sparkled in the ice boulders that nestled against the grainy green of the glacier. We used the last of the kerosene to light the primus.

17 & 18. The dogs find it heavy going at times over the ice ridges. The leads get so tangled that the driver has to stop every few miles to unravel them, before the dogs are strangled. It's a difficult job in the cold, as it has to be done with bare hands.

19 & 20: It can take two hunters over an hour to cut up a large walrus. The skin is tough and heavy, too thick for clothes. It is scraped and sent to Denmark. The tusks are sold at the store, and the meat is good for men and dogs.

After breakfast we upturned the sledge and all helped file the deep scratches on the runners.

The men arranged boxes at the back of the sledge to give me support. The dogs howled in excitement. The sea ice was good and we sped over it towards the island. I was excited as I told Geoff about the village and the people. We travelled fast, but there was time to daydream. I kept seeing Kari's face. I longed to cup it in my hands.

The hours flew by. As we approached the Point, Wally indicated the sledge tracks leading to the hunting grounds. A flotilla of bergs surrounded the tip of the island. Wally drove the dogs expertly through them. We rounded the end of the island. I knew it would not be long before we saw the village. Very soon a hut appeared over the brow of the slope. 'There's the village, Geoff,' I said excitedly. One after another the houses came into view.

'Which is yours?' asked Geoff.

'That is funny, I can't see it.' I was puzzled. 'Oh, of course, I haven't seen the village from this angle. It is hidden behind those houses on the rise.' As we ran abreast of the village the hut came into view. 'There it is, there it is—the red one in the middle.' We were about 400 yards from the village. I suddenly noticed that outside each hut there was a little group of figures. I waved frantically, and from all corners a host of hands returned the greeting. I felt a lump in my throat that nearly choked me. My eyes filled, blurring my vision. I looked for Kari but could not see her. But I saw a line of children tottering from the village towards the cove we were making for. It bounced and bobbed over the rocks as the smallest staggered to catch up. I loved them.

The tide crack had widened considerably in the last two weeks. The children called from the land and rushed on to the ice to join us, grinning from ear to ear. I slipped away while the men were untangling the dogs and picked my way over the uneven ground towards the village. I heard voices calling from the nearest hut. Nauja and another woman ran out to meet me. 'Oh, it is so good to see you,' they said, hugging me. 'We have been so worried.' I could not say anything. 'Kari is fine,' they reassured me. 'You go and have a look at her.' I waved to them and continued.

I was stopped further on by other villagers, who embraced me warmly, wiping tears from their eyes.

'Look, there's Kari!' They pointed to Maria's house. She stood outside with my little curly-headed girl in her arms. I could not stop the whoop of joy that broke from me. I thought my heart would burst. 'Hello, my little darling,' I whispered to the puzzled little girl. I whipped off my headgear so that she could see who I was, and followed them into the house. I threw down my wet clothing. Kari looked so very sweet and fragile. I took her gently from Maria and hugged her to my breast. A wave of sadness hit me, and I sobbed unrestrainedly. Maria looked calm and grave. 'I am so happy to see you,' she said quietly. 'We thought you were dead.'

15

Our return to Herbert Island lifted the depression that had settled over everyone in the village during our delayed absence. We told and retold our adventures. Maria told me how she had paced the floor with Kari, at times weeping and at other times laughing at her fears—after all, Wally was clever; but the winds were so violent, and continued for so long. It was possible that we would not be able to take it, or we would miss our way. And when the winds had died down and a full day had passed, and we still had not returned, they felt that all was lost.

Avatak had gone to Qanaq hoping to find us there. He had met Peter Peary on the way, who confirmed our absence. They decided they would give us till the following day—the 14th March—before they went to look for us, even though we were four days' overdue. The women urged the men to form a search party, but the hunters hesitated. On the one hand they wanted to give Wally credit for being able to look after his party : on the other they were concerned because the storm had been like nothing they had seen before.

Maria and Avatak had discussed the fate of Kari, and though they adored her, they realized she could not stay with them. Weeping and hugging her, they wondered who her new parents would be, whether she would have anyone to care for her at all. They blamed themselves for letting us go on our own.

The strain of sitting and waiting for us to return told on their nerves, and they had to get out of the house. But visiting could not distract them from their worries. Every day they hung up the meat to thaw for Wally's dogs, and every night it had to be taken down.

We were not long back when Peter Peary arrived to see if we had returned. He was very glad to see Wally, and understood that the trip would have to be postponed for a week or ten days, while Wally and Geoff sorted out the repairs and got their clothes and equipment in good order again.

Taitsianguaraitsiak and Suakuanguak visited and embraced us with tears in their eyes. The old man had had sleepless nights : he could not stop thinking and worrying about Wally. 'Oh, when the children rushed into the house to say your dog team had appeared, we felt a great load off our hearts. We are so happy now,' they said warmly.

The old man told us that he had visited Avatak every day to see Kari. He chuckled as he sucked on his pipe and gazed at the cot where Kari was asleep. A minute or two later a little head bobbed up and a sleepy-eyed girl looked out at them and exclaimed suddenly, 'Taku Ata, Arne,' 'Look, Grandad, Grandma,' the traditional name for old folk.

Geoff was popular with everyone. His friendliness was infectious and he greeted everyone in Eskimo which he had learnt on the trip from Dundas. While Wally went to Qanaq the following day to buy some things from the store, Geoff and I unpacked all the sledging bags.

There was a lot to be done before the men went off again. They expected to be away for about fifty days. The Eskimos were supposed to provide food half the time, but four men would still need a lot of food and pemmican.

Peter and Avatak were each taking a dog team, and Wally and Geoff were sharing one and taking a Skidoo part of the way to haul the pemmican and other heavy gear. They would leave part of this with the Skidoo for use on the return journey. Before they left they brought several sledge-loads of ice from a nearby iceberg, by Skidoo, for Maria and myself. We were thrilled : I had to have a special corral made for it, so that the dogs could not get at it.

The 20th arrived, the day Wally and Geoff were to set off for Canada. Everyone in the village had turned out to see the men off. They shook the travellers by the hand, because a journey to Canada was a serious business, and they admired the courage of anyone who would journey that far.

A couple of hours later the men were away. I watched through binoculars as they collected the Skidoo and dog team off the ice and started on two slightly different routes—a more direct one for Wally with the dogs, and a circuitous one for Geoff, because the other trail was too thin in places for the Skidoo.

I was in the store later that morning when I thought I heard the distant sound of a helicopter. 'It is the fire,' said the locals, but I thought otherwise. Soon there was no mistaking the sound, and we all rushed out.

As the metal insect settled, it was almost lost in a surge of snow. Sheets of driven snow swept towards us and plastered our huddled figures. The whining ceased and as the blades slackened speed the snow subsided to reveal the strange aircraft.

A door slipped open and four enormous men got out. I recognized two of them, Jim and Skip, whom I had met at the Airbase.

'Hi, are you stopping for coffee?' I greeted.

'We thought we might just drop in on you for a while,' Jim answered as he struggled into his parka. They followed me to the hut, while another figure followed the storeman to the radio, which he was to service. The visitors looked so big and incongruous in our tiny hut, and I had to keep reminding them not to bump their heads on the doors or ceiling.

I made coffee, and they asked about our adventures in the storm. 'It was only the second highest wind recorded on the face of the earth,' said Jim drily. 'Roofs were torn off buildings and rocks hurled through windows—it caused a lot of damage.' No wonder we could not travel in it. It was surprising that our homemade tent hadn't blown in on us.

As we chatted, the door opened and Migishoo and her husband shuffled in, clutching a couple of crudely carved brooches wrapped in toilet paper. 'Maybe the Kasdlunas want to buy these,' said Migishoo. Nobody really wanted them, but they were too polite to refuse. The villagers seemed shifty, without their usual dignity, and I felt uncomfortable on their behalf.

'They must have heard the Americans were here,' said Skip.

'Well, who could fail to know with that noise?' laughed Jim.

Both Jim and Skip were making their last flight before returning to the States after a year at Thule. I could never think of Jim without remembering the story he told of his first flight to the villages. He had come in rather low over some of the huts, and had blown out all the fires. When he got out of the helicopter he was greeted by a host of soot-covered Eskimos, who begged Orla later to tell him to come in at a different angle in future.

It was a good tonic to see them. They were off to Qanaq. 'Any message for Wally if he is still there?' asked Jim.

'Just give him my love and a big kiss,' I replied.

They laughed as they delegated the task to each other.

Wally had left one dog with me because his paw seemed very tender. It was good to have the dog for company. He was beautiful, black and white, and very good-natured. But it was going to be a problem feeding him, as there was hardly any sharkmeat left, and no other meat in the village except a little in the caches. This would be a lean month for men and dogs. Some of the villages had no meat left at all. Taitsianguaraitsiak offered to look after the dog when his paw was better. In return for the loan of the dog he would feed it. But it was a long while before the dog's paw healed. In the meantime I had lent him to Ilanguak, Avatak's son, to help draw his little sledge, together with a bitch and two of her pups that had also been left behind.

By 23rd March the sun was higher every day. There was no more night: between sunset and sunrise there was deep twilight. The ice was beginning to disappear from the windows.

The men were away for long stretches. Some went in search of polar bears and expected to be away for many 'sleeps'. Others hunted walrus, within a couple of days' ride, and returned to the village every week or two before setting out again.

In March the female bears nurse their newborn young in their lairs deep in the snowdrifts. By now the bear is beginning to feel hungry, after the long winter, and she begins to look for food. The new cubs are very vulnerable, because they are so tiny. Ironically their greatest predator is the wandering male bear, who would devour the young cubs if the female did not defend them. Meat is scarce in this month because the seals, too, are in lairs, nursing their young, and are not so easy to get at as later in the season, when they bask in the warm sun on the ice.

The Ringed Seal, which is the most common type found in Greenland, clambers up on to the ice through the cracks near stranded bergs, and tunnels out a cave under the snow cover in which to have its young. These caves are warmer than the outside air because the heat from the animals is trapped beneath the snow crust.

Sometimes bears can smell them out and burrow down to get them. Sometimes a good sealing dog can also smell out these lairs. The fur of the young seal is very beautiful and much coveted by mothers for making Amauts. There is a blue-black band down the back, flanked by glistening silver-grey.

March is the month when bears mate. The female bear only comes in heat every three years, and keeps her cubs with her till they are nearly two years old. A female bear will always have two cubs, and very often a hunter will bring back all three, as the cubs are very defenceless without their mother.

When a bear is sighted the hunter whips everything off the sledge and gallops after it. A few dogs are released, with a quick slash of their traces. They dart ahead, followed soon by others. If the hunter were to release all of them the sledge would come to a halt. Very often the dogs will surround a bear or drive it up an iceberg, where it is an easy target for the hunter.

Once, Avatak had killed a female bear and one of her cubs, but wanted to bring back the second cub to show his small son. But the dogs were hysterical with excitement, and he could hardly keep them back from the white bundle of fur perched uncertainly on the sledge. Finally, with great reluctance, he had to shoot it.

The village radio broke down again, not long after it had been repaired. It could not be mended without spare parts from Denmark. It was worrying sometimes to know that there was no way out of the village in an emergency, except by walking the eighteen miles across the frozen sea to Qanaq. With no men in the village, there was no transport. I could still receive messages over the transistor but I could not send any.

Now that the light began to creep into every corner of the hut I could see where the walls and ceiling had been discoloured by the lamps and fires during the winter. Washing down the woodwork was not enough— the whole place needed a new coat of paint. The women hung out their newly washed kamiks to let the frost bleach new life into them. Nauja washed mine, which had jaundiced and concertina'd after their mistreatment on the trip to Dundas. Old clothes were turned out of the house and lay in disreputable heaps on the dump outside.

When the chores were done, the boredom became acute and the women grew restless. The return or visit of an occasional hunter induced ribald jokes, which died when each home received his attentions. There was much curiosity as to whether I was a faithful wife. The Eskimos are remarkably tolerant of sexual indiscretions. Celibacy is a condition they cannot understand, and faithfulness is a perfection to be aimed at (so the priests tell them) but difficult to attain. 'Pissoktut angut', or 'Pissoktut arnak',—'Because of being a man', or, 'Because of being a woman', was the common explanation for anything remarkable.

On one occasion when Nauja had a visitor whose attentions she declined, he asked her whether I would be interested. 'You had better leave her alone or she will get her husband after you,' threatened Nauja. 'And

if you don't leave my house soon, I will get my husband after you too.'
With mock fear the young hunter left. This was not the only occasion
when someone suggested that I might need a bit of male company while
Wally was away.

I noticed a party arrive one day from Qanaq, with a young hunter
whom I had not seen before. Later in the day he arrived with some others
to pay a social call, as was customary with visitors to a settlement. I made
coffee and we chatted for a little while. When the time came for them to
leave, the hunter hung back, as if wishing to say something to me. I was
busy changing Kari so that she could go out and join her playmates. He
kept following me between the two rooms as I collected nappies and
various clothes. At last he said, 'Marie, when is Wally returning?'

'Oh, not for several weeks,' I answered.

'Ajor, what a bad man your husband is,' he said vehemently.

'Why?' I asked in some surprise, and not a little indignation.

'To leave you alone for so many sleeps—he is a very bad man.'

I did not know what to say. I wanted to tell him to mind his own business, but I didn't know how. I felt a strong dislike for this stocky man and
could not understand what he was saying about sleeping.

'I don't understand a word,' I eventually declared rudely.

He seemed deflated, and scratched his head, as if wondering how else
he could explain himself. However, with a final 'Ajor', he left the house.

A second later his stubbly face poked round the door. 'Maybe you could
teach me English?' He flashed a brilliant set of teeth at me.

'Maybe not,' I said firmly, closing the door behind him.

I learnt later that his intentions had been benevolent, to say the least;
he had heard that Wally was to be away for several weeks—it was lonely
for a woman on her own, more especially for a Kasdluna, and he thought
he would come and offer himself as a companion for the time Wally
was away.

I talked to Nauja about it and she thought there was nothing extraordinary in the idea. Of course husbands were jealous of their wives,
and wanted them to be faithful, but if they were going to be away for
several months they might occasionally agree to their wife 'being kept
warm' by another man—a friend of theirs, for example. These days things
were different, because the priests had taught the Eskimos that such practice was wrong. But the Eskimos could not really *believe* it was *wrong*.
It was really very natural and sensible.

In the old days when the Eskimos were more nomadic than they are now, before the villages such as Qanaq, or Kekertassuak or Siorapalouk were built, there were camps in these places, and in many other places throughout the district. When a man travelled for a long while he needed a woman to cook for him, scrape his skins, and make his clothes. If his wife were pregnant or indisposed he frequently had to take another woman—usually a friend's wife. His friend in turn would look after his wife.

She reminded me of an incident that had happened to her the year before. They had then been in another settlement where Nauja had a friend—not a real close friend, but a woman she had known for years. Nauja's husband had brought back three polar bears the year before and Tukumik had offered to help her scrape them. Tukumik was small and rather round, with a sickly husband. She was sometimes jealous of Nauja, whom she thought was lucky to have such a strong, good-looking husband.

The two women worked hard scraping the skins and Nauja was very pleased to have Tukumik's help. She wondered what she could give her friend to show her appreciation, and decided on the beautiful long mane hairs of the polar bear. This was a present that no Eskimo woman could resist, as they used the hairs to trim the tops of their long kamiks. The longer the mane, the prouder the woman, and this mane was really something special.

To Nauja's great surprise Tukumik refused her generous offer. Indeed she was most emphatic in her refusal. For a minute Nauja was quite put out. She had never known her friend to refuse a good offer and she was puzzled. It could not be that she did not think the present good enough : she had already admired them as the finest she had ever seen. She pressed the point. 'You have worked hard and helped me, why should you not have a gift in return?' Tukumik looked down as she said, 'I would like to borrow Inugssuak for a night instead.'

Nauja admitted that for a while she was surprised. After all the priests said you were not supposed to do this sort of thing any more. But she did not like to refuse. So she agreed provided her husband liked the idea. When Tukumik had gone and Inugssuak returned Nauja told him of the other woman's request. He grinned, not a little flattered at the idea. He had never given Tukumik much thought but she was not unattractive. He agreed.

One day when Maria was in the house we tried to imagine where our husbands might be at that moment. I got out an atlas. While I was flipping through it I came to a page with a colour picture of different kinds of precious and semi-precious stones. Maria remarked, 'Maybe we have many like that in Greenland. The Greenlanders do not know enough about them.'

I agreed there was always a danger of strangers coming and exploiting the country, but I did not think the Danish Government would allow it to happen.

'Maybe not now that the Minister for Greenland is a Greenlander,' she said. 'We are very glad to have him. The Danes think we have no brains and that we are inferior beings.'

We had a long talk about colonization. Greenland is euphemistically called a 'Province of Denmark'. However, the spirit in which the name was given was benevolent. No doubt there are Danes who think the Eskimos inferior. I tried to explain to Maria that, as a nation, Greenland was very young. The Greenlanders had a lot to learn, and the Danes were making a great effort to help them. But Denmark had to pour into the country millions of kroner every year to supply hospitals, schools, houses, and other essential buildings, besides the many professional and technical people involved.

To the Eskimos it might seem incredible that Denmark gets little in return : after all she gets their hard-earned skins and meat and ivory. I tried to make a comparison with the Canadian Eskimos. The Danes did not want to repeat the mistakes which had made the Canadian Eskimos feel displaced—people who could neither live the old traditional way of life nor accept the new.

'At least you still have your pride,' I told her.

She nodded, but said sadly, 'Maybe soon we shall lose that too.'

Few of the Danes spoke any Eskimo. 'They do not even try to learn,' Maria complained. I began to understand why the Eskimos seemed so arrogant at times. The Kasdluna did not know everything, especially when it came to living in the Arctic.

'It is so easy for you,' said Maria bitterly. 'A hunter has to go out in all weathers, and you just have to sit at home and write.'

At last she had said what we expected. The Eskimos did not really respect a man who was not a hunter. How could I begin to explain to a person, who had no concept of time, the pressures and disciplines of writing and filming or of any other creative work? How could I explain the stress and bitterness of the competitive world in which we lived?

'If we just sat at home every day, Maria, what should we write about?

If we had not worked hard before we came up here how could we afford the expense? If Wally does not produce anything worth "selling" after hours of thinking, which leaves him exhausted and mentally drained, how can he feed and clothe his family?'

She nodded. 'Yes, I understand. You too have to work hard, but it is work of the mind—not many people would understand that.'

I had decided to go to Qanaq, as Wally had suggested, for a couple of weeks at Easter. Orla was having house guests, and I was invited to join. There was to be a visit from two groups of Canadian Eskimos, arranged by Fr Guy Mary Rousselière, the Parish Priest of Pond Inlet. This was the first time such a visit had been organized, and it would mean that many relatives from the two countries could meet for the first time. Many of the Thule Eskimos had relatives in Canada. Everyone wanted to meet the Canadians, and plans were made in all the settlements to pay a quick trip to Qanaq.

Both Maria and Nauja wanted to go, but they had no transport and there was no one to leave the children with. 'Why don't you look after each other's children for a day or two, and take it in turns to go for a while?' It was not possible—there were too many children involved.

Orla came to collect me with his son Harald, by scooter. Harald and I sat in a Skiboose—like a miniature car on skis. Following the sledge tracks, we passed three newly born pups lying dead on the trail. Often bitches give birth during a journey. It is troublesome looking after these newborn pups and the bitch becomes difficult once she smells them, so they are often left to freeze and the bitch carries on.

Easter weekend coincided with the liquor ration, and there were many fights in town. I got a little note from Maria which read in Eskimo, 'Thinking of you very much, longing for you to get back, have a happy Easter, with love Maria.' I was very touched. I felt really happy to get it. I wondered how she was.

The Canadians were expected on 7th April. It was a calm, sunny day, and their plane landed on skis on the ice. They wore bright-coloured parkas, trimmed with rich braid, and their kamiks were a masterpiece of fine stitching. A long felt stocking turned over at the top showed above the outer kamik and was embroidered in marvellous designs. The pointed hoods of their parkas made them look like people out of a fairy tale.

The next seven days were given over to festivity. Dog-sledge rides, dances, and feasts were arranged. The first feast was given by the host families to the guests and various heads of the community. As Orla's guest I was invited too. We all assembled in the Community Hall around two large tables on which the feast was already laid out—plates and plates of mattak. We all dived in. Some preferred the black mattak from the tail of the narwhal, others favoured the greyish mattak from the young white whale. I remembered my lesson from Christmas and cut only the tiniest squares, which slid down easily. We sat sawing away at the tough hide, sharpening knives against each other's. The only accompaniments were salt and lashings of pepper. There was tea and coffee to follow, before the speeches.

The Thule Eskimos welcomed their 'forefathers', and they replied in glowing terms. There were requests for people to sing the old folk songs— or drumsongs as they are called. In Thule there are often no words to these 'songs'. A person will just sing 'Aya ya ya', to a tune tapped out on the rim of a small drum. Each tune belongs to the person who made it up and if you 'borrow' it you have to acknowledge its ownership. One young fellow got up to sing the song of an old man at the feast who was too shy to sing it himself. One of the women offered to sing, provided nobody looked at her. In reply the Canadians sang their own versions, which were more amusing and topical.

The following night the whole village was invited to a feast by the visitors. The small hall was packed to capacity. The air was heavy with the smell of skin, clothing and sweaty bodies, and a thick pall of smoke hung above our heads, smarting our eyes and making most of us cough repeatedly. Infants tottered between the chairs while their elders chewed on frozen raw salmon or caribou. There was plenty for everyone. I enjoyed mine, till the meat began to thaw in my hand—raw meat is marvellous if frozen but not so palatable when it thaws. It was fascinating to watch the two nationalities exchanging news and stories. There were differences in dialect, but generally they understood each other. They talked about people who had emigrated from Canada to Greenland with the great-grandparents of some of the present Thule Eskimos, but after a while in Greenland they had returned to Canada. It was a great event for everyone.

One Herbert Islander was so impressed by the modern amenities that the Canadian Eskimos enjoyed that for the first two weeks of her return she talked seriously of leaving Greenland and emigrating to Canada. 'You live like dogs,' she told her family.

When I returned to Herbert Island, Maria was waiting for news. 'It seems like months since you were here,' she said. 'Maybe I will go away now and leave you on your own for ages.'

There was hardly anything I could tell her that she had not heard already, but she insisted on hearing my version. 'I was very annoyed one day,' she told me. 'Migishoo came back from Qanaq, a little drunk, and shouted to me right out in the open in front of everybody, "Maria, the English Marie has found a new boyfriend—an old man—I saw them walking down the street together." I felt so cross,' said Maria, 'but just ignored it.'

I laughed and told her not to worry. I remembered the day I had met Migishoo—she was very drunk and greeted me loudly as I walked into the store with the visiting priest.

'Didn't she know he was the priest?' I asked.

'Oh, old people are sometimes nasty when they don't understand,' Maria said. 'Never mind, they will soon be dead!'

16

In April the song of the first snow buntings filled the air. Soon the land would be alive with new life. Fox trapping had ceased and the animals could breed in peace. Gradually more and more birds would make their way to their nesting grounds in the hills and cliffs. The ice was wearing thin and the hunters avoided areas of deep snow where they knew the ice beneath had been worn away by the current.

Kari enjoyed her daily excursions on the sledge. She gathered handfuls of the bright snow and dipped her tongue into its delicious texture. The children stayed in the sun all day, with occasional trips indoors for food. The Eskimos have no set times for meals. The children eat when and what they like. The parents believe the children know best what they need and that it is unthinkable to force a child to eat.

Like everyone else I hated leaving the sun to go to bed. I would creep into the sleeping bag at two or three in the morning. Kari seemed equally disturbed by the brightness, which even the curtains could not disguise, and it was midnight at least before she slept. The villagers visited at all hours, and we lived a crazy timetable.

The children's creamy complexions turned deep brown, and sledging parties returned almost blackened by the glare from the ice. Soon we would have to wear sunglasses to avoid snow blindness. It makes the eyes red and tearful. The effect of the light is like rubbing the eyeball with grains of hot sand, and a severe case can damage the eyes irreparably.

By the 23rd April the sun was still high in the sky at 11.30 p.m. Rasmus returned with three seals. He was very proud, and everyone was delighted. It takes skill to creep up on a seal without being seen. Seals are very wary animals. They sleep for a minute at a time and then lift their heads to look around.

One of our greatest delights these days when the men were away was to have coffee outside on a sledge, in a sheltered place, where we could feel the full benefit of the glorious sun. Coffee was considered a luxury, but I had brought plenty with me, and I used to make several pots so that whoever passed by could stop for a cup.

The ice around Herbert Island was breaking up in places and we thought anxiously of our husbands. We had heard that the men had arrived safely at Grise Fiord about two weeks ago, but soon after a party travelling from there by Skidoo had had to turn back because of bad ice. We were worried. Each year the ice conditions were different.

It was still possible to get to and from Herbert Island by sledge, but new routes were being used. And vast stretches of water had been reported to the north. We hoped our men would not be stranded, miles from a settlement, with no food. The time of year was approaching when men needed both boats and dogs, the one at times carrying the other.

Nauja's husband had come back with two polar bears. He had gone hunting on his own and had been away twenty days. He was a good hunter and often went north. Once, it was whispered by one of the women in the village, he had gone to Canada with another hunter and while he was there he fell in love with a young girl. He stayed with her for a month, during which time he became more and more loath to leave. His companion had to practically drag him away so that they would not hit the bad ice on the way home.

Inugssuaq had wept most of the way home, saying he had never met such a woman and that he could not live without her. He swore to return the following year and even talked of taking this woman for his wife and living in Canada.

But it was two years before Inugssuak could return. At Grise Fiord, among the crowd to greet him, was the girl he had come to claim. His heart leapt for joy and he felt his love for her stronger than ever. But he soon discovered the young woman had married in the meantime, and, what was worse, seemed quite happy. Inugssuak could never bear to visit Canada again. My informant laughed maliciously as she mimicked his dejected return.

After my return from Qanaq I painted out the whole house in preparation for the men's return. Maria called with her eldest daughter, Inoutdliak, and asked if I would like to watch the women scraping a polar-bear skin while Inoutdliak looked after Kari.

We bent double down the low passage into Kaudlutok's shabby hut and squeezed through the half-opened door into the small living room. A frame made of long beams of wood, laced together, formed a square almost as large as the room. The bearskin, with the inside turned up, stretched taut between a complicated cat's cradle of rope and string. A small child played in and out of the ropes, clambering over them and crawling under the stretched skin which balanced precariously on a variety of furniture and boxes. A few of the women in the village surrounded the skin. It had been fairly well scraped already, but was still wet and creamy. There was hardly room to move and inevitably the small child got jammed between the ropes and had to be freed. The women talked and joked. More children squeezed in and floundered across the frame. Their mothers yelled at them. Others pressed their noses against the window pane to look in.

Maria, Inaluk (Kaudlutok's wife), Nauja, and Aima all took a leg and started scraping the curved ulus against the skin with short thrusts, to remove the milky sap. It came away in stringy pieces and sometimes stuck to the ulus. The women wiped them clean with their fingers and dropped the sap into a tin. The sight of it turned my stomach. As I watched, Maria glanced at me and licked her ulu. I gave a screech of disgust. I really did feel sick. The others laughed and said it was very tasty. They all sucked the fluid from the milky strands and spat them into the tin; I had never felt any revulsion at their eating habits but on this occasion I could barely watch. My gorge rose and I was seriously afraid I might spew right over the precious pelt.

After a while Kaudlutok strode in. He sat back with obvious pride as he watched the women work. 'You are very clever,' I told him. He laughed good-naturedly. 'Pissoktut angut,' 'Because I am a man,' he agreed.

I persuaded Maria to take advantage of a lift to Qanaq for the day and offered to look after the children. When she left Nauja came in. She seemed depressed. She explained why she had not come to see us when we first arrived. She was sure we had witnessed her violent argument with her husband and they had both felt very embarrassed about it. 'We thought we could not come to see you,' she explained, 'because we had been drinking a lot. Inugssuak is very moody and sometimes likes to fight, and if I drink I get mad too. He doesn't understand I get bored just staying in the house all the time.'

I listened without interruption. She asked for a cigarette. The corners of her mouth sagged. 'Some days I want to cry and I do not know why. I want to visit you but I get a lump in my throat because I know you will leave one day and I don't know how I will feel when you go. So it is better I do not see you every day—then the parting will not seem so difficult.'

The ice was breaking up! There was a sudden flurry as visitors from other settlements hurried to load their sledges. Children were bundled into their clothes and thrown like another piece of baggage on to the enormous piles of bedding already on the sledge. Massana and his family were on the move. They had to return to Moriussaq. His sledge was very long and he had eighteen dogs. He was a big, broad fellow, the son of Kaviarssuak, with whom we had stayed at Moriussaq. Massana's wife was very beautiful. A tall strong-featured woman with green-brown eyes and fairish skin, she was one of Migishoo's daughters.

Everyone turned out to see them off. As the last four dogs were un-hitched from the picket, they careered down the rocks towards the on-lookers, dragging Massana's twelve-year-old son with them, on his seat. He clung on, digging his feet into the snow. No wonder the Eskimos always wear out the seat of their pants, I thought. A stray dog rushed at them as they arrived at the bottom of the slope near the meat racks. The boy scrambled to his feet as the dogs tumbled around him, yelping and snapping. The noise of the fight excited the other fourteen dogs, already attached to the sledge. They pulled round and made a lunge towards the others. Men bellowed, women shouted and children screamed. The women snatched up small children and scrambled on to the drums of fuel. The men hurled lumps of hard snow at the dogs. They grabbed anything that came to hand to beat them back. Massana caught the whip from his son's grasp and cut the dogs round the ears and hind parts till they screamed in agony. Eventually order was restored.

When everything was ready, Massana, red-faced through his dark tan, and bursting out of his tight clothes, led the team across the tide crack. Maria grabbed the smallest child from the sledge as it tipped almost vertically in the air. Another child clung on to the front, and Patdlunguak and her two sons brought up the rear. As they caught up with the sledge, a loud cry of farewell rang out to them from the onlookers on the 'shore'. We watched as they made a wide detour to avoid a stretch of dark, thin ice. It was sad to see them go. I could not help thinking of Wally and wondering how soon he would hit bad ice. There was no way of knowing where they were. I felt suddenly very worried and depressed.

A couple of nights later Maria was listening to the radio in my house.

'Don't you get tired of that?' she said at last, turning off the pop programme from Thule Airbase. I had to agree that I did, but we had only a few tapes.

We chatted till late. We discussed how customs had changed. She told me that before the missionaries came the Inuit men had grown their hair long and that if two people liked each other they would sleep together or live with each other without a ceremony. But the priests told them this was wrong, so the men cut their hair and nowadays everyone got married in church.

However, some of the young people in Greenland were beginning to live the way they had done before the priests came. They grew their hair and if they wanted to live with a person they did so without first going to church to say a few words. She could not see anything wrong in this. It was natural. She did not see what all the fuss was about. I told her it was the same in most countries these days, that the young people felt they had different standards of what was right and wrong to what they had been taught by their parents.

I asked Maria if the Inuit were better off before the priests came. She thought for a long while.

'Maybe not,' she said at last. 'In the old days there were a lot of murders and when one person was killed, his relatives would take revenge. Sometimes a whole village would be wiped out this way.

'In the old days a woman in labour was put outside in a snow house and she had to deliver the child herself. Occasionally an old woman who knew about such things might help her, but very often she was left to fend for herself.

'Also,' she continued, 'if a husband died, the wife and children were not allowed to eat meat for weeks. They sometimes nearly starved. There were lots of strange customs.

'But one very bad thing the white man brought,' she said vehemently, 'was alcohol. Why did they think we needed it?'

As we talked I kept stopping to listen. 'I am sure I can hear the sound of a Skidoo,' I said. She listened. 'It is the aerial. It always makes that noise.' It was the 28th April. In places the ice was very bad, and in front of the island there was a wide stretch of water. Recently a young hunter had fallen through the ice and been drowned near Siorapalouk. His body was not found. 'Sometimes even the cleverest hunters lose their lives on the ice,' said Maria.

I listened again. 'I am sure I can hear a Skidoo!' I whispered.

'You are hearing things. It is late. I had better go to bed.

'Sleep well,' she called from the door. It was 1 a.m.

I was very tired but could not sleep. I kept thinking about Wally and wondering if he would be cut off from the island by water. I must have dozed off. It seemed only a few minutes later that I heard a sharp tapping at my window. It was Maria. 'A snow scooter! A snow scooter!'

I tumbled out of bed, half dazed. It was 8 a.m. As I dashed outside I saw the yellow snowmobile racing towards the island like a beautiful beetle. A figure in furs half crouched astride the seat as the vehicle picked its way through the pressure. There was no mistaking the figure of Avatak. 'Atata! Atata!' the children shrieked in excitement. The newcomer wove his way through the village and stopped outside Maria's house. She rushed and hugged him, pressing her face close to his.

I ran across and clasped him by the arms. I was too excited even to say hello, I just beamed from ear to ear.

'I am going out again. Wally is quite a way out there.' He unhitched the heavy sledge from the Skidoo and turned on his tracks. As he left Maria proudly lifted two polar bear skins off the sledge. 'They got four between them,' she said excitedly. They had left Siorapalouk at midnight the night before and travelled all night.

'So I *did* hear the Skidoo,' I breathed to myself.

I scurried back to the house and tidied up. I mixed the yeast for new bread and took the duck I had been saving out of its hiding place. All morning I scanned the sea ice. Eventually Kaudlutok called to me to look through his field glasses. There, in the distance, to the north of the island, was a dog team. It was tiny but unmistakable. I was so excited I shook hands with him. I would have gladly hugged him. But instead I rushed off to put the bread in the oven.

With a group of children behind me I hurried through the village towards the hills. I walked along the ridge that led to the cliffs. There I sat with the children until the team came into view around the spit of land that stretched northwards. I watched them for about five minutes through the field glasses. They looked black with sunburn. As they drew level with the cliffs about three hundred yards away we all waved and began to run round the cove to meet them at the Parcol.

There seemed an enormous number of dogs. I realized there were two full teams, on an extended trace. Maria came across with her whip to get her team. I walked slowly to meet the advancing horde of dogs. I forgot that Avatak's team were sometimes vicious.

'Hi. How are you?' Wally whispered giving me a hint of a hug.

Geoff self-consciously tried to cover his mouth as he grinned.

'How did you lose your teeth?' I asked.

'Sledging biscuits,' he confessed.

'Oh dear, well, the dentist has arrived in Qanaq.'

As I spoke, figures converged on the scene from all over the village.

Everyone took a hold of the long trace behind Maria's dogs. She walked ahead swishing the whip from side to side. The power in the rope was incredible and it took the whole village to keep the dogs at a reasonable pace.

The men were exhausted. They had been travelling for the last forty-eight hours, with just a brief stop at Siorapalouk. In the last few weeks they had journeyed over treacherous glaciers, hacked through fields of gigantic pressure, and floundered through the slush of melting ice. The strain of the 1500 miles told in their lined faces and torn hands. There were dark patches of frostbite around their peeling noses, and a white halo around their brows where their hats sat. It was good to have them back.

17

The bear had come to life it seemed! Its feet splayed sideways and its head lolled from side to side, just out of reach of the hysterical dogs. Some snarled and bared their teeth; others howled in a frenzy of excitement. The clumsy creature lunged towards them. Six pairs of legs tangled in the leads and the large animal tumbled to its death.

The onlookers roared with laughter. Avatak's children limped to their feet, moaning and rubbing themselves where they had fallen against the jagged rocks. Pouline nursed a very sore spot: as the bear's 'rump', she had been an irresistible target for a well-aimed nip, and her pants showed the teeth marks only too clearly.

Maria and Avatak took the beautiful skin from the children. They rubbed it in the snow to clean it and then beat the pelt with sticks to remove the fine white granules. It had been scraped and washed and would now be stretched.

The children scampered off towards the steep banks behind the village. The snow was hard packed and marvellous to slide down. They each carried a small piece of skin to sit on. Some had skin from the head of a polar bear; others just a spare scrap left over after breeches had been made; another carried the creamy skin of an unborn seal.

May was a month everyone enjoyed. There was sunshine and warmth. The empty meat racks would soon creak under the seals and walrus. But, for a while, the dogs went hungry. After Wally's return they were not fed for almost two weeks. There was no meat in the village. In some houses the stench from the meat that had been cached all through the winter made even the locals comment—but it was food. Others subsisted on what they could afford to buy from the store. The children poured uncooked oats into their tea and ate it by the spoonful. Hard tack biscuits made up most of their diet.

Kari had still a plentiful supply of canned food. We had been given more than we really needed, in case of loss or damage, and I gave some to the children. They wolfed it down, without leaving a drop in the tin. The Eskimos always finished everything off their plates and drank the tea down to the bottom of the cup.

In May everyone thinks of summer camp. The Eskimos love living in tents and at the earliest opportunity the whole family will move down the coast or round the other side of the island. Those living on the mainland had many sites to choose from, and people freely changed location, depending on the type of food they most enjoyed. Different animals and fish are found in the various parts of the Arctic, during the summer months especially. Now there are permanent trading stores in each village, people are more inclined to stay put for most of the year, and do their travelling in the summer.

The snow melted off the roofs into a frieze of jagged icicles. School was over for another few months. 'At last the boys can learn something useful in life,' said the hunters. The aspiring hunters proudly put on their polar-bear pants to accompany the older men on the hunt. The boys spent hours improving their technique with the whip. By the age of eleven some of them could crack it with the left hand almost as well as with the right.

In the village Taitsianguaraitsiak sat outside on his sledge, making a circular net, which he attached to a long pole. I went and sat near the old man. He greeted Kari and myself with a warm smile and explained that he would use the net to catch birds later in the summer. The pole was about ten feet long and he swept it gracefully into the air, imitating how he would pick little auks out of the sky.

Suakuanguak appeared from the store and laughed. 'Here, catch this,' she challenged, and threw her sealskin mitt into the air. He scooped it up. We laughed and clapped, and he beamed delightedly.

After the trip to Canada, Avatak had asked for five of Wally's dogs. He knew we were going to sell them as they were too much of a liability during the summer. He suggested keeping five, in return for letting Wally use the team whenever he wanted. It seemed a sensible arrangement. It was a sad day for Wally though when a man came from Qanaq to fetch the other nine. Wally had acquired a few more than the original thirteen, and had let Ilanguak keep the one he had looked after. A group of sympathizers came and stood around outside the hut. 'They will probably come back anyway,' they said reassuringly. They laughed scornfully at the new driver, and shot sympathetic glances towards Wally, who watched them through his binoculars as they disappeared into the distance. I sensed his disappointment. We were suddenly immobile, and once again dependent on the Eskimos.

The ice in Qanaq would take much longer to move out than that around the island. It was still possible to make a wide detour to get to the other villages from Herbert Island, but often these days the men would leave with their boats on the sledge. It was funny to see them clambering into a boat pulled along on a sledge. When the hunter met water, he could reverse the procedure. The dogs would pile into the boat and the sledge would be balanced across it. Most hunters used smaller and lighter sledges during this season.

As the men got ready for their trips to the camps, they took the kayaks off their racks and examined the skins. It was a sociable occasion. A new kayak was usually made from the skins of the Ringed Seal, although the hide of the Bearded Seal was thicker and larger. The man made the frame, but several village women would help the wife to sew and stretch the skins over it. In the water it was a graceful craft.

There was great excitement as people began to leave for summer camp. The store was crowded with villagers buying flour, tea, sugar, oats, and tobacco. They rolled their eyes and smacked their lips as they talked of the birds—the little auks, the eider ducks, and others. What feasting there would be! Sledge after sledge trundled out of the village loaded with cardboard boxes full of bedclothes and the invariable pups strapped squealing to the front of the sledge. There was much shouting, laughing, and cursing, but at last the teams got away, and everyone waved and called goodbyes.

I went in to see Nauja before she left. I felt sorry to see her go. She and her husband and their two little girls started off on one sledge, and their two young sons aged eight and eleven drove a smaller sledge with five dogs. All the children from the village raced after the two boys and clambered on to their sledge, with the result that it came to a full stop. But eventually the sledge disappeared across land towards the east.

May was a month of startling contrasts. Frost smoke wafted up from the sea, to merge into the deeper layer of blue fog. As the sun cut a path through it, casting a brilliant glare on to the water, the giant icebergs towards Qanaq lit up as with the light from a million footlights. Veils of grey, now pale, now almost black, ebbed and flowed around the fortress of ice which like a mirage suddenly disappeared.

25th May was my birthday, and I asked everyone left in the village to come for coffee and cakes. We played an old Eskimo game with an 'aja-gak'. This is the knucklebone of a seal : the Eskimos carve a hole in either end and attach to the centre with a strip of hide a pointed stick, which the person holds in one hand while flipping the other part in the air. The object is to pierce either the small or the large hole with the stick as often as possible in succession. There are many fancy flips which only the more experienced know how to do.

Geoff and I had practised and we were delighted when he confounded the Eskimos with an amazing show of skill. He and Wally had become very irritated with the one-upmanship the Eskimos displayed repeatedly throughout the trip to Canada, and we secretly enjoyed scoring points against them now. The Eskimos often make fun of each other, and frequently ridicule the Kasdlunas, but they cannot bear to be laughed at by a foreigner. When the Eskimos, time and again, found some little thing wrong with the way Wally or Geoff made camp, the two men would cut them short by laughing at them.

That evening, before going to bed, I glanced out at the calm sky. 'The ice is moving,' Maria called out. I went down to the rocks by the shore to watch as the ice slowly and inexorably began to move past the island.

'Do you like to see it go?' she asked.

'In a way,' I replied.

'Oh, we are so happy when the ice disappears. We have the sea for such a short time. We love it.'

We sat on the rocks admiring the view. Maria told me how surprised they had been when we first arrived on the island. They could not understand why we should want to live in one of their little huts. Avatak had suggested to her that maybe we would feel lonely on our own and that she ought to come and talk to me so that I could learn to speak Eskimo, and in this way feel less lonely.

I told her how glad I was that she had tried so hard, and how marvellous it was for me to be able to talk to her in her own language.

'I think I will feel very unhappy when I have to leave,' I admitted.

'Yes, I think of it often, and tears pour down my face. The children ask what is the matter—I just say because I have been dreaming.'

We watched silently as the lead between the shore and the ice widened. The sun seemed to burn it away. 'This will be a "field" of little bits to-morrow—it comes and goes—sometimes the whole area is broken up, then again it is so calm, at times, that you can see the land in the water.'

I noticed Wally come out of the hut and scan the place with his field glasses. 'Goodness, Maria, it is 1.30. I had better go in. Wally is probably looking for me.'

'The children get so wet and dirty in summer,' complained Maria. She pointed to great pools of slime that began to separate the houses. The rubbish dumps, huge after the winter, breathed foul air into the atmosphere. The tacky grime from the blubber caked the children's rubber boots and stuck in dungy patches to the floor. Our thoughts turned to summer camp.

Maria had come back with Avatak and another couple to bring back walrus hides. 'There are lots of walrus there,' they said excitedly. 'Why don't you come back with us?' We had intended waiting till Wally had finished a script, but we persuaded him to bring his work along with him.

Before we left Maria gave me a present of a pair of kamiks she had just finished. 'You won't need these with you though,' she explained. 'It is so wet at the camp with such thick snow, you had better take rubber boots.'

We travelled along the thick band of ice that skirted the coast towards the north. I noticed the way she 'rode' the sledge, almost as one would ride a horse. She shifted her weight as we tipped over obstacles and clung on to Kari as we soared over ramps. When we met a bridge of narrow ice she leapt nimbly off and steered the sledge expertly through the parallel leads, jumping quickly on again once we had crossed the second crack. 'You will love it at the camp, Marie.' Her eyes were shining. I was delighted to see my friend so happy, after the months of being cooped up in the hut.

As we came abreast of mountains and fiords I had not seen before, I noticed a raised stretch of shingly beach, at the foot of a steep snow-covered hill. Four tents squatted next to a hunter's hut. A wide fissured wall of pressure separated the camp from the sea ice, on which were spread the remains of a terrible slaughter, a mass of congealed blood and guts. Maria pointed proudly. 'Avatak shot five walrus, a Ringed Seal and a Bearded Seal.' Further on another three carcasses lay on the ice. 'The dogs are bloated with meat,' laughed Maria pointing to the animals slumped on the ice.

'We have not slept all night,' explained Maria, rubbing her eyes. 'We worked so hard flensing the animals—the children have only had a few hours' sleep.' The camp life had its own routine. The sun revolved around the sky twenty-four hours a day. We would sleep when we were tired, eat when we were hungry and act as we pleased.

The pebbles clattered under our feet as we put up tent—a small one for Geoff and a larger one for the three of us. We used boards and stones to raise us above the thick layer of wet snow that lay beyond the shingly path.

Geoff and I soon sank into the easy life of the camp, while Wally tried hard to work. Although the sun shone constantly, there was often a sharp breeze. The children bounced with energy and health. Their laughter and squeals of pleasure could be heard day and night. Kari seemed to have inexhaustible energy and her cheeks glowed like peaches under the sunglasses I insisted she wore. The light was dazzlingly bright. When one first opened the tent flap after a night's sleep, the light pierced the chinks like a white flame.

It was lovely to have Wally and Geoff around after their long trip to Canada, and the atmosphere in the tent was very relaxed, especially at meal times, when we would sit chatting about the various activities of the camp. Sometimes the men went hunting with Avatak in the boat. On one occasion they got back from a trip at two in the morning, with four walrus. They had only time for a cup of tea before they had to go back out to the ice to flense the animals.

It is heavy work skinning a walrus and cutting up the meat, and very cold besides. At this time of the year, the animals often sleep on the ice and the men could see them asleep on floes that they could not get to. The walrus is one of the most dangerous animals in the Arctic, and many hunters have been killed when the animal either capsized their boat or drove its tusks through the frail skins of the kayaks. Even the polar bear will not attack a walrus in the water—though on land he is not so agile. The tusks are sometimes huge and they butt fiercely with their granite heads.

It was three hours before the men could return to the tent for food and sleep. I had sat up most of the night outside the tent watching the group on the ice. Maria pointed out the head of an animal with large tusks that she said was Wally's. Avatak had urged Wally to shoot when a herd of walrus had slouched off an ice floe into the water. Although foreigners were not allowed to shoot walrus, Wally salved his conscience by the thought that it was for the Eskimo. Avatuk very generously allowed Wally to keep the tusks as a trophy.

I was curious to know what it was like to scrape a skin. I had never asked to scrape a sealskin as it is easy for the beginner to tear it, and they were too valuable to waste. The walrus, however, has such a tough hide that I could safely experiment. Maria handed me an ulu. The skin of the animals had been slit down the front and back. We struggled and heaved and with great difficulty pulled it over the naked carcass. I was amazed at the weight of the skin.

We slithered in the pool of blood and blubber round the animal. My hands were cold and covered with oil. I had not realized that the blubber itself would feel cold. It was difficult to handle the ulu and the muscles of my hands and arms ached. We stopped for a short break and Maria lit a cigarette. We sat on the sledge and looked around us.

'I love working in the open,' she said. 'It's the best thing about summer.'

We got through the whole skin in an hour and dragged both halves to a pool of clear blue water around a nearby iceberg. The skin made a slurping sound as it sank in and we anchored the rope attached to it to an ice knobble. The skin would stay in the water till it could be taken to Qanaq to be sold to the Royal Greenland Trade Company. I was pleased with my effort. 'You can scrape the tusks later,' offered Maria.

There was a variety of food available for those who had the energy to pursue it. Long strings of eider ducks flew by, and every night flocks of little auks could be seen skimming over the water in the distance to gorge themselves on fish, before returning to the bird cliffs, near Siorapaluk, on the opposite side of the Sound. The Eskimos took a shot at everything.

The children amused themselves throwing stones at targets, and whirring others through the air from a sealskin sling. They pelted any bird that came within range, whether it was edible or not.

It was at this camp that Kari got her first real taste for seal meat and for the various birds. I too enjoyed the local meat, though some of the Eskimos were disinclined to offer us any, for fear of a rebuff. The disgust with which most foreigners received their food was hardly conducive to hospitality. But we were delighted on the occasions we were invited to share in the communal life of the camp.

It is in the camps that the good story-teller comes into his own. There are long periods of bad weather or when the catch has been so plentiful that people just want to relax. In the old days there were many great story-tellers, who handed on their stories to their sons and daughters. But now the young have lost some of the art, and they have to seek out the old folk if they want to be entertained.

Summer is a period of feasting, but for the dogs it is a boring time. The hunter has little use for them except to make the occasional trip to another settlement while the ice is still good. There were many occasions when the men had to run out on to the ice with harpoons or anything else that came to hand to break up the fierce fights amongst the dogs tethered on the ice.

One day a fierce commotion broke out among Avatak's team. It was a while before Avatak could reach the dogs. He screamed at the grappling animals, but the fight continued. Eventually he shouted to Maria, who hurried into the tent to get his rifle.

He fired two shots. Then I noticed him dragging an animal away from the team. I watched with horrified fascination what followed.

He separated a large white dog from the rest of the team and tethered it by a short lead—about three yards in length. Stooping down, he picked up an enormous piece of driftwood which he had taken out on to the ice. Slowly and methodically he cracked it over the dog's head. The creature darted from side to side to avoid the blows, and at times snarled and snapped, but eventually the blows began to daze it, and it ran in smaller circles.

At times Avatak hurled the wood at the dog, and caught the animal a sidelong blow. Every time the wood fell, the hunter walked slowly to pick it up before smashing it again at the dog's head. The dog yelped in terror and defiance. Soon its white head turned red and it slunk from side to side, its tail bent beneath it. The punishment lasted a full five minutes, till the creature cringed to the ground, at the feet of the exhausted man. Its head hardly moved as it received the full force of the last blow. Maria stood quietly, watching without emotion.

Eventually the man threw the splintered board away and plodded heavily back to the camp. He sat on the stones outside his tent and spoke tremblingly, as I approached with Kari. 'Kari, come here, I have been fighting with the dogs.' He took her lovingly and she nestled into his arm and took the pebble he offered her as if it were a delicate treasure. Her presence seemed to soothe him. He motioned to me to sit down.

Maria came and sat down with us. She seemed as if she would like to speak but did not know how. So I spoke first. 'Kingmek ajorpok?' 'Dog bad?' I asked simply.

Avatak gave an impassioned explanation for his behaviour. Three of his dogs had attacked the dog Wally had given him at Christmas. He had dragged it half dead away from them. It had been a strong dog and an excellent worker and he had been very pleased with it, especially as Wally had given it to him. Two of the other dogs had always been vicious. They had killed so many good dogs in their time and they themselves were so lazy that he had at last decided to get rid of them, so he had shot them. The third dog, the white one, was a good sledge dog but had a mean nature. He often badly mauled other dogs, but he was too good a worker to lose, so Avatak had to teach him a lesson. He was hurt, but he would recover, and it would be a while before he forgot the punishment.

'Come, Marie,' said Avatak. 'Would you like a look at the sea?'

'Yes, you go with him,' said Maria as she took Kari. I walked down to the ice where the awful beating had taken place. The dog which had been attacked by the others was lying near Avatak's boat, just out of reach of the rest of the team. It was badly mauled and bloodstained, and held on to life by the faintest breath. It died as we looked at it.

The white dog was also on its own, but although it too was bloodstained, it was on its feet and apparently not too hurt. The two carcasses lay together. Avatak put a cord through their harnesses and attached it to the back of the sledge. We drove the few hundred yards to the sea. The ice broke off suddenly and the waves lapped gently against the edge. The man unhitched the dogs and dragged them to the water. With a passionless kick he shoved them in. The tail of one still lay on the ice and slipped slowly after the body. 'Avek neke', he said with disgust, as he wiped his hands—'Meat for walrus!'

He turned abruptly and got on the sledge. I sat at the back. A tremor ran down my back, as if I had been partner to a grim execution.

At the beginning of June, all the adult Eskimos in the camp went to Qanaq by dog sledge. They had to make a wide detour to the good ice. Eleven children were left in our care and as it was a rather windy day we had them all in the tent with us for the whole day. We were glad when their parents returned to claim them. We noticed that they had brought their liquor ration with them. We wondered anxiously what the evening had in store for us. There was no door on the tent that we could lock.

As we had imagined we had a constant stream of visitors, starting with Avatak who woke the sleeping Kari with his singing and insisted on her sitting on his knee. He told us very seriously that he loved her very much and that we did not appreciate what a fine brain she had. She was worth the three of us put together. Kari yawned sleepily at him, as tears began to stream down his face.

Soon everyone in the camp had squeezed into the tent, each newcomer looking for the person who had arrived before them. A young hunter had his sleeve constantly tugged by his sulky lover. He wanted to enjoy the company, and ignored her. She perched on the box beside him with boredom written all over her face.

Maria came in breezily, but became more serious as the night wore on. She confided that she was obsessed with the thought of our departure and thought she would go out of her mind after we had left. Geoff chatted to a wizened old man who was almost incomprehensible without his false teeth. He confided loudly to Geoff that he was fed up with his ugly wife and felt tempted to get rid of her. Geoff gazed in amazement from the ugly wife to the complaining husband, and had an irresistible urge to giggle whenever he caught my eye.

We sat cramped and in earnest conversation for a couple of hours till the young hunter's girl rushed outside, taking her young man's kamiks with her. If he didn't come immediately she would leave for Qanaq. He hardly acknowledged her departure—till the sound of dogs whipping past the tent sent him out in his socks to have a look. She was driving his team in the direction of Qanaq. A few minutes later he was in hot pursuit with his father's team, and wearing his father's kamiks.

The excitement got everyone out of the tent. It was three in the morning. We did not bother to investigate the commotion that broke out when the hunter and his girl returned. He had avenged his honour by giving her a good beating and she had replied by throwing his clothes down the tide crack. He had retrieved these and beaten her some more. In the fracas the tent caught fire. Eventually, however, the fighting stopped and peace reigned in the camp.

The following day was little Etos' birthday. There was a celebration on the ice. Everyone gave her a present—a pair of socks, a packet of oats, a few sweets. We all sat round on the sledges and there was walrus meat, coffee and biscuits for everyone.

That afternoon I worked on the tusks, boiling them for a while to get the meat off the base, and then scraping to get the thick gristle off. I sat outside with Maria and followed her instructions. She gave me a wing from a bird she had boiled. It was delicious. Avatak came in later with some seal. The children stood round as he cut one open and handed them each a piece of raw liver. The twins each wanted an eye. Maria cut them out and handed them to the children who sucked them as if they were sweets—almost the size of a golf ball. After a while they handed them back to her and she cut the ball open with her ulu. The children squeezed out the almost colourless liquid which they sucked and swallowed. They turned the black fleshy cast inside out and chewed it, and rolled a small colourless ball, like a small marble, round in their hands for me to see before popping it too into their mouths.

Later in the summer I noticed Martha flip a tiny red jellyfish out of the water. She turned it inside out, sucked it and threw the skin back in the water. I sometimes wondered if there was any living thing the children would not eat.

18

It was 3.30 a.m. The sun was low now on the horizon and it was cold enough to freeze the surface of the sea ice which had been fairly slushy during the day. We had a four- or five-hour ride ahead of us to the scree-covered cliffs near Siorapalouk. In these cliffs the colonies of little auk, or 'agpaliarssuk', as the Eskimos called them, milled in noisy confusion.

It was safer to travel in the cool of the evening because there was less likelihood of going through the ice. But there was always the risk that the ice might break up and blow out to sea. There would be no escape if that happened, because as the floes meet the bergs, carried down by the current from Smith Sound, they break up into tiny pieces and melt in the heat of the sun.

In the last few days the Eskimos at the camp had urged that this was the best time to visit the bird cliffs. We had arranged to borrow our friend's team—only to have doubt cast in our minds by the locals, who now said that the ice might move out any minute. If that were the case it seemed foolhardy to take the risk, so we decided to postpone our trip, possibly till the next month, and then go by boat.

Avatak then decided he would go to the birds' cliffs that night.

'Well, is it safe or not?' Wally had asked with some exasperation.

'Imaka ajungilak,' 'Maybe it is all right,' was the casual reply.

'Well, in that case, we can all go,' continued Wally. We had waited five hours for our friend to sleep off the stupor of the day before. I had suggested to Maria that Wally and I should go on ahead and that Avatak could come when he was ready with Geoff, but she did not seem to like the idea. At last our friend woke up and got ready to leave. Just as Wally and I were about to set off, Geoff told us that Avatak had said he was only coming halfway, because the ice was bad.

Wally and I were furious.

. In spring seals come up on to the ice to sleep
the warmth of the sun. They have keen eyesight,
d the hunter has to hide behind a white screen.

22. Avatak's mother, Suakunguak, ties a newly-
scraped sealskin to a frame. It will be hung
outside, and should turn milky white. When dry
the skin is hard, and has to be softened by
kneading with the hands so that it can be sewn
as *kamiks*.

23. After the polar-bear skin has been scraped it is rubbed in the snow to remove surplus blubber, then beaten, stretched and hung out to dry —with the fur turned away from the sun, or it would turn yellow. The men and boys wear polar-bear trousers. From a very large skin you could get three pairs that would just cover the hip and reach to the knee.

24. The white whale is fast and difficult to catch. This mother stands proudly over the four whales that her son has caught. The meat racks in the background are bare except for a few pieces of dried whale meat. This is called *niko*, and has a strong nutty flavour. It is delicious with *mattak* —the skin of the whale, eaten raw as an Eskimo delicacy.

'Why the hell does he bother to come at all?' asked Wally. 'I don't need a guide. We have wasted five hours waiting for him, and now he thinks it is unsafe for him to travel but safe enough for us. What's he playing at?'

I tackled Maria. 'Why is Avatak only going halfway?'

'He thinks the ice might go out. He is a bit afraid,' she said sheepishly.

'Well, if that is the case why should we go—we would be "perdlerortok" to go out on the ice if the Inuit think it is bad.' I had used a word they apply to mad dogs. I hoped it would emphasize the seriousness of the situation. She gasped at the strange word and tried to laugh. Then realizing my anxiety she said seriously, 'Maybe it will not go out. Maybe he does not know anything.'

I walked out on to the ice towards the dogs without a word. 'Marie, inudluarit', 'Maria, goodbye,' my friend called sadly. I returned the farewell, trying hard to smile. Our eyes met in understanding. I did not want to hurt her.

No sooner had we hitched the dogs than they took off. They bolted like the devil over the ice, as if they wouldn't stop till they reached their destination. The only problem was that they were headed the wrong way. As Avatak's sledge came over the tide crack further down we passed him at right angles, bouncing across the smooth ice like jacks-in-the-box. As we whipped past, I grinned at Maria, who was behind the other sledge, guiding it through the pressure. She answered with a laugh. I waved cheerily.

In a couple of minutes the dogs had calmed down and Wally drove them back, at a tangent, towards Avatak's sledge. We ran parallel with the rim of the ice, about a mile from the open water. Except for a few cracks the surface was good. The two other islands just west of Herbert Island came into view, the nearest a paradise of beautiful snow-capped mountains.

About halfway we stopped for a tea brew. The atmosphere seemed cheerful. Avatak had decided he would go the whole way. We looked up into the blue sky at the flocks of birds high above our heads. Wave after wave of tiny birds sailed high overhead on their way inland after gorging themselves out at sea.

As we neared the cliffs, a tremendous tumult filled the air, like a million people shrieking, cackling, crying, clapping. High above us the birds rolled in in unending sequence.

We followed Avatak and Geoff up a steep bank to a broad apron of land at the foot of the cliffs. The two of them joined a group of figures who had watched our arrival. A booming voice greeted us with a loud hello. As I answered I sank up to my thighs in drift. Eventually I clambered up to find that the figure was Kissunguak, a jovial Eskimo who represented the Thule District at the Community Council in Godhab. Beside him was his beautiful wife, Pouline, whom I had met several times. She was the grand-daughter of Robert Peary and her father, Kale Peary, lived on Herbert Island.

At this camp we experienced the hospitable Eskimo at his best. Within seconds of our arrival a pot of tea was made and jam and sledging biscuits were brought out from their stores. As we sat around Pouline busied herself with a delicacy which is quite rare, even in the Arctic, the tiny clams from the stomach of a newly killed walrus. It is not often that a hunter will kill the animal at just the right moment after it has eaten, before the contents of its stomach have time to digest. The clams are heated in the juice from the stomach. We took them and peeled off the soft skin. The shells had been crushed between the walrus's flippers before they were eaten. I found them delicious.

The sun was overcast, and the hills became shrouded in mist, but still from time to time black specks appeared in huge numbers out of the clouds and added their chatter to the increasing babble.

'There are not many today,' said Pouline, 'but I think there will be many tomorrow.'

The best time of day to catch the birds is early morning, when they are fat and heavy from a good night's feed. We were very tired and slept till 2 a.m. When we got up Avatak and Kissunguak were sitting outside making nets like the one Taitsianguaraitsiak had showed me at Herbert Island. 'You can borrow this one,' offered Kissunguak. He showed me how to use it and explained that if I caught a bird I must twist the net so that it could not get out. I must be very careful hauling it in, as that was the time most people lost their birds.

The Eskimos catch these birds by the hundreds. They are very tasty, and are eaten in a variety of ways. They are sometimes cooked, feathers and all, in a large pan of water, weighted down with a flat stone so that they are completely immersed. This way the fat from the skin seeps into the flesh making it really succulent. When the birds are cooked they are then rubbed in snow to cool the feathers, which can be peeled off with the skin, like a sock, merely by pinching the down on the back of the neck and pulling gently.

Every part of the bird is eaten, except for the bones. That morning before climbing the cliffs we were offered this delicious meal. I watched Kissunguak as he cracked the bird's head between his teeth and rolled his tongue round the inside to get at the brains. The birds are so small that several are needed to make up a meal and the Eskimos stay up in the cliffs for hours catching them. I was excited at the prospect, and we practised throwing dead birds up in the air and catching them.

At 4 a.m. Pouline and I started towards the cliffs. Avatak had gone ahead, and Wally and Geoff followed him to film. As we looked up at the hills, their outline was blurred by millions of birds, like thousands of swarms of bees, circling, landing, taking off again, swooping gracefully towards another part of the cliff. Large black patches on the reddish brown rocks suddenly took flight. At times even the clouds were darkened.

The noise rose to a crescendo, as if hordes of spectators were cheering and clapping some spectacle. We sank into thick moss on the lower slopes. Avatak was hidden in a little nest of rocks, made by the Inuit in several places along the slopes. Pouline chose another and pointed out one for me. I sat and watched for a while as the birds wheeled and dived around us. With the speed of a whip, her net flashed into the air and chased the screeching creatures. Suddenly it turned sharply and a small bird fluttered in its grasp.

Time after time I watched Pouline snatch the birds out of the air, and time after time I tried to imitate her. We had been up in the hills for an hour. My neck was aching from twisting and turning as I watched the birds reel in dizzying circles around me. They came from every direction and perched on every rock and boulder, just out of reach of the net. They would sit for a while till an impulse made them rise as one and fly screaming away. Their places would be taken seconds later by another crowd.

Wally came and sat near me for a while. I missed a couple of birds as they dived straight at him.

'That one nearly got me!' he gasped, ducking as another skimmed the top of his head.

It was exhausting, but the satisfaction of eventually catching one was worth the sweat. As I stood, hardly daring to touch the flapping creature, Pouline scrambled up the rocks towards me and with deft movements folded its wings behind its back and placed her thumb on its heart. It died instantly.

'Nissuk,' 'Clever person!' she said as she handed it back to me. I laughed proudly.

As the hours wore on we followed the birds higher up the cliffs, till we were about 500 feet above sea level. I felt dizzy and tired and sat gazing out towards Herbert Island in the distance and the ring of mountains around. It was very beautiful. Three more birds fell victim to my net, but when it came to handling the creatures I got frightened and either Avatak or Pouline had to do it for me.

'If you catch any more you have got to kill them yourself,' said Wally. I promised I would try. The birds grew thicker and thicker on the ground and in the air around, and I found a secluded den which they flew over constantly, without seeing me. I reached up and caught one easily.

The sport had been tremendous up till now, but suddenly I felt different. I looked at the creature flapping in the net. It was really very pretty, with a black head and body and a white breast. Even its eyes were a velvet black. It looked so gentle. Avatak and Pouline looked up at me. I must surely know what to do, I had been shown four times.

I wished I could let it go, but I had promised Maria I would bring back a sackful. I did not like killing. It was bad enough to use a gun, but to do it with bare hands, when the creature was harmless, seemed cruel. I closed my eyes and caught hold of the flapping bird. With difficulty I extricated its claws from the net and held it round the neck. Its eyes were pleading. My heart pounded and my fingers shook as I folded the wings behind its back. My thumb felt for the heart. I could not find it. I panicked. The creature gasped. I pressed its chest, without reaction. Why wouldn't it die? Oh, God, was I hurting it? The eyes rolled upwards vacantly and its head hung limp—it was dead.

I sat down with the lifeless creature in my lap and gazed at the countless others whirling around me. My head suddenly began to spin and my eyes felt strange. Things became bright and blurred. I closed my eyes to blot out the constant movement in front of them. My wrists and neck ached. I had had enough of the bird cliffs. It did not matter if I had not caught my sackful—I wanted to leave—to get away from the deafening noise.

We started back to the camp at about half past nine. Pouline had caught 198 birds and Avatak nearly as many. The load was heavy and Geoff carried it for her. She was surprised and grateful for the help. Now she had enough to make a 'kiviak', she told me. I had already seen a hunter at the other camp carefully skinning a seal, so that the carcass was pulled away from the skin through the opening at the mouth. It was a tricky job. After the body had been dragged clear a complete bag was left which could be stuffed with as many as six or seven hundred birds. The opening at the mouth would be sewn up and a load of birds would be cached for several months under large stones so that the sun could not get at them. During this time the fat from the skin would seep through the feathers and skin of the birds, which were 'pickled' just as they were, feathers and all. The birds would ferment and later would be eaten raw. It was a great delicacy. 'Maybe if you visit us in the autumn you can have some too,' she offered graciously.

That night after a short sleep we decided to start back. Our hosts were most disappointed.

'Maybe it is because you do not like us,' teased Pouline. I hastened to assure her it was because I had to get back to Kari before the sea ice blew out.

On the trip back we saw many seal on the ice. But they slipped into their holes at the sight of our teams. It seemed a long ride, but a happy Maria greeted us warmly on our arrival. She laughed when I told her that I had not brought many birds because I could not bear to kill them. She admitted that she was none too good at it herself and that she usually knocked them over the head with a stone!

Wally had too many distractions at the camp to do the work he needed to finish by the time Geoff flew out at the beginning of July. We returned to Kekertassuak, and found we were the only people there. It was a marvellous feeling to have the place to ourselves. In the sanctuary of the village, alive only with birds, we had time to reflect on the beauty of the surrounding country. In places there were still ugly trash heaps and we spent ages tidying away the layers of blubber that had lain around our hut for years. From the hills the sound of birdsong mingled with the murmuring streams. Snow from the hillsides had melted to form melt-streams of delicious clear water. A small sea washed the bloodstained ice-foot beneath the village. The pools of fetid water between the dwellings had evaporated in the warm sun and in their place the loveliest minia-ture flowers appeared.

Greenland is rich in flora, and even as far north as we were—almost 78° latitude—beautiful little flowers appeared on apparently barren ground. The sudden appearance of a large hairy bumble bee had me scurrying out of its way. I had forgotten such creatures existed and the Arctic was the last place I expected to see one.

'Look,' exclaimed Wally one day, 'there are two snow geese.' There are so few of these birds left in Greenland that they are protected.

Geoff would often go for walks into the country and he reported an exciting find one day; an eider duck's nest with five beautiful green eggs in the greyish down. The bird was so well camouflaged that he almost stumbled on her before he saw her. We became very fond of this solitary female and hoped that when the Eskimos returned they would not find her; we knew that if they found it the nest would be looted and the mother probably shot.

The arrival of Avatak's family was exciting. The whole family came in for breakfast. They had had great fun, after we had gone, when they had all gone looking for agpaliarssuk on another tiny island west of Herbert Island. They had caught the birds by hand as they nested and they had brought back lots of eggs. They brought in a packet of hard-boiled eggs, greeny coloured and slightly mottled, with bright salmon-pink yolks. 'There should be eider ducks' eggs around,' they said excitedly. The three of us thought anxiously of our bird.

One day Wally and I went for a very long walk to a cape at the east end of the island. I took him up towards a spot in the hills where the ground was covered with beautiful purple saxifrage. He had his camera with him and wanted to take some photos, but we decided we would explore first. We passed inland lakes on which the black and white male eider ducks bobbed undisturbed. We avoided the place where we knew the female duck had her nest, meaning to have a look at it on the way back. We walked across large stretches of sandy ground and in other places patches of water-logged moss. We passed an ancient camping place, where there were stone rings to indicate where the tents had been. The ground around was strewn with bones. In a vast stretch of rubbly ground we noticed two graves. Within a stretch of a couple of hundred yards this was the only spot where flowers grew in profusion—purple saxifrage, white bell-like flowers, buttercups, and Arctic willow.

An hour's walk brought us to the camp-site to which the villagers would move a little later in the summer, to catch the white whales and narwhals that swim past the Point on their way to the nearby fiords. We hurried back to relieve Geoff who had offered to look after Kari. I just wanted a quick look at the eider duck to make sure she was all right. I remembered the tuft of grass that she had chosen for her nest—at least I thought I remembered where it was. But things looked different from the angle at which we approached. We moved as silently as two shadows, so as not to frighten her. At last Wally stopped.

'The eggs have gone—the kids must have got them.'

'Oh.'

'Honestly, these Eskimos have no idea of anything,' muttered Wally. 'Don't they understand that without eggs there would be no birds?'

'Geoff will be disappointed,' I murmured, as I looked at the silky down scattered among the stiff grass.

That evening when I talked to Maria, she admitted that the children had found them. 'Oh, and there was a little chick in one—it was very tasty!'

19

By the time Geoff left, most of the villagers had returned from their camps. They were as sorry to see him go as we were. The few days surrounding his departure coincided with a drinking bout in the village, the effects of which even Geoff must have felt. It seemed that one of the greatest evils that 'civilization' had brought to the Eskimos was liquor, and even they recognized this fact.

In Thule the 'disease' is not so virulent as in other parts of Greenland, but each month there are tragedies which leave a scar on the face of an otherwise peaceful society. In order to curb drunken excess the authorities allow each adult in Thule (Eskimo or foreigner) thirty points a month. For these a person has a choice of thirty bottles of beer, a bottle and a half of hard liquor or three large bottles of wine—or a mixture of all three. In the first few days of each month the whole ration is imbibed in one glorious swill. Overnight the normally polite and friendly Eskimo can turn into an uncontrolled and ugly brawler.

One evening the children rushed in to tell me that three of the old men in the village were singing the old drum songs. In the early days there were different types of drum song. There were those which were sung for entertainment and there were others which were part of a ritual, and there were fight songs. The ritual song was usually sung by an Angakok or Shaman during exorcism, where the Angakok would call upon the spirits, through his song, to help him. This type of song was condemned by the early Moravian and Lutheran missionaries. So was the drum fight song, which took the place of law courts in the old Eskimo society. In the case of complaint the prosecutor would summon the whole community to arbitrate between him and his opponent. They would then attack each other, not with weapons, but in song, with the most sarcastic and malicious invective. The winner would be acclaimed by applause. The two opponents would merge into a general song and dance.

These days in Thule the songs are only sung for entertainment. The drum has gone out of existence and any old plate and stick is used. The singer beats a steady rhythm, three beats at a time, and while he sings he moves his body from side to side as if dancing on the spot.

I thought I would try and record the singing, if the singers did not mind. I borrowed Wally's best tape recorder. Unfortunately, it was too large to be inconspicuous and I hoped I would not put everyone off. The merriment was taking place in Piuatok's house at the top of the village. As I struggled up the slope I noticed Aima coming out of the house and sitting down on one of the rocks outside. She seemed pleasantly intoxicated and very friendly. 'They are all singing in there,' she said, pointing to the house. The flashing smile that always charmed me gave way to a toothless grin which she tried to hide behind her hand.

She laughed as she told me she had come out for a breath of air. I began to have some misgivings, but it was too late to turn back. Kari was with Maria. Wally was down at the other hut away from the village and would not know where I was in an emergency. However, I followed Aima up the wooden steps.

Inside were a couple of old women. One of them slumped over the table. The other sprawled across the bench at the wall, her head propped at an awkward angle against the corner, her mouth gaping. She was old and very plain. Her few teeth stuck out of her swollen gums in a grimace, and her eyes looked dazedly out of half-closed lids. She was a visitor to the village and her husband, a skeleton of a man with a shock of greying hair, stumbled around the room clutching an almost empty bottle of aquavit. He spluttered and spat as he spoke and a dribble of saliva oozed down his stubbly chin.

The other man in the room was Taitsianguaraitsiak. He got up when I came in, and came over and shook hands. 'I feel a little bit drunk,' he apologized. But he smiled and motioned me to a chair. 'We have been singing,' he explained, 'but my throat is very hoarse from that awful stuff.' He pointed to the aquavit in the other man's hand. 'There is no beer,' he said. I asked him if he minded my recording some of the songs. 'Ajungilak, ajungilak asorssuak,' 'Of course, that is all right,' he said.

Taitsianguaraitsiak made many false starts but eventually he launched into a full-blooded song about his son who was away catching narwhals. It was lovely to see him, swaying from side to side, suffused with a great joy which lit up his face.

Suddenly he stopped, and sat down beside me. He dropped the coal shovel and rake he had been using instead of a drum, and leant over to confide to me that really he was unhappy. He thought, whenever he saw Wally, that a big stone would hang from his heart the day Wally left Greenland. He had come to think of us as his very own children, and when we left his family would be left without friends. It was very sad to see this old man weep. The scene was so incongruous. In the middle of the room the drunken hunter lolled uncertainly on his feet and staggered over to Aima. She avoided his clumsy embrace. The heavy breathing of the sleeping women filled the silence as the old man beside me wiped the tears from his cheeks. 'Kari is a real little Inuk,' the old man continued. 'She speaks the Eskimo tongue like Wally and yourself.' He made an effort to control himself and stood up again. 'This is a song I borrowed from my father, Kaerngak,' he said, naming him with great pride. He beat out a soft quick rhythm against the plate Aima handed him. 'Aya ya ya, Aya ya ya yai,' he started, increasing the tempo of the drum. As he sang, his face became transfixed with the same marvellous smile. The sound rose and fell like the surge of a wave. Even the other old man seemed soothed by its rhythm and managed to keep quiet for a minute or two.

The sound seemed as if it could go on for ever. But the door flew open and the stumbling figure of Piuatok, supported under the armpits by half a dozen children, appeared in the doorway. He flopped on to a chair that I pushed in his direction. The muscles of his face had dropped, and his eyes looked twice their normal size, ringed around with a broad white band. The singing stopped and Taitsianguaraitsiak sat down. I turned towards Piuatok. His vacant eyes fell on me and focused with difficulty He dropped his head heavily again and struggled to rise to his feet. With a tremendous heave he got to his feet and lurched towards me.

His face thrust towards me and he spat, 'Kasdluna huna piumavok?' 'White woman, what do you want?' I said nothing, but got up. Aima walked over and spoke to him, but he elbowed her aside and grabbed the hood of my anorak. I tried to pick up the tape recorder but he yanked so violently that I dropped it and jerked myself free. He lunged for me as I dived for the door, and I could hear him falling heavily against the chairs as he bellowed something at me. I stumbled down the steps in the wake of several scrambling, shrieking children.

'Can you just hand me out the recorder?' I asked one of the older ones.

'No, I am frightened,' she said, huddling against the others.

A cold sweat broke out on me as I imagined how I would explain the loss of the recorder to Wally. I started to creep up the steps, in the hope that I could persuade one of the children inside to hand it out to me. I was halfway up when a scream of rage preceded the lumbering Eskimo, as he rushed through the door towards me. 'Run, Maria,' screamed the kids. The man landed on the bottom step and bellowed with anger and pain. I dashed around the side of the house, as he yelled something obscene at me.

'Where is she?' he asked the children.

'We do not know,' they said, standing at a safe distance, but too curious not to watch. I hid in the shadow of the house. I had heard of an Eskimo chasing people with an axe in Qanaq a few months earlier and I kept well away.

Another bellow sent me running towards the hills behind the house. I heard a small voice calling, 'This way. This way.' A young boy darted round the back of the church, clutching Wally's tape recorder. He beckoned me to keep to the shadows, and we ran right round the church and down through the back of the village to my house. I could have hugged the little fellow as he handed over the tape recorder with the furtiveness of a conspirator. We were all out of breath as I locked the door. I could not help laughing when I saw the stricken faces of the children.

'If I had a gun, I would shoot Piuatok,' said four-year-old Eto with vehemence.

'He is very bad,' the other children chimed in. 'We were so afraid.' They all held their hands over their hearts to show me that they were still thumping. I had to admit that mine was pounding too.

They clustered to the window to look out, and they noticed Taitsianguaraitsiak coming slowly down the hill towards the house. I let him in and sent one of the children for Wally. It was almost midnight. The old man sat down in the kitchen. He seemed for a while lost for words, and when he spoke his voice broke. 'I am sorry. I had not the strength to stop him.' When Wally returned I fetched Kari.

The old man broke down when he saw her. He was always so dignified and yet suddenly he was like a child. 'Ajor, Wally. You will leave one day—it will be like losing a son. I came here to sing for you, Wally, but another time—my heart is too heavy.' He drew himself up to go, slightly unsteady but with great dignity. He was the last of the Inuit. For me he represented the very best in his people.

The faint chug of an engine stole over the fog-grey sea. I recognized the trim vessel as it pushed through the curtain of mist. Inugssuak and Nauja were returning from summer camp. There was something a little erratic about the boat's course. It seemed to be going far too fast, straight towards the rocks. Suddenly it swerved away and made towards the sea again. A woman's voice screamed at the figure at the controls. I could hardly believe it was Nauja—though something in the sound made me think back to that first violent scene in the village when we first arrived. The boat turned, checking its speed and dropped anchor. The harsh voice of the angry woman continued. Then she began to scream as Inugssuak grabbed her by the hair and slapped her round the face. He shoved her roughly back into the cabin. From inside the boat a child wailed, 'Anana, Anana'. I turned away.

Kari had been out most of the day and I went across to Maria's to look for her. When I entered the room Avatak was lying on the floor, with glazed eyes. Maria was sitting on the bench above him, talking to one of the older women. She turned to me and smiled gently, a slight rosiness in her cheek and a light in her sparkling eyes.

'Avatak, you have got a visitor,' she said. I brought a chair into the centre of the room and sat down. 'I am glad you came,' continued Maria. 'I was just thinking about you. I wondered if you would like to try a little drink?' I said that really I did not feel like any at that moment. 'That is all right,' she said graciously. 'I would not force you to have any.'

At this moment Avatak staggered to his feet. 'Ah, I feel bad,' he said. 'I keep thinking about the day when you all leave, and I feel very bad. I think maybe my heart will be broken when I see Kari go. I love her like my little Eto.'

He knelt down beside my chair and put his head on my breast. Tears streamed down his cheeks. I felt embarrassed. His wife sat just a couple of feet away. What could I say if Wally walked in the door? 'Oh, we will be back sometime,' I said casually, extricating myself and going to sit beside Maria.

'Why are you afraid of him?' asked Maria. 'I am here—there is nothing to worry about.'

I made room for Avatak to sit between us.

'I could not sleep last night,' she said. 'I kept thinking about you going away and my heart felt very heavy. I cried. Soon all the children were crying. We will have no friends when you go. Nobody visits. And they are our own people! How will we be able to live?' Her voice began to rise and she buried her head in her hands, like a soul in distress. I felt very wretched. I, too, felt sad. But the atmosphere was hysterical and I felt I must not let myself give in to the dreadful depression. I pinched myself hard to stop myself crying, but found that try as I could I could not stop a few hot tears running down the sides of my nose.

An influx of children brought me to my senses, and soon the others stopped weeping. They both talked to me at once for a long time.

The gist of what they said was that they had grown very fond of us. They were rather unhappy that Wally did not visit very often, and it was not very friendly of him to borrow someone else's boat for the summer, instead of asking for the loan of theirs: after all they were our friends. They talked a great deal about Kari and finished by saying that they hoped she would visit Greenland once more before they died. As a token of friendship they took down a photo off the wall that I had admired for a long time. A photo of Avatak as a little boy with his parents outside one of the old-fashioned skin tents. I felt my presence made them more emotional. I promised we would try and visit them more often.

That evening we decided it would be best to have an early night. But before I could lock the door, one of Nauja's children called me to go and see her mother whom she said was 'ajorpok', 'bad'. I took a little medical kit with me. My friend was alone in the room. Her face was swollen with crying and a large bruise shone luridly from her temple. There was a line of congealed blood at the side of her mouth. She hardly saw me. Her eyes looked inward in utter desolation. I sat beside her and touched her hand, to try to communicate some warmth. I noticed a gash on one finger. I took her hand, examined the cut, and pressed a plaster over it. As I did so she grasped my hand and sobbed piteously, her head bent into the crook of her arm. I sat for about a quarter of an hour with her, till Inugssuak staggered in. His aspect frightened me. I had no intention of getting involved in arguments, so with a whispered word to Nauja I slipped out.

The next morning the village seemed dead. A thick fog blanketed everything. It was about four in the afternoon when I found a hastily scribbled note in Eskimo stuck under the mat in the porch. It was only by fluke that I found it, as I took up the mat to mend a tear in it. It was from Nauja and read: 'My dear friend Marie. I am leaving home but will still be on Herbert Island. I have a wound in my face which Inugssuak did. Maybe I will see you sometime when you take Kari for a walk. I would like to see my little girls too. Goodbye.' A little diagram was drawn to show where she was. It was crudely done and difficult to decipher. On first reading it I had not understood that she had actually run away. Only when I saw the children had I realized she was missing. They had no idea where she was. She had left the house when they were all asleep. As far as they knew no one had been to look for her.

I could never tell how disturbed the children were. They were very composed as they told me the details of the night before. Their father was very bad to Nauja, they told me. He had punched her and had cut a deep hole in her face with a broken cup. One side of her face was swollen, and her nose was battered. We cried, they said. I asked where their father had got his liquor : he was supposed to be on the black list. They told me he had drunk Spirit (methylated spirit). He is still asleep, they told me. They seemed more serious than usual, but otherwise no different.

I made some tea in a flask, gathered some food, and packed it all in the bucket I used to collect water. I crept out of the house while the children were playing with Kari. It was 10 p.m. It was still foggy but not too cold. I had put on a wind-proof parka with a thick lining, which I could leave with Nauja, if I found her. I did not know how much she would have taken with her.

I walked through the village to the meltstream where I usually got water. I met a few people on the way and waved to them as if nothing extraordinary had happened. The stream was at the back of the village, up in the hills. I made directly for it and then skirted along the slopes of the hills, giving the village a wide berth. In a few minutes I was out of sight. The snow had melted, forming huge lakes and marshes. My boots stuck in the mud and almost pulled off my feet when I tried to lift them.

I imagined Nauja would be near the shore, at a very old camp-site which I had discovered recently. The ground was flat where the old tent rings stood, but there were some caves in the rocks which would provide a good shelter. I followed a little path round the side of a meltwater lake. A patch of bright green luscious moss ahead startled me. In the centre of it was a huge blood-red stain. I remembered how my friend had tried to throw herself into the sea when we first arrived. My mouth felt dry and my knees weak.

I approached the moss stealthily. I hoped I would find nothing, but I had to look. About four yards from it I stopped. It was blood red and vivid even in the mist, but it was nothing terrible—that was its natural colour!

I made my way towards the sea and followed the broken coastline. In places a narrow band of thick ice clung to the shore. Elsewhere small pieces of broken berg balanced precariously on a rocky mound, left by the tide. No sound disturbed the eerie silence.

I knew Nauja would not show herself until she was quite sure who it was. I presumed she had found a cave to hide in. I wondered how I could let her know it was me without actually calling. I did not know how I would explain my presence if I did meet anyone. It seemed daft to be going for a walk in the fog at that hour of night. At last I hit on an idea. I would whistle. The problem was what. It had to be something the locals were unlikely to know. At last I had the answer. I walked for three hours and whistled 'God Save the Queen'.

But my search was fruitless. I returned home miserable and worried. Wally and Kari were still awake. Neither had felt much like sleep. Wally offered to look for Nauja, but I did not think it a good idea in case her husband got jealous. Besides, she might want to talk. I tucked Kari into bed but felt that I had to make another effort. This time I would search the opposite coastline. Wally was reluctant to let me go. I told him I would only be away at the most for a couple of hours.

I set out again, this time in the opposite direction. I looked in all the old stone huts. I inched my way along the narrow ledge that led to the hole in the cliff. The snowdrift outside it was still at least thirty foot deep and sloped dangerously down to the sea. I tested the ground carefully. If I fell in the drift no one would think of looking for me there. The cave looked black and terrible. I almost did not dare look inside. I whispered Nauja's name. There was no answer, but I had to look, in case she was asleep or even unconscious. I crept to the mouth of the cave and looked in. There was no one there, and I inched my way back along the ledge.

My search led me further along the coast, to another old camp-site, sunken and boggy. As I approached, a strident screech startled me. Soon others joined the horrible alarm. It was a group of Arctic terns. The graceful stream-lined birds appeared from all directions and squawked angrily at me. I grabbed a curved bone from the many that lay embedded in the moss and waved it frantically over my head. The birds hovered over me. I yelled and hissed at them and whirled the bone over my head. But they kept at me. I snatched frantically at anything that I could hurl up at them.

My bucket fell into the water and the contents spilled out, as I lunged away from the screaming birds. They pursued me, hovering and swooping, till I had crossed out of their territory. I felt tired and lonely. I made a wide detour inland and then gave up. My friend was nowhere to be seen.

I got to bed at 5.30 a.m., and slept till after midday. Nauja's children were playing outside when I got up and I went out to speak to them. Nauja had come back that morning. She was unwell, and still asleep. Their father had gone hunting in his boat and would be away several days.

I waited till later that evening to go and see my friend. I wanted to take some flowers to her but the flowers there were too tiny to gather. I looked through all my things: I felt I had to take something to her as a token of my friendship. The only thing I had was an ornamental egg coddler. It seemed a ridiculous gift to give, but it was very pretty, with delicate paintings of flowers and birds on it. I wrote a little note saying how very much I felt for her. I had not enough words in Eskimo to tell her what I really wanted to say. I wrapped the small parcel in tissue paper and put it in my pocket.

Inside Nauja's house the children were playing quietly. The usually tidy house was littered with clothes and unwashed dishes. A spilt cup still lay on its side on the table, the liquid splattered over the plastic cloth. Cigarette ends strewed the floor and a few empty bottles were slung in a corner. The air smelt fetid.

I tiptoed into the bedroom. Nauja lay on the bed facing the door. Her jersey was stained with blood. Her eyes were open, but hardly flickered when I approached. Her face was swollen and ugly. I could hardly recognize the attractive woman of whom I had grown so fond. I sat on the chair beside the bed and smoothed her brow. I had nothing to say, yet I wished to say so much. There was nothing I could do. I put down my poor offering and left. An impenetrable barrier separated me from my friend. She was the victim of the most dreadful violence and because of this she suddenly represented that violence. I felt utterly desolate.

20

The tension in the village had become unbearable.

Our things were packed. Wally had already made several trips with various items of our gear to the narwhal camp at the eastern end of the island. All that remained was Kari and her various clothing and some items of hardware.

We were pleasantly surprised when an old hunter from Qanaq offered to take Kari and myself by boat. The vessel was loaded with an assortment of shopping. Various members of the family and relatives crammed into it. I had Kari on my back. It was a lovely evening: there had been so many foggy days I was beginning to wonder if we would ever see the sun again. The water slapped the rocks and set the boat gently swaying. The engine purred into life and the boat turned away from the village towards the bergs that dotted the Sound.

I had not seen the hills in summer from this angle. It looked as if the whole island had been covered with a layer of sand. On top of this a giant hand had poured a handful of black dust, which had slid down to form a wide irregular band along most of the lower slope. Then the same hand had thrown patches of crimson, which had settled haphazardly along the steep hillside, and crowned it all with an irregular snow cap.

A ride of about ten minutes brought us in sight of the camp. A cluster of tiny tents clung on to the edge of the land. We spilled over the side of the boat on to the pink rocks. A steep, natural staircase led up to the grass. The steps were sticky and slippery in places from countless summers of whale hunting. Thick pieces of blubber clung to our boots. Time had coloured it a deep saffron and a thick layer of black dust had gathered on top. A human chain hastened the passage of food and gear from the boat to the space above. As we climbed higher our shoulders touched the stiff black meat, drying in strips on the overhanging rocks. I had brought a little girl with me from the village to stay with her aunt. I was glad of some company for Kari.

There were five tents besides ours. Huge boulders rose like fatted whales out of the grass, blackened and polished by the layers of meat and blubber that had lain on them. Smaller rocks lay everywhere, and huge slabs of pink, stratified rock poked from the ground at an angle, forming a natural den for the litters of pups. There was little open space. We searched for a furrow where we could pitch our tiny tent. Everyone rallied round to clear the ground and to tie the guy ropes. We put down a couple of foam mattresses on the floor of the tent. It looked very cosy. There were several small children in the camp. They were a bit older than Kari and more sure on their feet. They tottered between the tents, tumbling over the rocks like puppies, gathering the various flowers and eating them.

The view was breathtaking. The sea surrounded us almost in a complete circle. Giant bergs growled and grunted as large chunks were torn off by the current. Huge waves splashed around them, sending out myriads of tiny ripples. Slabs of pack ice drifted by, becoming smaller every day as they collided and broke. The sun bored into the pieces till they became watery and grainy and finally dissolved.

Across the water to the southeast the chain of glaciers that we had crossed with Geoff shone like burnished swords. Between them and us the white whale and narwhal, the unicorn of the sea, surfaced for air. Near them, the silent hunter, at one with the sea, waited in his frail kayak. The chase would sometimes last for hours, even as much as a full day and night, but the hunter would not give up, though his head swam and the thousand shimmering lights that the sun reflected from the sea blinded him and burned into his mind. Exhausted by the victory, he would return to camp insensate with fatigue. He would strip a portion of skin from the victim and his family would devour it immediately. Then the hunter would collapse into deep sleep. The hunt was over—the spirit had satisfied the flesh.

The children ran around, threatening to fall any minute into the piles of trash or blubber that littered the camp. They picked up the threads of sinew which a woman was splitting into strands to use later for sewing skins. They held it between their teeth like long strings of chewing gum. They were given a smaller piece to split, like their mother. They sat engrossed in the task for a few minutes. The sinew frayed and broke and dropped in discarded whorls around them.

A beautiful white puppy strayed from the warm belly of a lean bitch. It waddled down a slope, landing on its chin near a chunk of meat. Tiny fat hands reached down. It was roughly caught round its middle, its head lolling and its legs stretched out unnaturally. It squealed and blinked. Kari plodded over. An agonizing tug of war broke out between the two youngsters. The pup continued bleating. The faces of the children blazoned with battle. Their cries mingled into a fierce scream. The pup was rescued—the children pacified with a couple of larger, sturdier specimens.

The Eskimo is at his most traditional in summer camp. Here the influence of the white man is apparent only in minor details; the primus stove replaces the old blubber lamps, steel knives are an improvement on crude stone and bone tools; fabric tents are lighter and brighter than old-fashioned sealskin; matches save hours of toiling with sticks. But in other respects camp life is real Eskimo life.

The men scan the ocean for game. The women prepare the skins. The sealskins are scraped on a board or flat stone. Skins are pegged out on the ground or stretched between a wooden frame. The whale meat is cut in thin strips and laid on the rocks to dry. From time to time it is turned to let the moist underside catch the sun. The meat turns almost black. It has a nutty flavour and a consistency like toffee. It is very good when eaten with blubber or with mattak. Neither Wally nor I found mattak particularly satisfying on its own. Eaten with the dried meat, however, it seemed quite filling. Its great merit is its high vitamin C content—important in a region without fresh vegetables or fruit. In the summer camps, where food was plentiful and varied, everyone contributed something to the meal: dried whale meat, mattak, eider duck or some other bird, seal, walrus, or even eggs from the numerous bird colonies around.

We were delighted and grateful to be included in the social life of the camp. At meal times we were always invited. We could not supply meat ourselves, but we made up for this by contributing a selection of luxuries which were quickly demolished.

The sun shone on the front of the tent when we went to bed. The light pierced the thin orange material, casting a warm glow over our faces. The hours of sleep were erratic. The men hunted at any hour of the day and slept when they were tired. The waking and sleeping pattern of the Inuit was like a seesaw: only for a few hours in the day was everyone on the same level—either horizontal or vertical.

We sank into our sleeping bags. Only a faint cool breeze stirred the flap of the tent. Nothing could disturb the tranquillity of the hour. Through my sleep I heard a droning, like the approach of a large aeroplane. The air seemed suddenly to come alive with the clamour of voices. I woke. Kari was crying. Wally was just stirring in his sleep. Outside people ran around and called. A hand whipped open the flap of the tent and a head jerked through. 'Ujarkat, Ujarkat!' called a small boy.

'Rocks, Wally, Rocks!' I yelled, shaking the sleeping figure. We shot out of bags and rushed outside. A great roar came from high up the hillside. A broad furrow of snow collapsed. As it opened up, torrents of water gushed down the slope carrying streams of rolling, leaping rubble. It looked as if they would gouge a highway out of the rugged earth. In its path a huge boulder presented the only shoulder of resistance. The water slammed up against it, sending showers of spume high into the air, divided and spread out across the flattening hillside. The rocks rolled to a halt and the water ran on past the camping site to the sea. The new sound of waterfalls rose in the air.

In many places in the Arctic the mosquito and black fly launch such an assault in summer that life is made miserable. In Thule we were plagued by neither of these. I had always imagined that the people of the north must get tired of seeing the sun twenty-four hours of the day. But I had not counted on the fog which creeps in from the sea. It forms a natural curtain from the incessant brilliance of the sun and supports the plants that draw moisture directly from it—mosses and lichens especially.

We had had two days of fog. One of the hunters had been out hunting narwhal for three days. People began to scan the sea for his return. Thin veils of fog swirled around the necks of the bergs. Sparkling necklaces of light reflected tiny gaps in the clouds. Suddenly, a faint humming vibrated through the air. A dark shadow took substance on the grey sea. 'Kaudlutok tikipok,' 'Kaudlutok is returning,' a chorus of voices spoke in song.

A frail stream-lined kayak lay across a small boat. The outboard engine chugged toward the rocks beneath the camp. Large chunks of meat stained the boards of the boat. Frozen drips of blood hung in suspended animation from the slats which supported the butchered carcass. The young hunter smiled as he caught our glance. His wife scurried to help him with his catch, while his listeners stood absorbed in the details of the hunt.

But we had decided not to stay too long at this camp as we wanted to go up the fiords to look for salmon, and film the narwhal hunt.

21

'The children are dancing on the backs of the whales!' greeted Maria, pointing excitedly towards the harbour.

They were indeed. Eight white whales lay in the shallow water of the cove and the children sat on them, jumped on them and cut slices from their flesh to eat. Avatak had killed them in a show of bravura, as he raced ahead of the other hunters in his boat and forced the creatures into the shallow waters. He had shot indiscriminately at them in rapid succession and eight had fallen victim. Two had sunk as he had expected. That did not matter, the water was shallow enough for him to retrieve them.

'I am the king's wife today,' said Maria joking, arms akimbo as she surveyed the scene.

The whole village had collected to help flense the creatures, stripping the grey-white skin from off the thick layer of blubber which covered the flesh. The women separated the sinews from the flesh of the spine to make thread, while the men cut the large carcasses into pieces.

We sailed away from the busy scene en route for Kekertat—an island down one of the fiords. 'You will love it there,' said Maria. 'The water is always so calm, and it is so beautiful.' Since our return to the village it had been tidied up in expectation of a visit from the Community Chiefs from Godhab—a marvellous transformation.

When Wally had gone salmon fishing I joined the women and children searching the mud under the seaweed for mussels and clams. It was cold and wet. I had armed myself with a spoon and a tin to collect the awful slimy creatures. I had never seen such horrible specimens. Whether it was their colour (they were mostly grey) or their texture (they were mainly fleshy) or their movement (they all wriggled) I did not know, but they all revolted me. Tiny pink heads stuck out of the slime and squirted streams of yellow liquid at me as I bent to dig them out. I shuddered as I dropped the nasty creatures into the tin. Thank goodness we did not have to survive on them.

I had helped Maria de-bone a salmon that morning and score the flesh before hanging it out to dry. In the sun it was a beautiful translucent red. The other 'niko' (dried meat) that the Eskimos made from the whale looked like bits of old bark. We had sucked the bits of cold flesh off the bones—it was delicious and tasted as if it had been smoked.

A spell of very stormy weather had kept us indoors for a week. On the 16th of August the sun sank below the horizon for the first time. It was the end of summer. New ice began to form in tiny patches on the sea. Now as we got into the open sea, friendly Harp Seals jumped out of the water, and the curious Ringed Seals inspected our boat and disappeared with a splash.

There was a lot of ice in the fiord. The island was low-lying and rocky, flanked by two beautiful green glaciers. The little huts stood haphazardly in front of a small lake. There was a friendly atmosphere and the locals greeted us warmly. From the village we could see the whole of Herbert Island, sixty miles to the west.

We were offered one of the empty houses to live in. It was sparsely furnished, with one chair, a very broad wooden sleeping platform, a chest of drawers and a coal stove. A few crumpled photographs hung on one wall and the windows were grimy and cracked.

Wally was anxious to get out and film the narwhal hunt but the ice had left the fiord late this year and there were not so many narwhal about. It was getting late in the season. There was little food in the village—stormy weather blew pans of ice into the cove which prevented the kayaks from going out. Even when the men could hunt they were away for hours before finding even one seal. This had not been a good summer for them.

At last Wally had a chance to accompany one of the hunters on a hunt for narwhal. The male of these sea mammals has a single tusk that grows out of the left side of its jaw. These magnificent spiralled tusks can reach lengths of as much as ten feet. Wally had to row for about six hours, and then wait like a hawk for the animals to appear.

While he was away I visited some of the villagers. A few I had met when they had visited Kekertassuak. There was something very un-usual about the place. It was off the beaten track, on the route to nowhere. Here I noticed mothers suckled their four-year-old children.

Of course the children ate as normal children, but on impulse they would run to their mothers and fumble with her clothes till she bared a breast for them. In the old days the Eskimos would suckle their children very late, but this was the only village I had seen it happen.

Kekertat was really kayak country. Because it was deep in the fiord, they were not permitted to hunt by motor boat, in case the noise disturbed the game. It was lovely to walk through the village. It was the cleanest I had seen. The kayaks were hoisted on light frames along the beach, which was cluttered with the bones of whales.

In one house I visited, a little boy of two sat perched in a kayak which his father had made for him. It was exactly half the size of a man's kayak and was perfect in every detail. It was suspended from a drying frame an inch above the floor. The child sat wide-eyed as he wavered in the gently rocking kayak.

A perfect sense of balance is necessary to handle the kayak. Each kayak has its own centre of balance, no two are exactly the same, and they are made to fit the owner as snugly as a glove. The slightly raised opening in the centre is just wide enough for him to squeeze through. With most of them it would be almost impossible to get out in a hurry and if it capsized a hunter could easily drown.

In Kekertat the children were trained from infancy, first in the home and then on the edge of the shallow lake or at the edge of the sea. On occasions a kayaker might lose his sense of balance through exhaustion, or sometimes permanently through sickness. Occasionally he might be afraid to go out in case he is overcome by the dizziness that afflicts a hunter sitting motionless for hours in the sun, dazzled by the water. Many young hunters have lost their lives this way.

Before setting out each man examines his craft carefully to make sure there are no tears or thin patches. The wife deftly sews a piece of skin over a worn patch, as a leak could be fatal.

I sat outside the hut waiting for Wally to return. It was sundown. The children played a dangerous game of floe-hopping on the beach. One floe broke and a child fell through, but the tide was low and she suffered no injury. Other children whirled and pranced on a huge boulder, silhouetted in gold against the setting sun. They laughed and shrieked as they tried to tread on each other's toes.

It was after sundown when the hunter and Wally returned. The cove was choked with pans of ice and the boats, with the kayaks along the deck, wove their way through to the beach. In the wake of the first boat was a narwhal. The villagers flitted silently down to the water's edge to help with the flensing. The scene could have taken place centuries ago.

On the way back to Qanaq we made a detour to a small settlement, where the parents of one of the women on Herbert Island lived, with a son of eighteen. The two old folk were well over sixty but the old man still went out in his kayak after seal. There were only three huts in this little hamlet, and they were all made of turf like the houses the Inuit used to live in long ago.

There was a pastoral atmosphere about the place. In a dip between rugged cliffs, rolling turf-covered hills formed a backdrop for the tiny shacks. A gentle trail of smoke rose from the chimney of the only house in use, while outside a few dogs rested in the spongy ground, docile as sheep. Behind the huts there were several ruined stone dwellings, now covered with grass. It must once have been a great camp, when the sea was rich in seal and whale. The ground was littered with bleached bones.

A magnificent berg stood a few hundred yards from the shore. Although the sun was at the wrong angle for filming, I begged Wally to try. While he did so, I took the tiller for the first time in my life. I cannot imagine what the old folks thought when they saw us arrive. For the few minutes before we floated on to the beach we had careered in circles, as I tried to control the speeding craft. It was not that it was unresponsive—on the contrary, the faintest touch of the tiller and it swung into action.

'For heaven's sake, practise a bit before going near that ice,' pleaded Wally, as he struggled to keep his footing.

I managed to hold to a speed just faster than a complete standstill, and we wove our way through the pans of ice towards the shore.

A wizened old man in polar-bear pants, clean anorak and peculiar peaked cap came down to the shore to greet us. I had met him once at Herbert Island, but now he was surprised to see us. His wife, a short woman of seventy-nine, waddled over to us from where she had been scraping a sealskin. They were very kind and took us into the house for a cup of tea.

The walls of the house were covered with pages of newspapers and magazines which looked as old as the house. I had an urge to browse round, reading them all. The old man's grey hair sat like a fallen halo around his head. He told me proudly he had caught three seals the day before. He pulled a small narwhal tusk from under the bed. He had captured it himself the year before. It was marvellous to see such a fit old man. He had no boat, but relied solely on the kayak in summer: in winter he used his dogs. His son was away in Kekertat and would return with friends in a few days. The old couple were lonely sometimes, but they had got used to living on their own. The land was good and there were huge salmon, as long as your leg.

We had brought them some supplies, as we knew they could not get to the village unless someone came to collect them. They were very pleased and just as we left the old man handed Kari his narwhal tusk as a present. I was moved by this gesture—it was his only trophy and might be the last narwhal he would catch.

We could not stay long, as we had a four-hour journey ahead of us to Qanaq. As we started the boat the old woman squatted on a stone and lit her pipe. An enormous meat rack—bigger than I had ever seen— loomed over her. There was plenty of meat on the rack. The old man was a good hunter.

The return to Qanaq seemed long and cold. The sun was setting as we arrived, firing the bergs with an iridescent glow. A kayak darted between the coloured ice-islands in the direction of the far glaciers. The whales were leaving the fiord. Another year's cycle was over, another season was complete.

22

Over a year had passed since we first came to Thule. For me the year had been tremendous. The challenge had tried my mettle and left me honed and rid of the superficial varnish of 'civilized living'. I had come to grips with life in an environment more hostile than I had ever known, but I had drawn from the people all the warmth I needed. I loved Greenland—her grandeur was inspiring as well as awesome.

In reflective mood I turned towards the hills one day in October. I stood for a minute beside a huge boulder embedded in the permafrost. It towered above me with its face covered with a brilliant orange lichen. I rubbed my nail idly over the flaky fungus—till I remembered that it took lichen years to grow. So many Arctic plants took years between germinating, growing leaves and stems, and finally flowering. It seemed a shame to pick them.

I climbed up on to the cold stone and sat in reverie. My eyes travelled full circle over the wild scenery. Pans of ice speckled the sea. The hunters' small boats picked their way carefully through the obstacles. They were out every day, as soon as it was light, to make the most of the hunting before they hauled their boats out of the water for another nine months. At the end of October the setting sun would salute a dying summer and another winter would begin. The salmon had already left the rivers and the water in the fiords was getting colder. Even the whales had left, sneaking past the watchful hunter in his kayak.

My thoughts travelled back over the thirteen months we had been in Northwest Greenland. I had lived with a sense of peril that members of an effete society have to pay dramatists to create. Like the audience of a Greek drama I felt purged in my spirit. I looked towards the little village. Most of the Eskimos on the island and those of the surrounding settlements had lived in Dundas before the Americans came in 1952, with their thundering machinery, to build an airbase. This massive military installation had accommodation for up to ten thousand men—a strategic airbase, a multi-million dollar investment in peace, with four radar screens on constant watch for long-range missiles directed from the Eurasian land mass at targets in the West. The Eskimos complained that the aeroplanes had driven the game away. They did not believe that a change in climate was responsible, as they were told.

Some families went south. A few came north to Murchison Sound, where they were offered small box-like wooden houses as compensation for having been uprooted. A cluster of such houses made up our village of twelve men, twelve women, and twenty-six children. None of them were aware of the protective umbrella of radar beams above their heads. Few of them were aware of the hatred and turmoil in the world, or of the great imbalance of poverty and wealth among the 3,900 milion people to their south.

A small village of people, north of all problems except their own—proud people whose problems are unique, for their tribe now numbers only 600. The last of the Inuit are descendants of what must surely be the hardiest and most adaptable race the world has known in half a million years of evolution.

Many people feel that this last unspoilt tribe of Eskimos should be preserved in their innocence—protected from anthropologists, from writers and film-makers, and from the whole insidious influence of our civilization. But it is too late already. Their fate was determined long before we came along, by the fortunes of the fur traders and the zeal of the missionaries. Had the tribe been geographically less remote or had the trade in furs been less profitable, the story might have been different. As it was, they were encouraged to stay where they were—north of all other people on earth—and in a sense hunt for money. From the trading store they bought knives, guns, matches, wood; they replaced their skin boats with motor boats, their stone dens and igloos with wooden huts, and their ancient drum songs with Christian hymns. Within three generations of being (as they thought) the only human creatures on the face of the earth, they have come to accept not only the white man but his system of commerce and his God.

'The phenomenon of the Thule Eskimos,' Wally maintained, 'is not the speed at which they became "civilized" but the fact that they alone among the Eskimos have remained convinced of the pre-eminence of their race, in spite of what they have seen or been told the white man has accomplished. It is their naïve conviction that a man is not a real man unless, like them, he is a hunter who drives his dogs on the thin ice of autumn and throughout the long dark winter. Only real men, like them, still drive their dogs thousands of miles in search of bears each spring and in the summer haul walrus and whales out of the sea, collect ice for water, move drums of fuel, and even shift their boats with the pulling power of their dogs.'

I wondered how much longer they could remain so proud and independent. In the past, whole tribes were wiped out by famines and epidemics, children were killed by dogs or accidentally suffocated on the communal bed. Cannibalism was not uncommon, nor in certain circumstances was it uncommon for parents to kill their newborn babies in order to reduce the number of mouths to feed.

As a race, the Eskimos survived, however, not in spite of the famines and epidemics but, ironically enough, because of them. For a hunter is not a man of free will, he is a child of nature, his very life dependent upon his observance of nature's strictest law that a predator must live in balance with his prey. For over a thousand years the population of the Thule tribe remained relatively stable : blood feuds, famines, and accidents kept their numbers in check. Then white men came with medical aid, and saved the lives of so many children that the population doubled in less than ten years.

As a hunting tribe they can now survive only by dispersing or by shipping their children to the fishing ports of the south. I remembered the discussion I had had with Maria about the future of our children. She, like me, knew there must be change—even her own son had whispered that he was afraid of being a hunter and that he could earn more money working in the store : her own daughters had complained that the duties of a hunter's wife were too hard and that they wanted to marry men with some other occupation. Change was inevitable.

Our sojourn in Greenland had been a happy time for Kari. Here there was an enormous natural playground to explore. There were no restrictions; no set times for meals, no hours or minutes or bedtimes, none of the discipline and pressure of learning to which so many European children are subjected, none of the stress and bitterness of the competitive world in which she would have to live.

We had grown used to the fact that she spoke only Eskimo. It amused and pleased the locals, but I felt some concern that she was not growing up bilingual. I did not want her to be at a disadvantage when we returned to England and I worried that it might slow her development. The stimulus the year in Greenland had provided was excellent but it was not enough for a child that would have to take her place in our western society. I felt that as she grew older she needed greater stimuli than she was getting, especially now that she was at an age when she could learn so much.

As the youngest child in the village, Kari was indulged by everyone and I hoped it would not spoil her. Her fingers were allowed to stray into every door and cupboard without reproach when she was in the locals' houses. It was therefore upsetting for her when she was forbidden the use of expensive equipment or books that were the essential tools of our trade. The villagers looked askance at my concern, for they, like Kari, were unaware of the value of things. The Eskimos take no pride in possessions : even their rifles were rusty and scratched. It was difficult to explain to my friends that Kari would have to learn manners, and that as she grew up she would have to live within a rigid system of law and order—these were concepts that were alien to the Eskimo mind. They practised no etiquette that conformed to our standards, and they acknowledged no chiefs.

It was natural that Kari, who spent so much time with Avatak and Maria, should, like their own children, call them Anana and Atata—mother and father. This did not bother me. But it did concern me that when she wanted her own way she should run to them for support—which was readily given. It was not a serious matter at this age but I felt it was potentially a problem.

These thoughts, together with our concern for our families, and the nagging ache in my back, made me think about going home for a few months with Kari. I wrote to my parents to say that I would be home for a while in the new year. Wally would stay on in the hut, and I hoped to rejoin him in May. There were still gaps in our filming which he hoped to fill before we finally left Greenland the following August.

Preparations for winter began as soon as the sea ice formed, but the whole village was impatient until it was firm enough to travel on. It set later this year than usual. The hunters sat fixing their nets till it was thick enough to walk on. This year everyone in the village laid nets beneath the ice and the catch was plentiful. The racks groaned under the weight of seal and the women boasted that it was like spring. Every day two or three seal were brought into the house to thaw. The pelts were not as pretty as those of the spring seals. The women combed their fingers through them for lice. I bought three to have an amaut made, and Migishoo took great pride in making it. I had always been fascinated by this garment which the women wore when they carried their babies on their backs. It looked beautiful, with its intricate pattern : but the smell was powerful, and even Migishoo joked about the reaction I would get if I walked into my parents' house wearing it.

This winter we made sure we would be better organized than last. Wally overhauled the Skidoo so that he could use it, as soon as there was enough snow, to drag the heavy barrels from round the cove to a ledge in front of the hut. Like last year the coal was stacked against one wall, but the stock of ice we had planned on fetching was difficult to find in the mass of broken pressure surrounding the village. All the ice around the village was salty and Wally had to drive a couple of miles to an iceberg to bring back some fresh ice. It was almost the end of November before we had the hut repainted, new curtains on the windows and a couple of new lamps to replace the old ones.

We planned a trip to Qanaq to do some shopping in the last few days of November. We wanted to be away from the island at the time of the new liquor ration. We had begun to dread these monthly drinking bouts, because now, unlike the first few months when the villagers had kept their distance during these sessions, they began to visit and to bring their drink with them. Their intentions were friendly enough but it was disturbing to see them reduced in their drunken state to pathetic caricatures of themselves.

With my first sledging trip of the season all the excitement of travelling swept over me again. I nestled against Kari as we passed the dark icebergs, with their jagged profiles. Qanaq seemed alive with people and the store was crowded with visitors from other settlements come to do their Christmas shopping. We stopped by the tiny office to collect our mail and hurried up the hill to Orla's home to open the bundles of letters and parcels.

The news of the death of Wally's father came as a sad blow to us. It did not take us long to realize that we might be needed at home. We felt we should all go home for Christmas, and then Wally could return to Greenland some time in the New Year.

There was suddenly a mad rush to get ready. We heard that there was a flight from Thule on 12th December. The commercial flights flew to London via Copenhagen but there was the problem of getting to Thule with Kari. We had the choice of going by Skidoo or by dog sledge. Wally favoured the Skidoo, as it would be faster, but a lot colder. There was one problem, however, there was no snow on the glacier and this might make it very difficult for the Skidoo. Ideally we needed a dog team to accompany us in case of emergency. There were many hunters who would only be too willing at a fee of £100, but we felt that Avatak might want to be the one to accompany us. On the other hand we did not want to ask him outright, in case, for any reason, he would rather not, but would be too embarrassed to say no. With these thoughts in mind we hurried back to Herbert Island to pack our things.

If we were to allow four days to travel in and a day at Dundas to recover, we should leave Herbert Island on 7th December—in two days' time. Wally had cabled his mother to say we would be home in time for Christmas, but as we followed the sledge tracks over the sea ice, England seemed a long way away.

We had not been back from Qanaq for more than a few minutes when Maria breezed into the hut. She was the new storekeeper and had been working in the store when we arrived. She shivered and hunched her shoulders, blowing into her cupped hands. Kari was over with Avatak as the hut was icy when we arrived and was only just beginning to warm up. When we got in it had been −14°C.

'What a lot of smoke,' Maria complained, screwing up her face at the acrid smoke belching out of the top of the stove. She slammed the door of the flue shut with her foot and looked at me as if I were a naughty child.

'It's the wood, it always smokes,' I excused myself unwillingly.

She nodded, with a half-smile, as if she had heard it all before, and peered over at the oil stove in the other room to make sure it had caught.

'There's a lot of walrus,' she said, proudly indicating somewhere to the northwest of the island. 'Maybe Wally would like to go hunting.'

It was the moment I had been dreading. 'We are all going home the day after tomorrow,' I blurted out. I tried to look busy as the information sank in. 'Wally's father has died and we must go. But we shall be back before the summer.' I glanced regretfully at her, sad that I had to bring back such news from our trip.

She nodded thoughtfully, and the light went out of her eyes. 'How are you going?' she asked, with concern.

'I don't know. Maybe by Skidoo, maybe by dog sledge. Maybe both. I am not sure who we will take.'

A heavy silence followed. There seemed nothing to talk about that was not upsetting. Maria seemed suddenly unsure of herself.

'We will be back,' I said, murmuring, 'if God wills' as an afterthought. I did not want to make promises that for some reason I might not be able to keep. I think Maria appreciated my honesty.

'I'll come and help you later,' she said with a great effort to be cheerful. Turning on her heel, she left the hut.

When Wally came in from outside, we decided we must pay a courtesy visit on Avatak to tell him the news. He and Maria looked grave when we walked in but they tried to act as if nothing had happened. A cup of tea was put before us. Kari and Eto were in high spirits in the bedroom and that seemed to emphasize the sadness of the occasion.

Wally explained why we were going away so soon. Our friends listened silently, except for the occasional murmurings of sympathy. We mentioned our travelling plans, but avoided the name of anyone specific to accompany us. With the promise of plentiful walrus there would not be many who would wish to travel such a distance when they could do some unexpected hunting instead. We talked about the hunting and Wally casually asked Avatak if he were going after walrus.

'No,' he replied without hesitation. 'It is too dark.'

This was another factor we had wondered about. It was getting near Mid-winter's Day, the darkest time of the year. Mid-winter this year coincided with a full moon, but it still meant that we would be travelling when it was very dark.

There was the safety of Kari to think about. Many Eskimo children travelled great distances by sledge even in the winter but that was with parents who had been over the route countless times and who themselves had travelled the same distances by sledge when they were children. With us it was different. We were not used to taking a child on a journey of that distance. The considerations were enormous. Would the Skidoo hold? Would we be able to pad the sledge sufficiently so that in the event of an accident Kari would be completely protected A hundred and one thoughts crowded our heads and we returned to our hut to try and sort them out.

Our efforts at packing were interrupted by Avatak and Maria, who suddenly seemed to have a change of humour. 'Avatak's been drinking a bit,' explained his wife, as he greeted Wally loudly, and handed him a package.

'Jutdle pidluarit', I could hear him saying. 'Happy Christmas'. There was the sound of rustling paper and a delighted gasp from Wally as he produced a beautifully-made sealskin anorak.

'Try it on, try it on,' urged his friend. Our visitors stood back in pride to examine their gift.

'My, that looks good,' laughed Maria. Wally had to turn round as we all commented.

'It is really beautiful,' I said to our two smiling friends.

5. Little auks come in hundreds of thousands to the bird cliffs of Siorapalouk.
The catchers climb the mountains of broken rocks and hide in small hollows . . .

There is an art in plucking the birds out of the sky . . .

There is even an art in bringing the net in . .   But after the sport—is it worth it?

26. There are only three old turf huts still occupied in the Thule District. This old couple live many miles from the settlement. One son of nineteen lives with them and helps the old man to hunt. Another visits in his boat from time to time and brings them provisions from the store.

27. Kari made friends with t old people right away. Insid the hut was lined with old newspapers and magazines. The old wooden platform serves as bed or seat and, a in all Eskimo houses, the teapot and coffee pot are always ready for use.

'Yes. We wondered what we could give Wally. But you had an amaut made recently, and we felt it only right that Wally should have something made of sealskin too.'

'I bet the people in England will want to take a photo of you in this,' added Avatak. He stood mockingly to attention as he mimicked the pose.

It was good to see our friends happier. I hurried to make a meal of fried caribou steaks. Maria called me outside to see her present for me. She had no wrapping paper and wanted it to be a surprise. It was a beautifully made hunter's stool. Occasionally, when the men were hunting at a blow hole they had to wait for hours for a seal and they sat on a three-legged stool. The seat part was made from the triangular shoulder bone of the walrus and the legs from bones from another part of the animal. Around the 'feet' of the stool they always placed a covering of polar-bear skin so that it would not scrape on the ice and frighten the game away. The legs were lashed with rope made from the Bearded Seal. It had to be securely made so that it would not creak.

Maria watched my face, and beamed at my compliments. 'I knew you wanted one,' she said delightedly. 'But we had such a job to find three male walruses the same size for the leg bones.' She mimicked Avatak rushing to measure them. He laughed with some embarrassment. He was never completely at ease when Maria made her jokes.

We were delighted with our presents, and of course we had some for our friends. Mysteriously Wally beckoned Avatak outside and showed him a type of two-seater tandem attachment for the secondhand snow scooter Avatak had bought recently off one of the Danes in Qanaq. Avatak came bounding back into the hut, clapping his hands and whooping with delight.

Maria sat laden with lengths of cloth for herself and the children, while Kari struggled to hand her the assortment of small items from her. 'Oh I am so pleased with these,' she admitted. 'I did not know what to do for their new anoraks. There is nothing worth buying in the store.'

The atmosphere was more relaxed. While I finished cooking the meal Avatak had a long talk with Wally and drew him diagrams of the route. 'There is hardly any snow,' he said gravely. 'It will be very difficult by Skidoo. You need dogs as well. I will bring my team and together we will make it.' He looked lovingly at Kari and leant towards her. 'I will take you to Dundas,' he confided, 'because you are my greatest friend.'

23

It was a clear day when we set off from Herbert Island on our journey to Dundas. Already in early afternoon the last of the twilight had vanished, to leave us in darkness, except for a vast canopy of stars. Within the orange shelter Wally had built for us on the sledge hung a hurricane lamp and Kari was bundled in furs and sleeping bags against the back, so hidden in the folds that the only clue to her existence was a little puff of vapour where her warm breath met the chill air.

Avatak waited for us on the ice. Occasionally his light flashed from the darkness. I could not find Maria. A crowd of well-wishers surrounded the sledge, and a tearful Migishoo shook hands with me. 'Safe journey, and may you return happily to see us,' the little hunter called.

The Skidoo roared into life. The exit in front of the village was water-logged in the high tide and we made a circuitous tour of the huts to look for a new route. 'This way,' called a voice out of the darkness: the lithe figure of Maria appeared in the headlight, pointing down to the ice. A few seconds later she was behind the sledge with me, helping guide it through the maze of rocks.

'Jump on,' said Maria, as we hit the level ground. Darting ahead, she sprang nimbly on to the boxes at the front. Wally glanced round and, seeing a figure on the sledge, assumed it was me. Before I could reach the front runners he quickened speed. I could only grab the handlebars as the vehicle sped past. I pounded along behind, shouting myself hoarse to attract his attention, but the engine roared mockingly and belched acrid fumes in my face. I was lost in the shadows behind the sledge and had to run very fast to keep up. My clothes were bulky. In seconds I was perspiring furiously. I gasped for breath and felt weak at the knees.

Maria leant across to see what delayed me—and burst into laughter when she saw what had happened. After a run of four hundred yards, we at last reached the pressure, and Wally was forced to slow down. I lunged frantically towards the front of the sledge and fell in a heap beside Maria. 'Oh, I am dead!' I gasped between breaths.

'However will you get up the glacier if that short run tired you out?' she asked good-humouredly.

I shrugged my shoulders. At the moment I did not care. Even the discomfort of finding I was sitting on the handle of a jerry can could not make me move off the sledge.

Once over the pressure we swept round in a wide arc in front of the village towards the waiting team. Twenty-eight tiny lights appeared in the dark as the eyes of the curious dogs turned towards the Skidoo. Seconds later the hunter leapt gracefully on to his sledge as it shot into motion ahead of us. The moment had come at last: we were away.

For a while Maria sat silently beside me. Her two sons appeared suddenly: they had run out from the village and they waved excitedly as we sped past.

'I am going soon,' said Maria calmly. She held out her hand. 'Inudluarit, Marie,' she whispered as our eyes met. A second later there was a touch on my arm and Maria slipped off. 'Look back,' she called as I waved. I turned and watched for several minutes where she stood with the brilliant beam of her flashlight directed towards us. As I gazed, the light danced and seemed to suffuse the person holding it. I blinked, and the vision vanished. The light came on one final time, and died. Dear Maria —how I should remember her: at first tough and resilient, like an Arctic plant, with its surprisingly delicate blossom, and finally, a symbol of peace, the only light in the darkness.

It was some time before I sought the shelter of the 'tent'. The ice was a jumble of splintered ramps which fell away in brittle confusion in every direction. The dogs were better on this surface than the snowmobile, which crawled tortuously between the maze of obstacles. I felt hot still from my exertions and the sweat clung to my clothes, making them clammy and uncomfortable. When the belt of rough ice was past I crawled through the flap of material and sank back against the slumbering Kari. I put a hand inside her clothes to satisfy myself that her face was warm, and a little jet of hot air fanned the tips of my fingers.

I was surprised to find that I had taken our departure so calmly. Maybe it was because I could not quite believe we had actually left the island. Or maybe I was so definitely sure we would return. The sledge jogged steadily forward for a while. I sat back and relived the last two days.

There had been no time to relax. Migishoo had come hurrying in after Avatak and Maria left two nights before. 'Ajor, you are leaving. Maria has just told me,' she said breathlessly. 'But it will be good for your family to see you. I know just how a mother feels.' She paused and looked at me sadly. Then, remembering why she had come, she demanded to see all our kamiks and fur clothes. I fished them out of the bags they had been stored in since the last winter and let Migishoo look over them with her practised eye. The Eskimos would always make sure that we had the right clothes before we went on a journey—they knew only too well that proper clothing sometimes meant the difference between life and death.

She peered myopically at them all and complained that she could hardly see a thing without her glasses. She would have to examine them more closely later. I found all the weak spots and we filled an enormous red sack with the stuff for her to take away. 'Nihima', 'Father Christmas', I teased her as she went out the door.

'Yes, I feel like him,' she chuckled.

'Don't you want any help with that load?' I asked.

'No, no,' she snapped. 'I am not decrepit.' I laughed. Migishoo hated any suggestion that she was not fit.

That night neither Wally nor I could sleep. At last he spoke, 'What's it with you?' he asked.

'Oh, just thinking about things,' I answered non-committally.

'How many times have you slid backwards down the glacier?' he asked intuitively.

I had to agree that that was one thing which had been bothering me. I had noticed, even in Qanaq, how the Skidoo slithered uncontrollably on ice. It was after all a snow scooter, and had not been designed to tackle glaciers. We were gambling on there being enough pockets of snow for it to hold. At least, if we did get stuck, we could transfer to Avatak's sledge. But that would mean dumping some of the baggage and making two trips.

I had wondered if it was irresponsible to take Kari such a long distance—over ninety miles—in the depths of winter. My memories of the trip I had made down the glacier with Wally and Geoff sent a chill down my spine. She would have to be strapped in maybe, on certain parts of the route, in case she fell off. What would happen if the sledge tipped over? How would we know that we were not wandering off the route? How often we had found we were going off at a tangent in the dark. The glacier changed slightly from year to year and the locals had warned that there were a couple of wide cracks this side of the col where there were normally none.

Coping with Kari would not be easy. We would have to make several stops for her. The covering on the sledge did not allow for much movement, so we would have to erect a tent to change her clothes and to let her stretch her legs in the warmth while we made a brew. There was the danger that she might get cold feet or hands. At least adults knew that it was important to keep the circulation going by wriggling these from time to time.

We spent ages working out the pros and cons of the trip. It was a great responsibility for Wally to have to take a wife and daughter that long distance. There was the fear of bad weather blowing up, the fear of difficult ice conditions and always the fear of the unexpected. But Wally was never one to shirk a challenge, and once he had satisfied himself that it was feasible and that he had worked out the answer to every kind of problem, the journey was on.

The following day we had invited the whole village to a little party— the children in the afternoon and the adults later. The hut was packed to capacity, but we managed to provide an unending supply of coffee and cakes. I had spent ages wråpping gifts for everyone in coloured paper. Geoff had sent most of the things up to me during the summer, and they had been hidden away till now. Everyone had brought a little token present for us which they had hastily carved or sewn.

With so many people inside and the fire roaring, to provide more water the temperature in the hut was stifling. There was an unusual stiffness about everyone, as if they felt the occasion called for a certain decorum. And when they left they all lined up with touching formality to bid us safe journey. I had a lump in my throat as I faced all these kind people. Their faces crumpled unhappily as they wiped their eyes.

The saddest moment of all had been that morning just before we left, when Maria's children had come to say goodbye to Kari. They were shy and unsure: they bent towards her, wondering whether they should kiss or shake hands. Maria turned away and wept, and I embraced the little children I loved so much. 'No crying!' I whispered, almost sternly. 'We will be back in summer and we will live in tents together like last year and hunt for birds' eggs in the hills—it will be great, won't it?' They nodded eagerly, wanting to believe it. I knew how upset they were to lose their little friend. We had all looked forward to a second Christmas together. I hoped it would not spoil their enjoyment of this one.

The night before we left Wally and Avatak had worked outside till midnight, when they joined Maria and myself inside for a nightcap. There was something intimate about the group and we talked together like people keeping vigil. Maria joked that Wally's sledge was so heavy that it would just get to the top of the glacier and slide back. Wally smiled wryly. He had spent ages fixing a tunnel-like covering to the sledge so that Kari and I would be protected from the wind. With the speed of the Skidoo the wind chill would be high. Avatak suggested lighting a primus inside the shelter as they sometimes did in their boats, but I did not like the idea of an open flame in such a confined space. We discussed how I should attract Wally's attention in an emergency, and decided I should have a flashlight which I could shine on to the snow beside him.

'Just write a few lines occasionally to let us know how you are,' asked Maria. 'A few words will do.'

I promised I would. Avatak contemplated his boots for a while in silence as he sat on the edge of the wooden platform. 'The weather's good,' he said at last, and glanced at Wally, who nodded in relief. Soon after they rose to leave. 'Sinitdluaritse,' 'Sleep well', they said, as if it was a word they had never spoken before, but saved for this special occasion. 'Sinidluaritse,' we returned.

On a short walk to the site of the other hut Maria and I had chatted about many things. 'I shall miss these hills,' I had confessed. 'I think we shall have to find a house in England that overlooks the sea.'

'Why, are there any houses that don't?' Maria had asked.

The question had surprised me until I remembered that most of Greenland was covered by the great icecap, and all houses had to be built on the comparatively flat coast line. In Greenland every house overlooked the sea. The thought of living in a place where you could not see it was appalling to Maria.

She chatted about the things I would find different when I returned, and suddenly exclaimed, 'Ah, Marie, you will see the sun !'

'Of course, I had forgotten,' I answered.

'What will you say when you see it?' she asked curiously.

'I shall say hello,' I replied, without thinking.

She laughed. 'How marvellous to see the sun in winter.'

I wondered whether Maria and Avatak would regret giving their friendship to us. How often they had been warned not to get too close.

'Kasdlunas would never make good friends,' they were told. 'They always go away and forget the people they have left behind.' I hoped they would not feel it too much. There was so little in their lives compared with ours. We had friends and family to return to and the promise of days full of activity. I must not abandon these people who had been so good to us.

My thoughts whirled ahead of me, as we jolted and lurched over the slightly uneven surface, towards the world we were returning to. It was a while before I could forget the scores of problems that buzzed in my mind. A sudden chill wind cleared my mind as I battled with the flap at the front of the tent to hold it down. The Skidoo had started to pick up speed now that we had passed the rough ice, and I began to feel the cold. I wondered how Wally was, without anything to protect his face. At that moment the vehicle slowed down. Seconds later heavy footsteps crunched towards the sledge.

'You all right?' enquired Wally from the darkness as he peered in.

I nodded and murmured a reply.

'I will stop from time to time to see you're O.K. Let me know if you want anything.'

He trudged back again. It was marvellous travelling with Wally—he was so attentive. I was so lucky to have been introduced so gently to the Arctic. I always remembered him explaining to me the secret of being a good expedition member, 'You should always try and do more than your share.' He certainly did more than his.

We made a stop a couple of hours later on the approach to the moraine in front of the glacier. The route around the side, which I remembered from the previous trip, was no longer the same. We had to cross a band of newly formed pressure before we got to a narrow ledge of ice at the foot of the moraine, which we had to traverse carefully, if we were not to slither sideways into the fractured ice. Blocks of broken floe and berg were held together by a waxy paste of new ice, which bent underfoot. The Skidoo ran at the slope and whined and trembled, stuck on the brink of a narrow chasm. The engine raced and the tracks stuck deep into the icy quagmire. Avatak skidded over the ice to help Wally, and the two men struggled to keep their footing as they hauled on the machine. I clawed my way up the pressure and tried to help by driving the snow-scooter while the men went to the back of the sledge to push, but the vehicle just bit deeper into the mush. As I stepped off I slipped, landing painfully on the ice.

'You had better go on up,' advised Wally, 'we will cope with this.'

I crawled the few yards to the moraine as the men tugged on the rope which attached the sledge to the scooter. It moved enough for the Skidoo to inch over the chasm. As it reached flatter ice it continued to creep forward and the sledge laboured heavily behind it.

I hobbled over the rocky ground, afraid to be left too far behind in the dark. The scooter sneaked round the rocky ridge and stopped. An immense roar filled the air above the noise of the vehicle—a sound that I had not thought I would hear again this winter : the sea. For there, in the bowl where we had pitched our tent after our dramatic trip down the glacier last time, was a boiling cauldron of black water. The light from the headlamps picked out the greeny white of the surrounding pressure and gave substance to the vapour which poured off the raging waters. The sight was fearful and the sound alarming. Beyond the river lay the glacier, silent and treacherous.

If ever nature seemed frightening it was then. I felt I was gazing on an outpost of hell through which ran the only exit to a tranquil world. This was the strange quality of the Arctic. Nowhere did reality and fiction merge in quite the same way, or life have the same substance as dreams. But unlike a dream, from which a waking moment could release me, from this adventure there was no escape.

'Marie, you climb up over the moraine,' ordered Avatak, as he un-hitched the sledge from the Skidoo. By now my eyes were accustomed to the dark, and I scrambled up over the rocks, as the men inched the sledge across a narrow bridge of ice. A careless move and the sledge with its precious burden would slither over the edge, dragging the two men with it. I froze in my tracks as I watched the delicate manœuvre. The light from the orange tent glowed warmly, illuminating it like an enormous magic lantern.

In a few minutes both sledges had been dragged to firmer ground. The dogs lay around in heaps, as if conjured into silence. I stumbled amongst them, but they did not react. I scrambled out of reach before they changed their mind. The men hitched up the sledges and as they did so the noise of moving pressure exploded out of the darkness from the direction we had come. Ice snapped and the bridge they had crossed moments before collapsed. It whirled and bobbed in the water below for a few seconds before being sucked against the broken floes and smashed.

With infinite care Avatak sounded out a route over the newly frozen ice which led to the foot of the glacier. The dogs trod the malleable ice carefully and then made a dash up a steep bank to the glacier. It took a while before we could find a route safe enough for the Skidoo to follow. The brew I had promised myself at the glacier would have to wait. As Kari was still asleep we decided to push on. The dogs disappeared after a while, leaving the Skidoo to flounder on the waves of ice without anything to grip on. I stood at the back of the sledge to push, but my efforts were no help. I felt uncomfortable at the back of the party in the dark and kept looking over my shoulder for signs of anything creeping up on me. I could see where the stars met the mountain's darkened rim, and where the glacier fell into the shadow of the rocks.

Wally transferred the Skidoo to a lengthened lead and at last we began to move. For a long while I had to walk behind the sledge to guide it away from the ruts. When the pace quickened I had to run, plunging into hollows and leaping over the ridges, till we got stuck and had to have the dogs to help us out.

Avatak had taken his lighter sledge a good way up the first of the four tiers before he returned to give us a hand. I was glad when I saw his flashlight appear over a rise. The air was still, except for the yelps of the dogs as they toed the line behind the swishing whip. The dogs were hitched to the sledge as the Skidoo pulled away to reconnoitre a roundabout route which could get it up the icy slope. I could hear it churning against the surface and it was a long while before it could follow us up.

The climb was gruelling for both men and dogs and on the steeper slopes of the glacier we had to use both snow scooter and dogs to drag our heavy sledge. At least the higher up we went there was more snow to give them a hold.

Kari's head seemed lost in the folds of the sleeping bag and I had some anxious moments when there was no sign of the little trail of vapour which showed that she was breathing normally. I ferreted inside the covers with a cold hand to make sure she had not smothered, and a peeved snort greeted my icy fingers.

Her cries for milk bothered us, but we were on a particularly tough stretch when the clamour began, and we had to wait till we found a safer spot to stop and erect a tent. I realized then just how much little children could suffer on these journeys. It was not always possible to feed them when they needed it. I had brought a bottle of milk, but somehow during the jostling over the tide crack it had fallen out. I had kept it inside my clothing till then to stop it from freezing.

Kari became frightened and hysterical. Avatak spoke to her and she begged him to take her outside. I was interested to see that on this occasion he did not indulge her. On a journey the Eskimos do not stop at the first signs of weakness. It is better to get somewhere safe before stopping to relax. We had to make sure we were off the steep slope before we camped, in case bad weather caught us out. The disciplines that children learn in the Arctic are those that nature impose.

The route we had used up the glacier last time was impassable; Avatak scouted a quick route with his dogs. For a while I travelled inside the covered sledge in an attempt to pacify Kari.

It was a strange sensation travelling in the night up a glacier which I knew to be dangerous and not to be able to look out to see where we were going. There were not many people I would trust in that situation. The strain on Wally must have been heavy. Despite my trust, however, I was glad when we stopped for a brew.

Avatak and Wally had a tent up in seconds and it was only a matter of minutes before I handed Kari a bottle of warm milk. Our frustrations were nothing compared with hers when she found it was not her usual brand of milk. In an attempt to cut down weight and space I had put in a tin of milk which we also could use. I am sure most baby-care books warn the mother against making such a mistake. Kari, however, had on occasions drunk this milk before and seemed to like it. I could not understand why she should take such an aversion to it now.

Our pause for relaxation turned into a nightmare of anxiety as we tried by every known method to pacify the baby. Wally was suffering from the noise and fumes of the snow scooter, which had given him a raging headache. Now Kari was screaming. With the greatest patience we eventually persuaded her to drink some tea. The only thing she would eat was frozen butter, picking at it and eating it like candy. I did not mind. At least the fat would help her to keep warm.

We all felt heartless when we bundled her once more into the tent over the sledge. 'Skidoo finished—let's go home,' she pleaded.

It was 2.30 a.m. when Wally pulled off the glacier into a hollow to pitch camp. We had been travelling for twelve hours. Avatak and he put up a tent over the other sledge which they built out into a platform with various boxes for the four of us to sleep on. In no time there were two primuses roaring, and we feasted on sledging biscuits and as much as we could chip off the frozen corned beef and liver paste. It was really warm with both stoves going and we stripped off our furs. Kari was much happier now that we had stopped and she pranced about the platform from one to the other. Avatak watched her fondly and for a while the two of them sat together chatting and sharing biscuits and chocolate. It would be hard for him to part with her.

There was a marvellous atmosphere to the tent, which was bright and roomy. Kari had slept so much during the day, that she was not too keen to go to sleep now that she had room to move, and for an hour or so it was a battle to keep her still, as our eyelids got heavier. At last she gave in and crawled between Wally and myself. Avatak was curled up in a thick cover from which it seemed nothing could disturb him. In the middle Wally stretched out beneath a double sleeping bag we had brought with us and I lay along the outside. I fell asleep too tired to think about anything.

I woke up feeling cold and cramped. The light from the hurricane lamp was still on, but the primuses had gone out. The men lit the primuses and I cooked the breakfast of porridge. I was glad when Kari ate some. We cleared away quickly afterwards and loaded our sledges without much trouble. The twilight was still quite bright and we noticed we had camped near the route over the moraine to the frozen river-bed which led down to the sea ice. Several sledge tracks pointed on further down the glacier but it was a hazardous route, Avatak told us, and especially dangerous with so little snow. It probably meant, however, that the Eskimos had gone that way because the route down the river-bed was bad.

It took an hour to cross the moraine. Rocks jutted out in the path of the sledges at all levels, and the men were flushed with the exertion of lifting the sledges over the jagged obstacles. The frozen river-bed offered no relief from the exhausting manhauling. At times it seemed we would be stuck for ever in the maze of rubble. The Skidoo shook frenziedly as the skis rattled against the rocks and it took both men all their strength to haul it over the boulder-strewn ground. For thirteen hours we toiled the five miles that led down to the sea ice over a snowless jumble of rocks and stones, till we were parched and shaking with the effort. Wally had expected we would slip down with ease in an hour and a quarter on the snow scooter. Instead it had almost broken the backs of the men and nearly wrecked the Skidoo. Kari was bored and tired of being confined and the constant relaying had exhausted the dogs. It was a weary party who arrived at the hunters' hut at the head of the fiord. The hut was damp and airless and the fumes from the primus stove stung our eyes. It was as grimy as the time we had visited it with Geoff, though I had not remembered it being so stuffy. Every few seconds we had to open the door to let the fumes out. The cold air rushed in in great billowing waves and the walls were wet with condensation. It was depressing and unhealthy and our sleep that night was fitful. The platform was still warped and the floor still wet where the snow fell in from the roof. The temperature dropped rapidly during the night and we huddled together for warmth. Our clothes in the morning were damp and our hair covered with rime.

Breakfast the next morning was a short affair. Kari was surprisingly cheerful, but I suppose anything was better than being cooped up on the sledge. Avatak set off for Moriussaq as soon as his sledge was loaded and we were not long following. The route down the fiord was flat, with enough snow for the Skidoo to get a grip without skidding. It was marvellous to be on the move again, and we were soon hurtling along at a good speed. The sledge bounced behind the snow scooter, setting the lamp swinging violently from side to side. Eventually I had to hold it. The wind whistled through the gap in the flap, but I did not mind. Kari was snug in her clothing and I had nothing to worry about.

We didn't know when we passed Avatak, as he had no light on his sledge. It seemed no time before we were at the Cape where we had turned back when we had come this way with Geoff several months before. Ahead of me I saw for the first time the lights of Dundas and of the Airbase almost side by side. Fifty miles in front of us, they shone brilliantly like the lights of a vast esplanade. It was an extraordinary sight—so pretty and unexpected.

Wally stopped for a while to let me enjoy it. We had taken just over an hour and a half to travel the length of the fiord that normally took about four hours by dog sledge. Moriussaq, the little Eskimo village where we had dried out our clothes after the great storm which had caught us on our return from Dundas the last time, should only be half an hour away.

I sat near the front of the sledge so that I could spot the lights of the village when they first appeared. Suddenly, as the tracks veered to the left, the lights flickered into view. They were very faint in comparison with the electric lights across the bay, but just as comforting. The noise of the Skidoo brought a score of figures out of their huts. They ran, bowlegged, towards the tide crack, their lanterns swinging in their hands as they pointed out a route over the pressure. Smiling faces peered at me, when we stopped and a dozen hands flashed out to greet us. Ituku and Massana—the tallest of the group—stepped forward to help us with our baggage. They were both sons of Kaviarssuak and Bibiane, and they urged us warmly to go up to the house. They swept up Kari and the bag I was carrying and escorted us up.

I could hardly recognize the little hut that had been so buried in drift the last time we had visited. Kaviarssuak had built an extension to it, which made it look twice the size, and it was still too early in the winter for the deep drifts that alter the face of the villages. The entrance was just the same, but I had forgotten how low the ceiling was in the porch, and it was with an aching head that I burst through the inner door to surprise Bibiane. 'Ah, you have come visiting,' she beamed as she opened her arms to welcome me. She clutched me to her as she would a daughter before stepping back to look at me and enquire, 'How are you?'

I could not stop grinning. It was so lovely to see this old woman again—I felt I was home from home. Kaviarssuak was equally friendly, as if we had known them for years. In no time Kari and the old man had established that bond so special between the old and young. He talked to her seriously and chuckled at her answers. Her initial shyness soon gave way to boisterous good spirits. There was no lack of playmates amongst the visiting children.

I chatted eagerly to Bibiane about our activities during the last few months. She gestured to the other room where the table had been laid for tea. 'I am cooking meat for later,' she explained. I looked admiringly at the new room and commented on its stylishness. 'Oh, it is not finished yet,' her husband explained. 'We have to cover in the roof.' The moment he had said it I knew why, as a large drop of cold water landed on the tip of my nose. Little spots of white hoarfrost patterned the rafters. As I watched, little beads of water formed overhead and dropped around me. 'It is so big now—your house is fit for a king,' I teased Bibiane.

She laughed good-naturedly. 'And I am the king's wife—fine clothes these are for the king's wife to be wearing.' She looked drolly at her faded dress and giggled.

I wanted to hug her. 'How have you been keeping, Bibiane?' I asked, as she sighed unexpectedly.

'Not so well,' she whispered. 'It is my heart—the doctor visited the other day—I was very ill, trembling.' The news alarmed me and my anxiety must have shown in my face. 'I am all right now,' she added confidently, but I felt suddenly unhappy. She was such a comforting person to be near, her presence seemed to give everyone strength.

Avatak arrived some time later and stayed for the meal of sealmeat. Kari rushed up gleefully to see him and he swept her up into his arms. The evening was relaxed. Often I would look at Bibiane and find her kind eyes gazing into mine—we did not say much but I felt we shared a rapport. 'Don't travel any further tonight,' she urged after tea. 'Stay with us. We have plenty of room.' A spare bed was brought into the kitchen and put beside the divan, which I was to share with Kari. From a cupboard our hosts fished out two sheets for us to lie on, and we covered ourselves with our sleeping bags. I could not have felt more at home anywhere—we were completely accepted by these generous people.

Before we turned in I was approached by Bibiane. She confided in whispers that I would not have to go out for a pee tonight, as there was something I could use in her son's bedroom. I looked towards the room where her son and his wife slept with their little boy. There in a corner opposite the bed was a portable toilet. I thought to myself I would make quite sure they were asleep before I used that.

It was marvellous to sleep on a bed in the warmth after the last two nights on the trail. I felt very content and fell asleep to gentle murmurings from the other beds. Nothing woke me till I heard the clatter of pots on the stove and the swish of water in the basin. The smell of fresh coffee was delicious.

We had arranged to be away by 10 a.m. Avatak was to accompany us across the bay to Dundas to make quite sure we got there. He had several boxes of ours which we could not have taken too easily on our sledge. We strolled over to Massana's house after breakfast to see them and to find out if Avatak was up yet. We liked Massana—a large florid-faced man with a round physique. He had been on Herbert Island during our first winter and had been great entertainment at the Christmas party. His wife Patdlunguak was the daughter of Migishoo—tall and slim, she was beautiful, with chiselled features and lovely eyes.

Avatak had just finished breakfast when we arrived. He looked tousled, as if he had just got out of bed, and his hosts joked about him being a great sleeper. They obviously liked him and he did not seem to mind being teased. They made coffee for us and ferreted around among the shelves and boxes to find a present for Kari. She sat on Avatak's knee happily chatting to him as she brushed his hair. He seemed absorbed in her and totally unaware of anyone else in the room. I thought of him returning alone to Herbert Island—the memory of Maria and the children and all the emotion of leaving suddenly welled up within me and I burst into tears. I tried to hide my face, as I gathered up our furs, but whichever way I turned I saw only the reflection of my distress in the eyes of those around me.

We made our way slowly down to the ice, my vision blurred by tears that would not stop. Half the village was there to see us off. Our farewells were brief. Finally I turned to Bibiane. She embraced me and kissed my cheek. At that moment I said my goodbye to Greenland.

I crawled into the shelter on the sledge. The flap fell over the entrance, blocking everything except the lights in the distance. The sledge slid on to the sea ice. Hands fumbled through the opening to bid me a last fare-fell. Ahead, in the shaft of light cast by the Skidoo, I could see Avatak. Resplendent in furs he sat, the whip in his right hand tracing in the air the movement of the sea as it broke upon the shore. With each sweep of the whip his dogs surged forward. Soon they were rushing headlong towards the distant lights of Thule, their shadows fleeing before them across thin ice already scored by the tracks of countless sledges.

Through the darkness we sped after him, the noise of our machine rending the silence of the Arctic night, as we made for the glitter of lights which marked the boundary of his world and ours. Beyond those lights he could not go. But I was no longer sad, because I knew that what kept him a hunter of the north was infinitely better than what we could offer him. My heart began to fill with pride for having known and loved these people.

Our arrival at Thule finally severed the link which had bound me for the last sixteen months to the past. The garish street lights cast a weird glow on us as we carried the boxes from the sledges to the waiting car. Overhead a jet screamed out of the darkness. We turned our backs on the dogs and stumbled towards the waiting car. As Wally held Kari Avatak stepped forward and buried his head in her neck. My hand reached out to comfort him. 'Inudluarit, Avatak, Goodbye.' The door slammed and the car sprang into life. I leant out of the window. 'Some time soon we will be back.' But as the engine roared, a weeping man turned away, and my words were lost in the night.

LIST OF CONTRIBUTORS AND SPONSERS

I wish to express my gratitude to the following sponsors and contributors to the Expedition:
National Broadcasting Corporation—New York
British Broadcasting Corporation—London
Sunday Times
Woman's Own

Mr Dudley E. Witting
Mr and Mrs Charles Turriff
Royal Air Force, Lyneham

Avon Rubber Company Limited	Rubber boat
BASF United Kingdom Limited	Audio/video tapes
Blacks of Greenock	Tentage
BSA Guns Limited	Rifles and ammunition
A. Baily & Company Limited	Sheepskin coats
Bombardier Limited	Skidoo snowmobiles
Eclair-Debrie (UK) Limited	16mm. cameras
Glaxo Group Limited	Medicines
Granta Boats Limited	Folding canoe
H. J. Heinz & Company Limited	Canned baby food and ready meals
Imperial Tobacco Company	St Bruno Flake tobacco and John Player Special cigarettes
International Wool Secretariat	Woollen clothing
Linguaphone Institute Limited	Linguaphone course in Danish
J. Lyons & Company Limited	Coffee
Ludlow Carpet Company Limited	Foam-backed nylon pile carpet
Donald MacDonald (Antartex) Limited	Sheepskin rugs
B. & S. Massey Limited	Ice axes
Frank O'Shanohun Assoc. Limited	Expedition brochures
Philips Electrical Limited	Cassette recorders
Rolex Watch Company Limited	Chronometer—Oyster Lady-date
Shell-Mex & BP Limited	Pink Paraffin
Sleepeezee Limited	Two-some space-saver divan set
Tate & Lyle Limited	Sugar
Graham Tiso Limited	Mountaineering equipment
Typhoo Tea Limited	Tea
Unigate Limited	Domo milk powder
'W' Ribbons Limited	Tubular nylon webbing
John Wyeth & Bros Limited	SMA milk